DREAMS OF A LITTLE CORNISH COTTAGE

ALSO BY NANCY BARONE

New Hope for the Cornish Farmhouse
No Room at the Little Cornish Inn

DREAMS OF A LITTLE CORNISH COTTAGE

Nancy Barone

HEAD OF ZEUS

An Aria Book

This edition first published in the United Kingdom in 2021 by Aria,
an imprint of Head of Zeus Ltd

Copyright © Nancy Barone, 2021

A CIP catalogue record for this book is available from the
British Library.

9 7 5 3 1 2 4 6 8

ISBN (E): 9781838938055
ISBN (PB): 9781800246188

Cover design © Cherie Chapman

Typeset by Siliconchips Services Ltd UK

MIX
Paper from
responsible sources
FSC® C020471

Printed and bound in Great Britain by
CPI Group (UK) Ltd, Croydon CR0 4YY

Aria
c/o Head of Zeus
First Floor East
5–8 Hardwick Street
London EC1R 4RG

www.ariafiction.com

This novel is dedicated to my beloved husband
Nick who is always by my side with a kind word,
coffee and cake.

Author Note

I have always been in awe of the so-called Sandwich Generation, i.e., those super-human beings who take care of their elderly and possibly frail parents alongside their own children. It's a very demanding position to be in, and only love and patience can give any hope of getting through it. I hope this book makes you smile and realise that you are not alone.

I

Man For Hire

'Hello? Mrs Amore?'

'Yes?'

'My name is Connor Wright. I'm calling about your ad in the paper.'

Finally. I cleared my throat, my heart pounding. 'Oh yes?'

'Are you still looking? The ad is a few days old.'

I was, but if his voice was anything to go by, my search was over. But still, I hesitated. Maybe this was a thing for divorced ladies, but it was a first for me.

Neil would freak if he knew, but the glory of it was that it was no longer his business – not since he elected to entertain himself with another woman, leaving me all on my own up here in this five-bed mausoleum dedicated to his allegedly noble ancestors. I was just glad that we didn't have any young children to fight over, both Lizzie and Sarah having moved to Truro to live with their boyfriends.

'I'm assuming you'll want to meet me first?' came the polite question.

'Er...'

A warm, hearty laugh filled the ether. 'Believe me, I feel as awkward about this as you.'

I very much doubted that. 'Well, then. When would you be available for an... interview?'

'I'm available from now onwards, if that's okay?'

Now? I gulped. I wasn't ready. In fact, I'd probably never be ready, but the time had come to inject some novelty and excitement into my life. Yes, it was time for a change. It was time for many changes, in fact. So I gave him my address.

'It's the first house on the coastal footpath up from Wyllow Cove, if you're coming from that way. Or the last on Abbot's Lane if you're driving?'

'I'm driving.'

So he wasn't a local. I'd have recognised his name. There were no more than a hundred of us in the village, pets included.

'Okay, I'll be waiting,' I said, wondering how fast I could change out of my clothes and into something decent.

'I won't be long,' he promised and rang off. Deep voice. Sexy, Irish accent. It all boded very well indeed.

Missy jumped up onto my lap, and I stroked her dark fur as she rubbed her head against my palm. Affectionate and dependent, she was more like a dog than a cat. The more attention she got, the happier she was. I had thought about getting a dog for years, but Neil had always been allergic, and when Missy showed up one day in the garden soaked to the marrow and shivering, it was love at first Meow.

'Are you hungry, Missy-Moo?' I cooed and opened a sachet of her favourite, Liver Delight, and dashed up the stairs to change from my yoga pants into a white sundress. Ten minutes later, the doorbell rang.

But as I moved through the entrance hall to open the door, I realised how stupid I'd been in giving a perfect stranger my address. Maybe we should have met somewhere first, to size each other up politely and walk away with no hard feelings if it didn't feel right. Because not only was I doing something I never ever thought I would do, I was also being completely reckless about it. The man now on the other side of my front door could have been a nutter. And that alone would have raised the criminal offences of Wyllow Cove of the past fifty years to two, not counting that sheep that went missing about ten years ago.

I should've gone through some sort of agency. Gone online and asked for someone with references. You could do that for this sort of thing, right?

Before I could think any more about it, I yanked the door open and standing on the threshold before me was a man – a *younger* man. The first thing that hit me was his friendly smile. Then came the dark mop of loose curls and the lashes so long he could sweep the floor with them. He was tall, but not overly so and there was an air of easiness to him, and even in a pair of faded jeans and a black Zenyatta Mondatta Police T-shirt, he looked formidable. I couldn't have hoped to meet anyone as gorgeous as this even when I was twenty, but now that I was thirty-nine? Pure fluke.

My friends and colleagues at *Lady* magazine had urged, nay, badgered me to go on a date, but I barely had the will to live, let alone to love or have a fling. But this man before me would rearrange anyone's perspectives. Perhaps even my picky sister Yolanda's. But this was my little secret, and seeing that I lived high above the village, maybe I had a small shred of a chance of keeping this under wraps for a little while longer. Of course, eventually, it would come out, but for now, I was my own secret agent.

He smiled amiably as he stretched out a lean but particularly muscled arm. 'Mrs Amore?' he said in that deep, velvety voice that had won me, literally, at hello. A voice so warm, like something you'd gladly wrap yourself up in. 'I'm Connor Wright.'

'Yes, please come in, Mr Wright!' I practically sang. Never had a name sounded so apt.

Not only because he was by far the most ravishingly good-looking bloke I'd ever seen, but also because there was something, well, undefinable about him.

It was in the eyes, and in the curve of his mouth – an innate kindness, a shyness that you didn't expect. We'd be a perfect fit. And I had got all that in the time it took him to step over the threshold? I must have been going mad. Or I must have been more desperate than I'd thought.

'Please don't mind the boxes,' I apologised as he stepped over the threshold and into the large hall. 'I'm putting my house on the market.'

'You're grand,' he simply answered with a dazzling smile and already I could feel my skin tingling with pleasure. Yes, this was going to work out just fine.

He followed me down the hall to the large kitchen extension at the back, the only area of the house where portraits of Neil's parents hadn't been allowed and that had been decorated according to my taste and not his. A huge Shaker-style kitchen done in white and grey with a large island dominating one end of the room extended into a bright orangery awarding a view to the enormous garden and beyond that, the sea. A tartan-style cream and duck egg sofa/daybed and armchairs occupied the opposite corner, with a low coffee table made entirely of driftwood I'd found on the beach below. It was clean, relaxed and airy, without the stuffiness of the empire-style drapes and thick carpeting everywhere else. And now there was not a gilt portrait frame or a coat of arms in sight.

'Very nice, and very tastefully done,' he said.

Bloody right. The minute I'd kicked Neil out, down came all the pictures of his ancestors that he'd so proudly displayed in the entrance hall without even asking my opinion. I sensed that Connor, too, preferred this to the grand entrance as he seemed to relax further. Hopefully he'd be more interested in the bedroom, because, truth be told, I had completely gone blank on all the conversation pieces I'd rehearsed.

'Thank you. Have a seat,' I offered, as I busied myself with filling the kettle and broke open a selection of biscuits, rapidly assembling everything on an Emma Bridgewater plate before him with a composed but friendly, 'Please help yourself.' I figured that if we agreed on this, certain formalities would have to be dispensed of, sooner rather than later.

'Thank you.'

'Coffee? Tea?'

'Coffee, please.'

'Coming right up.'

But when I switched the kettle on, nothing happened. I checked the power point and the 'on' switch. Still nothing.

'Mind if I take a look?' he offered and I moved to the side as he got up to stand next to me by the island, his head cocked at an angle while he removed the kettle from its cradle and examined the underside.

What a bad show this was. I couldn't even operate a kettle. I only hoped he didn't think...? 'I've paid my electricity bill, I promise!' I blurted.

'No, it's not that,' he said with a chuckle. 'The connection is a bit wonky, see?'

I craned my neck to examine it, which brought me closer to him. He smelled nice. Like fresh soap and clean clothes.

He fiddled around with the cord and then, satisfied, put it back down and switched the kettle on again. 'It's oxidised. Normally, I'm for repairing rather than running off to buy new when it's not necessary, but in this case, this one's on its last legs.'

'Ah. Okay, thank you,' I said, wondering where to start again, what to say next.

He, on the other hand, seemed at ease, his bright dark eyes twinkling with good humour and an undercurrent of naughtiness. Or perhaps that was just my imagination.

As the water finally boiled, I poured two coffees and placed the sugar bowl before him. Even performing simple, mundane tasks felt strange in his presence, let alone anything else.

'Cheers,' he said. 'Sugar for you?'

I shook my head. 'Not for me, thank you. I more than make up for it with my biccies. It's all yours.'

He nodded and scooped out three generous spoonfuls, stirring slowly, his eyes never leaving mine as he politely, but still openly, assessed me as he took a sip of coffee, swallowed and reached for a Jaffa Cake.

I was sizing him up, too, of course, imagining a whole (silent) conversation to match our gestures and faces:

Him: So, date much, Natalia? I imagined him asking me when his eyebrows raised with curiosity.

Me (lying through my teeth): Oh, yes, of course. But I prefer quality to quantity. And you, Connor?

Him: Me, too. He stared into his mug because, as handsome as he was, he was still somewhat shy.

Me: So what do you think about us? Are we not a perfect fit? Apart from the age difference, I mean.

And then he looked up at me again. Inquisitively. *Him: Yes, you look like you could fit the bill, Natalia. You've got proper manners, your own home. Not bad for thirty-nine, either.*

No, scratch that. I wasn't telling him my age. Let's not be too revealing.

Him: Pretty and petite. But with an impressive rack. Perhaps a bit too reserved, and in desperate need of a good sha—

'Is it just you in this great big house, so?' he asked, putting his mug down on the table and yanking me out of my fantasies. I came to, and his face was polite but still impersonal.

'Yes. If you don't count Missy, my cat.' And then, a thought: 'You're not allergic, are you? Or to anything else, like down feathers, or…' I faltered, ready to give up. Who was I fooling? What was I doing here with this pure hunk of eye candy, sipping coffee and eating him with my eyes?

Where was my staid self? I didn't want to give him the impression that all I could think of was sex.

I sat up. 'And you? Do tell me a bit about yourself, Mr Wright,' I urged after clearing my throat loudly. I did that when I was nervous. Of course I shouldn't have been nervous at the mere sight of a beautiful young man. After all, he really could have been my younger brother, couldn't he? Not that I had one.

He reached for another Jaffa Cake, which he popped into his mouth. 'Call me Connor. There's nothing much to tell, really. I'm pretty boring. I work in IT, mostly from home.'

'Interesting,' I said and immediately cringed.

He laughed and stroked his chin, lightly scratching his stubble, his long fingers cupping the lower half of his face. And what a charming face it was, so different from the cookie-cutter ones you saw around, with laughing, mischievous eyes so beautiful it was unfair. And at the corners of those eyes were tiny laugh-wrinkles, which appeared every time he smiled.

'And you? What do you do, if I may ask? I mean, not that running this lovely household isn't enough.'

'I'm a monthly contributor to a magazine.'

'Wow. Which one?'

'It's a female publication – you won't have heard of it. It's called *Lady*.'

'*Lady*? You're joking. All the women in my family read it! From my mam to my sisters-in-law. Hang on a minute – Natalia Amore – is it the column *That's Amore?*'

'Uhm, yes.' Heat shot up my neck. I wasn't exactly counting on being recognised. Plus all this beating around the bush was killing me. So I racked up my courage and said, 'Connor – I'm really sorry, but I'm rubbish at small talk, so if you don't mind, let's skip the formalities. Are you interested?'

His eyes flickered with amusement.

If 'out with the old, in with the new' was any divorce motto to go by, I'd certainly nailed this one. And that verb was used aptly, because I couldn't even remember the last time I'd had another man in the house besides Neil, let alone the eye candy now sipping coffee at my table and helping himself to my biscuits like there was no tomorrow. And to think that, hopefully, in a moment he'd be interested enough to go upstairs.

He pushed his mug away, clearing his throat. 'I'm more than interested. I'm excited. Shall we go upstairs?'

The coffee I was just about to swallow spurted out of my mouth and landed on his T-shirt, precisely on Sting's face.

'Oh, I'm so sorryyy!' I wailed, dashing to the island for some paper towel, but in my haste to get back to him, I tripped over my own feet and lurched towards him. As I hurtled through the air, he reached out a hand to stop me. Just like that, without even breaking a sweat. I liked men with good reflexes. There was something of the primitive in that, which attracted me on an instinctive level.

'Easy, there,' he said as he took the paper towel from me and dabbed at his chest.

'Oh, I'm an absolute disaster today! I'm not making a very good impression, am I?' I apologised.

'You're perfectly fine,' he assured me. Liar. But I wanted him to stay even more now.

'Thank you. You're very kind.'

'Do I pass muster too?' he asked with a grin.

'Well, uhm… the thing is, Wyllow Cove is a tiny village and I really don't want anyone knowing about our arrangement for as long as possible. Can you guarantee absolute discretion…?'

He crossed his heart with his index finger and sent me a knowing grin that made my chaste and very lonely white cotton knickers sizzle for the first time in years.

'Discretion is my middle name.'

I bristled. Of course it was. His clothes might have been plain, but his Jeep outside said a lot about his income, and I was thinking that at this point I probably needed him more than he needed me.

I moved my hands from the spoon on the table to my lap, out of sight. No need for him to see I was shaking like jelly, was there? After all, I called the shots. But if that was so, why couldn't I keep still? The idea of having such a handsome man at my disposal, and guilt-free, to boot (well, almost) was foreign to me.

'Are you single?' I blurted out.

'Divorced.' He grinned. 'We didn't see eye to eye anymore.'

And suddenly, I wasn't so sure. Up until a moment ago it had felt like a great idea – you know, after the divorce, get my freedom back and all that, but now? My friends were bound to find out and I'd die of shame.

'If you're not convinced,' he said softly.

I caught sight of his eyes, as dark as the unknown world I was about to jump into. 'It's just that I've never done this before, you see.'

'I know,' he whispered. 'But you have your reasons and you don't have to answer to anybody anymore.'

I snorted. 'You should put that on a business card.'

He grinned a sexy grin. 'I keep it on the quiet side. You know.'

I looked at him. In a parallel world, I should've been born ten years later – to say the least – and met him instead of bloody Neil.

They say that forty is the new twenty. So technically, I was only nineteen.

'What's your hourly rate for the uhm… extras I require?' I asked.

'It depends. Do you want me to fit you in as a regular?'

'Oh. Do you… have many other regulars?'

He hesitated. 'A couple. IT doesn't pay as much as you'd think.'

'But I get first dibs?'

'Absolutely,' he assured me.

'And we do this only if we both want to, yes?'

He smiled wryly, a set of dimples bracketing his firm but luscious mouth. Surely he must have known how dreadfully gorgeous he was?

He coughed. 'So, upstairs?'

'Yes!' I almost screamed. 'Follow me.'

Now, normally, I wouldn't have done this until I'd made a decision and, oh, but who was I kidding? The bloke had perfect manners, he looked clean and, let's face it, he was easy on the eye.

We passed into the hall and up the stairs, and I was acutely aware of him behind me, and even more aware of my thin sundress separating his body from mine. And apart from his own clothes, unfortunately. Goodness, what was happening to me? Had divorce finally flipped a switch inside me? Now it seemed I wanted everything I'd missed out on all those years, and with a vengeance.

I opened the door of the second bedroom and stepped back for him to enter. As he slipped past me with a smile, I sniffed at the air like a hound dog. We were completely alone in the world, and the only sound between us was the light padding of his feet on the carpet and the occasional creak of a floorboard.

My mind raced like that of a love-starved teenager, imagining all sorts of scenarios where he took me in his arms and kissed me, or where he toyed with the strap of my sundress and—

He looked around, poked his head into the en-suite bathroom and looked out the window down to the garden.

'It's perfect,' he said. 'I'll take it.'

I gushed, despite my thirty-nine years. 'Really?'

He grinned, warming me from the inside out. 'Absolutely. I'd be honoured to be your lodger.'

Of course, it would have been fun to continue pretending to myself I was interviewing him as a prospective gigolo, but the truth was, I needed a lodger to boost my income that had been halved since my other half left me for a woman half my age. Ah, life was so unfair, wasn't it? And so far, Connor seemed like a great choice, due to his – oh, who was I kidding? He was absolutely delicious, with just a hint of stubble you wanted to run your fingertips over, just to see what it felt like to be close to a man again.

Yesterday I didn't even know he existed, and all it had taken was an ad and a phone call to see him here, in the flesh, right in front of me. I wished I had the guts to go all the way and live life instinctively. To do whatever I felt. I'd been married for years and had always toed the line, never misbehaving, always doing the right thing, and never anything that might, God forbid, bring me any personal pleasure or enjoyment.

He pulled out a sheet and unfolded it. 'These are my credentials. Should I come back tomorrow?'

I nodded. 'I'll have the contract ready for you to sign and give you the keys and you can move your stuff in.'

He smiled in relief. 'Thanks. You don't know what it means to me to be able to start afresh.'

'Oh, I do know, believe me,' I answered. Having the house to myself, without Neil, having my own life back after all these years… was pure bliss. It had always been about him, his medical career, his needs. Now it was about me. But independence cost dear, so a lodger was the perfect solution. I was feeling good about this again.

'Yeah?' he said, but was too polite to ask why and I was certainly not going to volunteer any info as to what a woman my age was doing on her own, besides Missy, in a huge five-bed detached high above Wyllow Cove.

'Yeah,' I chirped.

'Okay, then,' he said. 'I'll be back tomorrow with my stuff.'

'Great. Welcome, Connor.'

'Thank you, Natalia.'

'Oh – it's just Nat.'

'Ok, then, Nat.' He eyed me one last time and instead of seeing him out and closing the door, I lingered on the threshold and watched him as he got into his SUV, drove back up Abbot's Lane, reached Sennen Road, turned left and out of sight. But not out of mind.

Wishing it was already tomorrow, I went back into the kitchen and started to do the washing up, when something on the table caught my eye. I squinted at the sugar bowl and grabbed my reading glasses. It had Salt written on it. I remembered that he'd put three spoonfuls in his coffee. The poor bloke. No wonder he was knocking down the Jaffa Cakes two at a time. With me as his landlady, he was in for quite the adventure.

I cut some fresh flowers and arranged them about and around the house, trying not to think how Missy and I rattled in this huge space. My own dream was to get rid of all the tat and downsize to a cottage in the village, just Missy, myself and a few family pictures and mementos, with a second bedroom for when my sister's little girls came to stay. And then I could start afresh, with only the things that I had chosen rather than put up with because they were or looked expensive.

I'd buy some essentials like a new bed (top of my list), a table and enough chairs for family dinners, a sofa and a writing desk. Neil would certainly turn his pseudo-aristocratic nose up at it all and say I'd lost my mind. If anything, I'd *found* myself, and a whole new future.

Because I didn't need a lot of stuff – and certainly not the high-class jewellery that I'd had to flaunt at dinner parties to make Neil happy. Emeralds, diamonds and rubies. All bought with his family's old money, and certainly not his own salary. Beautiful objects, indeed, but what did I need any of them for? The one time I went to the annual black-tie benefit for writers in London? Besides, I'd soon lost any interest in them the moment I'd realised that every necklace, bracelet or pair of earrings had been a silent trade-off, if not an apology, for each and every one of his indiscretions. The safe was full of the stuff. You do the maths, if you care to.

I had to get away from this status symbol, as the upkeep of a five-bed detached house and its grounds was expensive. Plus it was the last link to my life with Neil, if you didn't count the one good thing that had resulted from our marriage, i.e. our daughters Sarah and Lizzie.

I had always envisaged selling the place alongside all of its humongous, self-important furniture and family portraits that Neil had inherited from his grandparents, all pompous and impractical.

If, on one hand, I would miss the commanding views of the coast from up here, my ideal home would be something like Lavender Cottage down in Wyllow Cove, tucked away at the end of the quay. Empty, run-down and in need of a loving new owner now that Mrs Pendennis was gone, it was perfect, except for one thing. It was right next door to my mother.

I decided to leave the decluttering and packing away of all of Neil's stuff and spent the rest of the day sunbathing with my feet up and drinking iced tea while waiting for Gin o'clock (one must have some semblance of restraint) next to a stack of magazines.

Now with the rent money to tide me over until the house was ready to be viewed, I had both eye candy and extra income. The first thing on my list was to help Sarah and Lizzie get onto their own property ladders rather than renting.

The doorbell rang and I grinned to myself. Whoever it

was, they were too late. I was already all lodgered up with someone who had even agreed to have a go at my borders and disintegrating fences, to boot. Financial freedom, happiness and relaxation, pleased to meet you. Or so I thought.

2

Domestic Drama

It was Yolanda, my younger sister, with her twins Amy and Zoe. After the umpteenth time trying IVF, she and her (now ex) husband Piers had finally managed to conceive, and the result was not one, but two bundles of joy. It was a shame that Piers had decided he didn't want a family after all that, and that he left Yolanda for a younger woman. That was the story of the Amore sisters – no matter what we did in our lives, there was always another woman our men preferred to us.

It was lucky that Yolanda, a very popular celebrity chef with books and TV shows under her belt, had had a career to keep her going in every sense. When she was away for work, she depended on me to help her with the girls who knew my house better than they did their own. They even had their own room here, which I'd painted half pink for Zoe and half purple for Amy.

But these days, I could hardly help myself, and was beginning to resent the fact that Yolanda always took but never appreciated anything I did for her. It was like still being married to Neil. Of course I loved those two little girls like my own, and, to be honest, pitied them for going through a childhood with a mother whose ego was the size of a cathedral. I knew what that was like, as our own mum was a drama queen, a diva and a general all rolled into one still today.

And Yolanda was very much like her, breezing in and out of her daughters' lives and leaving the hard work for someone else to do. It sometimes made me wonder why she'd gone to all the trouble of IVF when she preferred being a celebrity to being a mother. My guess was that she wanted it all.

But I was the one who went to the twins' PTA meetings, volunteered for all their activities and ferried them around from ballet to football. It was a miracle they didn't call *me* Mum.

Luckily I worked from home and was able to be there for the girls and it wasn't a huge upheaval school-wise for them because Yolanda's villa was a hop from mine.

'Nat, I need you to look after the girls for a couple of weeks,' she said as she put her Birkin bag down.

Now, on any day, I'd have been thrilled. But I was on a deadline and this week was a bit tricky.

'Hi, Yolanda, nice to see you, too.'

'Oh, Nat, don't start on me. I'm on my way to Heathrow.'

'New York again?'

'Tokyo first.'

That was Yolanda Amore for you, jetting to all the best exotic places, cooking and taping shows. Nigella Lawson had nothing on her. Yolanda's divorce had done her a world of good, both financially and emotionally, while I was struggling on both levels.

'Auntie Nat!' Amy and Zoe hollered, hanging on to various parts of me as I steered them into the kitchen and made a fuss of them while Yolanda disappeared into my pantry, no doubt to give me advice or criticise the fact that my herbs weren't stored alphabetically, or that I didn't have pink Himalayan salt.

If there was one person who could make me feel bad about myself it was Yolanda. Richer, taller, thinner, younger, albeit by a couple of years, Yolanda had it all. And never missed out on the chance to rub my nose in it. Even my mother preferred her. And so blatantly, too.

Try as I might, I could not find a single memory of either of them doing something kind for me. My mother had always gone out of her way to please the beautiful Yolanda, the talented Yolanda, the graceful Yolanda, who only preened, the two of them completely forgetting my very existence.

Even when I had broken my leg at ten years of age and was being operated on, where was my mother? At a children's beauty contest with Yolanda. And when my children were born, she had been away on a cruise both times, while when the twins were born she had been knitting and sewing and stitching bibs and blankets from the day Yolanda told her she was pregnant.

Not even when I had had a miscarriage ten years ago had she been there for me because she'd preferred to be by Yolanda's side during her umpteenth IVF treatment. Need I say more?

'Darlings, why don't you two go into the garden and pick some more flowers for Auntie Nat's vases?' I suggested.

'Mummy's staying in New York for *ever*,' Amy informed me matter-of-factly as she helped herself to a Granny Smith apple and took a huge bite of it. A drop of the juice hit Zoe in the face and she protested. 'Eewww! No, she isn't!'

'It'll be fine,' I said, eyeing Yolanda who was still perusing my shelves from what I could see of her through the half-open door. She let out a huge sigh and shook her head, and already I could feel my resentment growing. Easy for her to criticise my life when absolutely nothing was missing from hers. Even her producer, Bill Evans, was sniffing around her.

'Do you want us to do the weeding for you, Auntie Nat?' Amy asked innocently, but I read her devious little mind. She was heading for my beautiful white roses, the rebel. The minute I turned away she'd be decapitating them with sinister glee.

'No de-weeding,' I warned her. 'Now go – and don't kick at the fencing again, Amy,' I reminded the wilder of the two of one of my rules, which she systematically disobeyed. Had she been my daughter, I'd have set her straight years ago, that was for sure.

Door closed and kids spy-proofed, I tried the kettle, which gave a huge cough and a wheeze before kicking the bucket completely. So I boiled some water in a pot and pulled out the biccies Connor had left, all the while waiting for Yolanda to bash me because I hadn't baked my own like she did.

But Yolanda was quiet, gathering her thoughts, and I left her a few minutes because I knew what it was like not to be able to hear yourself think with young children. When I put the steaming cup on the table, she came out of the pantry with a jar of powdered cinnamon. 'God, how can you even find anything in there? Try it with this.'

I poured two cups and let her shake – or was it fold? – the spice in.

Yolanda and I were not that close anymore, not since she had got married. And during her divorce, she had clammed up even more, to the point that now we were ships passing in the night, meaning we only saw each other when she dropped the girls off to stay the week, or the weekend. I swear I could name their teachers and the names of the other parents off the top of my head, but it didn't bother Yolanda, always too busy to notice anything but her own rising star, and gradually, our relationship had cooled to that of mere acquaintances. If she hardly had any time for her own daughters, what could *I* possibly expect? Weekend lunches or Saturday evening drinks were non-existent with her.

She stirred her tea and closed her eyes to enjoy the aroma.

'I'm thinking of taking a cruise the minute we wrap,' she said.

'Hey, maybe we could go together? I've got a stack of brochures somewhere. How about a cruise around the Mediterranean, or perhaps even the fjords or—'

'Sure, sure, whatever,' she said. 'I'll hire a nanny.'

'We can take care of the girls ourselves. We don't need a nanny,' I said, when instead I wanted to say: *Dear oh dear, Yolanda, get a grip and start taking care of your own children rather than hiring perfect strangers to do your job, career or no career.* But I bit my tongue. It was so rare to see Yolanda sitting at my table long enough to chat that I didn't want to ruin the moment.

'What about you?' she asked. 'Are you seeing anyone?'

'Me? I only divorced six months ago.'

'Exactly, Nat. You should get back in the game. Perhaps a fun man this time, rather than that mummy you married.'

'Yolanda—'

'I'm serious, Nat. Look at you. You could be absolutely gorgeous, with that early Natalie Imbruglia look – if you only took care of yourself, that is.'

My hand absently went to my short dark hair, raking across my longish fringe, which I usually kept behind my ear. Take care of myself. Easy for her to say. I just didn't have the time to look after long hair, and as a result, I looked like a tomboy while Yolanda looked like a princess. But I was okay with that. We had our own personalities, and although a tiny part of me envied her huge celebrity status, there was no way I would ever swap my quiet life with her hectic one, despite the millions. I had all I needed from my column, and now a lodger.

Yolanda, for example, would never settle for a cottage. She herself lived in a sprawling mansion made of glass and concrete, a huge monolith perched above the opposite end of the cove. I'd often joked we could send each other signals by switching the lights on and off, but she barely even phoned me. We were as different as Amy and Zoe.

I glanced at the girls outside. Zoe was following Amy's lead in a game of Frozen Statues, very much like Yolanda and I used to play. I was the quiet one, while Yolanda used to lord over me like Amy did over Zoe.

'You deserve better than Neil,' Yolanda continued. 'If he weren't the twins' GP I'd have told you to strike him off your phone directory, the cad. Yes, what you need is a sexy man to get you going again.'

'Going where, exactly?' I snorted into my mug, all the while thinking of Connor. He was perfect fling material – young, handsome, and on a short lease.

She took a last swig of her tea and glanced at her watch. 'Crap, is that the time? Girls, come and say goodbye to Mummy,' she called out into the garden.

They came in sopping wet, probably from a hose fight by the looks of them, trailing mud in from under their feet.

'Girls,' I said, because Yolanda sure wasn't going to. 'Please wipe your feet when you come in from the garden.'

Zoe obeyed while Amy pretended to take another step while gauging me for a reaction. So I said what I always say. 'Amy, you know that act doesn't work with me. Now do as you're told and say goodbye to your mum.'

Yolanda made an impressed face. 'See? That's why I trust you with my girls completely.'

Ah. I'd forgotten the compliments part of her game. She always buttered me up at the last minute just to seal the deal. I sighed.

'Bye, Mummy, I'll miss you,' Zoe said, throwing her arms around her.

'Don't forget to bring back pressies,' Amy reminded her as Yolanda pulled them into her arms and sniffed. Every time, and never a tear. She was much better at cooking than acting.

'Be good, do your homework and listen to Auntie Nat, okay?' she said. And then she got to her feet, scooped up her bag and headed down the hall.

'Any special instructions?' I asked from the front door as she was getting into her Merc.

She flung her hair to the opposite shoulder as she got in and flashed me a smile.

'The usual. For anything else, I trust you completely.' Which, coming from her, Mrs Know-It-All, was an enormous compliment.

She popped back up and called to me over the bonnet. 'By the way, your magazine wants to interview me.'

'Oh? Right.' How could I not know about this? And why hadn't I been asked to interview her? I was a monthly contributor after all, and she was my sister. Who better than me for the job?

After Yolanda sped off, I closed the front door and went upstairs to supervise the girls while they put their stuff away into their room. I made a note to call Hilary, our editor-in-chief. It was very odd indeed that she hadn't already called me to do it.

With an inward sigh, I watched as Zoe carefully folded her things while Amy shoved everything into the drawers. That girl would be the death of someone one day. She didn't have a drop of organisational skills in her. How to slowly teach her some despite herself? And then I got an idea.

'Amy, darling,' I cooed. 'We're going to play a game now.'

'What game?' she asked, her face lighting with interest.

'The Speed Game.' Amy loved anything fast and exuberant, and she had absolutely no patience whatsoever. She always spoke her mind without thinking of the consequences. Remind you of anyone? 'I'm listening,' she answered while pulling out a packet of crisps from her schoolbag.

'You're not eating those in here,' Zoe cried, her pleading eyes swinging to mine for help.

'Amy, you know it's against house rules to eat in the bedroom.'

Amy stared at her, then at me, chewing slowly, just to annoy me, but she didn't dare take another one out of the bag.

'So what's this Speed Game, then?' she prompted me.

I smiled. 'I call an item – say, "blue T-shirt", and you both have to rush to your drawers, and the first one to show me the item, wins.'

Amy's face fell. 'That's it? And what do we win?'

Oh, Jesus. 'A trip to... to... it's a secret for now. Ready?'

Zoe clapped her hands, back into the groove of being with me and much happier now, while Amy rolled her eyes, but moved into position, ready to sprint. She was highly competitive, and used to winning. Just like her mummy.

'I want you girls to bring me your... PE kit!'

And the drawers were yanked open, Amy burrowing like mad, leaving a pile of clothes as high as herself, whereas Zoe plucked it out of a neatly folded stack in her second drawer, along with her sports socks.

'Well done, Zoe!' I clapped, hugging her and kissing the top of her head.

Amy turned to stare at her with a raised eyebrow, and kicked the bundle under her bed, leaving the room with a slam of the door.

'Amy?' I called after her. 'Sweetheart?'

'I want to be alone now!' she called back.

I sighed. That was Amy for you. She'd come back when she was ready.

Who said this was going to be easy? And with Yolanda gone for a month or more, I guessed all my summer plans were more than on hold now. Good thing I still had rooms to let if I decided to rent another one out, I consoled myself as I went to answer the front door.

It was Sarah, my nineteen-year-old.

'Oh, Mum!' she sobbed the moment I opened the door.

'Sarah? What is it, sweetheart?'

'I've left Sam…'

I wrapped my arms around her and led her to the kitchen, her favourite room while she was growing up.

'Sit down and tell me what's happened,' I urged. 'Why?'

She sighed and reached for a napkin to blow her nose. 'You know why. Or at least you can guess.'

'The gambling.' Sam always had a soft spot for taking chances, and not only with money.

Sarah wiped her eyes and looked up at me. 'I was sick and tired of him spending all the money I made. And last night, he gambled our rent money and lost it. The landlord's kicked us out.'

I stared at her. She was watching me, waiting for me to gasp in indignation, but I couldn't. Because I couldn't believe my ears.

'That was our flat, Mum! *Where we were supposed to live together.*'

Oh. My. God. I took her hand, and she hung on to mine like a lifeline.

'So after I read him the riot act, I packed my bags and checked into a hotel…'

'Oh, darling, you should've come here straight away.'

She shrugged. 'It was late, I didn't want to alarm you.

And that's not all of it. He's completely cleaned out our savings account. As of today, I haven't got a pound to my name. Oh, no, wait,' she said, laughing and reaching into her wallet and unfolding an old pound note she always kept for good luck. 'I've got this. Fat lot of good it'll do me as it's not even legal tender anymore.'

'Hang on to it. It might be worth tons one day,' I said. Not that the same could ever be said of Sam, but, unlike my own mum, I kept my opinions to myself. Besides, what else could I say? I was still in shock.

'And in my haste to get out, I left most of my clothes there.'

'We can always go and fetch them. I'll come with you.'

'Thanks, Mum. And the worst thing is that some of the utilities are still in my name.'

I sat up. 'You need to sort that out today, love,' I said.

'I guess I'll have to organise the life I'd planned without him now.'

Welcome to the club, was the first thing that came to mind.

I stood up. 'You make those calls now while I go to the car and get your bags.'

'Thanks, Mum, I don't know what I'd do without you.'

'I'm here for you, love.'

She wiped her eyes and looked upwards as a crash ripped through the house. 'Jesus, is that the twins again?' she said.

'Sarah, you know how important they are to us.'

'Oh, Mum, I love them to bits – you know that. But does their own mother? That's the fourth time since Easter that you've had them.'

I shrugged. 'As a family, we need to stick together.'

She snorted. 'But you're doing all the together, while Aunt Yola does all the sticking. God, I'm so glad my own sister is not like yours.'

So was I, truth be told. I had made sure that my mothering was the opposite of my own mother's.

'Have you heard from Lizzie, by the way?' I asked. 'Do you know if she can make it for dinner tomorrow night?' By that time I'd have had enough time to prep my girls for the news of my new lodger.

'Yes, we were supposed to come down by car together, the four of us.' She sighed. 'But I'm already here.'

And she would be for as long as it would take to bounce back. 'Make those calls, sweetheart. Together we'll sort you out in no time.'

Her room was just the way she'd left it, with pictures of herself, friends and family and Sam practically all over every wall. When she left it she was Mummy's daughter, full of dreams of love.

That had been Sarah's world until last night, and now she'd been introduced to the nitty-gritty reality of relationships, and that not all of them lasted forever. And that if they weren't worth hanging on to, you might as well cut your losses and leave while you were still young. And now she was a broken young woman who had known the humiliation of not being loved in return despite having given herself completely to someone who didn't appreciate her.

That's what most women did. We gave men everything we had – our time, our work, our smiles, our patience, our last drop of energy and our courage and optimism for them to lean on. And they just took without giving anything back.

I wished I had followed my own advice. I should have kicked Neil out at the first signs of his overbearing temperament, or the first time he'd embarrassed me in front of his colleagues during a dinner we were hosting by saying that my Beef Wellington (which is a real bitch to make at the best of times) was too dry and that he would have been better off marrying the sister who could actually cook. As if she'd ever have him. I remember the dining room temperature suddenly dropping to an embarrassed zero degrees, and my smile freezing on my face while sudden coughs had filled the room.

It was safe to say that Neil didn't need anyone else to make him look bad. He did that very well all by himself. And now, thankfully, that part of my life was over. I was actually glad that he'd shacked up with that Helen. That meant there was no risk of him ever coming back. Not that he would. There was nothing between us anymore, and we had practically been living like brother and sister, with little love lost between us.

'Auntie Nat!' the girls called. 'Come!'

I raced to where they had assembled a game of giant Jenga and we played for about an hour. After that we had a nice meal of spaghetti and meatballs accompanied by a fresh garden salad. For dessert, we had the twins' favourite ice cream, and the four of us hunkered down onto the sofas to watch *Mulan*. But then Amy got bored and started a popcorn fight, which I promptly ended as, exhausted, Sarah had finally fallen asleep curled up in the corner of the sofa.

'Right, you two,' I whispered to my nieces. 'Time for bed.'

But they just looked at Sarah. 'What's wrong with her?' Amy said.

'Sarah is having problems with her boyfriend, pet,' I whispered. 'So we need to be really nice to her, okay?'

'Is she going to be okay?' Zoe whispered.

'Of course she is, darling. She just needs some peace and quiet.'

'And some pills,' Annie added. 'Mum can't sleep without her pills.'

Now that was too much information from someone who barely saw their mother. 'Bed,' I repeated. 'Now. I'll come up to tuck you in in a minute.'

As they made their way up the stairs, Amy mumbled something about just when it was becoming fun, while Zoe put her finger to her lips. 'Shush, Amy. Auntie Nat said to be kind.'

In the dimly lit living room, I watched my daughter sleep, curled up defensively. I could just drive over there and kill Sam right now. Slay all the dragons, solve all her problems for her, just once, to give her a break, and the chance to start afresh. I quietly sat next to her, wanting to hold her against my heart. I knew I couldn't wrap her up in cotton wool, so I used my best throw instead.

Sarah opened her eyes and looked at me like when she was little, and my heart turned over in my chest.

'You okay, pet?' I murmured.

She stretched and nodded. 'Mum...?'

'Yes?'

'How long... do you think before I get back on my feet?' she whispered.

I drew her to me and kissed the top of her head. 'As long as it takes, darling. You can't rush these things.'

She sniffed, wiping a tear from her face. 'What would I do without you, Mum?'

'You'll be fine, love. Tomorrow is another day.'

But not even Scarlett O'Hara could have any idea of what *my* tomorrow would be like.

3

Three's Company

The next morning Sarah looked much better. The purple shadows under her eyes had gone, and instead of the sadness, there was more of a combative air to her. Good girl. Stay mad, be strong.

'Hello, love. Come and have some breakfast with us,' I said cheerfully.

'I can't believe you really want to sell our home,' she said as she nodded back at the bubble wrap and boxes in the hall.

I looked up from the table where the twins were munching on scrambled eggs and toast.

'Well, I think it's a good idea,' I answered as I passed her a plate.

'So do I,' Amy said. 'This place is too big for you all by yourself.'

'Is there going to be room for us in your new home?' Zoe asked hopefully, watching me with those huge eyes.

I ruffled her hair. 'There will always be room for you two, my darlings.'

'What about Sarah here?' Amy asked. 'If she and Sam don't get back together again we're going to have to lug her around too. Make sure you buy a three-bed at least, Auntie Nat.'

I shot Sarah a glance. She put down her toast and turned to Amy. 'Never mind me, smarty-pants. I'm going to find somewhere else to live.'

'Don't be daft,' I answered. 'This place is huge. What's the use of it, if not to house my loved ones?'

'Amy does have a point,' Sarah said. 'Where are you going to live when you've sold up?'

Ah. 'Somewhere cosy, like Lavender Cottage.'

Sarah poured herself a cup of coffee from the carafe. 'Lavender Cottage? Isn't that the one next to Nana?'

Even Sarah knew that that was the only fly in the ointment.

'Yes. It's pretty run-down, what with Mrs Pendennis being dead ten years or so. But the harbour front is the ideal spot. I don't like being secreted up here. I'd rather be in the midst of it all. And I believe it would make a great home for me – for us,' I corrected myself. 'It has three bedrooms.'

'But surely you don't want to live next to Nana?'

Diplomacy was never our forte. 'It's not even for sale, anyway,' I said. 'I'm sure that somewhere there is the perfect cottage for me in Wyllow Cove.'

Sarah shook her head wistfully. 'Only a year ago we were all living together in this house. How things change.'

'Of course they do, love. Change is life. You and Lizzie both moved to Truro to live your own lives. No one wants to hang around Mum when there's so much out there to see and do.'

'I'm never going to leave you,' Zoe promised me loyally, resting her chin on my forearm.

'Oh, sweetheart, wait until you grow up. What a wonderful life you'll both have.'

'I'm not living with *her*.' Amy smirked as she shoved another piece of toast down her throat.

I sighed. Things changed indeed. It was a fact of life. And once the process started, nothing was ever the same again.

'What are your plans for today?' Sarah asked.

'After we get back from Truro, I'm going to enlist my precious little helpers here and bag some of what your father calls the family heirlooms. I want to get the house ready for a real estate agent to see.'

'Can't you show it as is?'

I baulked. 'Absolutely not. If they were to pop in now with the house looking like a medieval lair, they'd run for the hills.'

'Some people like this grandiose style. And you never seemed to mind it before,' Sarah said.

How little she knew me. How little I'd spoken up. It was my fault that Neil had dominated me in everything, from what I cooked to how we decorated. Like the goldenrod velour drapes which I loathed with a passion. They made the rooms look smaller and darker. If I'd had my way, I would have thrown everything out and started from scratch, but then Neil had come back with a couple of tables and a sideboard belonging to his grandparents and claimed that they had been *destined* to reside in this grandiose house. For goodness' sake – this place wasn't a castle. It was a huge arts and crafts home. Very pretty on the outside, granted, but quite stifling on the inside. The sooner I got rid of all this tat, the better.

'That's because they're hoarders,' I dismissed.

'That's what Mummy's last boyfriend said before he left,' Zoe said.

Sarah and I turned to her. How was that possible? Yolanda's home was as aseptic and pristine as they come.

'It's true,' Amy assured us. 'He said, "Yolanda, I've had enough of this bullshit. You're a right hoard."'

Sarah's eyes swung to mine and it was all she could do to not burst out laughing. I shot her a warning glance and she excused herself from the table.

'And he's never coming back,' Zoe said with a sigh.

I pulled them both to me and kissed the tops of their heads. 'Did you not like him, girls?'

'I didn't,' Amy sentenced, and Zoe reluctantly shook her head, too.

'He was always angry at Mummy for some reason or other. It's better now without him. And even better here with you.'

'Oh, my darlings. Mummy and Sarah and Lizzie and I will always love you above everything else. Will you remember that?'

'Even if you get married again, Auntie Nat?' Zoe asked.

'Of course.' Even if that prospect was highly unlikely. 'Right, now let's clean up before we drive Sarah to Truro. Maybe we can stop for lunch there?'

'Yayyy!' they shouted right into my ears, and I was instantly stereo-deafened.

When Sarah came back down, she was no longer grinning from the hoard misunderstanding. Obviously the idea of going back to the flat dampened her spirits.

'Are you ready to go?' I asked.

She nodded. 'My landlord told me that he gave my stuff to Sam who left a forwarding address. But the last thing I need is to see him again.'

By the time we got to Truro, Sarah was in a right state, poor love, her hands gripping the safety bar above her left shoulder, her body rigid.

I parked in front of the block of flats where Sam had apparently relocated and removed my seat belt. 'Tell you what, Sarah. You take the girls for a walk and I'll go. If he's there, he certainly won't start arguing with me.'

Sarah turned to me, and nodded, and in her eyes I could see the sadness.

I got out of the car, rang the doorbell and waited. After a moment, Sam opened the door, his hair sticking out in every direction. He emanated a distinct odour of hard liquor and smoke.

'Mrs Tamblynn-Lobb?' He gaped, stepping back in what could only be surprise. There had never been any love lost between us and the fact that I was here with three trolleys made it clear I hadn't dropped by for a social call.

'Hello, Sam,' I said civilly, while inside I wanted to rip him apart. But I realised that that would make me resemble him – unable to communicate and basically feral.

I stepped past him and turned expectantly to him. 'May I go through or have you got company?'

He blushed, then stuttered. 'K-Karen! Sarah's mum is here to collect her things!'

I was shown into the bedroom, which reeked of more alcohol, and there I stopped dead in my tracks. Karen, I presume, had pulled out all of Sarah's clothes and shoes onto the unmade bed and was trying them on, admiring herself in the finger-smudged and greasy mirror. So gambling had not been Sam's only flaw.

I turned to him. 'Have your friend box everything and mail it to my home. I'll let Sarah decide what to do with her stuff.'

And with that, I turned on my heel, the three trolleys bumping along behind me, hoping I'd scraped the walls in the process.

'Ew!' Sarah said while we were waiting for the girls to come out of the ladies' room at Wetherspoons when I told her why I had come back empty-handed. 'I never believed they were only work colleagues. They deserve each other.'

Good girl, I thought to myself.

Instead of going home to do some more decluttering, we spent the rest of the day wandering through Lemon Street Market, browsing over the artwork and artisanal vases. There was a beautiful pale turquoise ceramic dish that would look great in the entrance hall of my new home.

I gifted Sarah of a few outfits, which she tried to resist out of pride, but I gently took her to one side. 'Sarah. I'm your mother. I'm here for you. Now try some stuff on while I hang on to the girls. We'll be right here if you need me.'

At that, she blushed and kissed my cheek before she

went back into the stall. 'Thanks, Mum. I don't know what I would do without you.'

I smiled. 'Go. These two are getting tired.'

I took the girls to the food stalls and picked up some cheeses and focaccia bread along with some sun-dried tomatoes as a light dinner for when we got back to Wyllow Cove.

All in all, we'd managed to get through today, and would do the same tomorrow as well.

Later that night, my doorbell rang while I was getting ready for bed. It was Mags, my best friend and colleague at *Lady* magazine who covered fashion.

She dropped a bottle of Prosecco into my hands.

'Isn't it a bit too late for booze, even for us?' I quipped.

'Haven't you heard, then?' she said as she trudged through the entrance hall to the back of the house.

'Heard what?' I echoed, following her.

'Hilary is leaving, effective immediately!'

'Hilary? *Our* Hilary, as in our editor-in-chief?'

'The one.'

'Oh my God. We've been together since we started out!'

'And you'll never guess who's taking her place.'

'Anna Wintour?' I offered and she snickered. 'Yeah, I wish. Octavia Hounslow.'

I pursed my lips in thought, but the name didn't ring a bell.

She rolled her eyes. 'Does *Your Home* mean nothing to you?'

'My home?'

'No, Natalia – the magazine *Your Home*.'

'Oh!'

'Yeah. She used to contribute with a column called Girl Power – and now she's suddenly our boss. I can only surmise as to how she got this gig.'

'Don't be crass,' I said. 'If she worked at *Your Home* she must be good.'

I pulled down a couple of flutes from my cupboard as she popped the cork. I poured and we took a long swig. 'Ah,' she said, smacking her lips. 'Better already. More, please.'

I obliged, my mind racing, wishing she'd get on with it. To be over at that hour, even if she was a fellow villager, there had to be more news. And knowing Maggie as I did, the booze could have either been celebratory or consolatory.

'Apparently, Octavia wants to zing up our rag a bit. Meaning everyone forty and over is getting the boot. Unless they can provide a very good reason for being there.'

I gasped. 'She can't do that. That's ageist, let alone downright illegal!'

Maggie sighed. 'She's put a different spin on it, of course, but that's what it's basically down to. You know – out with the old...'

'But we've been writing for *Lady* forever!'

'Exactly. She thinks it's time for a change – to bring the younger generations in.'

I was dead. Absolutely, positively dead. While Maggie had alimony to support her, I didn't, as my settlement had been the house. Which was no good unless I could capitalise on it.

Karma already working its wonders on me for kicking Neil out, I wondered? But he'd cheated on me. What was I supposed to have done? Or, more to the point, what was I supposed to do now? All I had income-wise was my measly column, which was why I'd decided to take on a lodger in the first place, but to think that now my job was actually in danger simply because I was quickly approaching *The Big Four-Oh*? Like a bolt of lightning on a clear blue day.

Damn these power-obsessed twenty-something-year-olds. Why couldn't they just let women mature without fearing the worst? As if we already didn't have to contend with: wrinkles, spare tyres and bloody bingo wings.

'So what are we going to do?' she asked, swerving unsteadily, and I suddenly realised she had already had quite a lot to drink before she even got here. I put a hand at her back and shrugged. 'We try to keep our columns, whatever it takes.'

She groaned. 'What do I know about fashion compared to someone half my age?'

'Everything,' I said loyally.

'Christ, I need a time machine.'

'Chin up, Mags,' I said. 'Your best is yet to come. Think of all those ladies twice our age who are still *leading* the game.'

'Yeah, well, sometimes I feel like their grandmother.'

I knew exactly what she was talking about, of course, but I wasn't about to allow her the pity party. This was a time to stay chipper and be optimistic.

I shrugged. 'We'll send our résumés out.'

'Did you not hear? The world is being invaded by

twenty-year-old workaholics! Whatever happened to them partying, and lazing around on Mum and Dad's sofa? When did they suddenly become productive enough to take our place? This cannot be happening!'

'Take it easy, Maggie. There's a thousand things we can still do.'

She opened her arms wide, her drink sloshing dangerously around the rim. 'Like what?'

'If worse comes to worst, you can open your own accounting business like you trained for. Go freelance.'

'Freelance? But I'm not that adventurous. I need stability.'

I took a swig of my own drink. It tasted horrible now, after the bad news. 'Stability? I think that ship has sailed, Maggie. Look around you,' I said.

Because it was all at stake now. Stability, jobs, relationships, marriages. Everything was subject to change and no amount of resisting would ward it off.

'Do you think we're going to be poor?' she slurred drunkenly.

Well, I most certainly already was. 'Of course not, Maggie. We'll be fine. Would you like something to eat to soak up the booze?' I asked.

'No, I just want to sleep. Could you drive me home, Nat?'

'Of course, Mags.'

When I'd sufficiently reassured her and driven her back to her home in the village, I came back and went to bed.

Only I was up half the night, staring out into the darkness, listening to the waves crashing against the rocks, wondering what to do. If Octavia Hounslow was already firing forty-year-olds, it wouldn't be long before it was my turn. If I panicked, I was screwed, so I tried to stay calm and think about nice things. And so I thought of Connor Wright.

The next morning, with a sour aftertaste burning my throat, my head about to explode and my ears ringing, I – no, wait. It wasn't my ears. It was the bloody doorbell. I peeled my eyelids open and found my way downstairs. Sarah was still fast asleep on the sofa.

In the hall, I bumped my head against the doorjamb as I completely missed the doorway.

'Ow, ow, ow…' I moaned as I finally made it to the front door and opened it a crack. Who would hike all the way up here to Smuggler's Rest so early in the morning?

Standing there, with a gazillion-watt smile and a white and blue chequered shirt and holding a toolbox was, you guessed it, my lodger. Connor Wright. Even more gorgeous than I remembered. Bloody hell, what with Sarah and the twins, I'd forgotten he was moving in today. I clutched my aching head as huge silver spots did the hustle before my eyes.

'Hi – are you all right?' he asked as I crumpled against the wall, my head spinning, or splitting open, whichever came first. 'What happened?'

'Head… door…' I groaned.

He put his toolbox down and lifted my face to inspect my forehead. 'Hang on a second,' he said, half-walking, half-carrying me back into the kitchen where he sat me down and reached into the refrigerator for an ice pack.

'Ouch,' I moaned as he gently placed it against my bruised skin. Up close, even in my confused state, I could see his five o'clock shadow despite the early hour. And yep – his skin was still flawless.

'It's just a bruise. But you are going to have a bit of a bump later.'

'Thank you,' I managed, pulling down on my hem, suddenly aware I was practically starkers except for my flimsy nightie and a cardi. 'Did you bring your things?'

'Yeah.'

'Great. I'll go... get the contract and the keys,' I said. 'Throw some clothes on...'

'Of course, let me help you up.'

I let him pull me up gently and together we headed for the hall again. 'What's that?' I asked, eyeing a box he'd put down.

He grinned and twinkle, twinkle went those eyes again. 'A new kettle.'

It was my turn to grin, thinking of how nice it would look in my next home. 'Thank you. You didn't have to do that.'

He shrugged. 'I wanted to contribute.'

And that was when Sarah stumbled in, dressed in her Charlie Brown PJ shorts and T-shirt.

'Wha's goin' on?' she moaned, stopping short at the sight of a stranger in the house.

'Honey, this is our new lodger, Connor Wright.'

Sarah stared at him, and then at me. 'What? When did you decide this?'

Connor looked back and forth between the two of us. 'Sorry, I came at a bad time...'

'No, no, not at all,' I assured him. 'This is Sarah, my daughter.'

'Oh! Right. Hi.' He leaned over and offered his hand with that polite yet knicker-melting grin. 'Pleased to meet you.'

Why had he looked so surprised? Did he think I was too young to have such a mature daughter? *punches fist into sky*

'I need coffee,' she declared briskly, grabbing the box with a picture of a kettle off the floor, still not in her best mood. 'It's about time you bought a new one, Mum. That old thing had been here since I was ten.'

Connor smiled but said nothing.

'Coffee?' she offered him, remembering her manners.

He nodded. 'Sure, thanks. I'll, uh, go get the rest of my stuff from the car, then.'

'Make yourself at home,' I said. 'I've put out some clean towels for you, and I've already made your bed.'

'Thank you,' he called over his shoulder as he sauntered down to his SUV.

Sarah, more operational than me without the bump on her head, started to make toast and coffee as I ambled back into the lounge to retrieve her housecoat. After all, we couldn't just stand around in our smalls with a man in the house now, could we?

'So it's okay if I go up?' he called from the hall.

'Of course, make yourself at home,' I answered, listening to his light step on the staircase as he hummed a somewhat familiar tune I couldn't quite place.

'Make yourself at *home*?' Sarah hissed. 'Where the hell did you find him? And why, above all?'

I sighed. Here we were, already. 'I need the money, Sarah. This house is too expensive to maintain on one salary.'

'But you know how tiny Wyllow Cove is – everyone's still

talking about the divorce and you've already got a new man in the house? I'm fed up with all the gossip, Mum.'

'First of all, I've never cared what everyone else thinks. It was your father who wanted to impress everyone and anyone.'

She could not argue with that. But my argument was not with her. 'And in any case, Sarah, you'll be here to guard your mother's virtue – and the jewellery.'

Sarah rolled her eyes. 'Mum, I'm just looking out for you. What will Dad think? You've already thrown his stuff out—'

'Stop right there,' I said. 'First of all, I didn't just throw his stuff out. I told him I was decluttering, and to come get it before the pick-up lorry came. If he chose to ignore me, it's certainly not my fault.'

'But, Mum, he was only hoping you'd change your mind…'

I turned to look at her. 'Change my mind? We've been divorced for six months, Sarah. Plus he lives with someone else now.'

Sarah lowered her head. 'I know, Mum. But Dad still loves you.'

'Yes,' I snorted. 'He loves me so much he's gone and found a twenty-year-old bimbo on the side. I'm just sorry I only found out recently.'

She eyed me carefully. 'You… didn't know?'

And then it dawned on me. 'You did?'

She shrugged. 'Sort of.'

'Well.'

'Mum – I'm sorry. I was hoping he'd stop. I didn't want to hurt you.'

'Sweetheart, no worries. I know you only want me to be happy.'

'I do, Mum. But *that*—' she said, pointing upstairs '—is possibly the biggest mistake that you have ever made in your life. What the hell has got into you?'

I sighed. As much as I loved my eldest, she was a photocopy of Neil. Lizzie, on the other hand, was a bit more free-spirited like me.

'Nothing. I just needed a change.'

Sarah snorted. 'He'll change you, all right. He'll take you to bed and then break your heart.'

'Sarah! That is not the way to talk to your mother. He is just a lodger, nothing more. Plus, I'm stronger now than I ever have been. And you will be, too. Just give yourself some time.'

'I only hope you won't regret it.'

I looked at my daughter and wondered how long it would take for her to understand that there was a difference between looking out for your mother and interfering in her new life. Assuming I had a new life. Because unless I shifted this mausoleum and found a way to save my column, there would *be* no new life.

'I'm done,' Connor said from the bottom of the stairs as if to announce himself before entering the kitchen.

'Here, let me help you with that,' he said to Sarah as the kettle boiled.

'That's all right, I can manage, thank you,' she answered, banging cupboard doors open and shut.

Ouch. It was already not looking good. I could only hope that his presence would cheer her up a bit and that we could all become friends. After all, he was a nice bloke, with a ready smile that was contagious. I knew, because I couldn't help smiling back. Or maybe it was just me.

'That really is a nice garden,' he said, looking across the orangery out to the green expanse. Luckily it had been raining a lot in the past few weeks, because a green thumb, I did not have.

'Oh? Oh, yes, thank you. As I mentioned in the ad, it needs a little work. My fences are a disaster and I haven't been to the garden centre yet. Would you, uhm, like a tour before we...?'

He shrugged. 'Sure.'

Saved by the bluebells. I was glad to get him out of Sarah's line of fire, if only for a moment.

I pushed down on the handle of the back door, which suddenly came off in my hand.

'Oh, I'm so sorry about that! I must get it fixed.'

'I can do that for you. I'm pretty good with my hands. Have you got a screwdriver?' he asked.

'I'm sorry? Oh, you don't have to—'

'I want to,' he insisted. 'Wyllow Cove seems like a lovely, safe village, but it's always better to be safe than sorry, don't you think?'

'I think.'

I ducked back into the kitchen where I opened the top drawer and handed him the screwdriver while Sarah shot me a baleful look.

'Can I help in any way?' I asked him.

He was studying the door handle. 'It's just a couple of screws loose, nothing more. Can you hold this straight while I screw it back in?'

'Sure,' I said, putting all my strength into it, trying not

to stare at his lovely face only inches away from mine on the other side of the glass. The man truly did not have any pores to speak of, and his face was a mixture of youthful yet very manly beauty. Just how old was he? Twenty-five, twenty-six, tops? Only eight years older than my youngest daughter. *Shame on you, Natalia Amore.*

'Done,' he said, dusting off his hands.

'Okay, quick garden tour it is, then,' I said. 'Follow me.'

And out we went, where I nattered on and on about the messy borders, the fences that needed replacing and the tall grass and the tree branches that had fallen down last winter that I'd neglected to remove. As much as I loved the outdoors, since I'd have to let my lovely cleaner go, I just had no time for the outside anymore.

'Gorgeous oak tree,' he said, looking up as we reached the bottom of the one-hundred-foot garden.

I smiled. 'Yes, it's over three hundred years old and sturdy as they come.'

He smiled back, apparently enjoying the sound of the breeze as it whispered through the highest branches. It was going to be a warm summer. I could already tell.

Once inside again, I became even more aware of his presence that had been diluted outside, but back in the kitchen, however huge it was, I had no excuse but to look him in the eye. All under Sarah's critical glare.

'And what exactly are you doing in Wyllow Cove, Connor?' she asked as we gathered around the table for breakfast.

He ignored her tone and smiled. 'I needed a break – somewhere quiet. I have a friend in Little Kettering who told me about Wyllow Cove, and I have to say it's even more beautiful than I'd hoped.'

'Have you got any family?' Sarah persisted as she tore off a piece of toast.

'Yes, loads. They live on a farm just outside Dublin.'

'Girlfriend?'

'Sarah…' I said, mortified.

He wiped his mouth and smiled. 'Divorced.'

'Kids?'

'No.'

'Well, I hope you like them anyway,' she said, relish on her pretty face as a horrible crash ripped through the house. Connor looked up towards the ceiling, clearly wondering whether the roof was caving in and I wanted to warn him, but then the twins came in, looking so pretty in their pink pyjamas and housecoats that you'd forgive them anything.

'And who are you?' Amy demanded of Connor in perfect Sarah style, hands on hips.

Zoe simply stared at him, wide-eyed. I was sure even she could tell he was an absolute dish. I had my first crush when I was six, but maybe I was just precocious.

'Amy, Zoe, this is Connor, our new lodger,' I said, urging them to the table to say hello.

'What's a lodger?' Amy asked. 'Is that like a boyfriend? Auntie Nat, you've only been divorced since Christmas.'

Connor grinned as he put his coffee cup down.

'Of course he's not Auntie Nat's boyfriend, Amy,' Sarah answered. 'He's much too young.'

Turning beetroot red, I rolled my eyes at him while Amy plunked herself down to her breakfast, whereas Zoe plucked up the courage to go and stand next to him, her eyes huge as she looked up into his face.

'Hello, sweetheart,' he said softly as he bent down to her. But Zoe just continued to look at him in silence.

'Connor, these are my nieces, Amy and Zoe. Girls – say hello to Connor.'

Amy peered up at his face, whereas Zoe remained silent. I gave her a gentle nudge.

'Come on, darling, say hello to Connor.'

'Hello, Connor,' Zoe whispered.

'Hello, Zoe. It's very nice to meet you. Hello, Amy.'

'Hi,' Amy said back, amiably enough.

'Connor will be living with us,' I informed them, wondering how that sounded to a new pair of ears.

'Then he really is your boyfriend,' Amy said, her eyes flicking over him analytically.

'Amy…'

'I'm just a friend,' he answered politely.

'So are you staying here for free?' Amy continued and I slapped my hand over my forehead, forgetting my bruise.

'Amy – please don't be rude,' I scolded and mouthed to Connor, *I'm so sorry*, but he winked at me. *Winked* at me. Innocently, without any sexual subtext whatsoever. So why did my skin tingle?

Zoe was still staring at him and when he turned to smile at her again, she said, 'You look like Poldark. My nana loves Poldark. So does Auntie Nat.'

Connor threw his head back and laughed while Zoe climbed onto his lap and settled herself against his chest like a three-year-old, and, after a moment's surprise from all of us and an uncertain glance my way, Connor's hand rested on her little back.

I wanted to tell her that she shouldn't be so immediately trusting, and that the world was full of horrible people, but I couldn't bring myself to do it and break this instant idyll. It was like love at first sight – between them – and I didn't want to ruin it. Perhaps Zoe was the extension of me. I, too, would have loved to be able to trust a stranger – or any man, for that matter, but that ship had sailed for me a long time ago. I also wouldn't have minded sitting in his lap, either, but those privileges were reserved for people with nothing to lose.

If my husband Neil could up and leave me with no warning, and if Sam could gamble his relationship away and cheat on Sarah, what hope was there for me to ever start anew? No. All I wanted was to live my own life, away from the people who had hurt me, and Neil was in the top two.

'Zoe, darling, come sit here and let Connor eat his breakfast,' I cooed, and she obediently slid off his lap and into the chair next to me.

'That's okay,' he said. 'I don't mind at all. On the contrary. I have tons of nieces and nephews and I enjoy being around them.'

'That'd because they're your own blood. Give these two some time and you'll be running for the hills,' Sarah said, nodding at the twins who giggled.

'Sarah and the girls are going to be staying with us for a bit,' I explained to Connor as Amy started on her apple juice, not taking her eyes off him. Zoe was still watching him too, her eyes still wide in wonder. The kid had excellent taste.

'Ah, we'll have loads of fun, then,' he answered as the toaster popped up and he stretched a long arm to put the slices before us.

I lowered my head to kiss Zoe's forehead. 'Amy, would you like some toast with that juice?' I said, and she pulled out a chair right opposite Connor, suddenly interested in him now.

'Your name doesn't start with an N,' Zoe said.

Connor's eyebrows went up in confusion and he looked at me for help as I slapped my forehead again, this time avoiding the bruised spot.

'Oh,' I laughed nervously. 'It's just a family joke.'

'Sarah has Sam,' Zoe began to explain.

'Had. Not anymore,' Amy corrected her and Sarah groaned.

'Lizzie has Liam…' Zoe continued.

'Zoe, sweetie—'

'Auntie Nat had Neil, but he doesn't live here anymore.'

'Honey—'

'So you can't take his place unless your name stars with an N.'

At that, Connor fought to not snort coffee through his nose and fixed a benevolent eye on them. 'Can I keep my name even if I'm only going to live here for a little while?'

Sarah murmured something and shot to her feet, throwing the dishes into the dishwasher and then, wrapping her housecoat around her even tighter, charged out of the kitchen without another word.

'I'm finished, Auntie Nat. Can I get up from the table?' Zoe asked and Amy rolled her eyes.

'Of course, darling. Amy, have you got anything to say?'

'Same for me. Can I go?'

We played this game every meal time, and it was taking me longer than I'd hoped, but I was gradually managing to crack Amy and drum some manners into her.

'Yes, you may both go. But let's leave Sarah alone for a bit, okay?'

'Oh-kay,' Amy said, stomping her way out, followed by a light-footed Zoe.

I watched them go and then turned to Connor. 'I'm sorry about all that. They're normally good girls.'

'Nat,' he said. 'It's fine. I have two brothers and three sisters, and they all have kids under fifteen. I'm happy to be here. And your nieces remind me of my own. Marian and Emilia are like photocopies of yours. Amy and Zoe are adorable.'

'Thank you. They are, each in their own way.'

We sat in silence for a few moments. But it was a comfortable silence, with layers of common ground between us. We did have a lot in common, I was beginning to discover. Family was paramount to both of us. We were both divorced and starting over.

But while I was considering him as the perfect candidate for a fling, obviously the thought hadn't even crossed his mind. Why would it, with plenty of beautiful girls around? I was the landlady. Possibly a potential friend. But nothing more.

'I think Sarah will be the tough one to crack. She is very protective of you,' he observed neutrally.

'I'm sorry about her being so tetchy. She's just broken up with her boyfriend.'

'Sorry to hear that,' he said sympathetically. 'But I can totally understand why she would come back here. I don't know what it is, but there's something about your home that is so welcoming.'

I shrugged. 'It used to be, when we all lived here together, even with all the creepy portraits of Neil's family frowning down at us. But now that I'm downsizing, I think I'll be leaving a few of the family ghosts behind.'

'And some of your own?'

I looked up.

'I think that your new home, wherever that may be, will be a happier one without all the memories of what led you to the divorce. I know it was like that for me.'

'Well, you've got that right. My whole life would be made if I could move away from here and all the bad memories.'

'Ah, but you'll take the good ones with you in your heart. Am I not right?'

His voice softened as he said this, as if for a brief moment he'd had an insight as to what it had been like, living with Neil. Which, of course, he did, due to his own divorce. I guess sharing the same kind of pain made people more empathic.

'You're right,' I agreed, and there was another moment of silence as he watched me and I understood that he was silently, and perhaps even unconsciously, acknowledging the fact that we were both in that place where we were slowly but surely recovering from our darker moments.

'But I'm sure you're not interested in family drama,' I tittered, my eyes darting away as I spoke.

DREAMS OF A LITTLE CORNISH COTTAGE

He grinned. 'I come from an Irish family, Natalia. Drama is in my DNA.'

'Ah. Well, in that case, you'll fit right in.'

He leaned in. 'And for the record, Nat – I think your home has this feeling because of all your love for your family.'

'You really think so?'

He spread his arms. 'Look around you. You are the glue of this family. There's nothing you wouldn't do for them.'

'True. But I do hope they won't be too much of a nuisance to you.'

'Ah, really, Nat, you're grand. Unless things are now different for you? If this is a time when you need to be alone with them, I can always find somewhere else, no problem at all.'

'What? No, no, don't even think that, Connor. We'll be absolutely fine. The house won't be up for sale for another few months so if you're still okay with a short lease...'

'Absolutely. I won't go until you ask me to.'

'Oh good,' I breathed, and the warmth inside me returned. 'Not that I've even contacted an agent as of yet. And I'm still packing up Neil's stuff. He lives with his girlfriend in a tiny flat so he's going to have to put it all into storage. Sorry, too much information. I'm just an open book, unfortunately.'

He smiled, toasting me with his coffee mug. 'A lovely book.'

Now how was that as far as Irish charm went?

The rest of our day was spent in the garden with the girls horsing around with Missy who loved all the attention while Sarah ploughed through my back issues of *Good*

Housekeeping and of course, *Lady*. I pretended to be working by having my faithful notepad to jot down my thoughts in the very rare event of an idea. All this in conjunction with surreptitiously watching Connor at the end of the garden sorting out his tools in order to start on my broken fences.

See? Any other lodger wouldn't have agreed to do that for free now, would he? But, *elated sigh*, he wasn't just any other lodger, and I remembered the scene in the movie *Hattie*, where she is sitting in the garden, drooling while her new lodger, John Schofield, is flexing his muscles and flirting with no shirt on. I only hope we wouldn't end up the same way, i.e. him leaving her for someone else.

Connor was helpful but unobtrusive. Fun but not overbearing. But, also, apart from noticing how perfectly he fit into our routine, I couldn't help but notice how perfectly he fit into his *jeans*. Gorgeous but didn't know it. And I couldn't help but admire his arms as they flexed when he lifted a post. But when he got down onto his knees to inspect the base of the fence, I looked away, wondering if here were any tenant-lodger rules.

'You can look again, Mum,' Sara said hotly. 'He hasn't got plumber's bum, by the way.'

Busted. I lifted my eyes to her *gotcha* look. Christ, what was so wrong about having eyes? I was divorced and still under forty. Didn't I have a right to admire male beauty?

'Hm…?' I said distractedly, scanning my empty page while chewing on my pen.

'Don't *hm* me, Mum. I can see you, you know.'

I was determined to stick this one out. 'What's that, sweetheart?'

Her eyes narrowed and then, with her index finger, she

drew a circle before my face. 'You've got a look – the look of... Didn't you say after Dad that you would never be interested in men again?'

'Did I?' Bugger it.

'Yes, so you can stop swooning over Mr Bod over there.'

'Nonsense. I'm not swooning over anyone. And keep your voice down, please.'

She snorted, returning to her magazine, muttering something about forty being the new twenty, but only as far as foolishness was concerned.

'And what about you?' I asked. 'Are you slowly healing?'

Sarah chewed on her lower lip, a habit she'd inherited from me, and I could see the hurt on her face, but also the fire in her eyes and the determination to downplay it and recover as quickly as possible.

'There isn't much to heal from,' she said with a shrug, putting her magazine down. 'I thought that Sam was something that he's not. I'd put up with a lot from him even as I knew we were slowly fizzling into nothingness, and then he broke the last straw. I had to leave for my own sanity, Mum.'

I nodded. 'I know, darling, and you did the right thing, if I may say so now.'

The next Sunday morning was hot and sunny, and I couldn't wait to get out and about. Over the years, when Yolanda was away, the twins and I had developed our own Sunday morning routine. Neil would stay home and read the papers while the three of us would put together a picnic basket, slather ourselves in sunblock in the summer or cover up in woollies and wellies in the winter and head down the footpath to the beach where we'd do some rock pooling, followed by seal watching and some good old sandwich and sand munching.

They loved it down there, always finding something new to do, people to talk to (well, Amy, especially) and dogs to play with. After lunch, we'd go for a long stroll along the harbour front for ice cream and a chat with the fellow villagers who also enjoyed the afternoon sunshine on their faces while indulging themselves in a pint at The One That Got Away, the local pub on the fishing pier.

It was always lovely to see everyone away from their workplaces at least one day a week. They were all there. Dora, who owned The Rising Bun bakery, would ditch her apron for the afternoon while one of her daughters, usually Felicity, dealt with customers vying for that last slice of luscious, yet tangy lemon drizzle or that rich yet delicate carrot cake that only Dora could bake.

And Jim, the owner of the pub, who carried barrels up and down from the cellar with such speed as if the place was on fire, was simply lying out on the quay, arms outstretched like the Vitruvian man, without a care in the world.

Myrtle and Richard, the silver-haired couple who ran the post office/greengrocers named Fresh Lettuce 'N' Letters and who had been married for forty years now, were ambling along the beach, too, hand in hand like two sixth-form sweethearts.

'It's so lovely to see you with the girls, Nat,' Myrtle said, bending towards them without letting go of Richard's hand.

'It's lovely to see you, too, Myrtle. How's the old hip?'

She waved my concerns away. 'Bah, still attached to the rest of me, so it's okay! Yolanda away again?'

'Yeah,' I said as the girls skipped off to chase the seagulls. I watched as Zoe generously offered most of her sandwich up, which was why I always made her two, while Amy threw rocks at the feathered predators, not always, unfortunately, missing her targets.

'You're so good with them, just like you were with your own girls,' Richard commented.

'Thanks, Richard.'

'I suspect we'll be seeing more of you now that Neil's moved out?' Myrtle said.

I couldn't help but smile. 'Absolutely. And... I'm looking to buy in the village.'

'Good! There's a couple of cottages for sale on the far side of the quay, I think.'

'Oh? I'll definitely go and have a look, then. Thanks.'

Myrtle patted my cheek. 'It's good to have you back, Nat. That man was no good for you. It's time to get yourself one who actually likes people. When Richard sprained his ankle, Neil barely looked at it, let alone touched it.'

Pretty much how he'd treated our marriage, I thought to myself.

Neil did not like me mingling too much, as if I had suddenly become better than everyone else simply because my married surname was a double-barrelled one. The idiocy of it all. But being a doctor's wife kept me socially busy, hosting dinners and parties for his Truro colleagues, all the while pining for my people instead. And now that I was free, I wanted to move down back into the village near my friends, where I belonged.

For a hamlet of circa one hundred inhabitants, Wyllow Cove was Cornwall's best-kept secret, as the tourist industry hadn't sussed us out yet. Which suited us all fine. Not that we weren't welcoming. Of course we were, but the idea of being so tight-knit and knowing everyone since birth was heart-warming and reassuring.

While all the youngsters, like my own, had fled to Truro or gone the whole hog to London, you needed a reason to come to Wyllow Cove as it wasn't on the road to anywhere else. Which made me wonder why a certain handsome Irishman had chosen our little hamlet to live.

Yes, there was a core of young families that refused to go as they had the luxury of working from home, but what exactly was he doing here, in such an out-of-the-way place? Was he still nursing a broken heart?

He had mentioned he needed peace and quiet. But you could find that in most of the villages in Cornwall. So why Wyllow Cove?

In the old days, when I was still married to Neil, he never wanted to come down to the beach, so I always brought the girls with me. After an afternoon out and about chatting and laughing and just soaking in the relaxed atmosphere, the twins and I would say our goodbyes with a promise to have another lengthy chinwag the following Sunday, and scarper back up the footpath, picnic basket and all, exhausted and tanned and happy.

Once home, we'd empty our sandals of all the sand – or mud, depending once again on the season – and rinse them and our feet out with the garden hose and then I'd help them with their showers and getting changed into clean clothes. And then they would attempt to fill Neil in on the goings-on in the village. He'd listen for a few minutes and then his eyes would begin to glaze over and he'd finally give up on the book he was reading, only to try his luck by turning on the TV, louder and louder, to drown their voices out.

Shaking my head, I'd call the girls back in and explain that Uncle Neil was tired.

'From what, reading the papers all day?' Amy would scoff.

How did one answer such a direct question? As it turned out, I later found out that he was indeed tired, and rightfully so, but less from reading the paper than rolling around on the ancestral settee in his study with his floozy; I mean, his secretary. Could he have been more clichéd? And could I have been any more blind? It was a good thing that I had put it all behind me with a certain sense of relief, rather than wallowing in self-pity. Life wasn't long enough for that.

And then they'd help me prepare supper and one of them would bring Neil's out to the snug on a tray as he preferred to not interrupt his vision of all of the day's games and scores. It suited us fine, as we'd munch on our food and talk about all the things we'd done and all the friends we'd met during the day, making plans for the next Sunday.

Considering that now Neil and his acidic indifference were gone, I could only say that things had changed for the better.

The next morning Connor was planting some flowers in the garden as the girls mucked around in the dirt with him. They seemed to migrate to him whenever he was around.

Between you and me, after the divorce, when I had

trouble falling asleep, I always had the habit of forcing myself to think of something nice. And now I didn't need to force myself; nowadays, the moment I closed my eyes, Connor's smile would appear in my mind's eye.

And in the morning, I couldn't wait to see his smile. Just like now.

'You ready to help, so?' he called out to me.

'Me?' I called back, shooting to my feet. The garden was long, but I was down there in a heartbeat.

'You,' he said with a grin. 'All you do is work. Take a screen break, tell me where you want these violets.'

I looked at them, and then back at him. How the hell would I know? 'Uhm…?'

He threw back his head and laughed. 'Are you sure you're not a city girl?'

'I'm as Cornish as they come, only I don't have a green thumb.'

He looked at the girls. 'Did you hear your Auntie Nat? She rhymes! She really is a writer.' And with that, he bent to poke a hole into the earth big enough for his violets.

I shrugged. 'A writer without words, at the moment.'

He looked up, rubbing his hands to get rid of the dirt. 'Yeah? Writer's block?'

'I guess so. I need inspiration.'

'Then you need to do something new.'

Like him, a little red voice said inside me. *You need to do him.* If only he showed any interest!

Oh, be quiet, said the little pink voice on my other side. *She's a lady, not a—*

'Something new? Like, uhm, what?' I ventured.

Connor watched as the girls pressed the soil down at the bottom of the garden as he'd instructed them. Then he turned to look at me, his dark eyes twinkling.

'Something you thought you'd never have the courage to do.'

Ohgodohgod. If I hadn't known any better, I'd have thought he was flirting with me. He'd had more than one chance to, so far. But so far, no good. Maybe he was a late bloomer?

In any case, I sincerely liked being around him, so it was time to stop worrying about the lack of a looming romance – which was never going to happen between us – and just enjoy the present. I absolutely understood the girls' interest in him. But I would have to have a word with them about giving our lodger his space.

'We could find something to do all together,' Connor said. 'Like surfing. Do you surf?'

'You must be joking,' I said. 'I can barely swim.'

He stood up. 'What kind of a Cornish girl are you?'

'A very lazy one.'

'So it's decided. I'll teach you and the girls to surf.'

The mere idea of standing in front of him in a swimsuit, or worse, a wetsuit, made me cringe. 'Uhm, I'm okay with the girls learning, but we'll just have to see about me,' I answered as heat crept up my neck. Even the thought of *him* in a wetsuit was more than I could take. I needed my emotions with a pinch of distance.

He laughed. 'Okay, no pressure, so!'

No pressure? All I could think of lately was him. When I got back inside, I moved my desk so I could keep an eye on them and make sure they weren't pestering him (and, yes, okay, also to keep an eye on him as well), and sat down to write my article.

But it was no use. I simply couldn't concentrate, what with my career in danger and a half-packed-up house around me. There were a million things on my mind and when I got like this it was pointless trying to plough through the writing when I'd only be killing what little enthusiasm I had. Better to spend my time by actually being productive and getting my errands done. I stood up, debating on whether to bother him by involving him in the insignificant minutiae of my household. In the end, courtesy, and the will to get to know him better, took over.

'Connor?' I called softly through the French doors, leaning against the door jamb. 'I need to pop out and get some cartridges and some more bubble wrap. Do you need anything?' I offered.

He looked up and smiled. 'I'm all right, thanks, Nat.'

'Okay. Zoe? Amy? Put your shoes on, we're going into the village.'

'Awh, Auntie Nat – we're having fun!' Amy called back, as for once Zoe nodded her agreement. 'Can't we stay with Connor?'

'No, my pet, you can't. Connor is busy and doesn't have time to keep an eye on you.'

'You can leave the girls with me if you want. I'm not going anywhere,' he offered.

'Oh, no, I couldn't do that.'

'It's fine, Nat,' he said and the twins looked at me expectantly.

I debated. I had never left the girls with anyone, let alone someone I'd just met. Granted, I had all of his details and all. He wasn't actually a stranger per se. But maybe I should leave my trip until later. Sarah was home too, though, so I wasn't leaving them solely in his care.

Connor dusted his hands off and came to stand opposite me, followed by the girls who gravitated around him like metal shavings to a lodestone. In her haste to reach him, Amy almost tripped but Connor's hand instinctively shot to his side to steady her. Did this man have eyes at the back of his head?

'Go,' he said. 'The girls will be helping me here. Won't you, worker bees?'

Well, they'd certainly be safe, that was for sure.

'Yes!' the girls agreed, Amy, who never liked to be told what to do, agreeing even louder than Zoe. Hm. His influence on her could be a breakthrough out of her fractious ways.

I bit my lip. 'Really?'

'Absolutely.'

'I wouldn't be imposing? They can be a handful,' I warned him.

He grinned and turned towards my nieces again. 'Girls? Can you promise Auntie Nat that you won't tear the house apart while she pops into the village?'

'Promise!' Amy hollered as she came to a halt right in front of me, giving me a military salute.

I swallowed. 'Well, okay then. Thank you, Connor. I owe you one.'

'No problem, Nat. We'll be here when you get back,' he said softly, almost as if only for my benefit. Then he smacked his hands together loudly. 'Now who wants to help me dig up this old woody bush and plant new ones?'

'I do!' the girls chimed in unison and he grinned up at me as his curls tumbled over his eyes and he flicked them back with a toss of his head. 'See? Piece of cake, I tell you. Now go.'

'Well, if you're sure, then. Thank you.'

And after that, things were never the same again.

4

Mummy Dear

While I was down in Wyllow Cove, I bumped into my mother's neighbour, Mrs Locke, the village busybody and quite frankly, a nasty piece of work. It was no wonder she and my mother got on like a house on fire. Not having any choice but to stop as she'd already spotted me, I paused for what to the poor untrained sod would seem like small talk. Because I knew that, as soon as I turned and went my way, she'd dash back to my mother's to tell her how I was *literally* fifty yards away from her home but had chosen all the same to not pop in.

And now you'll think I'm a bad daughter. But if you had lived with my mother Beryl for the best part of twenty years and managed to grow up into a happy adult *despite* her, you'd get me completely.

I had had absolutely no attention whatsoever while living in that house. Nothing I ever did was good enough to mention – not my good grades, not my extra-curricular achievements – nothing. And you'd think that being the eldest of two, I'd at least be considered for that much. But from the day Yolanda was born, me being only two, I had literally faded into the background among the geometric patterns of the old Fifties wallpaper of our home.

'Droppin' in on yer poor mum, I expect,' she told rather than said to me.

'Uhm yes, of course,' I managed. 'I've got some errands to run first, but I'll be popping round later.'

She glared at me as if I'd said I would rather die than see her and stalked off.

I sighed and paid for my cyan and black cartridges and picked up some cinnamon buns – Mum's favourite – at The Rising Bun.

Mum's cottage, once our family home and where she now lived alone, was a small, three-bed terraced house right on the harbour front, but towards the end, so she was in the midst of it, but had her privacy. There was a bijoux front garden and a good-sized back garden. For years I'd tried to get Mum to renovate; not to bring the old fisherman's cottage into the twenty-first century, but at least to let it not fall apart in the next few years, but she was adamant. The Artex ceiling was staying, along with the single glazing and the Economy Seven electric heater. Which brings me to the huge bubble of water hanging from the ceiling right over the settee, caused by a leak in the upstairs bathroom that she refused to fix.

'Mum,' I'd said to her countless times. 'You have to get rid of that. Your beams are going to rot and the entire roof will collapse in time if you don't.'

To which she'd reply: 'Your father was the only man had

ever touched this house – and me, for that matter. So when it goes, I go. Together we stand, together we fall.'

After various attempts, I'd got Yolanda to lure her out of the house for a few hours and had a competent builder sort it out. But when Mum got back home, did she even notice it? No. Mum only noticed the negatives.

As I rang the doorbell and let myself in as usual, it turned out that Mrs Locke had actually beaten me to it, and was now glaring at me again like I'd just punched her in the face. Not that I wouldn't want to, nosy old cow. All my life she'd looked down on me like I was dirt, and God only knew what lies Mum had told her about me, or worse, about how wonderful Yolanda was.

And that was when I noticed the crutch against her armchair. 'Mum! What happened to your leg?'

She looked at me, then shrugged. 'It's me ankle. Sprained it.'

'Why on earth didn't you call me?' I asked, rounding to take a better look, but there was a bandage on it.

'What for? What could you have done?'

'I could've taken you to the hospital for starters!' I said. 'Are you sure it's not broken?'

'Of course it's not broken. I'd be howling in pain if it was, wouldn't I? Now stop fussing over me.'

'But does it hurt? Have you taken a painkiller?'

'Just a moment ago,' she answered, rolling her eyes at Mrs Locke, as if I was the intruder. Go figure.

Mrs Locke's eyes were now sizzling with delight at the sign of some more potential domestic tension. Was it me or was this not pure ostracism at its best? You'd think that a mother would always side with her family. And you'd usually be right. Only in my mum's case, you'd be wrong.

I stared Mrs Locke down, and then turned back to my mum. 'How are you going to get upstairs to go to bed then?'

She looked at me, then looked away. 'I was planning to sleep on the settee.'

'What? That's crazy, Mum.' I headed for the stairs.

'Where are you going?' she called after me.

'I'm packing you a bag.'

'A bag? What for?'

'So you can come and stay with me, of course.'

'I don't need to come and stay with you, Natalia. I'm perfectly fine on my own here.'

'No, you're not, Mum,' I argued from the top of the stairs. 'You can't hobble around the house on one foot – and the neighbours have their own lives and business to tend to. Don't you, Mrs Locke?'

'Well, I could pop in a couple of times a day,' she said sourly.

'Nonsense, you have your TV programmes. I'll take care of my mother, thank you very much.'

But on the way back to my place it was all *Why didn't you leave me there* and *I can manage on my own* and *I don't want to be a burden.*

Oh, if I'd only known then what I knew now.

'Connor?' I called as we got in.

'I thought your cat's name was Missy,' Mum said.

Connor was in the orangery juggling at least five oranges while the girls shrieked in delight. I paused, waiting as my mum stopped to catch her breath and I couldn't help but smile at this picture of serenity.

'So this is what's been keeping you busy,' she observed coolly.

'I bet you can't do six!' Amy challenged as he continued.

'I bet you I can!' he countered.

'Okay, then, what do we win if you can't?'

'What do you want?' he asked as the oranges continued to whir around his head and he made funny faces.

'Ice cream!' Amy negotiated. 'If you drop the oranges, you take us out for ice cream!'

'Deal!' he agreed, turning to acknowledge our presence and wink at me. It was just a tiny muscle twitch, but it instantly made me warm and fuzzy all over. What was happening to me?

He suddenly dropped all the oranges, one by one.

'Haaaa!' the twins cried. 'Ice cream it is!'

'All right, all right, you little pixies, pipe down, now,' he said as he bolted over to us at the sight of my mother on crutches. 'Hey, let me help.'

'Thanks, Connor, thank you so much. This is my mum, Beryl. She's sprained her ankle and will be staying with us for the next few days.'

Mum removed her glasses and looked him up and down. 'Very dishy.'

'Mum!' I hissed, but Connor smiled and held out his hand. His voice was respectful but warm at the same time. How did he do that? 'Pleasure to meet you, Mrs—'

'Beryl. Call me Beryl. I'm not that old.'

Connor grinned. 'Okay, Beryl.'

'And besides – the pleasure's all mine, I'm sure,' she murmured, and I couldn't tell if she was serious or not. Because Mum didn't do warmth. Nor did she ever laugh. Come to think of it, I couldn't even recall the last time I saw her smile since Dad's death.

'Right. Mum,' I said, taking charge. 'I'm going to move you into my study so you won't have to climb the stairs. There's a really comfy bed in there and you can see all the way down to the sea.'

She looked at Connor and gestured towards me. 'She doesn't understand the word *no*, this one. Fine, Nat. I'll stay. Just for a few days and to shut you up.'

Connor grinned. 'My good old Irish luck, so,' he said. 'We'll have great fun together, you'll see, Beryl.'

'Oh, I intend to,' she threatened him.

A little later, as I was transferring a few writing supplies from the study to the orangery off the kitchen, the doorbell rang.

'I'll get it,' Connor offered as he was coming down the stairs. After a moment of silence, he poked his head into the orangery. 'I think it's your GP?'

Neil? Oh my God in heaven. Just how had *he* found out about Mum? Ah. Mrs Locke must have blabbed.

'What's all this?' Neil said as he came in, spotting all the boxes and bubble wrap.

'Hello, Neil. This is Connor, my new lodger. Connor, you've met my ex-husband Neil.'

'Hi,' he said politely, extending a hand that Neil took rather reluctantly, turning to me for further explanation. Not that I owed him any.

Connor caught the drift and with a light cough, excused himself from the room.

'What are you doing?' Neil demanded in a hiss.

'Packing up the rest of your stuff. Isn't it obvious?'

'Besides that – what the hell is going on? Why is there a strange man living in our home?'

'My home, Neil. And all this,' I said, waving a hand over what could only be considered the tiniest portion of the entire collection of the Tamblynn-Lobb family heirlooms, 'is your stuff. I'm saving a couple of things each for the girls, but you can take the rest.'

'But I haven't got anywhere to put all this stuff!' he said, panicking. 'My flat is tiny…'

I shrugged. 'So? I certainly don't want it. Put it into storage.'

'Storage? With all the room you have here, you want me to put our forebears' stuff into storage?'

'Forebears? Please. It's just your grandparents' old tat.'

'Natalia, why are you doing this to me?'

'Because I'm selling the house.'

'You *what*? You can't do that! I forbid you!'

I snorted.

'But it's our family home!' he insisted.

'Was. It was our family home. Before you wrecked it. Now it's just an albatross around my neck.'

'What the hell are you talking about?'

I sighed. Neil and I had never been on the same wavelength. 'Forget about it.'

'You're throwing our whole life away and you want me to forget about it?'

'Neil,' I said, breathing deeply. 'May I remind you that

you were the one to throw our life away. So now, if you don't mind, I'm starting afresh and I certainly don't need any memories of you or your bloody forebears.'

'What about the girls?'

'They respect my decision.'

He rolled his eyes. 'I meant that they are a memory of me.'

I shrugged. 'Luckily just the good bits, Neil.'

'And can't you just remember the good bits? For old times' sake?'

I looked over at him above the sea of bubble wrap and boxes. But all I could remember was the humiliation, the never being good enough, let alone his superior frostiness towards me, especially in front of our dinner guests every single Saturday. He had been ashamed of me, despite the fact that I had become a master in hosting dinner parties. He had taken me for granted, shunned me, embarrassed me, and cheated on me. And I was supposed to forgive all that?

'Bring some boxes next time you come over, Neil. I haven't got enough.'

'I can't change your mind?'

'No.'

He heaved a huge sigh, a forlorn look on his face. 'Have you actually put it on the market yet?'

'Not yet. I'm getting it viewer-ready.'

'By packing everything up? Viewers want to see a lifestyle.'

'Well, certainly not your lifestyle. Plus I'm just emptying all the cupboards of old tat.'

'I wish you would stop talking about my ancestors' belongings like that.'

Again with the ancestors. But for the sake of civility: 'Right.'

'So where would you live?'

'Down in the village somewhere.'

'With the rest of the villagers?' he almost squeaked. The thought of his ex-wife living with the commoners made his skin crawl. And it made my heart sing.

'Yes, Neil. Down in the village, among everyone else.' The way it should have always been.

'But you're a Tamblynn-Lobb. We don't live among the commoners.'

'Not anymore, I'm not. Besides, I've never had – what did you use to call it – the class of your nobility?'

'You're still the mother of my children and I'll not have you mixing with the villagers.'

I snorted. 'You're their GP. You see them every day. How can you talk like that about them? They are all lovely, salt-of-the-earth people who work hard for a living. If it weren't for them, you'd be a poor, derelict medic.'

'If you're doing this to spite me—'

'Neil – get over yourself. It's not always about you. You may think that having an old surname, a coat of arms and some old furniture makes you better than all the rest, but it doesn't. Now if you'll excuse me, I've got work to do.'

He eyed me, his mouth crooked and his nose out of joint.

'Right. I'm going to check on Mum. How's her ankle?'

'She's not your mum, Neil. She never was. In any case, you tell me. You're the doctor.'

'Why didn't you call me straight away?'

'Because she had someone else look at it in the A&E a few days ago.'

'Days? And you didn't think to call?'

I huffed. 'I've only just found out myself. She never mentioned it any of the times I called her.'

'You mean to say you haven't seen her in three entire days?'

Three days of bliss, actually. But what did he know about our relationship anyway? From the start he'd decided that she was right and I was the thin-skinned wimp. But not anymore.

'Dad! Hi!' Sarah boomed as she came downstairs.

'Hello, sweetheart! How are you? Where's Sam?'

Sarah's eyes swung to mine for help. Neil absolutely loved Sam – and so he would.

'Sarah's visiting for a few days,' I volunteered.

'Ah, Sarah, that's nice of you to keep your Nana Beryl company, seeing as your mother hasn't got any time to spare.'

'Neil? I've got stuff to do, and you're only slowing me down and annoying me, so if you're going to check on my mother in the study, please do. Otherwise, you can start taking these boxes out to your car.'

He stopped at the door of my study where I had set my mother up and said, just about loud enough for her to hear, 'You have become so bitter over the years, Natalia.'

Bitter? It was all his handiwork. I had been perfectly happy before him. 'Don't forget the boxes on your way out.'

He eyed me at length, but I refused to rise to his bait and turn around to continue the argument. When he saw that I was actively ignoring him, he let out a loud sigh and then knocked on Mum's door.

'Hello, Mum,' he said and disappeared inside.

'Neil – get yer ass in here. What took you so long?' she chided him, but I heard him say, 'Keeping your spirits up as usual, I see?'

Now, if you thought that a mother would always side with her daughter rather than the cheating ex-husband, you'd usually be absolutely right. But not in this case. Mum always sided with him because she couldn't understand why a woman would want to divorce a doctor.

I went outside for a breath of fresh air and to check on the girls – yes, okay, and Connor – who were busy pulling worms out of a hole. Or rather, Amy was, and Zoe was begging her to put them back and leave them alone.

At the end of the garden, Connor was on his knees digging something up. It was like he and the earth were one. He obviously enjoyed getting his hands dirty and keeping busy, and I wondered if it was his way of getting through the day without hurting too much after his own divorce.

'Connor!' Zoe cried for help. Not to me, her Auntie Nat, but to a total stranger. 'Please tell Amy to stop!'

Connor went over to kneel before them, his huge hands dangling between his knees. 'Amy, do you think you might let the poor little fellow off? He's probably got little kids waiting at home for him. Hm?' he cajoled.

'At least they'll see their dad tonight,' she huffed, but, as if under a new, mysterious spell, she obeyed, and Zoe quickly sprinkled some earth back on top of them, making sure he wouldn't get squished.

I felt myself blushing as I walked down to where they crouched. 'Thank you, Connor. They seem to listen to you more than they do me, lately.'

He shrugged, and his dark eyes twinkled. A twinkle that touched something somewhere deep inside me. 'That's not what I see.'

'Oh? And what, uhm… do you see?'

'I see a wonderful aunt who would do anything for her nieces. And nieces who adore their aunt.'

And there was that warm, tingly sensation again. 'You're too kind, Connor. Listen, uhm, while my ex-husband is here with my mother I'm going to pop into Wyllow Cove to get some of her stuff. Could I leave you with the girls again? For just ten minutes? Cheeky, I know… But Sarah and my mother will be here if you need help.'

'Absolutely, Nat. Go ahead.'

'Thanks so much, Connor, I normally wouldn't ask, but…'

He grinned, pushing his hair off his face. 'No problem. Kids love me.'

Not just kids, I wanted to say, but thought better of it.

'Is that all right, girls?' I asked.

'Yay!' they shouted in unison.

After a few moments, Neil came out into the garden.

'Uncle Neil!' the girls cried, rushing to him. Even if he had never been top of the list for affection, strangely their loyalty to him had not dwindled. Although it was for the best, it told me just how love-starved they were.

'Hey, you guys!' he called. 'Look how much you've grown!'

I watched, completely disenchanted as he fussed over them for a few seconds, then followed me back to the kitchen. 'I heard you're going out?'

'Just to get some of my mother's stuff. Why?'

Neil's eyes widened. 'You were going to leave our nieces here with a stranger?'

Oh dear. 'He's not a stranger. I have his references. And I'll only be a minute.'

He crossed his arms. 'Sometimes it only takes a minute.'

'Neil, what are you on about?'

'Nothing. Take your time. *I'm* staying with our family until you get back.'

I ignored his territorial stance. Mussolini couldn't have done it better.

'Do I need to get a prescription for something while I'm out?' I asked, trying to change the subject.

'Just ordinary Disprin for the pain,' he answered.

'Right,' I said, poking my head into Mum's new room where she was reading *Good Housekeeping*. 'Mum, do you want to come and sit in the orangery while I'm gone? I'm going to get your stuff. Is there anything particular you need?'

'Just my recliner,' she answered without looking up.

I stopped. 'Your recliner? But we have a perfectly good recliner here, Mum.'

'Yes, but it's not mine, is it?'

'Mum – it's too big for the car...'

At that moment, Connor came in for a glass of water. He snapped his head back as he swallowed and then looked over at us, as though not sure whether to intervene or not. 'If Neil is staying with the girls, I can drive you over in my Jeep, Nat,' he offered.

Neil's jaw snapped open. 'What? I'm sure we don't want to inconvenience you.'

'No inconvenience at all,' Connor answered with his usual charm.

'That's a wonderful idea, Connor, thank you,' Mum said, then looked at me. 'See? Sorted. Plus, Neil's offered to wait until you get back.'

Neil looked back and forth between Connor and me, then nodded curtly. 'Don't be long. I have patients waiting.'

'Oh?' I said. 'We don't want to keep you.'

'It's fine,' he snapped. 'Just don't take forever.'

So I scooped my house keys out of the mother-of-pearl dish in the hall and we left Neil in charge of the twins and Mum for the five-minute drive to her cottage down in Wyllow Cove, my mobile phone in my pocket, just in case.

Connor drove with ease, giving way even when it wasn't necessary, earning him waved thank yous from the villagers whose eyes popped open when they saw who was in his passenger seat. I guessed there was a difference between knowing that the village GP had been kicked out by his wife and seeing her in a car with another man. I almost giggled to myself at the thought of the rumours.

'What gorgeous seascapes,' Connor marvelled as beyond every turn we were regaled with better and better views of the horseshoe-shaped harbour piled with pastel-coloured cottages, one of which was Mum's. And of course Lavender Cottage, with its pretty front garden.

'Where am I going?' Connor asked, slowing down at the entrance to the village.

'Uhm, sorry, just drive through to the very end of the High Street, then turn left for the quay. It's the second-last cottage.'

'Nice…' he said. 'I always wanted a little cottage facing the sea.'

'You and me both. That's why I'm selling.'

'Good for you. I mean, your home is beautiful, but it's not you.'

'Meaning?'

He shrugged. 'I imagine you in a lovely little bright and cosy cottage with lots of blues and creams and greys, driftwood and tiny lighthouses.'

'You just described my dream home,' I said. 'Up here, that's Mum's.'

I took out Mum's keys and opened the door while Connor adjusted the back of the Jeep and then followed in behind me. I went upstairs to her bedroom where I gathered some clothes, her spare pair of glasses, her bathrobe and some other necessities while he had already manoeuvred her recliner into the rear of the Jeep on his own.

'Wait – I can help you with that,' I said, scrambling to his aid, but in one swing he hauled it into the back of the Jeep and shut the door. He had extremely strong back muscles, apparently.

'Done!' he said, smacking his hands together. 'What next?'

'Uhm,' I said, holding up the carrier bag. 'Just this.'

'Nice place she's got, your mum. Very quaint. Did you all live here while growing up?'

I nodded. 'We did. Dad was the village baker and my sister and I shared a room because the box room was Mum's hobby room. When my dad died, I wanted to take over the bakery with my sister, but she went off to cooking school and I... met Neil at college instead. And that was the end of that.'

'You sound wistful. Ever think of opening your own bakery?'

I sighed. 'No, The Rising Bun – Dora's bakery – is more than enough. There's barely a hundred people here in Wyllow Cove, but it also supplies the neighbouring towns of Little Kettering, Penworth Ford and Perrancombe. Plus I'm busy with my column.'

'Oh, yeah, can't wait for your next one.'

I stopped. 'You really do read it, then?'

'Bloody right I do. The women in my family were going on and on about it, so I read it to see what the fuss was all about. And I got hooked.'

I laughed. 'How could a bloke possibly be interested in a romance column in a magazine called *Lady*?'

'You laugh? I learned a lot about women over the years thanks to you.'

'I hardly think you need to read to get to know women, Connor.' *I mean, look at him.* I was positive he never suffered a shortage of them.

'Oh, I don't mean meeting women. I mean understanding them. That was the tough bit, until your column came to the rescue. And now your deep, scary and mysterious world is a little less scary for poor blokes like me.'

'Well, Connor, thanks for that, but I genuinely think that you're the only bloke who reads my column.'

He grinned, his eyes twinkling as he leaned in to speak into my ear. 'Entirely their loss. I can certainly say I'm your greatest male fan.'

Now *you* try and be indifferent to a comment like that.

'How is she?' I asked Neil as I came in through the door,

eyeing Connor as he hauled the armchair into the orangery where Mum would be spending most of her time.

She liked to be in the middle of the action, and as the orangery was an integral part of the kitchen and led to the garden, I knew it would be her favourite place. From here I could keep an eye on both her and the girls in the garden or the living room where they liked to watch movies in the evenings.

'You've taken your sweet time,' Neil observed sourly, shutting his medical case with an audible snap, but I was not in the mood for any of his usual attitude. He seemed to think that cheating on me still qualified him to lord it over me. I always tried to make a point of being civil, which was best done by not speaking to him, lest I tell him what I really thought of him, but Mum had insisted on keeping him as her doctor, much to my annoyance, so I had no choice. As long as we stuck to the question at hand – her health.

'Well?' I prompted.

Neil removed his latex gloves, shaking his head. 'We need to run some in-house X-rays to see if anything's broken, even if it doesn't seem so.'

'Okay. How long will the results take?'

'A couple of days at the most.'

'That's good. Fast. I like fast.'

'I noticed,' he said, sliding me a crooked glance.

'I beg your pardon?'

'That…' he said, his eyes indicating Connor who was now swinging one girl off each bicep, '…was fast.' I watched as Zoe began to slowly lose her purchase and just like Tarzan, Connor caught her fall in mid-air by bringing up his thigh to boost her up back to his arms before she even noticed she was slipping. There was certainly something to be said for his reflexes. Neil would watch things fall without moving an inch. 'Too fast even for you.'

Oh, so was that how he wanted to play it? Fine by me.

'You were faster. We were still married.'

'Ouch. That hurt.'

'Good. So did you.'

'So now your revenge is sleeping with a younger man?'

'Why does everyone think I'm sleeping with him?'

'Aren't you?'

'Oh, you lost the right to ask me that quite some time ago.'

He put down his bag and came to stand in front of me, his eyes on my face.

'Nat – I made a mistake. A huge mistake…'

Well, he sure got that right.

'…but don't we owe it to ourselves to forgive ourselves?'

I smirked. 'You mean don't I owe it to you to forgive you? No. I don't owe you anything, Neil. Not anymore.'

'Nat…'

I opened the front door and swept aside like one of those grand divas. 'Call me when you're ready for me to bring my mother in.'

On his way out, he opened his mouth to say something, but changed his mind. 'Right.'

I closed the door and heaved a huge sigh of relief.

And now it was the six of us: Connor, my mother, my two nieces and my daughter Sarah and I. Three generations of females packed into one house and one male guest. So much for my dreams of downsizing to a little cottage. My mother would have to stay until she was self-sufficient again. This place was starting to look like Hotel California. I only hoped the line about never leaving didn't apply to her.

5

Hotel California

The next day I knocked on Connor's door.

'Come in,' he called from inside, and, hesitantly, I poked my head in. He was at his desk, banging away at his laptop. The room smelled of fresh laundry and there was not a piece of lint in sight.

'Hi, Connor, sorry to disturb you...'

He got to his feet and opened the door wider. 'Nat, hi! Come on in. Like what I did with the place?' he asked as I looked around. The bookcase was stacked with his books and CDs. And there was a picture of an elderly woman who had his same charming grin.

'That's me mam, i.e. your number-one fan.'

I smiled. It was nice to know the faces of my readers. I rarely got a chance to meet any. And she was the spitting image of him, with long dark curls and winged eyebrows and the same endearing smile of someone who loved life. She must have been missing him a lot.

'Connor, I'm just going to run into town to get some

food. Can you keep an eye on the girls? And my mum? She's reading and won't be needing anything. I'll be back in a jiffy. I'm so sorry, this seems to be becoming a habit, but Sarah works long hours and I've no one else to ask…'

'Sure, Nat. You go on ahead. Beryl and I will be fine.'

'You're very good with her,' I said gratefully.

He smiled wistfully. 'She reminds me of my own mam.'

'Really?'

'Yeah. They have the same sense of humour.'

Only, I suspected, Connor's mum actually liked him. 'What's she like?' I found myself asking.

He sat back. 'Good-natured. Strong. Bossy. She loves us all fiercely. A real matriarch. She saved the family from drifting after my dad died. She just told us to roll up our sleeves and get on with it.'

'I'm glad you don't feel too lonely without them.'

'Are you kidding?' he said. 'Amy and Zoe are just like my own nieces. So it's like I never left home.'

In that case, I sincerely hoped I didn't remind him of his sister. If I couldn't have a fling, at least I could still have a *fantasy* fling in my head. 'Thank you so much. You don't know what it means to me, to be able to ask someone and not feel guilty about it.'

He stood up and came to my side. 'You're grand. Go.'

Just standing next to him heated me up. 'Have… you got any requests for dinner?'

He beamed at me. 'I'm fine with anything. Oh – except for mushrooms or truffles. I'm allergic to them.'

'Oh? Okay, will keep that in mind. I'll be as quick as I can.'

'Take your time.'

'Okay, then. Off I go.' Only I didn't want to go. I wanted to stay home, with the twins and Connor. And Mum, funnily enough. I wanted to soak up the soft, warm feeling of his presence, strong but discreet. The exact opposite of domineering but at the same time useless Neil.

When I got in from my grocery shopping, I hung my bag around the newel post as usual – something I hadn't stopped doing just because I had a lodger. I had trusted him instinctively and was giving myself a pat on the back for that because Neil, who had been my family and who had dealt me the biggest blow of my life, had not broken me after all. In a way, he had not turned me into a jaded, angry divorcee. So in a way, I was still whole.

'Hello!' I called dragging the groceries down the corridor into the kitchen. I really should have got into the habit of using the back gate. It was much more practical, but coming through the front door like this always gave me a sense of having a hold on my house, something that I'd never felt.

Coming into the house post-Neil, my ears would always automatically strain for the customary sounds, like the dishwasher slushing away, the clock in the hall and twins nattering on, or Sarah's voice instructing them about something, or even Mum's television set.

But now, I heard nothing. How odd.

'Girls?' I called out. 'Auntie Nat is home! Zoe? Amy? Connor?'

Nothing.

'Mum?' I called, and still nothing. She was not in the living room or the orangery, so I had a quick peek in her bedroom and was relieved to see she was fast asleep, her tiny form rising and sinking under her rose-patterned summer quilt cover. I closed her door slightly, just enough to block out the louder sounds of the household for when they made their appearance.

A quick look at the garden told me there was no one there, and at that point, an unsettled feeling began its journey up my limbs like ice in my veins. I closed the French doors behind me and walked out and across the lawns to scan any hidden areas, all the while reaching for my mobile to call Connor. I knew that by phoning his mobile, I'd seem overprotective to his eyes, but he had certainly not mentioned that they would be leaving the house.

I checked to see if I'd missed any messages, both SMS and WhatsApp. Apart from one from Maggie, which I ignored, there was nothing there. As I dialled Connor's mobile, I leapt up the stairs and checked every single room, his included, which I never accessed for obvious reasons. I walked across the floorboards to his window and looked out at the cul-de-sac, which was deserted. Surely I'd have seen them when I got in?

I waited for the call to connect, but instead there was silence. I checked the screen and pressed the call button again. And still nothing happened. We had an iffy connection at the best of times in Wyllow Cove, but still you'd get a message from your provider. Here, nothing was happening. Had he lost his phone? Highly unlikely, seeing that it was always in his pocket. It sounded as if it had been completely disconnected.

The possibility of someone stealing Connor's phone was also very improbable. Not with his sense of alertness.

He had a sixth sense and awareness of his surroundings that made him turn before anyone entered the room, or that allowed him to catch objects in mid-air without even trying. You had to get up very early in the morning to get one over him. Which was one of the reasons I'd been comfortable leaving my nieces with him for brief spells. And now? Now what could I do?

There was no one else to call. If I called Sarah or Lizzie who were at work, I'd only alarm them as there was nothing they could do either. Neil was out of the question for a million reasons, and Maggie always panicked in situations like these, so I was better off not alarming her especially.

By now I was in full-blown panic mode and began to pace his room, looking for clues as to where he might have taken them. Was his laptop here? His trainers, sports bag, jacket? I needed anything that would indicate he hadn't gone far, so I opened his closet and almost fainted when I saw that his duffel bag was gone. And gone were most of his clothes. I muffled a scream and went through his drawers in a panic, pushing aside ties, belts and a watch he never seemed to wear.

A cry from the street made me jerk my head out the window and, thank you, God, there they were, piling out of Connor's SUV, all giggles and laughs. They were back! And safe!

I quickly straightened the contents of his drawers again with shaky hands and descended the staircase, pasting a serene smile on my face, trying not to look like I was going to shake myself apart and collapse from relief at their feet.

'Hey, you guys!' I called, hugging the girls as they came

in, holding them perhaps a little too tight and for a little too long.

Connor was lugging his empty duffel bag and a picnic bag as he came in behind them.

'Hey,' he said, flushed, and I couldn't help but wonder what he'd been up to. 'Shame you couldn't make it. Didn't you get our message?'

'Me?' I almost shouted. 'You're the one who's been incognito. Where have you been?'

His face fell. 'I'm sorry. Your friend Maggie called with a picnic basket, so we decided to have a picnic on the beach. I tried calling you but my phone had no signal so I asked your friend Maggie to send you a message for me. She's a real darlin'. Made the girls laugh themselves silly with her funny stories.'

'Maggie?' I echoed, grabbing my phone from my pocket and scrolling back to her message:

Hey, just swung by yours as I wanted to take you and the girls on a picnic. Why didn't you mention the dish??? We're going down to the cove with tons of food. Come join us! M xxx

Okay. He'd called me to let me know he'd taken the twins out. He'd tried, and when that had failed, he'd let me know through Maggie, my best friend. It wasn't his fault I hadn't read her message. Crisis averted.

'Oh,' I said, too relieved that he hadn't turned out to be a kidnapper or something of the sort. Of course he wasn't. I realised how silly I'd been, jumping to all sorts of stupid conclusions. I guess I was just an overprotective aunt who thought the worst in extreme times. I internally Zenned myself up while the girls gabbed on about the seals and the waves as we all gravitated towards the kitchen.

'What's with the duffel bag?' I asked, and he looked down at his wrist.

'This? Oh, I dropped off some old clothes I don't wear anymore at a charity shop.'

Still taking deep breaths to calm myself, I put on the kettle as the girls ran out into the garden to hose off the sand from their sandals. I turned to face him. He was looking at me with those twinkling, kind eyes that were incapable of any bad thoughts, let alone actions, and once again I was overcome with a warmth that was a mixture of relief and, well, something else. How could I have doubted him for even a moment?

He leaned in and took my elbow. 'You seem... frazzled. Are you okay? I left Beryl asleep in her room as you said we could, once she's had her afternoon pill.'

'I'm sorry? Oh, of course, that's fine...'

And yet, however I looked at it, I couldn't help shake the knowledge that I didn't have everything under control and that I never would. Sometimes bad things happened to good people, and we were lucky that this time everything was okay. But life teaches you that the minute you let your guard down, things happened. And the girls were at their happiest in their young lives, despite the fact that their own mother had buggered off to the other side of the world to make sure that she added another million to her bank account. They were vulnerable, and I had to make sure they'd be okay.

But Connor, with his kindness and generosity, was to be trusted. I knew it.

'What is it, Nat?' he asked, moving closer to me. 'I felt that shift. Are you angry because I took the girls out without your permission? I apologise, you are absolutely right. But Maggie said you'd meet us and the girls kept going on and on about me owing them that ice cream because of the bet I lost.'

'A bet you lost on purpose,' I said, and he helped me to a charming, helpless shrug.

I sighed. 'Yes. No, I'm not angry, although I confess I did panic.'

'That's what I told Maggie, but she said nonsense and that all we had to do was leave you a message. Plus, I knew you trusted me.'

I looked up into his face and smiled. I knew him a little better now – and his little kindnesses. The world was not a place full of only bad people. There was good and caring to be found within the vast oceans of everyday indifference. Connor was living proof of that. He was a giver by nature, and the confirmation of that allowed me to curl up in that thought, like a child in a warm blanket.

'You all right, so?' he asked as he slid me a cup of tea across the island top. 'Is it something else, then? You look pensive.'

I looked up from my cup. 'Pensive? No, I'm okay.'

'I've got to say, Nat, that I'm in awe of you,' he said.

'Me? What for?'

'For doing, no – *being* who you are. There's not many women I know besides my own mam who can keep a family together like you do.'

My cheeks started to burn at the sound of his words that had on me the effect of a physical, delicate caress.

'Awh, and look at you – you're also the only woman I know who is still capable of blushing.'

His eyes caressed me kindly, and something warm began to course through me, soft and sinuous, like the feeling of sinking into a nice hot bath. At first you're tentative lest the water scalds you, but then you relax and bask in the pleasure. And it hit me over the head like a brick. I was *more* than simply attracted to Connor. It wasn't simply an *oh, he's so handsome* attracted, but a viscerally *it's too late to deny it* kind. And I just knew I was going to get hurt.

I tried to clear my throat softly, but made a huge loud mess of it. 'Ah... sorry, uhm, oh? What exactly do you, uhm, mean?'

'I mean that you sacrifice yourself for your loved ones even beyond the call of duty. But what about you? What about the Nat inside you, the one who wants to break free from all her fetters?'

I swallowed. How did he even know that I kept her deep under wraps? *I* hardly even knew she was in there, somewhere, and Connor, what did he do? He reached inside my head with the delicacy I'd come to know him for, and plucked the chords of my thoughts, fears and hopes.

'I'll bet you can't even see all that you're worth,' he said softly. 'You should stand tall and not be afraid to reach out for what *Nat* wants.'

What I wanted. What *did* I want? What everyone else wanted. For my family to be happy. To find a little cottage. And... perhaps... a big love. But for now I counted my blessings.

I took a deep breath. 'I guess I just want time to think. And heal and just... be. Peace, I guess I want peace.'

'Nat! Nat!' Mum shrieked from her bedroom and we both put our cups down to rush over to her, dreading seeing her sprawled on the floor the one moment I'd turned my back. 'Mum! Mum?'

But she was still in her bed, drumming her fingers on the side table, her eyebrow raised at me. 'I want to go home.'

Here we go again – classic Mum. When she was down in Wyllow Cove, she'd always say that she never saw any of us and why didn't I invite her over? And when I did, she would start to moan and say she wanted to go home.

'But, Mum, you only just got here…'

'Well it seems like I've been here forever.'

I sighed. She was never happy. 'Mum, I need to know you're okay. So for the time being, you're staying with us.'

'But I don't want to. I want to go to my own home.'

'Come on, Mum – just for a few days? You're always complaining how you never see the girls anymore. Here's our chance to spend some time together.'

'For how long?' she asked.

I took her hand. Hell, she was my mother after all. 'As long as it takes.'

She huffed. 'Well, then, in that case, I'll need my wool jacket and stockings.'

Never mind that it was almost twenty-six degrees outside, the hottest that it had been for two years. 'Okay, Mum. I'll get them for you. Where are they?' I asked.

'In my dresser.'

I opened the dresser and peered inside. 'I don't see them. Actually, Mum, I don't remember packing them.'

'That's because you didn't. They're in my dresser at home, silly,' she said.

I rolled my eyes at Connor who hid a grin behind his knuckles, having the time of his life, it seemed to me.

'My word, he's delicious, just like the Poldark chap on the telly, isn't he?' she said.

'Mum – he's sitting right there. He can hear you, you know!'

At that, she turned around to address him directly. 'Connor, you remind me of my husband. We lived together for fifty years. I loved him so much. And now he's dead.'

'Ah, you're breakin' me heart, Beryl!'

She squinted up at him and gently patted his cheek. 'Yes. You remind me of him. And all the sex we had. Yes, you look just like him – a luscious, scrumptious sexpot...'

'Mum!' I gasped but couldn't help laughing my nervous laugh at the same time. At least *she* had the courage to say it. 'Connor, I am so sorry!'

But Connor took her hand. 'You watch yourself, Beryl Amore, or one day I'm going to take you up on it. And then we'll see what you're made of.'

'Oh, you naughty, naughty boy.' She cackled in delight. 'I'll be ready. I was born ready.'

'Don't tempt me.' He laughed, then: 'Fancy a brew, love?'

'And a biccie or two,' she agreed.

'I'm on it,' he said, getting up and going to the kitchen.

'Mum, what's the *matter* with you?' I hissed before I got up to follow him. 'Connor, I'm so sorry! I don't know what's got into her lately. She's never like that.'

He shrugged. 'Let her have her fun, Nat. She's not harming anyone. Besides, I really enjoy it. Makes me feel good about myself after so long.'

'I doubt you need a seventy-year-old woman to tell you

you're...' I swallowed back the words I'd be sorry for. Well, if not sorry, embarrassed about.

Because once you said something like that, you couldn't take it away, and I didn't want to be sued for harassing my own lodger, or, worse, making him think I was just like my mother. Which I wasn't. At least I hoped not. So no, there would be absolutely no comments about his looks or sex appeal from me. But it was interesting to think that someone looking like him could not feel good about himself. And yet, there was a mirror upstairs in his bedroom. Did he not use it?

At that precise moment the girls came in from the garden, traipsing past us and through to their nana's bedroom with a handful of flowers. Amy may have been a terror, but she did love her nana.

'They're lovely girls,' Connor said as he prepared some biscuits for Mum on a tray.

'They are. Amy's a bit of a handful, but it's Zoe who worries me as she's a bit more fragile, I think. I just hope they—' I bit my lip. Had I said too much already?

'They look perfectly fine to me, Nat. It's just that age. I was a terror when I was a kid, in and out of the headmaster's office. What about their parents?'

'Their mother, my sister, is away for work a lot. She's a very famou... er, busy chef.'

Yolanda had made it very clear that she didn't want her girls' lives to be affected any more than necessary by her fame. Personally, I thought that ship had already sailed. I just hoped he didn't connect the very few missing dots.

'Then she's lucky to have you to fill in for her. They seem very at home here.'

'Oh, they are. My sister divorced a long time ago and her ex isn't interested in family, so all the girls really have is us. And now with Sarah and my mum, we're an all-girls club.' And then I stopped, realising that hadn't sounded very welcoming at all towards him.

'Nat, listen, I've been meaning to mention this. Despite your previous assurance, your circumstances have changed since our agreement, and I'm not sure this is the right thing for you, now,' Connor said, wiping the counter of some spilt sugar with a sponge. 'So if you need the room back…'

I just *knew* he'd say that again. This was not what he'd bargained for. He was looking for a quiet house where he could unwind and live in peace, not *Romper Room*.

The trouble was, I didn't want to interview anyone else. The process of waiting for someone to answer my ad, and the worry about who I'd end up with in my home had been painful enough, not to mention the humiliation of having no other choice, and I didn't want to have to expose myself to all that again. Okay, confession: I didn't *want* anyone else. Period.

'Oh, of course not!' I said.

'Are you sure? It's such a delicate moment for your family and I'd only be in the way.'

'I'm sure, Connor, thank you. But I'll need the income even more now – you know. But if we're too noisy…'

He sprayed the counter with Dettol and wiped it down again, rather than just pushing the sugar off the edge of the counter and onto the floor like Neil used to when he thought I wasn't looking. And to think he was a doctor. But Connor? A man after my own heart.

'No, it's not that. I'm happy here. But I'm wondering

whether you might all need your privacy? I understand that Sarah is going through a difficult time, too.'

'Which is why we need cheery people like you around,' I concluded with a smile before he could continue.

He rinsed the sponge out under the tap and squeezed it before placing it in the draining basket by the window to dry. Oh, wasn't he absolutely *perfect*?

He looked up. 'Are you sure? I will be working from home a lot and don't go out much.'

'Connor,' I said. 'You are most welcome to stay. Otherwise I'd have found a way to politely mention it to you, believe me.'

He stopped, studying my face, and then broke out into a smile. 'Okay, then. Thanks. But if at any time, should you change your mind…'

'I won't, Connor. Thank you.'

'Excellent.' He stuck out a huge hand. 'Shake on it?'

We shook, my hand completely disappearing in his warm one, while a funny feeling shot up from my legs through my stomach, unsettling and exciting at the same time.

'And now,' he said with a wink, 'let's get that brew to your mum, or I'll have to play Strip Poker with her.'

I nodded and watched him walk back to my mother. If I was unable to ignore the warmth in his eyes and his voice, I was completely unable to ignore the lean hips below the low belt. *Strip Poker, indeed. Oh, get a grip, will you, Nat?*

You see how nice he was? Anyone else would've fled this nest of females like a bat out of hell. But Connor? He fit in perfectly with us, and the idea was totally heart-warming.

I got to my feet when he returned. 'Right. I'm going

to start on prepping dinner for tonight. My daughter Lizzie and her boyfriend Liam are coming over. It'll be a chance for you to get to meet them.'

'Cool. Need any help?' he offered.

I shook my head. 'No, thanks. I want to impress everyone tonight by myself.'

What I hadn't considered was that Connor would have done all the impressing without even trying. He and Liam, the only males in the house, had gone off together to the garden to do that Male Bonding thing, while Lizzie, who was more a hindrance than a help in the kitchen, was still looking at him even after the introductions.

She picked at a piece of cheese broccoli from the oven dish. 'So, what's he all about, Mum? Is he yours or did you get him for Sarah? I'd say he's too old for her.'

'He's not mine, and no, I didn't *get* him for Sarah.' The cheek!

Sarah snorted. 'He may not be hers, but she's got the hots for him.'

'Ooh, Mum, you naughty girl, you!' Lizzie teased as she craned her neck to have a good look through the glass of the orangery. 'Well, in any case, the goods are all there.'

'Lizzie,' I said. 'Stop taking the mickey. He's *just* a lodger. Nothing more.'

And that was when Connor looked up and his eyes met mine in a huge grin visible from across the garden. Luckily, he hadn't heard over the din the twins were making. He just did that eye contact thing with me very often, making me all jittery inside.

'And a gorgeous lodger at that,' Lizzie hissed under her breath.

'He's also in his twenties, for Christ's sake, Lizzie. Look at him,' Sarah said.

I'd have readily agreed if I hadn't remembered that his personal information was on the contract. He was thirty-three next October. Still, I enjoyed the girls' musings.

Lizzie studied him. 'Nah. He's got to be early thirties. But I'm telling you now, if I were to break up with Liam, and if Mum wasn't interested in him—'

'I'm not—'

'I'd know exactly where to go looking now.' Said by the young woman who had sworn her eternal love to her boyfriend only last month.

Sarah shrugged. 'I don't ever want to see another man as long as I live.'

A clear, manly laugh rung out and the three of us looked through the glass again at Liam and Connor chewing the breeze over their beers. Not to be mean, but Liam didn't have a patch on Connor.

'Single?' Lizzie asked.

'Divorced,' Sarah answered.

Lizzie thought about it and nodded her approval. 'Gorgeous face and bod. Sexy smile, too. And what does he do?'

'He's an IT expert. He works from home,' Sarah answered, elbowing her sister. 'And Mum has barely left the house since he arrived.'

'I thought you didn't like him, Sarah,' I reminded her.

'It's not that. I've nothing personal against him. Have your fling if you must. But do it discreetly.'

Lizzie guffawed. 'Discreetly? In this house? And in Wyllow Cove? Good *luck*.'

'Even if I have my doubts on whether it's the right thing to do at this point in your life, Mum,' Sarah said.

'What, take on a lodger, you mean?'

'Along… with everything else…'

'Nonsense, Sarah,' Lizzie said. 'You want Mum to be celibate for the rest of her life?'

'Ew…' Sarah said and I stared back and forth between them, trying to get a word in.

'Don't "ew" me,' Lizzie replied, nodding towards the window. 'Can't you see he's got the hots for her, too? He keeps looking over at her, and did you not notice? He's like her shadow.'

Which, I had to admit, was true. But maybe that was just the way he was. Attentive. It didn't necessarily mean he was attracted to me as well.

'And why shouldn't she go for him? She's only thirty-nine, for Christ's sake. And still smoking hot.'

'Hello? Your mum is still in the room?' I said. But I didn't mind the compliment, even if I knew that Lizzie spoke out of love. Because smoking hot, I was not. After the divorce, I had forgotten how to smile. And how to groom. I needed a makeover pronto. Especially if I was to impress my new boss, Miss Chic Extraordinaire.

After dinner, drinks and more conversation, Lizzie and Liam drove back to Truro and Sarah took the girls upstairs to sort them out for bed. Mum was in her chair in the lounge watching Corry, and Connor dried the dishes that I churned out of the sink at breakneck speed.

'Lizzie and Liam are a lot of fun,' Connor observed, still grinning to himself about the jokes they had cracked.

I smiled as I passed him a plate. 'Yes, they are. They are such a good couple.'

'And they're so lucky to have found each other at such a young age. My ex-wife and I had been childhood sweethearts, and we gradually just grew out of each other.'

'The same happened to Neil and I. We were students when we met. He was very different back then,' I said, trying to justify myself in his eyes. Why, I didn't know.

'Divorce happens.' Connor sighed. 'But I'm glad I gave Mel the house. She always loved it more than I did. And I'm glad you got this house.'

I sighed. 'It's too big for me. Or rather, it was. I guess that it's a good thing I hadn't already downsized. I was going to buy myself somewhere smaller, but it'll have to wait.'

Because I'd really have to put myself on the backburner until I could get the family sorted out. Mum needed me for at least another three weeks. Sarah could stay here as long as she wanted, but the twins needed me indefinitely, so there was no way I could go anywhere right now as I had literally been sandwiched in somewhere between three generations. They should have called me The Sandwich Girl.

When I was done washing up, I dried my hands and turned to tidy the pile of real estate brochures on top of the fridge, and binned them in one sweep. Connor's gaze flicked over me, but he said nothing. Good man.

6

The Hounslow

'Auntie Nat, why is Mum always away? Doesn't she love us anymore?' Zoe asked the next morning right out of the blue. Yola had only sent video messages due to the time difference, and the girls were starting to feel neglected by her.

I took her onto my lap. 'Oh, sweetheart, of course she does! She'd love to be here. Do you remember what we talked about last Easter when you came to stay with me?'

Zoe nodded. 'That she loves us very much, but she can't be here right now because she's *working.*'

'That's right, Zoe,' I said. 'Mummy loves you so, so much, and she really misses you.'

'So then why *doesn't* she come back?' Zoe insisted. 'We don't need all that money.'

At that, Amy rolled her eyes. 'Because our nanny says when you're rich, it's never enough, Zoe. How else do you think Mum's going to pay for all our nice things?'

Zoe was not convinced. 'But we never *see* her. What if she can't make it for our birthday?'

Amy shrugged. 'It wouldn't be the first time.'

But Zoe shook her head. 'Not even Daddy loved us. He left before we were even born.'

'Sweetheart...' I said, caressing her hair. 'Your mummy and daddy were having problems, but they both love you very, very much, you know?' What else could I say? All I knew was that Piers and Yolanda's marriage had been on the rocks for quite a while, and I had always wondered why she'd insisted on IVF in the first place. And then one day Piers simply filed for divorce. And we hadn't heard from him since. I only hoped that Yolanda would sort her love life out soon for the girls' benefit. It must have been very lonely for them to not have a father figure to refer to. Perhaps that was why they'd latched on to Connor so quickly, although he was more of an uncle figure.

'Yeah, right,' Amy snorted. 'He never gave a toss about us.'

'Amy...' I gasped. 'Where did you learn such language?'

'At football, Auntie Nat.'

'Well, please don't talk like that. It doesn't become a smart little girl like you.'

'Sorry,' she said. 'I'll try to remember your rules.'

'And anyway,' I said cheerfully, 'we all have each other, haven't we?'

'But even if Mum does marry again, we won't be the bloke's kids, will we?' Amy insisted.

From her chair, Mum harrumphed. 'God knows how many kids their father's had all over the world.'

I turned to glare at her.

'What?' she said. 'You don't think he's got enough kids for a cricket team by now?'

At that, Zoe's lower lip wobbled and her eyes filled with tears, but she remained silent as they plopped down onto her sundress.

I wiped them away. 'Sweetie, just look at how many people love you! There's me and Uncle Neil and Nana and Sarah and Lizzie and Liam,' I assured her. 'You're surrounded by love!'

'Both of us?' Zoe wanted to know.

'Of course, you silly sausage!' I said, pulling her closer and blowing raspberries into her neck until she giggled and finally threw back her head in a fit of laughter.

'I love you, Auntie Nat. I wish you could be our mummy instead.'

I bit my lip. I wished so, too. At least they wouldn't have to go through all this. 'Oh, but your mummy is very special, Zoe,' I said. 'She's intelligent and beautiful and kind and famous. And she cooks the best dishes anybody's ever had.'

'Speaking of, when's lunch?' Amy said. 'I'm starving.'

'I've got everything ready. Do you girls want to go and get the plastic containers from the fridge and set the table? I'm sure Connor's hungry, too. Isn't that right, Connor?' I called, twisting around to see him coming up from the bottom of the garden.

'Ravenous,' he called back, pulling his gloves off with his teeth.

As the girls ran off into the kitchen, I watched (along with Mum) as he scrubbed his hands and face and arms in the outdoor sink, but I blushed and turned away at the sight of a beautifully tanned and taut chest as he pulled on a clean T-shirt he had brought with him outside. He liked to sit at the table as clean as possible. *Do not think about his chest and surfboard tummy.* His dedication was admirable. *Nor that twinkle in his eye.* I wished I had the same stamina with my own work. *Do not think about his outrageous sex appeal. Think about practicalities. Like Mum, the twins, Yolanda, my finances – anything else but him.*

'I guess no one realises how tough having kids is until you have them,' Connor mused as he smoothed his T-shirt down over his abs and I gave my absolute, undivided attention to straightening the tablecloth on the patio table.

'Does their father not keep in touch at all?' he whispered as he sat at the table. 'Sorry for being so nosy, but it seems to me that you are being both their mum and dad.'

'No, he left before they were even born.'

'Shame, such lovely girls.'

'I know,' I said, choking up.

'I'm sorry, Nat...' he said. 'I should learn to keep my mouth shut.'

I shook my head. 'It's okay, Connor. We just have to deal with it, is all. I just worry about the effect on the girls. Zoe is losing her self-confidence and Amy is overcompensating her losses with a hard heart.'

'Who broke up – Yolanda and Piers?' Mum said, out of the blue. 'The tosser. When?'

'Years ago, Mum, don't you remember Yolanda telling you?' Was her medication messing with her head?

'No one ever tells me anything in this house,' she muttered as she leafed through her magazine, squinting. 'Can't see a damn thing here, without my glasses,' she said.

'They're on your head, Mum. And please don't use those words. Now I know where Amy gets her potty mouth from.'

'Bollocks,' she spat and Connor snorted water through his nose, reaching for his napkin to wipe the front of his T-shirt down, his eyes twinkling as he glanced at her and then grinned at me.

'When's lunch?' she continued. 'I'll tell Yolanda you're starving me.'

At that, Connor reached out and took her hand. 'Come on, luv – you're treated like the queen that you are, here. Look at your granddaughters coming back with all that food!'

I relieved the girls of their piles of plastic food containers and filled the serving trays up.

'We got pretty much everything that was in the fridge,' Zoe explained.

'I can see that, darling,' I said as with a couple of swipes of my hand I arranged all the plates and forks into place. Connor rose to cut some daisies and put them in a glass in the centre of the table.

'That looks nice,' Mum said, beaming at him. 'You always think of everything, don't you?'

I smiled as I uncovered more containers of potato salad, stuffed peppers, cold roast beef, a mixed green salad and a bacon and cheddar quiche.

Connor poured the lemonade and then disappeared into the kitchen to return with Mum's pillbox. A sense of guilt for forgetting, but also gratitude for someone else remembering, flooded me. 'We'll save these pleasure pills for after lunch, what do you think, darlin'?' he cooed and she giggled.

'Oh, you naughty boy, you.'

'What did he say?' Zoe wanted to know.

'It's a little game between him and Nana,' I offered and she shrugged as she reached out for some potato salad, whereas Amy went straight for the meat.

After lunch, while we were all still lounging around lazily, my mobile rang and I checked the screen to see who my caller was, my heart immediately shifting into overdrive.

It was my work, *Lady* magazine. *Lady* magazine *never* called me. Factor in the new boss firing anyone with a four at the beginning of their age, and that I was currently thirty-nine, logic told me that this call could not be good.

It was Hilary's (now Octavia Hounslow's) PA, calling me to a meeting with the boss herself on Monday morning in London. See? I knew it. Based on what Maggie had told me, it was only a matter of time before I got sacked myself. But I was determined not to make it easy for her.

I hung up and huffed.

Connor looked up from his lemonade. 'Is everything all right?'

I slid him a glance. '*Lady* magazine is cutting down and my new boss wants a meeting. Which is never good.'

'Maybe she just wants to meet you.'

'They have conference calls for that. No, she must want to sack me.'

'Sack you? Why?' Connor asked.

'Because I'm almost fort— Never mind.'

He put down his glass and sat up, studying me as I took a nervous sip of my own lemonade.

'You know what I think, Nat? You are an amazing writer

and should be proud of what you have achieved. And I'm sure she is only dying to meet such a bright mind.'

Bright? Me? Good one. If I hadn't had my column, I don't know what I'd have done in life. I have no particular talent. I can't play any instruments or fix things. In our family, Neil was the one who shone, and initially I had been happy to support him throughout his career while simply sending in an article or two until I had received the offer for this fixture years ago. Which had been and still is my lifeline.

And even Connor was clever. There was nothing he couldn't do, nothing he couldn't fix. And he was an absolute child whisperer, as Amy and Zoe seemed to get along better when he was around.

'You're the bright one, Connor. *And* you're good at DIY.'

He continued to study me. 'Everyone is good at something, Nat. And besides the fact that you are a brilliantly funny writer, you're an amazing cook. I have rarely eaten anything so good as the food you prepare. It's restaurant quality.'

I shrugged. 'I'm not that good.'

'Oh but you are, Nat! And what about how good you are with people? Look at the girls, and Sarah – look at your mum. You're the perfect nurturer.'

My cheeks began to burn. 'That's very kind of you, Connor.'

He continued to look at me. 'It's the truth, Nat. You have an astonishing number of good qualities. I want you to believe in yourself. Will you promise me you will?'

Well, put that way... 'Okay,' I promised. 'I'll try to believe in myself more.'

'Great,' he said, squeezing my hand before he got up. 'Back to work now. You go and write your next cracker of an article. There's thousands of people all over the country waiting for it.'

'No pressure, then,' I retorted with a grin, my skin still tingling at the contact. Imagine if he actually *caressed* me!

He gave me a thumbs up and headed down to the bottom of the garden to resume his tasks. And for a while, it was as if my whole world had suddenly lifted from my shoulders. Maybe Connor was right. Maybe Octavia wouldn't fire me after all.

But that evening at dinner, I couldn't manage to eat a bite. If Connor had boosted my confidence earlier, now I wasn't so sure anymore. He'd gone out somewhere, and I was glad he didn't have to see me down again.

It went without saying that I didn't sleep half a wink over the entire weekend, tossing and turning while conjuring up all sorts of scenarios where I got sacked just because I was getting long in the tooth compared to my boss.

What could I possibly say to save my neck when all of my colleagues, the very same ones whom I'd started out with, were getting the boot? What cat's chance in hell could I possibly have?

On Monday morning, after one and a half showers – I'd had to go back in because I'd forgot to lather my ears – I raced back into my room where my outfit awaited me. Only I realised too late that it had a reddish oil splotch across the chest – probably from my previous lunch date with Maggie during which I'd spilled some *penne all'arrabbiata* down the front. Hadn't I washed it out? That was karma getting back at me for my laziness.

It was way past the baby powder hack as that only worked with fresh stains, and only before washing, so I scythed my way through my wardrobe until I found something next to suitable, i.e. my infallible LBD. Which had, would you bloody believe it, a great big hole in the seam at the neckline. What now? Everything else was still in my toss pile, which I had already started in a bid to downsize and move.

It would just have to be my usual navy blue dress. But this time I jazzed it up with a gorgeous white gold necklace in the hope of mollifying Octavia as she was obviously obsessed with jewellery.

And it was then that I looked at my watch and panicked, grabbing my bag and throwing myself down the stairs.

'Ooh, I'm late, late, late! Girls, please do hurry,' I urged them, raking my hands through my hair as I faffed around looking for my keys and trying to steal a look at my reflection in the oven door in the hope that it would make me look younger and trendier than my real mirror upstairs, which was cut-throat accurate.

Connor looked up from his breakfast as the twins were still dunking the toasty soldiers into the eggs I had prepared for them at least twenty minutes ago.

'I can run the girls to school if you want?' he offered.

I stopped mid-faff. 'Really? I couldn't ask you to do that.'

'Why not? I'm happy to help. It's the one up the road, isn't it?'

'Oh, I can't possibly... Oh, Connor, are you sure?'

'Natalia – I can take care of two eight-year-olds. Now go.'

He cleared the table and gently nudged the girls just with

a gesture of his head, then slipped on a pair of marigolds which, rather than making him look girly, turned him into bloody Superman to me.

'I don't know how to thank you, Connor!'

He put the plates in the sink, which he'd already filled with hot water and washing-up liquid and as I was wringing my hands, he leaned forward and said, 'You're already late. You look great. Everything will be fine. Go get her.'

I blushed. 'Okay. Thank you. I'll make it up to you.'

He shrugged. 'There's nothing to make up for. I'm happy to do it. Go!'

So I kissed the girls, made a huge effort not to do the same to Connor, and went. I had ahead of me a four and a half hour train journey into Paddington Station, hopefully enough time to come up with plenty of reasons why she shouldn't sack me. When I could think of nothing, I tried to work on my next article, but there was a man opposite me who was talking very loudly into one of those earpiece phones so I gave it up as a bad idea and just resorted to people-watching in the end, my mind absolutely incapable of stringing two thoughts together.

By the time I got to HQ and was finally admitted into the new boss's office, I was soaked in my own anxiety. And as it turned out, she was worse than I'd thought.

'I see you've been here many years,' she said, instantly diving into the purpose of her meeting without so much as shaking my hand or welcoming me or even thanking me for coming in at such short notice. 'You're one of the old ones. *Literally.*'

So now it was my turn to get the boot, apparently. Only she couldn't risk being seen as ageist, so I was curious (and horrified) to see what kind of a spin she was going to put on this.

'And you've been writing this column some time now,' she said as if it was a genuine accusation.

'Yes,' I said. 'I've been writing *That's Amore!* for thirteen years and haven't missed a single month.'

'Hm.'

I eyed her. It wasn't looking good. The fact that she looked a lot like my perfect sibling Yolanda wasn't doing her any favours either. If my instinctive antipathy for her was not obvious, hers for me definitely was.

She sat back, her thin, bejewelled arms and hands dangling over the armrests.

Compared to her I looked like a yeti. And this was me *trying*, because ever since Connor had moved in, I had suddenly stopped wearing tracksuits or, worse, pyjama bottoms and had even started wearing make-up again. But all my old tricks didn't stick compared to this monument to fashion. In fact, Octavia could have given Anna Wintour a run for her money.

'You see, Natalia, my agenda is to *rejuvenate* the magazine.'

Bingo. She wanted to give me the boot completely, just as Maggie had warned me. I was too old for them, apparently. Her new target audience didn't want to read about HRT, or premenopausal mindlessness. They wanted to read about how to tell if their next date was The One, or how to start up your own online business. I knew nothing of either. I couldn't even get my own finances into gear.

And I'd thought that after the divorce, my life would start all over again. *Forty is the new twenty* and all that, but now a real twenty-something-year-old was telling me that I was redundant in this brave new world. That I was over the hill. Octavia was young, and she wanted to read about young women, not dinosaurs like me.

'Looking at your figurehead above the column, you do look much younger.'

'That's because I was,' I answered. 'Thirteen years younger.'

'Yes, well.'

Next, she'd be summing up the reasons for my dismissal. I took a deep breath and bit the bullet. 'Miss Hounslow, we seem to have a problem here. You can't just fire people because of their age or looks. That's discrimination – which is against the law. And apart from the fact that my column is one of the backbones of this magazine, I write what women like to read.' And at that, I recoiled in horror at my own words. When had I suddenly become confrontational? I had never spoken to anyone like that before in my life. Well, looking back now, perhaps I should have. Perhaps I should have never let Neil speak to me the way he did. Maybe it would have spared me tons of heartache.

'Well, the target market has changed.'

'I beg your pardon?'

She leaned forward, and I swear it was almost with glee that she said, 'I told you I am rejuvenating the magazine. My target readers will be in their twenties, and it'll be all about jobs, technology, relationships, cosmetics and fashion. Stuff for women in their twenties. Not their mothers. I hear you have a daughter in her twenties? You could even be *my* mum.'

I gave her my signature hairy eyeball. How dare she? 'I

have two daughters. Sarah is almost twenty and Lizzie is eighteen – much younger than you.'

'Well, then, I need their point of view, not their mother's.'

I was dead. Utterly dead in the water.

'So what are you saying? That you're going to fire me because I am almost forty?'

She assessed me. 'Of course not,' she lied. 'Tell you what. I'll give you one chance. One article to show me you can write something like a woman in her twenties.'

'But I'm not a woman in my twenties.'

'Then write something that might interest them.'

'Such as? How to Tell if He Likes You?' I said before I could stop myself. I really had to do something about this new sarcastic streak of mine.

'Exactly! I'm sure that as a mother, you've had these chats with your daughters. You've been through all that with them. Tell me what it was like. Maybe you could write this from a mother's perspective. A woman trying to reach out to her would-be daughter readers.'

Oh my God in heaven.

'Miss Hounslow, I need your assurance on one thing.'

'And what's that?'

'There are many, many talented people who have been contributing to this magazine for years. You need to promise me you won't let them go.'

She sat back and stared at me. How dare I speak to her like that? 'I beg your pardon?'

'Miss – well, seeing that I could be your mother, I'll call you Octavia,' I said, enjoying the raising of her eyebrows. If she was going to fire me, at least I'd get a word in edgewise. 'You just can't afford to send these writers straight into the arms of your competitors. They'd wipe you out over the weekend, believe me.'

She sat up. 'Excuse me?'

I got to my feet. 'I know you're new here. I was once new, too. But if you want to succeed in this job, you have to know it's all about connections, and building a rapport of trust with everyone around you. And you're not going to do that by threatening people the minute they turn forty.'

And before she could kick me out, I excused myself as I had a train to catch. Let her see that along with age came clout and intelligence.

When I got home, Connor and the kids were sitting around the kitchen table playing cards. Amy was so excited about winning that she couldn't sit still.

'Auntie Nat!' Zoe cried and threw herself at me. 'You missed dinner! Connor cooked steak and risotto with vegetables!'

'Sounds yummy,' I said, peeling my jacket off as Connor got up to pour me a glass of wine and turn the microwave oven on.

'Thank you for taking such good care of my girls, but now—' I turned to them '—it's bedtime.'

'But—'

'It's a school night, remember? No staying up late until Friday night.'

Amy's shoulders slumped. 'But I was just winning!'

'You were *cheating*,' Zoe corrected her.

'Was not!'

'Were too!'

'Girls, girls,' Connor cooed. 'Let's give Auntie Nat some peace, okay? Now go. She'll come up to tuck you in in a minute.'

Moaning, Amy headed for the stairs, followed by Zoe.

I slumped into a chair as the microwave pinged and he sat down across from me to keep me company while I ate.

'Hmm, Connor, this is really good. Thank you. And I can't thank you enough for taking care of the girls. How's my mum?'

He laughed. 'We get on like a house on fire. She proposed Strip Poker again.'

I sat up. 'Oh, Connor, I'm mortified. How'd you get out of that one?'

He grinned. 'I told her not in front of the kids.'

I snorted wine through my nose and he burst into a laugh alongside me, hugging his knee, a gesture of his that I had become familiar with. It was also very endearing, just like when he put one foot on top of the other when seated, or my favourite, when he bit on his lower lip in concentration.

'Oh, Connor, you are absolutely priceless. I don't know what I'd do without you. I mean, what I'd have *done* without you. *Today*, I mean.'

He waved my thanks away. 'So! How did it go?'

'I kicked her ass today, Connor! I told her what I thought about her methods and it felt great!'

'Good girl!' he exclaimed, high-fiving me.

'And before I left her office? I even told her how to do her job!'

Connor let out a hearty laugh, his dark eyes twinkling. 'Good for you!'

'You should have seen me, you wouldn't have recognised

me. *I* didn't even recognise me! Even if I do get fired, it will have been worth it!'

'You won't get fired. I'm so proud of you, Nat. It's so lovely to see you happy and full of confidence again.'

I blushed. 'Thank you, for your pep talk, Connor...'

He waved my thanks away. 'You deserve everything you want, Nat. And actually, if there's anyone that needs anyone, Octavia needs you, and not vice versa.'

I rolled my eyes. 'I wish.'

'Are you kidding me? You do know that your column is the main reason why people read *Lady* magazine, right?'

That made me laugh.

'I'm not kidding! The whole country buys it for you – take it from me. It's the first thing people go in for on a Monday morning. I can literally see them. Is it in yet, is it in yet? I can't wait to read *That's Amore!*'

'Shut up...'

'I'm telling you the truth, Nat. I have to wait in line at least ten minutes for my mam's copy.'

And then that warm, fuzzy feeling washed over me again, like I could do nothing wrong. It had been a while since someone encouraged me to do something. Usually it was me cheering everyone else on, and I was grateful for the change.

'Thank you, Connor.'

He shrugged. 'You're grand, Nat. I'm only happy to help.'

Ah, this miracle of a man who had popped into our lives, out of the blue. All thanks to a random ad. How lucky was I?

'What?' he said, grinning. 'What are you smiling about?'

I realised that in effect, I was grinning like a loony. 'You know all about us.' Well, almost. He didn't know that I was the sister of the famous Yolanda Amore, although Mum had blabbed her name out several times. I only hoped he hadn't made the connection. 'And I know nothing about you.'

He took a sip of his wine as he sat back, biting his lower lip in thought – there it was, another one of my favourites. 'There's not much to tell. I'm pretty boring. You know I'm a lawyer, and that I'm divorced.'

My eyes popped out of my head. 'You're a lawyer? I thought you were in IT?'

'I am. Corporate IT law. But I also have a personal work project,' he said sheepishly.

'Which is, if you don't mind my asking?' What the heck, he knew practically everything about me.

'Of course not. I want to start my own legal aid website.'

'But that is amazing! You must be super-smart. And there was me thinking you were just a young geek.'

He laughed, pushing back a curl that had escaped his man bun. 'Not so young, Nat. I'm going on thirty-three.'

As if I didn't know.

'And now you're opening your own online business – how does that work?'

'It's partly online, actually, connected to my blog.'

'You have a blog?'

He laughed. 'Sort of. It's more of a legal aid site. I just want the law to be available even to those who can't afford it, you know?'

I found myself beaming at him. 'You have a heart the size of a cathedral, Connor! Your mum must be so proud of you, and I can't understand how your ex-wife—' I bit my lip. Trust me to ruin such a carefree moment. But he only cocked his head at me and smiled.

'I mean, you even have time to cheer me on, humour Mum *and* play *Twister* with my nieces?'

'That's part of my down-time. Plus, I've actually taken some time out to dedicate myself to my real calling – the sea.'

'Ah, the surfing, yes.' I only hoped he wouldn't offer me swimming lessons again.

'Not just the surfing, but any sports related to it. I love being in it, under it, over it, by it. I love the flora and the fauna. My family makes fun of me – they call me Flipper.'

'Sounds like you have spent more time in the sea than on dry land!'

He grinned. 'I need to get rid of all the nervous energy I accumulate. At school I couldn't learn anything because I couldn't sit still long enough. My mam's amazed I managed to get a degree at all!'

'And what brought you to Cornwall? Didn't you have enough beautiful villages in Ireland?'

'I needed a fresh start. After the divorce, you know.'

I still couldn't understand what woman in her right mind would want to leave Connor. He was everything a woman dreamed of. Looks of a god and the heart of an angel. I wondered what his faults were, because, for the life of me, I couldn't see any yet.

He was silent, evidently thinking about her. Then he shook his head and looked up. 'You think you're building something, you know? And then you're left with nothing.'

I sighed. 'I know the feeling. Sometimes I think that

maybe I should have concentrated on my career. If I hadn't married Neil, I'd be my boss's boss by now, and not vice versa. But in the end, I opted to have a family instead.'

'How did it change your life, having your children?' Connor asked.

I grinned. 'It actually gave my life meaning.'

'I'll bet,' he answered, then rolled his eyes. 'Not that it didn't before, what with your busy life.'

'Is that something you wanted? Children?' I ventured, feeling my cheeks go hot.

His hand stole to the back of his neck. 'Children deserve the right attention and love. They need to come first. In our marriage, let's say they weren't an option. And besides, I don't know if I'd be any good as a father.'

'Trust me, Connor, if you can deal with my nieces, you're very good. Fantastic, actually.'

'You think? Babysitting the twins is a treat. But I can only imagine the responsibilities of being their main carer. A child is forever.'

I studied him as a smile formed on my lips. 'I think you'd be brilliant. If you have the main ingredient, love, you're already two-thirds of the way there.'

He thought about it. 'I guess you're right. Besides, how can you not love those two?'

'Oh, yeah, especially when they fight,' I agreed and we laughed and toasted to them.

'Well, maybe I will have kids, one day after all. If I find a woman who will put up with me.'

As if. All he had to do was stick his head out the door and there'd be swarms of women, young and old. My mother was living proof. And well, so was I.

*

The next day Mum wanted to sit in an armchair in the orangery, so after I'd returned from the school run, I joined her and began planning my next article. Something that would hopefully interest a younger woman.

I looked out to the garden for inspiration. Despite the bushes teeming with new floribunda roses and another couple of pots that had sprouted the purple agapanthus I'd been waiting for all spring, and Mum's incessant nattering about everything and nothing, it seemed empty and lonely without Connor pottering around in the distance.

After breakfast he'd gone back upstairs like most mornings where he worked until lunchtime. I checked my watch. Only ten o'clock. Pretty soon Mum would lapse into her usual pre-lunch nap. She would sleep for at least two hours without moving a muscle.

Connor. Now *he* would interest a young woman. I wondered whether he'd met anyone else in the village. Apart from Tuesday evenings and Thursday mornings and the rare times he popped out, he didn't seem to go anywhere, which made me think that he wasn't seeing anyone – a woman – on a regular basis.

'It's a gorgeous day, Mum,' I said. 'What do you think, would you like to go down into the village? Mum?'

She answered me with a loud snore and I chuckled under my breath. Ten thirty on the dot. Big Ben had nothing on her.

Sighing, I looked down at my empty pad of paper. All I needed was one good idea. Just one.

'Hey,' came a whisper from the doorway.

I turned to see Connor tiptoeing into the kitchen, and grinning down at my mother. 'You could set your clock by her.'

I chuckled again. 'That's exactly what I was thinking.'

'Care for a walk around the village?' he asked, flexing his back against the island. 'I need to stretch my legs.'

'Gosh, I was thinking that, too.' I glanced at Mum and chewed my lip.

'Just a quickie,' he urged. 'We won't be gone for long. She'll still be asleep when we get back. She's perfectly safe, look. She can't fall or anything.'

'Well, uhm…'

'Nat,' he said. 'As important as you are to this family, it won't fall apart if you go take a short break every now and then.'

'I guess you're right,' I conceded, grabbing my pouch from the countertop and sneaking out the back door he held open for me.

We took the footpath that led right down to the cove in a gymkhana of twists and turns among gorse, heather and marram grass. Connor was light on his feet, keeping up as I negotiated the tricky parts.

'I knew you were fit, Nat, but Christ, this should be an Olympic sport!'

I laughed. 'Don't tell me you don't have any cliffs in Ireland!'

'Oh, we certainly have – the Cliffs of Moher are our most breath-taking, but you wouldn't want to be there on a blustery day. Take it from me!'

When we reached the end of the coastal path, as always, joy filled my heart. There was something about the pastel-coloured cottages lined up in neat rows and the tiny shops on the quay front. As I watched in complete satisfaction, the villagers – all my friends – milled around, stopping for a chat or waving.

'Hi, Nat; hi, Connor!' Geoff, the village vet, called out in passing.

'You know Geoff?' I asked.

'Yeah, we played squash together last week.'

'Wow, you seem to have fit right in,' I observed.

'Yeah, everyone is so friendly here. Plus, you know me by now, I just can't sit still. Hey, fancy a pasty?' he asked.

'I'd love one!' I answered and together we ducked into The Rising Bun where Dora and Felicity were serving their customers with such efficiency you'd think they were on the deck of a cargo ship.

'Mornin', Nat; mornin', Connor!' Dora said. 'Your usuals?'

I turned to look at Connor. Obviously he was at home here, too.

'Just two pasties, thanks, Dora,' Connor said as Felicity slid him a coy smile from the other end of the counter. I couldn't blame her.

'Mmh,' I swooned. 'Dora, I don't think I could live without your famous pasties!'

She cackled in delight. 'I'm glad, pet. So, Connor, how's it going? Did you sort yourself out?'

He slid her a tenner. 'Yeah, thanks, Dora. Keep the change.'

I looked at him, but he didn't elaborate. 'Let's go sit on the quay,' Connor suggested, practically steering me out of there before I could say *bon appétit.*

We ambled down to the very end, passing children on bikes, tourists armed with cameras and couples strolling hand in hand. Of course, it would have been nice to have been part of a couple, too. With Connor, I mean. Fantasising about us had become a regular thing for me, but every time I had to tell myself to wake up. Because soon enough, Connor would go back home to his own family. And we'd be nothing but a blurred memory, like old Polaroids in a box at the back of an unopened drawer.

How silly of me to even fret over it. Connor's life was elsewhere, and it certainly didn't include us. And still, whenever I thought about him leaving, a weight descended into my stomach.

But he was here now, and I was determined to enjoy his company, so we unwrapped our pasties and I took a huge bite of mine.

He grinned and nudged me. 'Crikey, hungry much? Where the heck do you put all that food, so?'

I covered my mouth and nodded happily. 'I love Cornish pasties.'

He took a bite of his own and sighed as he looked out over to the horizon from where seagulls were coming in on the scent of our food.

'I love everything Cornish,' he said and ducked out of the way, bringing me with him. 'Except for these little buggers!'

'Get used to them, they never give up!' I warned him.

'It's nice, though, to just sit here, isn't it? And so rare to have you all to myself,' he said, taking another bite.

Now *that* was the kind of talking I liked, but when I hoped he'd continue flirting, all he said was, 'Just two adults chatting and eating good food.'

I had been too optimistic. Connor, in all fairness, had never shown any interest in me in that sense. I willed my heart to calm down.

'Enjoy being single and not having any children,' I said. 'Once they come, your life gets a *little* more complicated.'

'I'll bet.' He took another bite. 'So, besides buying the cottage of your dreams and telling your boss to sod off, what else do you desire?'

You, I almost blurted out had it not been for the huge chunk of pasty in my mouth.

I swallowed again, all too aware of his scrutinising dark eyes on my face. It was getting quite hot now.

I shrugged. 'For my family to be happy,' I offered.

'Would you ever remarry?'

'Not making that mistake again,' I answered. 'Unless, of course, I find someone irresistible who loves me and respects me for *me*...'

'Well, how hard can that be?' he wanted to know.

'Harder than you think. For now, I'll just see what's what.'

'You mean a fling?'

I stopped chewing. 'Why not? If I find someone I fancy enough.'

'Is that so?' he said, taking another bite, his dark eyes studying me.

'Can I ask you something?' I ventured, trying to change the subject.

'Anything.'

'I understand the new start and all but why, of all the places, did you choose to come Wyllow Cove?'

'Ah.' He laughed, turning red. 'Good question. I did it for love.'

I waited for him to explain, but judging by the look on his face, that was all he was prepared to say.

Of course. Silly, stupid me, how could I not have realised it? He had a woman down in the village. It had all been too good to be true. And then I couldn't help but wonder who it was.

7

The Ex Always Returns

The next day, I took advantage of a moment during my mother's nap to sit down and actually try and write and save my career. I did work well under pressure, but not so much pressure that my job was in danger. I'd have to think of something that would amaze Octavia and shoot me up to her circle of Untouchables. And there was me thinking that I had been safe before she came along.

So I sat down at the patio table with my laptop and started making notes. It was a beautiful day and I could hear the sparrows, goldfinches and blue tits flitting back and forth between the trees. The sun was warm and the sea breeze refreshing.

Of course my choice of working space had absolutely *nothing* to do with the fact that Connor was also in the garden, working on my fences. I should've known I wouldn't be able to concentrate with him bending and stretching in only a pair of shorts and a tank top that rose to reveal his spinal cord at the back, along with a very narrow waist. I didn't know why I continued to torture myself this way, but then I figured it was good for my soul – stay young at heart and all that.

And in that precise moment, instead of ringing the doorbell like every other human being, Neil appeared at the back gate, peering through the gap in the fence, convinced no one was there. And then Connor suddenly stood up, making Neil jump.

'Y'all right?' said Connor, unlocking the gate to let him in. Neil glared, then nodded at him, making a show of stepping over his tools strewn across the lawn.

'Yes, quite all right, thank y-aaaah!' He slipped and lurched forward and would have gone flying across the garden had it not been for Connor who caught him by the arm.

Composing himself, Neil eyed me to make sure I hadn't seen or heard anything as I was some way up the garden, so I buried my face behind the lid of my laptop to save him at least one shred of dignity. I was after all a kind woman despite what he'd done to me.

'Hello,' he said sourly as he came up the path, all one with his leather bag. 'Enjoying the *view*, I see.'

Seriously? I had pretended not to see him out of kindness and he was actually allowing himself to be sarcastic with me? I made a show of looking up and being surprised to find him there. 'Hello, Neil. Come to see my mother?'

'I have.'

'Well, then, maybe you want to use the front door next time. It's safer.'

From the corner of my eye, I saw Connor flash me an

amused grin before he placed another new panel into its slot.

'How amusing for you. I will,' he said. 'Is Mum up?'

'When are you actually going to stop calling her that?'

'But I've always called her Mum.'

'Yes, well, she's not. So kindly use her name.'

He sighed. 'Anything else?'

'She's in her room.'

'Right, then.' Neil's eyes swung to where Connor was now banging in a new post. 'I shan't be long. Wouldn't mind a cup of tea when I'm done.'

I raised an eyebrow at him. 'Don't you have tea in your own home? Or can't your new girlfriend even boil water?'

I knew I sounded bitter, but I was sick and tired of him commanding me, left, right and centre. For twenty years I'd baked, slaved, cooked and cleaned so he could look good in front of his colleagues without so much as a word of thanks as I delivered, served, poured, displayed in servile silence. And now that I was done with all that, he could make his own bloody tea. Preferably in his own new home.

'Well, she's not my girlfriend anymore, Nat. It was a mistake.'

'A mistake that lasted years, apparently.'

'Nat—'

'Don't you have your rounds to finish?' I said. 'Besides, I'm busy working.'

'Yes, I see how you are working,' he retorted, shooting Connor a disapproving glance before he went into the house. 'You might want to tell Adam over there to put some clothes on. There are ladies in this house.'

I shrugged, relishing being one step ahead or on top for once. 'My mother absolutely adores him. Particularly when he lounges around in his smalls.'

Neil's eyes popped out of his head, and then he huffed when he realised I was only teasing him. And then, without further comment, he stomped off inside the house.

'Sorry about that,' I said to Connor who came to the table for a glass of lemonade from the tray. 'I think Neil resents the fact that you have fit in so well.'

'None taken. He still loves *you*, Nat,' he said as he gulped down half a glass in one swig. 'Hm, very nice, did you make this?'

I nodded, glad that someone appreciated the things I did around the house. 'He doesn't, actually,' I corrected him. 'Love me, I mean. He just likes to think he does.'

He made a face. 'Why would he want to do that?'

I shrugged. 'Because now that I'm out of his life, he's started to understand just how much I did for him.'

'Do you think he's out of your life?'

'He only comes for Mum. When she goes back to her own place, I won't be seeing much of him.'

He swallowed the rest of the lemonade and wiped his mouth with the back of his hand. 'Fancy a drink tonight?' he said, straight out of the blue.

'A… drink?' *It's not a date*, I told myself. *Just a casual… thing.*

'Yeah. You know, that thing that friends do?'

You see? That kind of drink. What had you expected, a hot date? Really, Natalia, you should get your act together and start acting your age.

'There's a nice place just over in Little Kettering. It's called The Old Bell Inn and they have a good bar.'

I knew The Old Bell Inn. It had bedrooms and all. To go, or not to go, then? That was the question. If I didn't go, he'd think that I didn't want to fraternise with him, which I did. Oh, how I did! But if I said yes, how could I stop myself from really falling for him when he didn't seem interested in anything more than friendship?

Up until now, the girls and Mum had acted as a buffer between us. But the two of us, out at night, alone, all the while I fancied the pants off him, pun intended? What if we drank too much and something... happened? And if, rather than an insane, ongoing passion for me, he instead blamed the booze? I couldn't live with the heartache.

'I, uhm, I can't. I'd need a sitter and all.'

'You don't know any?'

'None that I can call on such short notice.'

His beautiful face fell. 'Oh. Okay, then.'

'Maybe next time?' I suggested, not wanting to kill his enthusiasm altogether. At least not until I figured out what I wanted. And how to go about it without getting hurt.

'Don't forget, though,' he said, pulling back his hair into a man bun. In doing so, his tank top rose to reveal his washboard tummy and a trail of fur leading south. Either he was the most drop-dead gorgeous man I'd ever seen in my entire life, or I was lonelier than I thought. I gulped and turned away.

'Also because,' he said, pointing at me as he ambled backwards to his fences, 'I know where you live.'

I chuckled, pushing my hair behind my ear and giving him,

I confess, a look halfway between flattered and incredulous. Call me Bashful. What the heck was happening to me?

'Hmmm...' I sighed to myself happily once he was out of earshot.

'Your mother is fine, in case you're still interested,' Neil snapped as he stopped on the threshold of the French doors, making me jump. Busted.

'I know,' I snapped back. 'I see her every day.'

He glared at me, then turned to go, swinging his damn leather bag so hard I thought he'd fly off into the air with it like Mary Poppins.

Neil being able to access my home again, albeit for a few weeks, was definitely something I hadn't factored in when I had brought Mum to live with me. Nor when Sarah had moved in. She absolutely loved her father. But I had the feeling that since Sam's stunt, she was beginning to understand my reasons for kicking him out. I had to find a way to limit his visits, or at least not be there when he came round. He still had the power to annoy me tremendously as he had neither truly apologised for what he'd done to me, nor had he suffered any consequences apart from losing me.

Which maddened me. He still hadn't realised what a horrible thing he'd done to me, and thought it was more a question of me over-reacting rather than him being a right shit. I just didn't need to see all that much of him to remind me how he'd humiliated me for years and then given me the final shove by choosing a lover whom he'd actually brought to our home while I was out.

Besides, Mum's ankle was much better. In a couple of weeks tops she'd be able to walk around like before and she could go back to being independent in her own home. Where Neil could continue to visit her if he so pleased.

'I suggest you hang on to him.'

I looked away from Connor, the vision fixing my fences, to Mum who had hobbled into the kitchen and was now precariously perched on her crutches like a bird on its trestle.

'Mum – why didn't you call me for help? You know we don't want you slipping and hurting yourself again.' All we needed was one more fall and then I'd never be rid of her.

I helped her onto a chair in the garden and poured her a glass of lemonade.

'What a drip,' she said.

'How do you mean, Mum?'

'That Neil. I don't know why you ever married him.'

I stared at her, absolutely gobsmacked. 'But I thought you loved Neil, Mum?'

'Paaaa!' she scoffed. 'Love. What is love, if not a constant state of turmoil?'

I looked at her closely. Now that was a change. Where was this even coming from? I was seeing her with new eyes. Well, almost. It had to be the medication talking. I'd noticed that sometimes it made her drowsy or a bit loopy.

I went into the kitchen to check her prescription and read the side effects. Ah. *Can induce hallucinations and variations in behaviour.* I knew that there had to be a scientific explanation for that one. People like Beryl didn't just mellow like that from one day to the next.

'You all right, darlin'?' came Connor's voice.

Beryl's face brightened instantly and she lifted her frail arm to wave at him.

'I'm proper happy to see you – and as much of you as I can, love,' she called out to him, then as an aside to me: 'That was my new, what do you call them, doober ontonders, by the way. It's supposed to be, ehm, subliminal.'

I covered my face, not knowing whether to be amused or horrified. 'That—' she said to me, indicating him with her chin '—that is something worth a sleepless night or two.'

'Oh, Mum.' I sighed as I dug out my mobile phone and moved off into the hall. I just didn't have the energy today. And what little I *did* have left would have to be spared for my phone call to Yolanda.

Not that she could do anything about it, but it was only right she knew that Mum was staying with me, just in case she decided to break the habit of a lifetime and actually ring her up. After a few rings, her answering machine kicked in with the jingle of one of her cooking shows and I rolled my eyes. She was always so blatant in everything she did. It must be her Italian half, although it was my mum who'd always done all the pushing and she was from Rotherham. I was tempted to hang up, but then I'd only have to do this all over again. So I bit the bullet and left a message.

'Yolanda, it's Nat, hope everything's okay. Just wanted to let you know that Mum's living with me at the moment. She's sprained her ankle, but not to worry. I thought you should know in case you tried to call her on her house phone. We'll talk when you get back to me. *Ciao*.'

There. That should do it, although I didn't think it would be enough to induce her to call back immediately. I was wrong.

'Nat.'

I moved into the privacy of an unused reception room that

I hated because it was always cold and mostly inaccessible. The perfect place to talk to my sister. 'Hi, Yola.'

There was an unnerving delay in overseas calls that always made me impatient, as if the person I was speaking to wasn't really listening, or even disapproved of what I was saying. And with Yolanda it was worse than with anyone else, as we communicated badly even in person at the best of times.

'How's Mum doing?' she asked.

'She'll be okay, it's just a sprain. I've put her in my downstairs study to make it easier.'

'Right, right. And how are my girls? I *miss* them!'

'Then why don't you call when they're at home?'

A sigh from the other side of the ocean. 'Don't start on me, Nat. This was my first break all day.'

'Yola, you're the star of the show. Can't you at least choose your own break time?'

'Nat, it's not that simple.'

'Whatever. They're fine. And Zoe is really coming out of her shell with Connor.' Shit. I had been hoping to get away without mentioning him. Now you know why I could never have a secret affair.

'Oh, is he a new play friend?'

'No, uhm, he's my new lodger.'

'Sorry, can you say that again. It sounded like you said *lodger*.'

Oh, hell. Me and my big mouth. 'I did.'

'What? You mean my children are under the same roof with a total *stranger*? Who is he, and where did you find him? Oh my God, Nat, what the hell is wrong with you?'

I bristled. 'He's not a total stranger.'

'So how do you know him, then?'

Blast her, she always found a way to suss me out. My only way out was always to distract her until I found something else to upset her and she completely forget her original attack. It had worked since we were kids. But not this time, apparently. 'I, er, put an ad in the papers.'

'You *what*? Nat!'

I knew that she did have a point regarding having strangers in the house. But when I took him in I didn't know that I'd have the twins at the house again.

'Yola – I can assure you that they absolutely love him.'

'Oh, my God. Are you sleeping with him?'

'Of course not, don't be silly.' And on a lighter note, I added: 'But Mum's considering it.'

'Mum? Okay, now you're just plain lying.'

'I'm not, honest. Mum kind of has a crush on him. She flirts with him like crazy. They have this sexy banter thing going on. I don't recognise her anymore.'

'You mean they talk dirty? In front of my girls?'

I rolled my eyes. 'Of course not in front of the girls. And besides, it's not dirty talk, it's just a bit of teasing. What do you think this is, Sleaze Central?'

'Huh,' was all she said.

'I resent that. And I resent you telling me how to live my own life. If I want a lodger who is kind to the girls, then I'll have a lover – I mean *lodger*.' Suddenly my face was going hot. 'In any case, they like Connor, and you will too, when you come back next week.'

'About that,' she said. 'I was going to call to tell you. I won't be home for another two months at least.'

'What? Are you kidding me? The girls miss you. And they need you!'

'I know, I know, Nat. But I can't just drop everything and run. I have a job to do here. Responsibilities.'

I snorted. 'Responsibilities? You want to talk to me about responsibilities? Yola, you know I love the girls like my own and I'm more than thrilled to have them in the house with me for as long as you need me to. But what will they think when you don't come home when you promised?'

'Nat, chill, will you? I'll come home when I can – two months. Three months, tops. Okay?'

Unbelievable.

She sighed. 'I promise I'll do my very best, and I'll come back loaded with presents.'

I shook my head. I didn't know why she'd bothered going through IVF all those years ago when she knew she didn't have time to be a mother. She knew she was on the fast track to being a celebrity and still she'd insisted on doing it. She knew that it would mean sacrificing her own children, and yet, she went ahead with it anyway.

'Nat? Are you still there? You haven't hung up on me, have you?'

'Of course not. I'm here.' As always.

Her voice softened as it did when she knew she was in the wrong. 'I'll do my best to come home as soon as possible. I'll keep you posted. Give the girls my love, will you?'

'Why don't you post another video message to them at least?' I suggested. 'Or better, call when they're home from school.'

'Sure, why not,' she said. 'I'll do that. Take care, Nat, and see you.'

See you. That was the closest she'd ever come to saying thank you. Not that she needed to. I had always been there for her and the girls, and always would be.

'Okay, Yola. See you,' I said, and hung up.

'Who were you talking to?'

I turned around to see Mum hobbling on her crutches again.

'Mum, how many times do I have to ask you to call me when you want to get up?' I said as I helped her onto a chair. 'It was Yolanda, in any case. She sends her love.' Pointless telling her that her favourite daughter wouldn't be back for another two to three months.

'Yolanda? Who's that?' she said. 'And where the hell is your father? He told me to put dinner on hours ago.'

8

Just Like Family

'It could be a momentary lapse, due to her medication,' Neil said over the phone.

'No, Neil. Mum could forget everything in the world – even her own name. But she would never, ever forget Yolanda. Nor that my dad is long dead. And she's looking a little loopy, actually.'

'Surely it's just the painkillers. I'll come over as soon as I can.'

Connor, who was bent over Mum, taking her blood pressure with her monitor, was keeping her distracted from my conversation with his usual banter. 'So I bet you can't beat me at checkers, Beryl. Want to have a game?'

'Eh?' she said, looking at me. 'Nat, tell your brother to stop foolin' around.'

'Have you got a brother?' he mouthed to me. I shook my head.

'Neil, I'm worried. It's like she's here one moment and completely out of it the next.'

'I'll be right over.'

I sighed with relief. If anyone would know what to do, it was him. 'Thank you, Neil.'

'Her blood pressure is perfect,' Connor said, unravelling the strap from around her arm.

'Where did you learn to do that?' I asked.

He shrugged. 'My mum has one of these. It's not rocket science.'

'Neil's coming over to check her out and I'm going to pop round to her place to turn off the utilities for now, clear her fridge out and whatnot. I can't let her go back to her home in this state.'

'I'll come with you as soon as Neil gets here.'

'You don't have to do that,' I said in earnest.

'I want to, Nat.'

'Okay, then. Thank you. If you're sure.'

A few minutes later, the doorbell rang and I raced to get it.

'How is she?' Neil asked as he hurried past me.

I shook my head. 'Still loopy. She's in her room.'

'Hello, Mum?' he called as he disappeared down the corridor. 'How are you doing?'

'Neil? Is that you?' she asked as I caught up with him. Sitting up, she seemed perfectly fine again.

'Can you tell me where you are, Mum?' Neil said, sitting on the bed next to her and taking her hand.

Mum leaned forward to peer into his face. 'I'm at your old house, Neil. What's the matter with you?'

I needed to help her, to do something useful for her. 'Neil, I'm just going to pop by her place and get some more of her stuff.'

If Neil's nose was put out of joint for using him as a babysitter again, he didn't show it. On the contrary.

'I'll be here, don't worry,' he assured me.

'Thanks,' I said and his mouth dropped when Connor followed me out the door.

I got into his Jeep and sagged against the soft seat in a heap. What was happening to her? Was it a stroke? Bad circulation? I'd never seen her act like that before, and it frightened me.

Connor took my hand and squeezed it. 'It'll be okay, Nat. Your mum'll be fine.'

I shook my head. 'Thank you, Connor. I sure hope so.'

On the quay, Connor parked and I descended, surprised to see a woman coming out of Lavender Cottage, i.e. 'my' cottage next door.

'Hello?' I said, knowing I had no right to poke my nose into the business of Mum's late neighbour.

She smiled at me, and upon seeing Connor, her smile broadened. 'Hello, Mr and Mrs Pentire? So glad to see you! I was told you might not be able to make it.'

Connor and I exchanged looks and only then did I notice the sign in the tiny front garden. For Sale? *No, no, no!* Not 'my' little cottage!

I grabbed Connor's hand, not missing the widening of his eyes. The terrified widening of his eyes. So much for him ever having any interest in me. 'Sorry for the misunderstanding,' I apologised breezily. 'Traffic.'

'No worries. Shall we start our little tour, then?'

Connor tugged at my hand and when I turned to look at him, he shook his head *no*, but it was too late.

I'm sorry! I mouthed, joining my hands in prayer for him to not give me away. *I love this house!*

'Yes, please,' I said, forcing myself to not push past her in my haste to finally get in there again. I had tried over the years, but since old Mrs Pendennis had died, there had been no one around to speak with. And now it was finally for sale!

Connor eyed me, unsure, but in the end followed me obediently.

The woman held out her hand. 'Hannah Williams,' she said.

'Pleased to meet you. I'm Nat and this is my husband Connor.'

If the words *younger man* occurred to her, she didn't show it, while I could feel Connor's uneasiness, but when would I ever get a chance like this to see the cottage again?

'Right, then,' she said. 'Well, as you can see, it's a lovely stone fisherman's cottage in a prime location in this beautiful little bay, in the midst of it but quite private as well. You can walk to all amenities, and you have your own front and back gardens.'

Have you ever stepped into someone else's home and known that it would one day be yours? That's what had happened to me with Lavender Cottage.

She opened the gate of the white picket fence and picked her way among clumps of tall grass and weeds and hardy perennials that seemed to have thrived on years and years of abandonment. We followed her to the pretty blue door that led onto a small porch where an old wooden bench stood over a shoe rack, still covered in Mrs Pendennis's tiny slippers, poor dear.

I remembered pulling flowers out of my mum's vases and passing them to her over the fence at her startled but amused face as she laughed and said, 'Oh, dear, love – yer mum'll be proper angry with you!'

And then she'd invite me over for lemonade and biscuits to thank me, and Yolanda would run to Mum and tell on me. Every time I needed a friendly face, it was always Mrs Pendennis who consoled me. Perhaps that was why I always fancied living at Lavender Cottage instead of in our own home that didn't even have a name. And when Mum would chastise me for something I hadn't done, it was always Mrs Pendennis over the fence who told her to go easy on me. I missed that dear old smile. My only accomplice while growing up.

Connor squeezed my hand gently and when I looked up at his face, his eyes gestured that we should be following the real estate agent.

'This is the entrance hall, and straight down onto the left is your living room with a lovely bay window and a large open fire...'

Exactly the way I remembered it, only now it was dark and smelled musty, while when Mrs Pendennis was alive, she always had a fresh bunch of daffodils on the windowsill.

'There's a lovely bathroom down here,' she said, opening the door to a powder room with a beach-themed shower curtain.

'Look, honey,' I said. 'Lighthouses, your favourite.'

He cleared his throat. 'Yes, darling.' He couldn't have sounded any more fake if he'd tried.

'And here, from the living room we go straight into the kitchen diner, with a lovely AGA and French doors onto the garden. As the garden is huge, you could actually extend the kitchen out, and maybe even put in some skylights,' she suggested, gauging our faces for a reaction.

'It's lovely,' I murmured, wishing I could just put my bag down and move here now. All it needed was a good clean, some airing and a bit of TLC.

'And upstairs there are three bedrooms, one en suite,' she informed us as she led the way, and up we went. The master bedroom faced the long garden that was simply crying out for rescue, drowning as it was in bramble, and overgrown shrubs.

Stone walls were visible here and there, and there were clumps of agapanthus, and honeysuckle and hostas and lilac and buddleia and roses crept up the doorframe. Here and there butterflies flitted and preened, getting close to us and shooting away as if beckoning us to follow them. I would do anything to fly in their wake.

Downstairs, at the bottom of the garden I stopped to smell the sea air. It was much more pungent down here in Wyllow Cove, whereas, like many other things, it arrived up at Smuggler's Rest somewhat faded. Living up there was like being the princess captive in her tower. I longed to live among people and just pop out for even five minutes for a quick chat, whereas now I had to scarper up and down the footpath or get into the car to be down here.

'I love it,' I said, feeling my face flush with excitement.

'Good!' Hannah Williams said. 'Naturally it will need some redecorating. But there is a special surprise for you out the back.'

Surprise? This property was the mirror image of my mum's. Where could the surprise possibly be? We followed the agent all the way down the garden. On the left-hand side, there was a gate, where she stopped and turned with a broad grin.

'Careful, now,' she said and hopped over a two-foot plank where there was a tiny, gurgling brook.

'Wow,' I whispered, 'I had no idea there was a leat here.'

'That's not the surprise,' Hannah said triumphantly. 'This is… your secret garden! Isn't it amazing?'

'*Oh…*' I breathed. It was vast, studded with fruit trees fed by the tiny leat. All these years had gone by and I'd completely forgotten about it!

Suddenly memories surged and I actually saw myself, like in a dream, as a child, sitting on that very same plank and dangling my tiny feet in the brook to cool off on a hot summer's day, not understanding why my mother was always so angry with me. All those long-lost sensations that I'd never thought I'd relive, and just like that, I was ten again, with all my fears, and my dad calling me to tell me lunch was ready.

'It's beautiful,' Connor said, squeezing my hand as if to pull me out of it. 'Honey, are you okay?'

And I realised that my cheeks were wet.

'Now *that* is the reaction I've dreamed of my entire career,' the agent said with a smile. 'Thank you, Mrs Pentire.'

'Thank you,' I said, eyeing Connor. 'But I have a confession to make. It's all my doing. We're not the Pentires.'

'Oh?'

'I'm sorry. My mum lives next door. I lived here my entire life and hadn't seen it since Mrs Pendennis died ten years ago.'

Her face fell. 'Oh.'

'But I really am interested in buying this cottage!' I assured her. 'And I have a large period property to sell.'

Her eyes shone with interest again. 'Oh? Where?'

'It's above the cove. It's called Smuggler's Rest.'

She gasped. 'You mean the five-bed detached at the end of Abbot's Lane?'

'That's the one.'

'I've always wanted to have a look inside! And it's yours?' She wanted to make sure.

'Yes. Sorry for lying earlier, but when I realised someone else was coming to view Lavender Cottage, I panicked. I'm sorry,' I said both to her and then turned to Connor, whose eyes shone with forgiveness as they caressed my face.

It took all my effort to drag my eyes away from him and back to her. 'I do want this house. Truly I do. I just need to sell mine first.'

She studied me, confused. 'You have a five-bed detached above Wyllow Cove and you want a three-bed cottage that needs work?'

I couldn't blame her. If I didn't know me, I'd have struggled to understand as well. But continuing to stay where I'd lived with Neil was not an option. I wanted somewhere I could call my own. And what better place than my old, secret haven, the place I'd always run to for protection?

'Downsizing and rebuilding a new life,' I explained cheerily.

She reached into her bag and gave us a card each. 'Okay, then, call me and we'll set a date for next week.'

'Thank you,' I said, then stopped. 'What if the Pentires reschedule?'

She shrugged. 'You'll just have to make an offer the estate can't refuse.'

Easier said than done. 'Okay. Thank you.'

After we said our goodbyes and watched her drive off practically singing 'We're in the Money', Connor stood in silence, staring at what to him could only look like a ramshackle dump.

'Oh, all right,' I said. 'I apologise. I should have never passed you off as my husband. I could see it in her eyes that she didn't believe me for one minute.'

'Of course she did. Why wouldn't she?'

For the simple reason that you're almost seven years younger? I wanted to say, but kept my mouth shut.

He chuckled, shaking his head. 'Hell, even I almost believed you for a minute. Although, I have to say I can see why you love it so much.'

'Fat lot it does me,' I mumbled sadly. 'If the Pentires offer before I can, I'll have lost it forever.'

'Nat, if this is what you want, you should go for it.'

'How? I need the space for Sarah and the girls and my mother now, too. I don't know that I can sell the bloody place anymore.'

'Nat,' he said softly. 'I don't know a lot of people who would have shouldered the burden of taking three generations under their roof. Isn't it time to start thinking about yourself, too?'

'But they're my family.'

'And that's great that you could do that. But what about you? I keep asking you, what do you want?'

I shrugged. 'It's not that simple, Connor. Too many things have to happen.'

'Like what?'

I eyed him. 'Well, my sister needs to sort herself out with

her work. She's always away and I'm not leaving the girls in the hands of some nanny who slags my sister off for being rich.'

His face softened. 'Maybe she will sort herself out.'

'And Sarah – she needs me right now.'

'The cottage has three bedrooms; there's room for her. And the minute you put the house up for sale, it'll fly off the shelf.'

'Really, you think so?'

'Of course! Now that you've got rid of every Tam… what's your ex's surname again?'

I grinned. 'Tamblynn-Lobb.'

'That's it. Without all that crap the house really shines. I'll help you with anything that needs DIYing, and Bob's your uncle.'

I put my hands to my face. 'You'd do that for me?'

'Nat, who wouldn't? You're a lovely girl and it's time you had your share of freedom.'

What a gem this man was. And now for the painful part. Oh, my aching heart! 'And… you wouldn't mind cutting the lease short, in case?'

'Nat, of course not. You *deserve* Lavender Cottage.'

I thought about it. Sad that he was all too happy to see the back of me, because I knew that I would miss having him around, with those twinkling eyes and that hearty laugh that warmed me from my toes up, not excluding some very particular areas. Ah, if he only knew!

But one thing was sure. 'You know what, Connor? You're right. After what I've put up with from Neil all these years, I do deserve to be happy in my own little place that doesn't reek of old money and snobbery.'

'That's my girl! You go for it. I'll help you any way I can.'

'Oh, Connor, thank you, I can't thank you enough for giving me a push,' I said and began to fumble in my bag for the key to Mum's front door. If only I really was *his girl*.

Inside Mum's cottage, if at first glance it looked exactly like the last time I was there, after about two minutes of opening drawers and cupboards, the alarm bells began to go off as I soon discovered that behind the apparently normal home, behind cabinet doors were items that didn't belong there. Stockings in the cutlery drawer, shoes in the fridge along with what was once food, newspapers and flyers. In the microwave there was a tub of melted ice cream and a pair of bed socks, and on the windowsill she had neatly stacked her underwear, which I snatched and stuffed into my bag before Connor could see them.

What the heck was going on? Mum had always run a very tight and squeaky-clean ship, making us leave our coats and shoes in the porch so as not to bring street dirt inside. Everything in the house had to be in its place, and every time a mug was used it would have to be washed, dried and put away immediately.

Dad would have to shower in the bathroom in the cellar where she kept his clean clothes, and only then would he be allowed up inside the house.

And so this? This was not my mother's usual behaviour. Every room was screaming that something was definitely wrong with her and that it hadn't just been a side effect or a mere isolated moment. What did it mean? Had she just given up? Or worse, had she forgotten she'd left it like this? Or had squatters taken her home over in her absence? That would have been the best-case scenario, but deep down, I knew what was most probable. Mum's mental health was failing her.

Fingers of fear licked at my insides, spreading up into my lungs as shock kicked in immediately, and all I could do was lean against the counter for support, perfectly still and useless, in the middle of the home I'd grown up in and that had always been spotless.

'Nat? What is it?' Connor said as he came into the kitchen.

My knees shaking, I sat down. 'Connor, would you mind? I need you to have a good look around.'

'Of course. What am I looking for?'

I lifted my hands helplessly, trying not to shake. 'Whatever you want. You won't find it where it should be. How did I not notice this before?'

He climbed the stairs as, with a huge sigh, I turned to make some tea and scrubbed two mugs, all the while wondering what I was going to do about this. When Connor returned from his recon, he sat opposite me and took a sip of his tea, his eyes never leaving mine. 'I'm so sorry, Nat…'

'It's not just old age, is it? Oh, Connor, she has always been super neat, and now this?'

He pursed his lips. 'You should have her run some tests.'

'What do you think it could be?'

'It could be anything. I'd rule out depression, though. She's pretty much always chipper. Maybe something neurological?'

I put my head in my hands. 'But she's only seventy. And fit!'

Connor put a hand on my shoulder. 'Let's not jump the

gun, Nat. Just take her in tomorrow morning. It could be something much less serious. My mum had a mini-stroke.'

'Oh, Connor, I'm sorry.'

He shrugged. 'After a couple of days in hospital she was up and at 'em again.'

And then a thought. 'Oh God, what if it's dementia? Or Alzheimer's?' I dropped my head in my hands, already seeing a dismal future for us. 'She's only got me. Yolanda hardly has time for her own children. How am I going to tell her? How am I going to be enough for my mum?'

'Easy, Nat. There's no point in worrying yourself sick with all sorts of horrible thoughts. Tomorrow I'll keep the girls while you bring her in for some tests. And then you can give your sister more information. How does that sound?'

Not removing my face from my hands, I nodded, mumbling a muffled 'Okay.'

'Here, chin up,' he said, taking my wrists and looking into my eyes. 'Everything's gonna be all right, okay? I'm here.'

'Thank you,' I said, knowing it had been just words, and that he couldn't make the problem go away, but still.

I sat at the table, staring out the window into the front garden and, beyond it, the sea. I was utterly unable to think anymore. And then, feeling like I was a hundred years old, I dragged myself to my feet, reaching for a sponge.

Connor, too, rolled up his sleeves. 'Right. I think I've still got a roll of bin liners in my Jeep from when I moved out of my own place. Be right back.'

Bin liners? We needed a *skip*. How could she live like this? Did no part of her scream out in protest? Or, my God, was that part of her disappearing? Would she never be the same again?

When Connor came back inside, he helped me dispose of all that shouldn't have been there, including stacks and stacks of TV magazines and old newspapers, not to mention boxes of biscuits and porridge that were at least six months old. Was that when it had all started? Because Mum would constantly check her cupboards for something that was nearing its sell-by date and chuck it out.

Connor held the bag open as I stood on tiptoe, and in went pretty much all of the contents of the food cupboards, while I retrieved rotting items of clothing from inside the washing machine, refrigerator and oven, and at every new quaking discovery, I forced myself not to shake my head in dismay, but inside I was panicking. And chastising myself.

How could I have not seen what was going on? Granted, Mum was fit and she had her own life with all her friends coming around. But none of us had delved into her life and home enough to see the horror that was happening under the surface of afternoon mugs of tea and biscuits. If I had deigned to have a closer look and delve under the surface of All is Well, I'd have seen that, alas, it was anything but that.

And I'd been so easily fooled with a smile or one of her usual wisecracks about minding my own business, and the likes of now that I was divorced, was I actually that bored that I had to go through her cupboards for amusement?

So I'd maintained a certain distance, or a certain discretion if you will. She had always hated me going through her cupboards or the refrigerator even when I lived there as a child, so no surprise that it annoyed her particularly after I'd moved out. But this... I had no idea.

I went upstairs to go through the bedrooms and removed the coverlets to find that she had no sheets on the bed, despite having an entire wardrobe full of new and unused ones. I stripped all three beds of their covers and pillows and divided the bin liners between a Wash pile and a Toss pile, feeling like the whole world was sitting on my shoulders.

After that, I left the mattresses bare and the drawers and cupboards ajar to air, leaving the bathroom for another day. We even swept and washed the floors and I sprinkled what was left of the baking soda before I hoovered the carpets.

After Connor and I cleaned as much as we could of the house, we moved down the narrow staircase and back to the living room, which looked a lot better.

'Thank you, Connor, for letting yourself get sucked into this. You could've just dropped me off but instead you stayed and—'

'It's okay, Nat. It's been a long afternoon. Let's go home now.'

I nodded and with a last, longing look, closed the front door and turned the key. The rest would have to wait. What was supposed to have been any other day had turned out to be pretty rubbish, and I appreciated having someone by my side, even though I knew that my troubles were only just starting.

When we got home, I apologised to Neil for taking so long and explained about the mess in the cottage, and he shook his head.

'The evidence is there. I'm so sorry, Nat, but it's going to be an uphill battle from here on, whatever it is.'

Didn't I know it.

*

The next day Sarah and Connor stayed with the girls while Neil drove Mum and me to Truro to see his friend Dr Simpson, a specialist in neurological disorders of the elderly.

Mum sat in the front, and I reached forward to hold her shoulder in a gesture of comfort.

'Will you stop poking me, Nat?' she suddenly said, then turned to Neil. 'Your wife is always so clingy, so needy. Why don' you give her a good—'

'Mum!' I groaned.

Neil looked at me in the rear-view mirror. 'I'd be delighted to, Mum, but she won't have me. Could you maybe put in a good word for me?'

'I would, Neil, but she's busy a-shaggin' someone else these days.'

'Bloody hell!' we both swore as he swerved just in time to avoid a bollard.

'...every night and every day, those two are at it,' she continued. 'I hardly ever see them anymore.'

'That is so not true!' I said, but stopped. Enough. I didn't need to justify myself. I was my own woman now, whether these two liked it or not.

When we finally got to the hospital, I helped my mother out of the car and into the wheelchair. At the door, she squeezed my hand with incredible force. To think that she had to go and break her ankle to come and spend some time with us. And that if I hadn't convinced her to do so, I would have never known, except perhaps for a smarmy Mrs Locke, that my mum was in this shape.

Dr Simpson had a private chat with us first and then with Mum on her own, after which he decided to run a few tests, and all the while I was waiting I couldn't help but pace up and down the long corridors.

'Nat, you're going to bore a trench into the floor. Come and sit down,' Neil said.

I knew he was right, of course, but couldn't bring myself to stop. When had all this started? Had it happened before and I'd never noticed? What a terrible, terrible daughter I was. Mrs Locke was right to hate me. God knows I had never had the relationship my mum and Yolanda had, and I resented her for it, but never, ever, had I wanted my mother to be ill. I swallowed and sat down next to Neil. Good old Neil, boring and sturdy. He, too, loved Mum. And I'd also resented the fact that they got along better than I did with either of them. So I guess I was the problem.

Maybe that was it. I was the odd one out. I was the reason that Mum never loved me as much as she loved Yolanda, and I was the reason Neil had cheated on me. I pushed people away. I didn't mean to. I had merely been trying to stand up for myself after years of getting the slack off everyone. For years I'd practically slaved for him, and when I hoped to have some kindness in return and didn't get it, I made my stand. I guessed it was time to come off that stand now, for Mum's sake.

'So what happens now?' I asked Dr Simpson as he ushered us back in. Mum looked tired and drawn, and I knew she couldn't wait to get out of there.

'She'll stay for the night, and we'll run some more tests tomorrow.'

I nodded. 'Thank you, Dr Simpson.'

After a few more helpful tips, he let us out, patting Neil on the back.

When he'd closed the door and we were alone in the corridor, I turned to Neil. 'I'm going to call Sarah to let her know what to do for the night with the girls. They'll be worried.'

'Nat – there's no need for you to stay. They have top-notch nurses doing the rounds constantly,' he answered.

'No, I want to stay. I'll wait in the visitors' lounge.'

'No, Nat, they won't allow that. Now let me take you home. You're much more useful to the girls than to Mum right now.'

I wished he'd stop calling her that. But for once, I kept quiet. He did love her. I knew that. It was me he had stopped loving.

'Nat?' he asked quietly. 'Can I ask you something?'

'What?'

'How are you?'

'I'm worried sick, of course. And I'm dreading telling Yolanda whatever is wrong with Mum.'

'No, I meant... how are you? Are you happy? Besides this, I mean?'

'Happy?' I echoed.

'With your life, the way it's turned out?'

Did he mean was I happy that he'd cheated on me? And he asked me this now? As I was trying to understand where he was going with this, my mobile rang. It was Connor.

'Sorry, I have to take this,' I said as I jumped to my feet and began pacing down the hallway again.

'Nat? How is she?'

'They're running some tests. She'll be here overnight.'

'Okay. I'll come and get you then.'

'No need. Neil is still here; he'll drive me back.'

'Okay. I'll keep your dinner warm for you.'

'Thanks. How are the girls?'

'Sarah and I have just put them to bed. You've got a really good daughter, Nat.'

I smiled into my mobile. 'Thank you, Connor. Sarah is an amazing girl. I'll see you in a bit.'

'Take care. And, Nat?'

'Yeah?'

'Don't worry about your mam. I told you, mine had the same spells and now she's absolutely grand.'

'Thank you, Connor, I hope you're right.'

'I like Beryl. She's a real character. And a trouper.'

'She sure is. Thank you, Connor, for being there to help Sarah. And for all the other things, too.'

He chuckled. 'No problem. I'll open a bottle of red for when you get in.'

'Okay. Later, then. Bye, Connor,' I said and reluctantly hung up. Because the moment I did, the air went flat and heavy with misery again.

'Nat?' Neil called.

I turned and saw him standing with Dr Simpson so I ran down the corridor, my heart in my throat.

'Easy, easy,' Neil said. 'It's fine.'

Dr Simpson smiled. 'I just wanted you to know that she's sleeping now and tomorrow we'll be running some more tests. We'll call you when we have the results.'

'Thank you,' I said, relieved. I didn't know why, but I had expected it to be bad news. Mum had never, ever been in hospital before and the idea of her lying there helpless made me want to bawl like a baby.

The doctor shook my hand. 'Pleased to have finally met you, Natalia.'

Strange how, in all my years of catering Neil's dinners, I had not met him. 'Thank you, Dr Simpson. Thank you so much.'

When I got in, I went straight into the kitchen where Connor was drying the dishes, bless him.

'Hey... how is she?' he asked as I sank down into a chair.

'She's okay at the moment. Tomorrow they'll run some more tests and get back to us.'

'Okay, good. You did the right thing to not waste any time.'

'How are the girls?' I asked as Connor turned on the microwave oven.

'Absolute gems,' he said, sitting down opposite me and pouring me the wine he'd promised. 'Sarah and I tired them out with a game of Twister.'

I giggled despite myself. 'I can't imagine you pretzeled up with Amy and Zoe.'

He pushed the hair away from his face, revealing a high, intelligent forehead. He really was beautiful. 'It was fun! Of course they beat the crap out of me.'

I chuckled, and he leaned forward, taking my hand. 'Nat? It's going to be fine. I'm here for you, okay?'

I looked at his hand, a sweep of deep heat enveloping me, and I suddenly knew what women meant when they talked about hot flashes.

'Thank you, Connor. You're so kind. I don't know what I did to deserve a lodger like you.'

He stroked the back of my hand with his thumb. 'You're you, and that's enough, Nat.'

He looked deep into my eyes. Was he finally, *finally*, going to kiss me?

Before I could answer, the oven pinged and he let go of my hand to retrieve what was inside. 'I made lasagne,' he said, placing the fragrant dish before me.

It was better that way, otherwise I would have never known if he'd done it out of pity, or just to cheer me up.

'Mum – sorry, I fell asleep,' Sarah said as she padded into the kitchen rubbing her eyes. 'How's Nana?'

'She'll be okay, we think. She's resting now.'

'Oh, thank God,' she said as she sank into a chair opposite me. 'When can she come home?'

Home. This was, indeed, everyone's home, no matter how long they were going to stay, and the thought that I could still provide a safe haven for my loved ones filled me with pride. The downsizing would have to wait.

'We don't know yet, probably in a couple of days, just to make sure they have the time to run all the necessary tests.'

'Eat up, now' Connor said. 'I'll be upstairs if you need me.'

He had sensed that Sarah and I might need some time together as I rarely saw her these days. 'Thanks, Connor.'

'*Buon appetito!*' he said as he went.

Buon appetito indeed, I thought, inhaling the fragrance. It looked home-made. I popped a huge forkful into my mouth and nearly swooned. It had been made from scratch. Was there any end to this man's talents?

'How did things go here with the girls?' I asked as I washed down my mouthful with a bit of *vino rosso*.

Sarah grinned. 'It was great. Connor kept them busy all day without a moment to spare. I'm beginning to understand what you see in him besides his looks.'

'I'm glad. That you're getting along, I mean.'

'He also gave me some advice about Sam.'

'Oh?'

'Financial and legal advice, mainly. He told me how to trawl through the web to see if there were any forgotten or hidden accounts where Sam might have had money. Maybe that will begin to cover what he owes me.'

'Brilliant, Sarah, I'm glad.'

'I wanted to thank you, Mum.'

'For what, love?'

'For taking me in and all.'

'Sarah – this is your home for as long as you need it.'

'Thanks. But things are better now. I'm still angry with Sam, but I no longer love him. It's like a blindfold has fallen away from my eyes. I finally see him for what he is – a dirty, lying scumbag.'

I was glad she had said it and not me.

'I'm off to bed, now,' she said, getting to her feet. 'I'm exhausted. I don't know how you do it all.'

'The same way I did it for you and Lizzie – with love. Are you up early tomorrow?'

Sarah nodded. 'I have a meeting. You?'

'I'll have to go in and see about Nana.'

'Is Dad going with you?'

I hesitated. I didn't want to get her hopes up about us

spending any time together. After all, she was still on his side. 'As Nana's GP, yes.'

'Okay, that's a good thing. He still loves you, you know?'

I made an effort not to snort but she tactfully changed the subject.

'Is Connor babysitting tomorrow as well?' she asked. 'Because I have to work.'

'Yes. I should start paying him instead of the other way around.'

Sarah chuckled. 'Yeah. Night, Mum. Good luck for tomorrow, and send me a message.'

I got up and washed my plate and fork, leaving my glass half full. 'Will do, darling. Have a good day.'

Before turning in, I checked on the girls. They were fast asleep, completely knackered by Connor's games. Where did he find the energy to keep up with them? All day and every day it was Connor this, and Connor that, *Connor, look* and *Connor, come!* And how selfless he was.

I hoped he would stick around a little longer. I didn't know how the girls would do without him now.

The next morning, Neil came to pick me up to go to Truro and consult with Dr Simpson again.

'Pete – how is she?' Neil asked before his friend had even settled in his chair opposite us.

Pete took a deep breath and my stomach sank. 'We're looking at a diagnosis of Alzheimer's disease. The symptoms are all there.'

'Alzheimer's?' I echoed. Fear grew inside me like flames

licking at wood. Would Mum lose all her memories, first her recent ones, and then finally her youth, until she could remember nothing at all?

I had read some articles on dementia in passing, but had never really stopped to think that this would affect my family, and so soon, to boot. We never think that these things can happen to us, touch us so soon. And then, bam – they do. My entire world crashed onto my head as I tried to digest the information.

Alzheimer's. I'd heard what it did to people. All the horrible transformations it brought about, wreaking havoc on the brain cells. She had started off loopy, and then she had become downright strange and at times even absent. And soon, she wouldn't even recognise us.

'It's not that advanced yet, but she will have moments where she'll seem to be lucid and then a moment later, she'll be absent.'

I let out a breath and raked a hand through my hair. Neil's arm circled my shoulders. 'The girls will be distraught, and especially the twins. How can I explain this to two eight-year-olds?' I said. 'I have to call Yolanda.'

He nodded. 'You go and wait for me outside. I'll get some more info off Peter.'

I shook my head. 'No, I want to know every little thing first-hand.' I swallowed. 'She's... *my* mother.'

'Easy, Nat, don't get upset. We'll deal with this, one day at a time.'

I dashed a hand across my eyes. 'I'm sorry, Doctor Simpson. I'm ready.'

'Well, what we do know about Alzheimer's is that it is a cognitive impairment. Not all cognitive impairments lead to Alzheimer's specifically. Clinically speaking, there are five stages of the disease. Many people may already suffer from it without any evident symptoms.'

'So you're saying that this started long before I realised what was going on, right?'

He nodded, and I buried my forehead in my hand.

'Don't blame yourself. It is often undetectable in the beginning,' he said.

Don't blame yourself. As if I couldn't not blame myself. Who else was responsible for her? And all these years I'd considered myself much more put together than Yolanda and therefore more responsible. Some daughter I was.

Amidst my misery, another half hour was spent listing the mainly unknown causes of the disease, what it entailed and what could be expected for the future. I had heard pretty much most of it before from second-hand sources. But I never had thought that it could happen to my mum. Strong, scathing Mum. After years of demanding the best from everyone, she had in the end reached her own breaking point. And I had no idea how to deal with it.

So that evening I called a family meeting with them all, explaining to the twins what was happening, and Zoe almost fell apart, her lower lip trembling. 'Why won't she recognise us, Auntie Nat? Doesn't she love us anymore?'

'Oh, sweetheart – Nana loves you two more than anything! She's just a little confused at the moment, is all.'

'Is she going to start dribbling and wearing her clothes inside out?' Amy said. 'Because Candace's nana does that and it's absolutely disgusting.'

'Amy!' Zoe cried.

'Of course not,' Lizzie said, taking Amy onto her lap. 'Mum is going to take really good care of Nana, you'll see. And we'll do all we can to help, won't we?'

Zoe nodded firmly, while Amy made a face. 'What can we do?'

'Well, darling, you can start by being really nice to Nana and bringing her flowers and make drawings for her. And sitting in the same room with her as much as you can. She loves to have you around.'

'But what if she doesn't recognise us at all? Candace's nana doesn't even remember her own name.'

At that, Connor and I exchanged glances. 'Your nana isn't that bad, girls, not to worry,' he said. 'And especially with all of us, she'll have everything she needs and she'll never be lonely. Right?'

'Right,' Zoe said.

Sarah nudged Amy. 'Right?'

Amy drew out a long sigh, as if she was eighty years old and exhausted from a long life of difficulties. I knew exactly how she felt. 'Right. But she'd better not smell like Candace's nana.'

'She won't,' I promised them. 'She'll be as clean and beautiful as ever. I'll take really good care of her.' And that was a promise.

But I couldn't help but wonder – was this the beginning of the end? Was this how it went? One day Mum forgot a name, or a date, and the next day, a little more, until one day she wouldn't even recognise our faces? Were we on our way to becoming strangers to her?

9

Someone Like You

When Neil and I got home with Mum, everyone was waiting in the living room to allow us to manoeuvre her wheelchair as her ankle was still not completely healed, plus she'd had dizzy spells so we kept the risk of her falling to a bare minimum.

Connor and the twins had made a huge, colourful banner reading *Welcome Home, Nana!* Surrounded by big pink and red hearts. Lizzie and Sarah had flung open the French doors to the garden and set the table in the dining room and there were fresh flowers everywhere.

'Look, Mum,' I said, bending to her. 'Look what a lovely welcome party for you!'

The girls wrapped their arms around her, pleased to see that she still smelled good, while Sarah and Lizzie fussed over her, pushing her wheelchair over to the dinner table where piles of presents were stocked.

Mum looked up at me. 'Are they staying long?'

Silent glances bounced around the room, and even the twins had the sense to be quiet.

I bent down before her and caressed her cheek. 'No, Mum. Are you hungry? There's a lovely roast, look, just for you.'

But Mum shrugged and rested her jaw on her knuckles. 'I'm not hungry.'

Amy turned to her. 'Nana, is it true that you're losing your marbles?'

'Amy…!' Sarah said.

Amy shrugged. 'That's what my friend Josh says.'

Mum cackled. 'You tell your friend that it's better to lose your marbles than your balls!'

'Oh my goodness,' I moaned. 'Whatever happened to trying to make Connor think we're not weird?'

Connor laughed and gave her a bouquet of flowers. 'I love weird. Welcome back, Beryl. I missed you.'

She patted his jaw affectionately. 'I've missed you too, Ross.'

'Mum – that's Connor, remember?'

But she turned to glare at me. 'What's the matter with you? Can't you see that's Ross Poldark? I saw him galloping on his horse along the path the other morning.'

Silence filled the room as my daughters eyed each other.

Neil coughed. 'I, uh. I'd better get going.'

'Aw, Dad. Stay for dinner. There's all this food. Can't he, Mum?' Sarah asked. As if I could say no in front of everyone. And I owed him.

'Yes, please do stay, Neil.'

But Neil looked at Connor. 'No, thank you. I'll call you later to check on Mum.'

'Dad, come on,' Sarah said, while Lizzie abstained. She was not a fan of her father, and never had been.

Mum pointed at me and we all settled to hear what she had to say. 'Put the telly on, Yolanda. *Doc Martin* is about to start.'

During the next few weeks, her condition worsened. She became irritable and aggressive, lashing out at me both verbally and physically. She'd even bitten my hand once. Other times she'd sit in her armchair, possibly brooding, possibly empty-minded. I needed to stimulate her constantly, I'd been told. So I went up to the attic, found the box I was looking for, then to the kitchen for a quick rifle through the drawers and skipped back down to the living room.

'Look what I've got here, Mum,' I said, showing her my find, i.e. the girls' old baby monitors. It was the only way I could think of to keep my eyes and ears on her at all times.

'See how this works, Mum? It's like a two-way radio or a walkie-talkie.'

'What the hell do you need that for?' she asked, eyeing it as if it was a three-headed monster.

'It's for parents to listen in to their babies' rooms to make sure—' I bit my lip. I had almost broken one of the golden rules. Never humiliate or be condescending. 'It's so you can call me if you need anything, or if you feel lonely, and we can have a chat from two separate rooms. What do you think, Mum?'

'Hm. Sounds like just an excuse to be lazy to me.'

I clamped my mouth shut. This humouring and being patient thing was proving to be much more difficult than I had thought. *Come on, Nat. You can do it. Do this for her, now. She's your mother, for goodness' sake.*

Of course I was going to do it, no question. Although I couldn't help but think that even if I had been a feisty child, there was no comparison with what I was having to put up with now.

I was doing everything by the book. I was being patient, kind, reassuring, never putting her on the spot with her memory loss, obviously, and always repeated things in the exact same way so she wouldn't get confused. I broke down instructions into bite-sized tasks. *Please stand up. Please raise your arms. Please be patient while I change your nightgown. Please sit down. Now pull your legs up. Now lie down.* I was doing everything I could and more, to make sure my mother never felt hurried or harried.

I waited patiently for her to eat her meals, and when she refused to eat and demanded something else, I cooked it. I never flinched when she threw her food at me, or when she swore at me or bit me. Who said it would be easy?

When she was settled, I went back into the kitchen and pulled out a bottle of wine and a wine glass from the cabinet. I set them down on the coffee table at the other end of the orangery and bent to the bottom shelf of the wall-to-wall book unit. I pulled out a box of pictures that I had been meaning to sort out and put into photo albums one day. There was a complete mish-mash, from my childhood to our last trip together as a family just before the divorce. I hadn't taken a single picture since then – not even a passing selfie.

I took a sip and began sifting through them, trying to put them into some semblance of order, when I heard the front door click and a few moments later Connor ambled into the orangery, his black leather bag dangling from his wrist.

'Hey,' he said, a huge grin on his face.

I looked up from my glass of wine. 'Hi. How was your evening?'

'It was good. Yours?'

Lonely without you, I wanted to say.

I held up my glass. 'Care to join?'

'Sure,' he said, putting his bag down in the corner and going to the cabinet for a wine glass.

'What have you got there? Family pictures?'

'Hmm, yes. A little stroll down memory lane.'

'Mind if I have a nosy?'

'If you like. Most of them are of Sarah and Lizzie growing up.'

'None of you?' he asked, sitting beside me, and that usual warmth filled me. It had to be the wine.

'Not really. Mum was never one to take pictures.' Except she took loads of Yolanda, but I wasn't going there. It was time to forgive and forget, especially now that she was so vulnerable. She probably didn't remember a thing now, anyway. What good would it have done to rake over the coals?

I picked up and oldie but goodie. 'This is Yolanda and me at Christmas when we were little. My dad had just given us a doll's house each.'

'Look at you two, so sweet.'

I snorted. 'Don't let the blue eyes fool you. And this is Sarah and Lizzie at Christmas with their new doll's house. I had always dreamed of giving them mine but—' I bit my lip.

He looked up from the picture and I began to heat up under his scrutinising gaze. 'But...?'

I shrugged. 'Mum gave it away to Mrs Locke, her neighbour.'

Connor's eyebrows shot up.

Ancient, unshed tears pricked my eyes but I managed to harness them at the last second. 'I was mad at her for weeks.'

'You really loved it, didn't you?'

I nodded and swallowed down the tiny pebbles in my throat. 'My dad had made it for me.' And I thought of everything I'd had to give up after he died – my collection of Beatrix Potter, my rag doll Nettie. All sold to put food on the table and because I'd had to grow up fast.

'Oh,' I said, laughing it off. 'Look at this – Lizzie on her first birthday! Look how beautiful she is...'

Connor peered into the picture, studying it. 'She looks just like you.'

'She's very like me on the inside, too.'

'You mean kind and generous?'

'I mean a free spirit. Never worried about appearances too much... And you? What's your relationship like with your family?'

He rolled his eyes. 'Can't live with 'em, can't live without 'em. I adore them, especially my mam. She's the number one in my life.'

So no other woman, after all? I'd wondered about his reasons for being in Wyllow Cove, and that maybe there was a woman on his mind.

'Do you miss her?'

'Like crazy. I miss them all, especially Old Mary – my mam. But we talk every Sunday afternoon. She fills me in on all the happenings at home. My sister-in-law Celia is expecting again. They'd been trying for almost two years now.'

'That's so lovely! Then I guess you'll be going back for the birth. How... long will you be staying here in Wyllow Cove?'

His long lashes fluttered. 'As long as it takes.'

'To...? Sorry, I didn't mean to pry.'

'To sort my life out.'

'And how is that going, if you don't mind me asking?'

His eyes narrowed and then he grinned enigmatically. 'I'd say it's going preeeetty well at the moment.'

Ah. Meaning he wasn't letting me in on his little secret.

'And who's this gorgeous little girl?' he asked, singling out a picture of me standing on the cliffs.

'I remember that day,' I said. 'My father had taken Yolanda and me on a picnic. Actually, not far from here. I remember him teaching us to fly a kite.'

'You still miss your dad greatly, don't you?' he asked softly.

'Yeah. I was my daddy's girl. I miss him every day.'

'But at least you had some good years with him, right?' he asked.

'Yes, I did. I looked up to him. There was nothing he couldn't or wouldn't do for us. He made our lives... secure. Stable, you know?'

He looked into my eyes as if studying me. 'Just like you with Amy and Zoe.'

'Yes, well. I'm all they have at the moment. But I, uhm, noticed that they really listen to you, too. They seem to quarrel much less ever since you moved in.'

He grinned. 'Really? I have that effect on my own nieces and nephews too.'

'My sister could have taken them with her, but we believe living here in Wyllow Cove is certainly a more stable life for them. But who says it's a better life?'

At that, he smiled. 'A simple life is always a better life.'

Oh, how much better my own life would be if you only realised I existed, Connor. But that was a completely different story, somewhere in between the realms of fantasy and science fiction. Because men like him weren't interested in women like me.

The next day I got another call from *Lady* magazine. Two calls in the space of a week was definitely not good. Octavia must have decided she wouldn't be spoken to like I had spoken to her.

'Natalia, Octavia here. I'll need that article sooner than we discussed.'

'Oh?' I hadn't even decided what it was going to be about, let alone started it, what with being busy with my mother. How was I going to slap together my job-saving attempt out of the blue?

'I want a special edition coming out to mark my takeover. And to announce my new and rejuvenated agenda.'

Oh, how she loved to flaunt that word!

'So I'll need it on my desk by the end of tomorrow.'

'So soon? But—'

'No buts, Natalia. If you can't do it, I'll just have to find somebody else.' Pause for drama.

'I'll do it, of course, Octavia.' Even if it killed me, I'd do it.

'Good woman. This will either make or break you.'

Hm. How to explain to her that writing a successful column for thirteen years and still going strong meant that I had made it to where I wanted to be? I didn't want much more, except for maybe a double-page feature. That would have been nice. 'Got it. You'll have it by the end of tomorrow.'

'Make it four o'clock.'

Jesus. 'Right.'

I hung up, wondering just how I was going to pull that one off in so little time. Mum needed round-the-clock care now, meaning shower, setting her hair in rollers, then styling it every single morning and then getting her dressed and then making her breakfast just to start. And that was before the twins even got up and I'd have to ferry them off to school. But the time I actually got a cup of coffee down my own throat and sat down at my laptop it would be at least nine thirty going on ten. Meaning I didn't have much time to pull a masterpiece article out of my hat. But I was all she had, and I was not going to fail her.

'You okay, Mum?' I asked, getting up from my desk.

'Of course I'm okay, why do you ask?' she asked back.

'Because I love you,' I said, sitting on the edge of her armchair and hugging her gently.

Which was more than I could have ever said about her. She was the exact opposite of a normal mother. At least for me. While she had been ever-present in Yolanda's life, she had missed all the major milestones in mine – my confirmation, my graduation, and even on my wedding day she was late for the ceremony. Dad had smiled uneasily making feeble excuses.

After that, she'd missed Sarah's christening, so after Dad's death, I didn't even bother to invite her to Lizzie's. Which had caused a storm.

'What have I ever done to you?' she'd cried. 'Why didn't you invite your own mother?'

'Because you wouldn't have come!' I'd shot back. 'You miss everything that's important in my life! You missed my wedding, my graduation – but you didn't even miss a hair appointment when it was regarding Yolanda!'

Her mouth had dropped open. 'You're jealous of your baby sister? I can't believe this, you, of all people?'

'What's that supposed to mean: me of all people?'

'You have had the treatment of a lifetime! I've made so many sacrifices for you above all people.'

'Oh, you mean, losing your figure? Were you so embarrassed you didn't even take one picture?' Had I been such a burden to her that she hadn't even wanted to remember it? But when she'd been pregnant with Yolanda, there had been all sorts of happy pictures, mostly colour ones, and some even blown up and displayed around the cottage in old silver frames. Even now it was still a shrine to Yolanda and her success as a celebrity chef, whereas I don't ever recall her making any comments about my writing career.

And now she was here, in the home of the very daughter she'd shunned, while her favourite one traipsed around the world, bouncing from one shooting set to another with her famous smile, oblivious to any filial responsibilities, whereas I never got a break. And still, I did it with constant love.

'Are you working on your next column?' she asked out of nowhere, her eyes now lucid.

It felt so strange to just be like this all of a sudden, when for years neither of us had ever had much to say to the other. Apparently we were entering a good phase again. 'I am.'

'And what's it about?'

I smiled. This was just lovely. 'I'm not quite sure yet. But it has to be good and ready by tomorrow afternoon.'

'Maybe you could write about motherhood. *Lady* magazine readers are mostly mothers.'

I studied her. Not only was she being kind and attentive, she was giving me what to her was good advice. She had no way of knowing that things had changed since last month's edition had come out and she had been a completely different person, as sharp as a razor. And the last thing I wanted was to share my worries with her.

'Good idea,' I said. 'Are you hungry yet?'

She shook her head. 'I think I'll read while you finish your article.'

'Okay, then,' I said and sat down, arranging my stuff around me just the way I liked it – mug to my right, pad of paper and coloured pens, my mobile on my left along with my family pictures. Ah, the life of a writer. If it could only be as easy as it looked. By the head shot above my column you'd think I was this successful, happy woman without a care in the world. Little did anyone know that it all came at a huge cost, and even now, as a result, I had only hours to save my career.

And just as I was settling into writing, the biggest distraction of my life came down the stairs for the second time that day. Every single time I sat down at my desk, he went to work in the garden. Coincidence?

'Hey Beryl!' he called as he went past us. 'My, you're looking younger and younger every day!'

At that, Mum chuckled. 'Go on with you, lad! You're just teasin' a poor old lady!'

He stopped in the middle of the room, hands on hips, a mock-hurt expression on his face. 'Now would I ever do that to the love of my life? Would I, Beryl?'

But Mum chuckled even harder, slapping her hand against her armrest. 'You listening to this, Nat? Isn't he a charmer?'

'He absolutely is.' I smiled at him, feeling my face go beetroot red and diving behind the screen of my laptop.

He pushed his hair away from his face. 'I needed a screen break, so I thought I'd continue on the fences. Is that okay?'

Did he mean, would I rather watch him than stare at my own blank laptop screen? He actually needed to ask?

'Knock yourself out.'

'Cool. Girls get off to school okay?' he asked.

'Yes. And Sarah will be late as she's had to go into London.'

'I hate London with a passion,' Connor said. 'Nothing but pushing and shoving, seemingly mitigated with a *sorry* that actually means *out of my way*. Not for me.'

'I used to live in London,' Mum said.

I sat up. 'I didn't know that.'

She shrugged. 'It was a terrible time. Yer dad was workin' as a baker and I was sewing to make a few bob. But we both realised that we could make a better go of it here at home. So we both quit, and with a little help from our families, we opened the bakery. The freshest, most fragrant bread you ever tasted.' And then she pointed the remote to her TV set, a sign that the conversation was over.

I nodded. It had been very good, I remembered. With a pang in my heart. *Oh, Dad.*

Connor stopped at my desk on his way out. 'Working on your next article?' he asked.

'Yes. And hopefully not my last.'

He frowned. 'What do you mean?'

'You remember me telling you that my boss gave me an article to write?'

'Yeah?'

'Well, she's brought my deadline forward and if I can't demonstrate that I can be as hip as a twenty-year-old, I'm out.'

He crossed his arms. 'She can't do that – it's illegal.'

'Not if she's giving me a chance to write like she wants. She says it has nothing to do with age. And I've got until tomorrow to write the article that will save my career.'

'Bloody hell.'

Mum cackled, now absorbed in her favourite morning show. 'You idiot,' she said. 'No Italian has ever cooked a chicken like *that*!'

Connor glanced at her, then turned back to me. 'So what are you going to do?'

I shrugged. 'No idea.'

'Well, if anyone can do it, it's you, Nat.'

'Awh, thanks, Connor.'

'If you need legal advice, I know a good guy.'

'Thanks, Connor. One day I hope to make all your kindness up to you.'

'You're grand. Now, if you'll excuse me, those bushes aren't going to tend themselves.'

I nodded and watched him as he sauntered down the length of the garden and immediately absorbed himself in his work. He was unfathomable. One day he seemed interested in me, and the next, he treated me like a good friend. Which was it? And if he was a good friend, how could I ruin it by intimating I wanted a fling? Because now, I wasn't so sure a fling would have been enough for me.

As if sensing my thoughts, he looked up and grinned that boyish grin of his, then turned back to his work.

Work, right. But I kept getting distracted every time he bent down or reached up to hammer the posts in. At one point, he reached into his pocket for something and pulled back his hair into a tiny ponytail, revealing a strong jaw and neck. He was truly beautiful beyond words. And speaking of words, I should really have been getting back to the ones – or the lack of them – on my screen.

But before I really got stuck into it, I had to tell Yolanda about Mum's condition. I'd been putting it off for weeks, lying to her, telling her that everything was okay, and even vetoing the twins from mentioning it during their video chats.

Not wanting Mum to hear, I picked up my mobile, closed the French doors behind me and sat at the patio table.

It was early in New York, but Yolanda was always up at four to shoot. I only hoped she would answer her phone.

'Nat?' came her voice across the Atlantic. 'Is everything okay?'

'Hello,' I said, trying to sound cheery, but not too much as to deceive her. Just enough so she wouldn't worry about the girls. 'Everything's fine. The girls are at school.'

'So what's up? Because if you've called to nag me about coming home—'

'Yolanda – Mum has been diagnosed with Alzheimer's. Neil and I took her to a specialist. It's in its early stages, but it's definitely coming.'

A silence followed, but I couldn't tell how much of it was part of the technical delay, and how much was shock.

'Oh my God! Is she okay? Is she lucid?'

'She is at the moment, but it comes and goes, you know? One minute she's discussing the shopping list with me and the next...' I swallowed, raking a hand through my hair. I spared her the fact that Mum had at one point actually said, *Who's Yolanda?* That would break her heart and worry her no end.

'Oh my God, Nat. You must be overwhelmed with the girls as well. I'm so sorry.'

'It's okay. Sarah and Connor are helping out a lot.'

'The lodger, you mean? He sounds like he's becoming practically indispensable.'

'He is, trust me. The girls love him to pieces and would suffer terribly without him. And he helps a great deal with Mum, too.'

'Okay, I guess that's her best option for now.'

'Also, I think it's a good idea to put her cottage up for sale as soon as I can get it all organised,' I said.

'The cottage? You can't! It was our home for years!'

'Yola, maybe I didn't make myself clear. She's not going to be getting any better.'

'But to sell the house? Why?'

'To pay for her medical expenses?'

'You're not putting her in a home, are you?'

'Of course not,' I said hotly.

'Good. Because at the end of the day, you've already got the girls. What harm could one more person do?'

I sighed. Of course she was clueless about caring for the elderly, particularly the fragile elderly, when she had no idea of what her own daughters needed.

'Yola, I said I would take care of Mum. But never for a moment think that it'll be easy, financially speaking.'

'And you're already complaining. Jesus, Nat, what do you want from me?'

'A bit of understanding.'

'Just because I don't want you to sell our family home?' she bit off.

I raked a hand through my hair again. At this rate I'd be bald by the end of the day. 'Look, Yolanda, I'm under a lot of pressure right now and I really don't want to argue.'

'Why, what else is wrong?'

Any other sister would have shared her fears and anxieties, but I was well aware of the fact that Yolanda only pretended to want to know. As soon as I'd open my mouth, her mind would start to wander to something else. Because no matter what I did for her, how much I encouraged her, et cetera. Yola and I would never be close, because we never really had been, which was sad. Our mother had always pitched us against each other by comparing us, and I was seldom the one who came out on top.

'Nothing, Yola, don't worry about it.'

Luckily I was my own person, but I couldn't deny that

my insecurities were childhood-deep. So I did everything I could to make sure that I hadn't made the same mistake with Sarah and Lizzie. And I'd be damned if I would let the same thing happen between Amy and Zoe.

I also wondered why I'd even bothered telling Yola about Mum. There was nothing she could do, except for aggravate me.

'In any case, the money would go into her bank account to pay for everything she needs.' I certainly couldn't afford to pay out of my own pocket anymore. I was barely surviving, what with the huge grocery bills I ran for such a packed house and Connor's rent was more than warranted.

'What if I sent you some money for Mum's upkeep?' she suggested. 'It's only fair – you're doing everything on your own.'

If anything, and knowing my situation from the start, she should have at least asked if I was okay with the expenses for her own girls, seeing as she was a millionaire and I only had my column, if even that now.

Not that I would have accepted any money from her, otherwise. I had my dignity and was happy to take care of my nieces when their mother was away. We'd been doing it for years. But not once had the thought even crossed her mind, just like a *thank you* had never crossed her lips. She'd bustle in, kids in tow, telling me how harried and stressed she was, and would I be a darling and take them? It was all about her and her career and her schedule and her flights and her brilliant life. To her mind, I should have been happy basking in the reflected light of her glory.

Don't get me wrong. I'm still very proud of Yolanda, as, brought up by our mother, it was no surprise we achieved our goals in life. I had been the one to teach her how to cook, truth be told, and I'd got her interested enough to go to cooking school. I had been there for her since we were kids when all Mum did was order me around while doting on the 'little one' who was still too young to know what she wanted to do with her life. I had been the one to actually support Yolanda's choice. But that had been lost in the sands of time, along with every other good deed of mine.

But private specialists for my mother were a cost I couldn't face on my own. Besides, she was Yolanda's mother, too.

'If you wouldn't mind?' I said. 'Because actually, I don't even have her PINs to access her own money. Plus, I don't think she even knows where her bank card is or how to use it, to be honest. She likes to go in there and chat with the tellers. But now that you mention it, I'm going to have to sort it out, and also do a direct debit for her utility bills.'

'Right.'

'In any case,' I continued, 'I'm going to speak to a lawyer first. I have no idea how these things work, but I suspect that in order to be her executor, I'll have to get a certificate or report of some sort from Mum's doctor. And then we'll see what's what. Naturally I'll keep you posted and cc you in on everything, so you should probably open a folder in your email account.'

'You're going to have her declared incapacitated?' Yolanda shrieked. 'You can't do that to her! She's our mother!'

I bristled. 'I'm not doing anything of the sort, Yola. I want to understand how to better serve her. Somebody's got to take care of her, and unless you can get Scotty or someone else to beam you back here this very moment, it's going to have to be me.'

'Oh, for God's sake, Nat. I'll buy you out of your share of the cottage,' she snapped.

'What?' Damn. There had been nothing I had wanted more than to buy Lavender Cottage for myself, and now she wanted to buy the house *next door*? I had never factored in Yolanda buying Mum's place and thus becoming my neighbour. 'But you have your villa on the clifftops. What would you do with an old cottage?'

'Oh, probably renovate it and turn the entire ground floor into a set for my next cooking show. You know, Yolanda's Little Cottage Dream or something like that. People are gaga for everything small. Why on earth, I don't know, when you could have a million-pound home.'

As she did. Mine didn't count, as I was having to sell it because I couldn't afford its upkeep. And I was one of those people she ridiculed, because I wasn't particularly ambitious.

I was happy with something more me-sized. I actually wanted a smaller life. Lavender Cottage would surround me with its history and the warmth of my better childhood memories. I would renovate it and make the master bedroom my sanctuary, maybe even put in a roll-top bath by the window where I could look out to sea while I had a leisurely soak.

'Besides,' Yolanda said, 'the crew could slum it upstairs.'

There was no way I was going to live next door to a set, what with all the coming and going and vans and bright lights and stuff. Could you imagine me trying to squirrel myself away in Lavender Cottage next door to write with her mob around twenty-four seven? And once again, it was looking like her decisions trumped mine.

'Why don't you find another place?' I asked, but then bit my lip. She would misunderstand as usual.

She snorted. 'Why, do you want it?'

'Maybe,' I bluffed. 'As soon as I sell my place.' *Come on, Nat. Tell her the truth.*

'Send all the paperwork to my lawyer. He'll sort it out. I have to go now.'

'Yolanda, wait…'

'What?'

I cleared my throat. Sometimes it was like she was Amy and I was Zoe. 'If we're going to put her house on the market, I don't want you to buy it because I want to buy Lavender Cottage next door and I don't think that a TV crew would be my ideal neighbours.'

'You want to buy Mrs Pendennis's old home? With what money, exactly?'

'I told you, I'm selling The Mausoleum.'

She snickered. 'Are you? And where is Sarah going to sleep? And Lizzie, when she splits up with Liam?'

I gasped. 'That is a horrible thing to say!'

'Nat – don't you get it? The Amore girls are all cursed in love – so much for the promising surname.'

'We are not cursed!' I shot back.

'No? Look at us. Look at Mum – Dad died while she was still a young woman. And you? Neil treated you like shit since the day you met. And Sarah, whatever's happened to her, I'm sure Sam hasn't been back to whisk her away. And me? Piers couldn't give a flying—'

'I get it,' I said. 'The Amore women are unlucky in love. Well, maybe I don't believe that. Look at Lizzie. She and Liam are like two peas in a pod.'

She snorted. 'Until they won't be.'

'I believe in love,' I insisted. 'Maybe it won't come my way, but there is so much of it around, Yola…'

'You really do live in la-la land, don't you, Nat? Do you really think that we're all going to fall in love again and be happily ever after?'

'I do. And besides, don't you and Bill—?'

She cackled. 'You crack me up, Nat. Truly, you do. Right, gotta go. We'll talk about the cottage next time.'

'Don't you want to speak to Mum?'

'I've just said I've got to go. Give her a hug from me, and give my girls a kiss,' she said hastily and hung up before I could take my next breath.

As always, my call to my younger sister left me with a bitter taste in my mouth. Would there ever be a time when we got on, when she didn't have to belittle me or show off or simply hide her fears behind her successes?

I looked up to see Connor making his way up the garden, bending slightly to wipe his face with his T-shirt. 'I'm done for today. You okay there?' he asked as he washed his hands under the garden tap.

I shrugged. 'My sister. She's being very uncooperative.'

'Yeah? Why's that?'

I explained it to him and he pursed his lips. 'That's not fair, with you doing all the hard work and her getting the power. Sorry, I didn't mean to meddle.'

'No, you're absolutely right. She's always been like that

but now I've had enough. What does she know about Mum's needs anyway? She doesn't know anything about her anymore.'

Connor nodded. 'No, you are definitely the right choice for Beryl. Listen, I'm only corporate law, but I have a few mates who are in family law. Do you want me to ask?'

'No, that's okay. I'll figure this out somehow.'

He studied me. 'Tell you what. I'm going upstairs for a quick shower, and when I come back down I'm going to cook you a nice dinner. How's that?'

'Oh – you don't have to do that, Connor...'

'I want to,' he replied. 'You just relax, pour yourself a drink and I'll be right back.'

Could *you* have said no? Exactly.

For dinner, Sarah had taken a tray up to her room. She worked practically every evening these days, bent as she was on getting her promotion. She spent more time barking orders into her phone than receiving them, which boded well, and I could only be proud of the determination she was showing. It seemed that we were all changing – except for Amy.

'Amy, sweetie, leave your sister's ears alone and eat your food,' Connor said as she made an attempt to shove a piece of shepherd's pie into Zoe's ear as Zoe swatted her sister's hand away. Only a few weeks ago Zoe would have buckled, but she was, thankfully, developing a sense of strength that I never knew she had.

From upstairs, we could hear Sarah shout, 'Just get to work – now!'

'She's gonna become her boss's superior if she keeps this up,' Connor said with a chuckle, reading my mind.

I grinned. 'She's bound to. I don't know anyone as strong and determined as her.'

He put his fork down, his eyes caressing my face. 'You don't? I do.'

'Oh, well, I uhm...' My cheeks burning under his gaze, I whipped to my feet and brought out the apple pie I'd bought from Dora's.

'Come on, girls, finish your dessert, then get ready for bed.' I couldn't have them witnessing their Auntie Nat blushing at Connor's compliments.

'Can Uncle Connor tuck us in?' Zoe asked, her eyes swinging to his. Which in turn swung to mine with the message *I don't know where she got Uncle from, but I like it.*

'Of course, if that's what you want,' I said. Uncle Connor. It was safe to say that he was definitely one of us now. I only hoped they wouldn't suffer too much when he went back to Ireland.

'Come, then, Uncle Connor, Auntie Nat,' Zoe urged, pulling both our hands until we stood up. Connor's eyes twinkled as he grinned at me.

'Me last,' Amy ordered as they skipped up the stairs before us. 'I want to be the last one up!'

'You'll be the first one down if you don't stop bossing people around,' I warned her, but couldn't help smiling. Zoe tittered, satisfied, and Connor laughed.

'Can you read us *Little Red Riding Hood*, like when we were little?' Zoe asked me.

'Goodness, aren't you too old for that now?'

'We like the voices!' Amy said. 'Uncle Connor, you do the Big Bad Wolf and Auntie Nat can do Little Red Riding Hood.'

'Or…' I said with a devilish grin '…we can do it the other way around.'

Connor's face lit up. 'Sure,' he said in a wobbly falsetto. '*I'll* be Little Red *Riding* Hood!'

'And I'll be the Big Bad Wolf!' I howled.

The girls shrieked with laughter for the entire story, hardly listening to the horrible events unfolding, and just waiting for the spoken parts.

'This'll keep 'em up all night,' Connor commented, rolling his eyes and laughing.

'All the better to eat you up!' I roared, pretending to pounce on Connor (not that I hadn't ever thought of that before) while he pretended to shrink away from me, wailing: 'Help, someone help me, please!'

'There's no hope for you!' I barked until Zoe sat up to make sure I wasn't actually taking chunks out of Connor.

He sensed her fear and looked up, caressing her face. 'Auntie Nat's good at acting, isn't she, Zoe?' he asked.

Swinging her eyes from him to me, she nodded, then exhaled in relief. 'I knew that you weren't really killing him, but it looked so real,' she said as Amy rolled her eyes.

'Enough. Time to sleep,' I said, kissing them both. 'Next time we'll tell you a happy story, a nice, happy fairy tale about mermaids and tropical islands.'

'And Connor, too?' Zoe wanted to know. 'Will he tell us more stories?'

Connor looked at me, then smiled. 'For as long as you like, sweetheart.'

'They are absolutely precious,' Connor mused as we went down the stairs.

'And hard work,' I added. 'Care for a glass of wine out on the patio?'

He grinned and spread his arms out. 'Yes, please! I thought you'd never ask!'

I poured what was left of the wine and smiled as I sat down opposite him, facing the length of the garden. The sky was still a luscious lavender colour with hints of orange at the edges, while the opposite end of the sky was a dark, dark blue, almost black.

'The days are getting longer,' I mused, raising my glass to my lips.

Connor leaned forward. 'To longer days,' he toasted.

'To longer days,' I echoed, taking a sip and trying to not think of when he would return to Ireland.

'Better now?' he asked.

'Mmmhh, yes, much better, thank you, Connor. Dinner was fantastic and I truly appreciate not having to do everything on my own.'

'You're not alone, Nat,' he said softly.

My eyes swung to his. I still didn't understand where we stood. Was I just a friend? Sometimes, like in that moment, when he looked at me with such intensity, I almost thought that there was something between us, and if we only let our barriers down, the wild horses would stampede out of their enclosures and show their true colours. For deep inside, I recognised in him a kindred spirit – a free, more liberated side that was dying to break free.

I took another sip of my wine and looked across the

garden he'd so lovingly restored. 'What an amazing job you've done,' I said.

He followed my gaze. 'Yes, it's coming along quite nicely, isn't it?'

'Is there anything you can't do?' I said with a light chuckle.

He thought about it for a moment. 'I can't mend a broken heart.'

'I bet you could,' I said without thinking.

His eyes swung to mine. 'Is your heart mended?' he asked. 'Are you completely over Neil?'

I blinked. 'Absolutely. For years, now.'

'That's good,' he said, slowly turning his glass on itself, completely absorbed by the task.

'And you?' I ventured. 'Are you over your divorce?'

He looked up. 'Me? Yeah. For years, now, too.'

My heart shook. *Easy, Nat. Even if he's over his wife, that doesn't mean he's interested in you.*

We spent the next hour or so chatting quietly until we finished the bottle, the tea lights had all died out and there was literally no excuse to keep going.

'Well, I guess it's time to hit the sack,' I said with a nostalgic sigh.

'Yeah, it's late,' he agreed.

'Well, goodnight, then,' I whispered, getting up to go inside, but at the same time willing him to ask me to stay a little while longer.

'Nat...?' he whispered all of a sudden.

I turned at the door, my heart hammering. Was he finally going to make the first move?

'Yes?'

He lowered his eyes. 'Nothing. Sleep well.'

I groaned inwardly. 'You too, Connor.'

And that was the end of that. One minute he seemed to be really into me and the next, absolutely not. Had I completely misread the signs, the smiles, the caressing tones of his voice? Was it that I had completely mistaken his intentions, and he had no interest in me whatsoever, the one time I decided to finally liberate myself from the shackles of loneliness?

10

The Noughty Boys, Pun Intended

'You wrote an article about twenty-something heart-throbs disguised as male geeks?' Octavia barked over the phone a couple of days later. 'How exactly is that going to fly in a young women's magazine? Where's the levity, the flirting, the *sex*?'

The sex? Excellent question. But lately I was not in a very sexy mood.

'Dear oh dear, Natalia. If you don't pull up your socks, we're going to have to let you go definitively.'

Okay. Maybe it hadn't been such a great idea after all. But I'd poured my heart into it. And it was funny, how I'd described them.

'The new, twenty-something Clark Kents of the Twenty-twenties? The new Noughty Boys?' she continued. 'Good Lord, I've never read such dross!'

'Have you read it to the end?' I asked. 'Because it would be nice if you had read it all before criticising it.'

'I have read it all. It's absolute rubbish, Natalia.'

My heart sank. 'Oh.' Well, that was that, then. I had just botched my last chance of keeping my job, and now that was it. *Finito*. I was dead. After thirteen years of being the golden girl, I had been put to the door, and I was now mentally packing up my virtual desk – jar of pens, family picture and my stash of Reese's Pieces. All going offline.

'I, uhm...' What could I possibly say or do? Beg for my job back? To what purpose? Octavia Hounslow, or The Hound, as Maggie called her, was seriously bent on getting rid of the dead wood, and making a huge bonfire with it. And she was making no bones about it. She was making a mission of her mission statement.

'Gotta go, I'll deal with you later,' she snapped and hung up on me.

Images of the future flashed before me, where I would have to sell the house and downsize sooner than planned. I would have no choice. It was either that or move to some godforsaken iffy area where meth and violence were the norm. Imagine raising Amy and Zoe in that area. Because, as far as Yolanda was concerned, I was completely on my own in this one. I wouldn't even have time to sell Smuggler's Rest, possibly.

And Sarah? She would need a place to stay – there was no way she could ever get on the property ladder on a single income.

And Mum? I could never afford home care, nor would I put her into a home, even the best one. God knew she could afford it with the sale of her house. But I couldn't even bring myself to consider the option, despite Yolanda's opinions of me. Sometimes I wondered if she really knew me at all.

Because if she did, she would understand how important

it was for me to achieve financial independence and to settle down in a place I had always loved and could call my own. And Lavender Cottage represented that for me. I would have easily settled for Mum's place if it hadn't been for the tiny patch of dirt she called the garden. Lavender Cottage, on the other hand, had the magic that Mum's place lacked. Plus, the brook and the secret garden? No contest. But Yolanda would never be able to understand any of this, and she was definitely not someone I could turn to for help or advice – unless I wanted to lose my dignity as well.

Because losing The Mausoleum ahead of schedule had not been part of the plan. Everyone would suffer for it. Even Connor would be inconvenienced as he'd have to go earlier than discussed. But in all honesty, I think we would suffer his loss more than he ours, because, let's face it – I knew *he* would be absolutely fine with finding somewhere else – he didn't need us. One landlady or another was all the same for a tenant, but what about the effect his absence would have on the girls?

After years of being shy and closed to most people, Zoe was finally opening up and Amy was at last calming down. They seemed to be getting along better than ever, Amy being more patient towards Zoe, and Zoe not resenting Amy so much. The unnatural antagonism between them had, under his influence, gradually decreased. All because they wanted to please him. There was no activity he offered that Zoe wasn't confident in doing, and nothing that Amy found in the least boring. With Connor's easy, natural charm and warmth he had unwittingly brought my nieces closer to each other, especially in this time during which their mother's absence was prolonged. He was the absolute child whisperer.

But not only children loved him. Mum was like young girl again in his presence. I'd never seen her act like a *woman* woman, only a mother. An exhausted, disillusioned, disenchanted mother who had given up encouraging us and who found it easier to chastise and take sides. Connor, with his naughty banter, had reawakened the girl inside her. He had given her back the smile she'd lost. He'd given her back a piece of her life.

Even Sarah, who had seen him as the enemy from day one, was finally warming to him. Although she still did continue to fight in Neil's corner, convinced that Mummy and Daddy were just going through a rough patch and that one day we would start going back to our family picnics under the rainbow.

I understood where she was coming from, of course. Truly, I did. But just how healthy was clinging to a false idea of her parents' idyllic marriage, especially when she had the dregs of her own relationship as testimony that nothing was forever?

And myself? What effect did Connor have on me, besides the obvious? And moreover, how long could I continue ignoring the way my body reacted to him whenever he was around? Quickening heartbeat, sweaty palms and dry mouth could no longer be ascribed to stress only. Not when all he had to do was smile and I was mush.

And there was me thinking that after the divorce things were finally going to go well and that I'd have it all together. If anything, I was an absolute emotional disaster and in total shits-ville.

The doorbell rang and I went to answer it. It was Neil, with that huge leather bag of his, come to check on his *mum*. Again.

'Good afternoon, Nat. You're looking very lovely,' he said. 'New haircut?'

'No. Mum's in the living room.'

'She likes it in there a lot, lately.'

I followed him to where Mum was sitting with an unobstructed front-row view of Connor at work in the garden once again. He was on a mission, and after erecting the fences and creosoting them, he was planting flowers in the flowerbeds and tidying up the borders. He was doing a great job, actually. My garden had never looked this loved.

'Does that man not own any trousers?' Neil asked. 'And has he not got a job to go to?'

I suppressed a grin. 'Connor works from home. And he's committed to taking care of the garden.'

Neil's face looked like he'd been sucking on a sour lemon. *He* would be very happy if Connor went, of course. Neil would *also* be pleased if I had to sell the house, too, because, as much as he loved it and missed living here, it would once and for all prove what he'd been claiming for years – that I couldn't survive without him. And that I had made a mistake of biblical proportions in leaving him, when instead I should have grinned and borne being his doormat. In his twisted, male chauvinistic mind, what woman wouldn't want to be married to a GP who has a great yearly income? In his mind it was all about the money and the success, leaving no room whatsoever for dreams, the soul, and love.

'Good afternoon, Mum. You're looking very lovely today. Is that a new dress?'

I rolled my eyes. He seemed determined to get back into our good books. It was a shame he had no originality whatsoever. Mum shot me an amused glance and I was happy that for the moment she was lucid.

'No, Neil. I don't have the money for a new dress. This one here—' she nodded in my direction '—keeps me in rags and feeds me garbage for food. You'd think that with my nest egg I'd be living like a queen, but does she let me?'

My heart shot to my chest. 'Mum, what are you *saying*?' And in front of him, to boot!

Neil turned around and gave me an inquisitive glare.

She must be having one of her moments, I mouthed to Neil, who didn't look at all convinced.

Neil turned to take her blood pressure.

'You'd think *she* was the rich one, the way she spends all my money,' she continued.

'Mum, you know that isn't true...' How could it be true? I would never in a million years do that – steal her money. I knew she was ill, but to even hear the words leave her mouth, and to see the way she was looking at me after I'd struggled in vain for so many years to make things better between us?

I hadn't even been to the bank yet, but had paid her bills out of my own pocket just to save time. And this was what I got?

When Neil was done, I jerked my head in the direction of the kitchen, and he snapped his bag shut and followed me.

'It's ridiculous, what she said, of course,' I told him.

His face was impassive. 'Then why defend yourself?' he asked and my head snapped up to stare at him.

'You think it's true? Do you actually—'

'It doesn't matter what I think, Nat. You told me very clearly that your life is your life. Are you spending Mum's money on him?' he asked, nodding at Connor outside.

I felt my jaw drop. '*What?*'

'Because I don't see you suffering too much for our divorce. And if anything, you are much too preoccupied with yourself to take care of your mother,' he sentenced. 'And this bloke – The Face – what the hell's going on between you? Are you sleeping with him or not?'

I felt my left eye twitch. 'What's it to you?'

'Meaning you are. Christ, Nat – you've known this bloke what – five minutes? He could be anybody!'

'He's not anybody.'

'Then who is he? What do you exactly know about him?'

I knew a lot about him. I knew about his goals and passions. I knew that he loved his family, his job, the sea, all kinds of sports. And helping others. I knew that he was kind and caring and manly and handsome and helpful – more than Neil had ever been.

I sighed. 'I'm truly grateful for you being there for my mother and all, Neil, but as far as my private life is concerned, I don't owe you any explanation. Not anymore.'

'Because if you're doing it for the money,' he insisted as if he hadn't even been listening to me, 'take me back and I'll take care of you.'

I did a double take and nearly snorted. 'What?'

'I'm serious, Nat. I made a mistake. You've made

mistakes, too. Let's forgive and forget and get back to how we used to be.'

'First of all, *you* made the mistake. I was always loyal to you, God knows why. And second of all, I don't want to go back to how we *used to be*.'

'So you'd rather be with Mr I-can't-find-my-clothes?'

'Why do you hate him so much, Neil?'

'Because he's bad news, Nat. He's no good for you.'

I rolled my eyes. 'What are you on about? You are greatly mistaken about Connor and me. Not that there *is* a Connor and me, but even if there were, it would still not be any of your business.'

A flinch belied his passive face. 'You are my business, and so is Mum.'

'Again – she is not your mum!'

'Who's taking care of her? Me. I'm her GP and I'm responsible for her health.'

'That doesn't give you the right to make her decisions – or mine.'

'Nat – I'm just worried about you all. Look at this poor family since you kicked me out. Sarah's split up with Sam, Lizzie has moved in with a bloke she hardly knows—'

'Liam is lovely and he loves her,' I defended. 'And her choices are her own. I won't be like my mother who would dictate my private life.'

'—and Yolanda has definitely decided to dump her problems on you,' he continued as if he hadn't even heard me. 'As usual. And even your mum is rebelling. Why do you think she's like that?'

My eyebrows shot into my hairline; I could feel them.

'You're blaming our divorce for Mum's condition? Do you even hear yourself, Neil?'

He shrugged. 'Tension and stress lower the immune system, opening the body to all sorts of illnesses.'

'Neil – just so you know, the person who was the least stressed and troubled by our divorce was my mum. Now, if you'll excuse me, I've got work to do.'

He turned to glare at me as I walked him to the door and practically threw him out. Gosh, that had felt good.

I sauntered back into the orangery, feeling rather proud of myself.

Mum looked up at me with those incredibly blue eyes and for a moment, it was like she was herself again. I could only hope that it would last a little longer than two minutes this time. And then she turned her head and looked out into the garden, her eyes losing focus as if her lucidity was slipping away again.

'Mum? Are you okay? What are you thinking about?'

'I'm not thinking, I'm drooling.'

'Drooling?'

'Over the hot new gardener.'

I followed her gaze to where Connor was. 'Mum, he's not a gardener.'

'You've got that right. Never seen such dry lemon trees.'

'Mum, that's a Japanese maple.'

'If you don't water them, they'll die, you know.'

I sighed. *God, please give me the patience to be up to this task, especially as things get worse and worse.* By the looks of it, she was running pretty quickly through Dr Simpson's stages.

*

'Nat, I was thinking,' Connor said later as I was making soup and sandwiches for everyone's lunch. 'The girls are going to be here all summer, right? And what with your mum and work and all, I was wondering if you wouldn't mind if I built the girls a tree house around that huge oak tree at the bottom of the garden?'

I looked up from my cutting board. 'Tree house? Connor, that's very kind of you, but isn't it a lot of work? And what happens when I sell the house?'

'It can be taken apart and reassembled somewhere else,' he said. 'The girls could help me. My treat.'

'But I can't accept that, Connor – it's too much money.'

'It won't cost much if I build it from scratch. But I insist on paying for it. As a way to thank you for opening your home and family to me. What do you think?'

I debated. 'Undoubtedly it would keep them out of trouble. But wouldn't you like some more time to yourself to do what you like? Your surfing or…?'

He grinned, reaching for a pile of plates from the cupboard. 'This is what I like, Nat. I'm a family man at heart. I miss my own family and nieces and nephews. With all of you, it's like I never left home.'

'Okay, then. If that's what you want to do, I'm more than grateful. But no pressure. If you get fed up, you send the girls back to me, okay?'

He nodded towards them. 'How could I ever get fed up with them? Just look at those little darlings. Be right back. I'm going to check the winds.'

'The winds?'

'Yeah. I need to see how sturdy the tree is, and figure out at what height to place the tree house.'

'Oh. Okay. Check away.'

He slid me a grin and sauntered off down the length of the garden, stopping a few yards before the tree and lifting his head to watch the higher branches swaying in the wind.

At that exact moment, my mobile rang and I glanced at the screen. My heart jumped into my throat. Octavia The Hound, returned to take another bite out of me.

I went outside and sat at the patio table. 'Hello, Octavia?'

'No, it's Trish, Miss Hounslow's new secretary.'

New secretary? Whatever had happened to Cathy? Well, apparently this was the week of Out With the Old and In With the New.

'Oh yes?' I knew The Hound would have left the dirty job of sacking me to someone else, and it didn't really matter whether I got canned by a twenty-something-year-old editor-in-chief or her PA.

'I've been asked to call you in to London. You need to sign some, er, papers. Tomorrow morning at nine?'

Meaning I'd have to get up at four in the morning just to go and get fired in person. Jesus in heaven.

'I'll be there.'

'Goodbye, then,' she sing-songed and hung up. Of course. What did she care if I got sacked? I was no longer indispensable. I was almost forty going on a hundred and three. God, how I missed Hilary.

I never needed an appointment to speak to my old boss, and we'd often have lunch together and she'd sound my new ideas out and nod enthusiastically, cackling in delight.

She had always loved *That's Amore!* and because of that I'd always had free rein to do as I pleased. My readers had always loved my column. But now my readers would never be able to read it again.

At this point I'd have to prepare my goodbye statement, the one where I'd be telling my readers that I wouldn't be in the next issue. They'd flip through the magazine and it wouldn't be there. I'd flip through the magazine and see that all my ideas and jokes weren't there. The idea I'd had for the sexy house-husband. Or the one about trying to NOT keep up with the Joneses.

Thirteen years of what had been considered a witty contribution on my behalf. And thirteen years of validation, when everyone else around me, from Neil to Yolanda to my own mother just shook their heads. And before I knew it, a lump formed in my throat.

I looked up to see Connor pulling his working gloves off with his teeth and coming to sit opposite me at the table, placing his hand on my shoulder.

'Hey, Nat, what's that face? Are you okay?' he said, taking my elbows.

I nodded, making an effort to breathe evenly.

'You're all right, just take a deep, deep breath...'

I did as I was told. In. Out. In. Out.

'Better?'

I looked up at his concerned face and made an effort to smile as I lied. 'Better. Thank you.'

'No, you're not, Nat. Stop trying to be brave.'

I rolled my eyes dismissively. 'I'll be okay. It's just all piling up and I'm – I just got a call to go into work. Probably to get sacked.'

'Awh, geez. Do you want me to call that lawyer friend now?'

I shook my head. 'No, that's okay, Connor, thank you, but if my editor doesn't like my work, there's no point.'

He shook his head in sympathy. 'I don't understand what's wrong with it. It's funny, witty and so mischievous. How can she not like it?'

'Again, it lacks the modern, sexy edge, I guess.'

'And that's what sells, huh? But what about the adorable, sweet, quirky women who don't care about any of that crap?' he said, and when I looked up into his face again, it was as if he'd figured me out already.

I felt the blush creeping up my neck and into my cheeks. 'Women like us are not modern and sexy, I guess...'

At that, he chuckled, that twinkle back in his eye. 'I wouldn't have any doubts about the latter, Nat.'

I stared at him in surprise. *Now* he starts flirting with me? Not that I minded the attention, of course, but we both knew he could have any twenty-something-year-old he wanted. Why bother with me?

'Nah,' I said. 'You want modern and sexy, you choose my sister Yolanda. She's the kind of woman Octavia would swoon over. Always perfect, and never a hair out of place, always perfectly made-up.'

'Well, she may be pretty, but she's nothing compared to you,' he said.

I sat up. 'Me?'

'You,' he simply said, and I couldn't help but notice his ears were turning red.

'Thanks, Connor, but I'm not. I used to be, when I was a girl.'

'Well, I can imagine that you were pretty as a girl, but if I may say so without seeming forward, you are a downright stunner now.'

Flames began to lick at the base of my neck, spreading into my ears. 'Sto-op,' I said, giggling, silently willing him to go on.

'I'm serious. Do you actually look at yourself in the mirror? You could easily pass for Sarah and Lizzie's sister.'

I snorted. 'Yeah, good one. But thanks, I appreciate the boost.'

'And you're talented as hell. I'll bet your boss won't fire you. So stop worrying about it. Try to relax.'

'I will, thank you.'

He studied me. 'There's something else bothering you, Nat, isn't there?'

I huffed. 'You're right. It's not just work. It's my sister. She's thinking of buying Mum's cottage and turning it into her workspace.'

'But what about your mum? Surely you don't want to sell her home?'

'I have to,' I whispered. 'Her pension isn't enough and until I can sell my own home I can't afford her upkeep.'

'Shouldn't Yolanda be helping out?'

'Yes, well, this is her way of helping. And if she does buy it, there's no way I can buy Lavender Cottage with her staff constantly working next door.'

'So what are you going to do?'

I shrugged. 'I don't know. Yolanda usually gets what she wants. She's the one with the money and until I can shift this house I can't buy the cottage. I really don't need this huge mausoleum to remind me of... Anyway, I also wanted to give Lizzie and Sarah some money to get onto the property ladder themselves.'

He nodded back in agreement. 'That's so you, Nat,' he said softly. 'Always thinking of everyone else first.'

'I'm a mother, a sister and a daughter. Of course I come last.'

'But you shouldn't, Nat. When are you going to realise that?'

I opened my mouth to reply, but it clamped shut. What could I possibly say to that?

'Sorry, that was uncalled for,' he apologised. 'I have a feeling everything will fall into place.'

'Natalia!' my mother called from inside. 'Get in here.'

I jumped to my feet. For a minute I had completely forgotten about her. I'm not all that selfless, you see? What a terrible daughter I could be sometimes.

Connor took his cue to get back to work and I took mine to be a better daughter. I opened the French doors wide. 'Yes, Mum? Are you hungry yet? It's almost lunchtime.'

But she simply shrugged. 'I want to go home now.'

I took her hand. 'I'm working on it, Mum.' And that was a promise. I made a mental note to give that Hannah Williams a call. Only an agent could tell me how much I could get for Smuggler's Rest, and only she could help me get Lavender Cottage.

When I went to change Connor's bedding later that afternoon, I found his room as spotless as usual, minus the crunched-up sheets of paper covering his desk, as if he was trying to write something over and over again. It looked like a battlefield, where some thoughts had prevailed over the weaker ones.

Being a writer and familiar with the painful process of the birthing of words, I wondered whether I could help. (Oh, all right, I was being a nosy cow.) I had never ever put my nose in anyone else's business, but those sheets of paper were practically glowing with an energy of their own, beckoning for me to read them. I just wanted to see if they were the attempts at a love letter. Connor looked like the kind of bloke who would write a good one. Only not to me.

I picked a ball of paper up and flattened it atop his desk, just for a quick look. It only had one sentence. Which almost blew me away.

Dearest Nat,
  Before my words hurt you, I wanted to tell you how happy I am to be here...

It was a letter for me! But why would his words hurt me? What was he trying to say? Did he have feelings for me or not? A huge knot began to form in my stomach, replaced by cramps as I picked up another one. And again, only one sentence.

Dear Nat,
  I wanted to thank you for taking me into your home...

I picked up another, and then another, but they were all one-liners. That said absolutely nothing. What had he been trying to say?

Dear Nat,
  I can't keep taking advantage of your hospitality…

Dear Nat,
  I hate myself for doing this to you…

Dear Nat,
  You must know how much I admire you…

Dear Nat,
  I hope you will forgive me…

Forgive you for *what*? My mind screamed. *What have you done that needs my forgiving?*

I sat at his desk, rereading the scraps of paper and trying to put the puzzle together. Connor was trying to tell me something, but I couldn't understand what it was. And then it dawned on me. He was leaving. Why couldn't he tell me personally? Unless… was he planning to disappear into thin air?

'Nonsense,' Maggie said when I cracked and called her for some advice. She should have headed the Agony Aunt department, she was so good with relationship tips. 'Don't go thinking dramatic endings.'

'Then what am I supposed to think?' I demanded. 'You should have seen those letters. There was no direct message, and yet, the tone was so, so sad! What if something's happened to him?'

'Like what?'

'I don't know!'

'Have you tried calling him?'

'His mobile phone is off!'

'Nat,' she said. 'You need to calm down. He's probably just writing you a love letter.'

'A love letter? No – love letters begin with things like: My dearest, my sweetheart and all that stuff. There is nothing in these letters about being in love. But there's bloody fifteen of them. Why would he be writing me something that he could simply tell me over lunch? Unless he can't simply tell me?'

'Tell you what?'

'That he's figured out I have feelings for him, but that he's seeing someone in the village? He did say that love had brought him here. Maybe it really is Felicity, or some other younger woman, and he's trying to let me down gently?'

'Oh, dear, Nat. I'm sure it's nothing serious. Try and relax. He'll tell you when he's ready. You have to respect that.'

Easier said than done.

Later that afternoon, Connor came to lean against my desk as I worked. I can assure you it was utterly distracting as I could smell the freshness of his soap and shampoo. He smelled like his room, fresh and clean, and all I could see again were those letters. This was going to drive me insane.

'You know what you need?' he said. 'A distraction.'

I looked up. 'A distraction?'

'Exactly. Let's go for a walk.'

Had he finally decided to give up writing that letter and tell me in person whatever it was he had been trying to write me? Was he going to tell me that he was involved with someone else, and that he was moving out to be with her? Or had I completely misunderstood, and he did have feelings for me after all, but was a bit shy? Was I ready to hear it, either way? What would my reaction be?

'A walk? But – the girls – my mum—'

'Sarah will be home from work soon.'

'But she might have plans.'

'Then ask her.'

'Just like that? I can't load—'

'Nat – they're her family too. She won't mind. Just ask for once.'

I thought about it. Surely there'd be no harm in asking for a little help, every now and then? I picked up my phone and dialled Sarah's number. 'Hello, love. Are you on your way home?'

'Yes, do you want me to pick something up on the way?'

'No, I just wanted to know if you would babysit the girls – and Nana – for me? Just for a short while.'

'Hot date?' she said.

I chuckled as if to say what a silly thought that was. 'Of course not.'

'Okay, no problem. I'll be there in ten minutes, Mum.'

'Thanks, love,' I said and hung up. 'Sorted.'

Connor grinned. 'Cool. Now get your walking shoes on.'

'Walking shoes?' I asked, a little deflated, as if I had been expecting an invitation to dinner. 'Where are we going?'

He took my hand. 'To one of the most beautiful places on earth,' he said softly, his eyes twinkling.

When Sarah arrived, her eyebrow shot up at the sight of Connor and I in walking gear.

'When did you discover the great outdoors?' she quipped, taking in my rucksack.

'Since I had a day like today,' I quipped back. 'I'll tell you later. I need some fresh air. Dinner's in the oven. Don't wait for us to eat.' And we left, leaving Sarah with her blank but at the same time disapproving face.

The south-west coastal path was a beauty to behold in early summer. The grass-blanketed cliffs rolled out like waves of granite, contrasting with the cobalt sea, outlined by a white, violent foam that sprayed the land. There was nowhere on earth like Cornwall. It was truly a world of its own.

I took a deep breath and soaked in the salt air, the wind ruffling my hair and the sunshine warming my face and bare arms. It felt good to be out here, far from it all. No problems, no bosses, nothing but me and Cornwall. And Connor, of course.

'Happier now?' he said softly.

Happier? This was perfection – my beloved Cornish coast, and a bloke like Connor at my side.

I wondered if he'd taken me here in this isolated place so his girlfriend wouldn't see us, whoever she was. I mean, he disappeared often enough, presumably to spend time with her. But he always slept at home, which I presumed to mean she didn't have her own place. Was she married? Or, even worse, was she just too young to have her own place? In any case, it was someone from Wyllow Cove. This was such a tiny village, and a gossipy one at that. How could I have absolutely no intel on this at all? Was I not, after all, a journalist? I'd have to get on it, if I wanted to find inner peace.

'Feeling better, then?' he tried again and I realised I hadn't answered him.

'Sorry, Connor,' I said. 'I'm just trying to not slip.'

At that, he took my hand and chuckled and a strange feeling of happiness coursed through me. I could have started worrying what and how and why, but decided instead to award myself this moment where we just chilled, and he swung my hand like it was the most natural thing in the world. Which it wasn't, for oh so many reasons. But my mind refused to deal with it at the moment, as it only wanted to enjoy the solid, reassuring fingers entwined with mine.

He said nothing else, just holding my hand as we ambled up and downhill, simply taking in his surroundings with that peaceful expression on his face.

Down below the village of Wyllow Cove lay nestled in the inlet, sheltered in a glistening bay that protected it from even the worst winter storms. But today, it was glorious.

'Look,' he suddenly said, shielding his eyes against the sun. 'A Cornish chough! I haven't seen one of those in a long time! Did you know that they are featured on the Cornish coat of arms?'

I looked up, completely clueless.

He chuckled. 'Sorry. I'm a bird nerd. I love anything with wings. I used to watch them all the time from my tree house when I was a lad.'

'Oh?' I said. 'I know absolutely nothing about birds, though I did once nurse one that had a broken wing for about a month, and when it flew away, I was heartbroken.'

'Is that why you don't get too attached to things?' he suddenly asked.

I stopped in my tracks. 'Attached?'

He, too, stopped, still holding my hand. 'Yes, Nat – attached. I'm hoping that's the only reason why you—'

And just then, a gust of wind swept into my face, and my hand shot to my eye as the pain enwrapped it completely.

'Ow… ow…'

'What is it, Nat? Something in your eye?'

'Yuh,' I barely managed. Oh, God, it *hurt*!

He placed a hand on my shoulder. 'Let me have a look.'

'I can't – it hurts too much.'

'I promise I can help,' he said and I removed my hand, my eye staying shut.

'May I?' he asked, and I nodded.

Gently, with his index and thumb, he pried my eye open, his other hand under my chin to keep me still, and all I could see was a blurry, wavy image of him as he neared me with puckered lips. Before I knew what he was doing, he was gently blowing into it to dislodge whatever was still in there causing the pain. It hurt, but not as much as before.

'Better?' he asked softly, still holding my chin as he examined my eye.

'Better, thanks,' I said, wiping it with my index finger, and we both stood there in silence. But as they say in cheesy moves, our eyes spoke for us, or rather, his did, as I only had one eye to speak with at the moment.

'Nat…' he said softly, his fingers gently caressing my cheek now.

Here it was. He was going to tell me about the contents of the letter he'd never written. Was I ready for it?

'Well, fancy bumping into you!'

I jumped as the familiar voice filled the space between us. Maggie.

'Hallo, pets. Connor! I haven't seen you for a long time!' she called as she ambled over to us.

Well, thank you very much, Maggie. You only went and ruined what could have been a lovely moment. He had almost kissed me, right? Or had I been imagining it all? Or should I actually be grateful? Because I certainly don't know what I would have done if he had. Thrown my arms around his neck, along with all caution and *que será, será*? Or gently but firmly pulled away, seeing as he was here for another woman?

'Oh, right. Connor, you remember Maggie.'

'Good to see you again,' he said cheerfully, holding his other hand out without letting go of mine. I saw Maggie's eyes dart to our entwined fingers and she grinned broadly.

'Nice to see you, too!' she answered, pumping his hand up and down like a wrestler. 'So! How's living with Nat?'

He smiled at me. 'Pure heaven. We get along like a house on fire.'

Maggie guffawed. 'I'm sure you do! You single?'

Not if Felicity could help it.

At that, he stiffened ever so slightly, but never lost his grin. 'Uh, for now.'

She clapped him on the back. 'So is Nat – so you'd better get on with it. There's plenty of men wanting to snap this one up. Isn't that right, Nat?'

I baulked. 'Actually, uhm, no.'

Connor turned to me. 'I'm sure Nat has a lot of men waiting in line.'

Just not me, he seemed to want to add, but luckily, he didn't. That would have been a tad embarrassing for us all.

'Cooeee!' Maggie chirped. 'Right! Must dash, I've got a dozen cinnamon rolls that have my name on them!'

'Take care,' Connor said.

'You, too, Connor! I'll say hi to everyone at The Rising Bun for you,' she as she sauntered away. 'And get that letter finished!' she called over her shoulder.

I think I must have turned beet red, while all colour drained from his face as we glanced at each other in panic.

'Oh.' I laughed. 'She means a letter I'm trying to write my boss!'

He exhaled, his colour returning. 'Oh! Right? What kind of letter?' he wanted to know.

'Oh, nothing important – just telling her to get her finger out and clear my position up once and for all. I think it's awful to leave people hanging, don't you?'

At that, he coughed and looked out to sea again. So much for the big reveal.

II

Toy Boys and Porky Pies

And speaking of hanging, I'm assuming you know what four and a half hours of agony are. If you don't, try taking a train into Paddington Station knowing it's only to get fired in person. Add the humiliation of having your sacker be half your age. You get the picture.

By the time I got to the fifth floor of my quasi-former workplace, I was covered in a sheen of sweat. I stopped in the ladies' just to wash my face and hands, unheeding of the blusher that had already slid off my face somewhere between Plymouth and Taunton, and of the mascara that had caked itself between my lashes, gluing my eyes open like Miss Piggy, even if I was dying for a catnap.

With nothing left to do, I went into reception where the new PA was tapping away on her keyboard, not even acknowledging me, and I sat down, waiting for my turn to see The Hound.

Over the space of twenty minutes, three of my colleagues came and went, and when they left – escorted by security, no less – they looked at me with the face of communal disappointment. And when Dave from Graphics came out with a face like the devil and looked my way, he even drew his thumb across his neck in the throat-cut gesture to warn me. We were falling like flies and there was nothing I could do. It was a bloodbath.

'Mrs Amore? Miss Hounslow will see you now,' the PA said, flicking a red-taloned hand in the direction of the door. As if I didn't know where the editor-in-chief's office was. Up to last month, my editor Hilary and I used to spend hours poring over pictures in there because she always wanted my opinion even after Graphics had completed the job. And now look at me – quivering on the edge of my seat, clasping my bag in terror of the ineluctable.

I eyed the new PA one last time as I took a deep, deep breath. And dived straight in.

The first thing that hit me was the starkness of the newly painted white walls. Octavia had wasted no time in redecorating. Everything was different – the desk, the chair, and even the carpeting was gone and there were mirrors everywhere. Three colours dominated the room – white, off-white and pearl white. Even her dress was white.

She gestured to me to sit down as she barked into her white mobile phone.

I swallowed and waited for her to demolish the poor sod on the other end so she could start on me.

'I said I'm not even remotely interested, Darren!' she said, rolling her eyes and swivelling her chair around to the wall so her back was to me. Jaw-droppingly rude, to say the least. 'Now pull your finger out and get on with it!' Judging by her mood today, this was going to be very ugly.

Without another word, she rang off and slammed the mobile down onto her glass desk with a 'Bloody fool! You!' she barked. 'Natalia!'

I jumped despite myself, angry that I let her scare me like that. She was already giving me the sack – what else could she possibly do to me?

'Why didn't you say you had a sodding toy boy?'

I gawped at her. The words *I beg your pardon?* tried to come out, but all I managed was a 'Huh?'

'Don't be coy with me, old girl! I know about you and the Adonis! Who is he and where the *hell* did you find him?'

I cleared my throat. 'I'm sorry, Octavia, I don't understand what you mean?'

But she was thumbing through her mobile. '*This* is what I mean. Maggie also sent me a video.'

'Video?' I repeated stupidly.

'Yes, the two of you walking hand in *hand*,' she said impatiently – or excitedly. It was difficult to tell the difference with her. 'Maggie said he's absolutely delicious and that he's your brand-new bloke. Is he your toy boy? Spill!'

Brand-new bloke? Was that what Maggie had thought when she saw me with Connor? Well, judging by the photo where he is gazing into my eyes just before blowing into one of them, his lips just a breath away from mine, it was no wonder they thought what they thought. I'd always told Maggie that she'd be great at handling the Gossip features.

'No, uhm,' I croaked. 'It's not like that, Octavia.'

At that, Octavia cackled in delight. 'Ha! Good one, Natalia! And I can only say, congratulations. He's quite the eye candy. Come, Natalia – don't make that face! There's nothing to be ashamed about. We all salute you! The unassuming forty-year-old bags a banger.'

'I'm still thirty-nine, actually,' I corrected her. But she was beside herself with what I could now see was excitement as she planted her huge eyes on me and I almost detected a smile.

'It would make a great topic for the June issue: Forty-something-year-old women and their toy boys.'

'You want me to write about toy boys?' I croaked. Oh my God in heaven.

'It'll fly like a kite. I want to warn our twenty-something readers what they're up against with cougars like you still lurking around.'

'C-cougars?'

'Women like you, you muppet!' she honked with a dazzling smile on her face. 'Look at you, in your boring navy blue dress and neutral lip gloss, all quiet and low-key. While the twenty-year-olds are busy trying to sort their careers and images out, women like you – the *older* woman who already has everything – crawls out of the woodwork and snatches the guy at the eleventh hour! Hey, that would be a great title – The Eleventh-Hour Date!'

Good God, she wasn't going to start a column just to humiliate me, was she? Not even she would go that far, surely?

'But I don't have a t-toy boy,' I faltered, hoping she'd come to her senses. This was insane.

'It'll be a huge success. You write an article about how to catch one of them and, most important, how to keep one. What's not to love?'

'Have you even listened to what I've said, Octavia?'

'Yes. But have you been listening to what I *haven't* said, Natalia?'

So she was threatening me again, and through a very thin veil. 'You can't be serious.'

'I am dead serious, Natalia. Of all the articles you've ever submitted, this will be the best. I can't imagine anything more interesting. Or anything worse than your last one about bloody Clark Kent.'

Well, if she thought I wrote so badly, then why was she giving me another chance? Surely there were plenty of women around the country flaunting their own (and real) toy boys and willing to write about it? I thought of Connor, and his kindness. But he hadn't so much as flirted with me, not even by mistake. How was I expected to just invent a relationship that simply wasn't there?

Octavia harrumphed, shaking her head, disappointed that I hadn't jumped at the opportunity. 'Have a think and call me tomorrow,' she said, standing.

Meaning: 'You can go now, because that's all I'm interested in negotiating,' and that it was either her way or the way of The Job Centre. But just how could I pretend Connor was my toy boy? It would never work, plus he would never in a million years agree to do something so sordid. And let's not forget he read my columns – and so did all the women in his family. How could I ever look him in the eye again? Plus, I would never agree to lie through my teeth just to keep my job. But then Lavender Cottage flashed through my mind. Or would I?

There was so much at stake. I needed to keep my job, no matter what happened. There was a possibility that the house might not sell for months. And now I had Mum to take care of and the twins. So, for the sole sake of survival, I'd have to doctor the truth. Could I do it? And, more importantly, would Connor agree to do it, assuming I gathered up the courage to ask him to do something so wrong?

I left the building in a right state, but by the time I'd settled myself into my seat on the train back home, I'd half-convinced myself that I owed it to everyone to at least ask him. If he agreed, my job would be safe. Surely it was worth a shot?

Once settled on my train, I called Maggie. Whether to chew her out, or to thank her, I still didn't know.

'You're *welcome*,' she said when she picked up.

'Hi,' I said, my voice dying in my throat. She may have acted recklessly with my personal privacy, but she had saved my job. And my life. My entire family's life. So who was I to be picky about her indiscretion?

'Please tell me you're going to do it?' she begged. 'I can't imagine you not working there anymore.'

'And you?' I asked. 'What are you going to do?'

'I'm already in talks with *House & Home*.'

'Oh, Maggie, that's fabulous, I'm so pleased for you!' Maggie was the best fashion reporter that *Lady* had ever had, and The Hound was an absolute fool to get rid of her just because she was forty-two. Really, what kind of business sense was that? But she was savvy, Octavia, because legally no one could reprimand her for it, as she had also sacked some of our younger members of staff just so no one could actually come out and accuse her of ageism. She'd say it was purely coincidental and random.

'And thanks for doing what you did, Maggie. I may not approve of your methods, but your heart was in the right place. And it got me a second chance.'

'You want my advice, Nat? You jump on that bandwagon. Octavia is here to stay, like it or not. And unless you win the lottery, I suggest you stick with her.'

She did have a point.

'And besides, I'm sure Connor won't mind you talking about your relationship. Did he tell you what was in that letter that never was?'

'No. Nor will he ever, I'm beginning to think. He's just my lodger. And a friend.'

'I wouldn't mind being his friend.' She cackled. 'How's Neil taking it?'

'Oh, he's not a happy camper. He's still hoping I'm going to beg him to come back. And with my mum now like this? He comes over practically every day to check on her – and to try to talk some *sense* into me, all the while glaring at Connor.'

'And Sarah?

'She's a tough nut to crack, too.'

'I figured as much. And what about your nieces? They get on like a house on fire from what I saw that day on the beach.'

'They are nuts about him. Although I worry about them, Mags. He's practically acting as their babysitter, games master, big brother, uncle, and everything in between. What happens when he moves out? They'll be devastated.'

'Then don't make him move out. Tell him about Octavia's ultimatum, and see how he reacts. You two looked awfully chummy on that path yesterday. I'm sure it won't be a problem for him.'

'Ha-ha.'

'Oh, and Nat? The black-tie benefit? I heard that *Lady* has already booked rooms for commuters at the Langham Hotel. Obviously you and Connor will be expected to share a room.'

'*What?* Maggie, I don't even know if I'm going to go for all this, and she's already booked rooms?'

'Be smart, sweetie, and play the game to save your ass. And bring your best nightie. You never know.' And then she hung up.

I stuffed my mobile into my pocket, my mind in absolute deep freeze. Assuming I decided to go ahead with this, Connor would probably not want to play along. Even when I had pretended to be Mrs Pentire to get into Lavender Cottage he had been uncomfortable about lying. Imagine trying to pass him off as my toy boy. And to share a room – and possibly a bed – with Connor? He would never agree to do it and I wouldn't get through the night without having a stroke, because sharing a house was bad enough – how the hell was I expected to not make an absolute fool of myself while lying prostrate anywhere near him? Not that I wouldn't have, well, you know... but let's ask for one miracle at a time. For now, I'd be happy to keep my job.

When I finally got home, with my heart in my throat, to be quite honest, I went straight to check on Mum. She was fast asleep in her favourite chair, and the telly was on at a low volume. I'd taught Sarah that trick – keep it on and Nana would snore away for hours. But turn it off and she'd wake instantly. She needed that background noise as a comfort factor. She'd always been like that.

I reached over and, although it was almost summer, I placed a light throw over her and brought it up to her chest and removed her glasses. She didn't stir.

How young she looked in her sleep, without the frown lines and the judicial glare. Now, sitting in the slanting rays of a summer evening, she looked, well, fragile. Helpless. And she was depending on me to take care of her. I was all she had in this world now. If I was going to carry out this farce, it was for her, too, as well as Sarah and the twins. I bent over her once again and kissed her paper-thin cheek.

In the kitchen, Sarah was finishing prepping dinner, her fancy bag and shoes already in pole position.

'Hi, Mum, how did your meeting go?'

I hadn't told her about the risk of losing my job. 'Splendidly, love. And how are things here with the girls?'

Sarah grinned. 'They spent a long time at the park with Connor. He's been teaching them to play rounders and now he's just got back from B&Q. I swear that man is like bloody Duracell.'

'B&Q?' I said.

Sarah nodded towards the garden and I went to the window. Not far from the tree was a huge pile of planks. 'He mentioned he's going to be building the girls a tree house?'

'Oh, yes. He asked and I said it was okay.'

She sat down as I began to peel zucchini for my quiche.

'I'm starting to think I was wrong about him,' Sarah said after a while, pursing her lips. 'He's so kind and patient. And he seems to really have eyes for no one but you. So from now on, Mum, I promise I won't interfere with your stuff.'

I raised an eyebrow at her. 'What stuff?'

She rolled her eyes towards the ceiling. 'Your budding romance with Captain Poldark up there.'

'Sarah, there is nothing—'

'Mum – I get it. You're single again and he's quite easy on the eye. So I say, if you want to have a fling, then go for it. But be discreet.'

'There's nothing to go for, darling.'

'No? You should tell him that,' she said.

'You can, uhm, sleep tight, Sarah. There is absolutely nothing going on between Connor and me. Nor will there ever be,' I assured her.

Not at this rate, anyhow.

'He wants to sleep with you so badly, I can see it in the way he stands next to you, the way he touches you.'

'I'm not sure this conversation has any bearing on reality, Sarah. You see things that aren't there.'

'Poor Dad,' she continued. 'How is he supposed to feel comfortable with Connor in the picture?'

I sighed. 'Sweetheart, for the record, Connor is just a friend. And you know what happened between your dad and me.'

'Can't you forgive him?'

'No, Sarah. Even if I tried, I just couldn't. I'd be lying. But don't you worry. Your mum is nowhere near falling in love with anyone, let alone the tenant.' *And the nomination for Best Actress is… you guessed it – me.*

She shook her head. 'I want you to be happy, but I don't want you falling for someone who will end up hurting you.'

'Darling – I'm not falling for anyone.' I gently nudged her towards the hall. 'Now go out and have some fun.'

She studied me at length. 'All right,' she said finally. 'It's just the girls, anyway. Don't wait up. And behave yourself.'

'The girls?' I said as I switched the kettle on. I was in need of a good strong brew. 'Not a bloke, then.'

She stopped. 'Mum, you must be joking. After what Sam did to me? I'm off men for a bit.'

'Okay, pet. Forgive me, I figured as much, but I just wanted to make sure you were okay. You too seem so lonely lately and you're working hard most nights.'

She shrugged. 'You know I'm up for promotion, Mum. I have to work hard. Plus, it helps me be less angry.'

'Sweetheart, if there's anything you need…'

'I know, Mum. Thanks. And you, too. If there's anything I can do to help.'

I frowned. 'What do you mean?'

'With the girls and Nana.'

'Thanks, love. You already help enough as it is. It's my responsibility.'

She snorted as she grabbed her bag and slid her feet into her pumps. 'And Connor's. He sure seems to have embraced his position in this family.'

'Sarah, honey, Connor is a good tenant and friend. To all of us. Even you said you were starting to like him.'

'I was – I am. He's a great bloke, Mum. I do like him. But he's not relationship material.'

She sounded just like her dad. 'I never said he was.'

'Well, tell him. All he ever talks about is you.'

'Nonsense, Sarah…'

'It isn't nonsense, Mum. You need to make sure you let him down gently *afterwards*.'

Hello, where had this conversation come from? Relationship? And *I* had to let him down gently? He was the one with the mysterious girlfriend in town, and Sarah was worried about how he'd take *my* not wanting *him*? Huh.

I must have really looked cool and calm on the outside. It was all part of my half-British stiff upper lip, I guess.

But before I could comment, Connor's soft humming – his usual way of letting us know he was around – echoed in the air.

'Hey, how did it go?' he asked as he came into the kitchen, a towel flung over his shoulder, his hair wet and giving me such a hot smile my bra burst into flames. It was a shame he was completely dressed.

'Right. I'm off,' Sarah said, grabbing her keys off the counter. 'Thanks for taking the girls today, Connor.'

'No problem, Sarah. I enjoyed it.'

Sarah gave me a 'Remember What I Said' look, and left.

I waited until I heard her car leave and then I turned to Connor.

'It was an absolute bloodbath,' I answered, my cheeks burning at the thought of writing about him as my toy boy.

'Please tell me they didn't fire you,' he said, joining his hands in a plea. 'I can't give me mam that kind of bad news. She's your number-one fan.'

'Well, thank your mam for me,' I said as I turned to the forgotten kettle and made two cups of coffee. 'But unless I can write what they want, then I definitely get the boot.'

'Thanks,' he said as I passed him his mug and we both sat down at the kitchen table. 'What is it they want, so?'

My eyes met his. 'An article about toy boys. Precisely, *m-my* toy boy.'

His dark eyebrows shot up.

'Maggie – when she saw us on the coastal path yesterday, when I had that thing in my eye? She got the wrong idea and actually, uhm… gave my boss a suggestion for a new column for me.'

He said nothing, just blowing softly into his coffee and studying me. He must have really thought I was a pure-bred loser. I plodded on. It was now or never.

'She… she thought that if I could write about having a new – younger – boyfriend, it would save me from getting fired during this whole rehashing of staff.'

'Would it? Help?' he asked as he attempted a sip.

I shrugged. 'Octavia – my boss – has made it very clear to me that if I don't do it, she'll sack me.'

I took a long, long drink from my coffee, wondering how to get out of this one. If I could have crawled into my mug and disappeared and reappeared into a parallel universe where this wasn't happening, I definitely would have. Because except for writing, I wasn't good at much, according to Neil.

Connor looked at me and blew out air from his cheeks, his eyes mirroring the magnitude of what I was asking him. Perhaps this was a bad idea after all.

'I'm so sorry, Connor, I don't even know why I'm telling you. It's so bloody embarrassing.'

And there was his usual stubble-caressing gesture again. If you didn't know him you'd think that it was a ruse or a device to attract attention, but I now recognised it for what it was. Shyness. How I longed to reach out and caress his face myself, but that would be creepy from his landlady.

'Well, Nat, I'd be embarrassed if I were her, to underestimate a main contributor like you. I don't even think she actually understands how many fans you have,' he said, getting to his feet to go to the goodie cupboard and retrieving the biscuits, which he put onto a plate between us.

'Thanks,' I said as I reached for one.

'Thank me later,' he said.

I looked up at him. 'What do you mean?'

'Once you've given her what she wants and you get your own column back.'

'You mean you don't mind me making up... oh, no, you know what? I don't think I can do it...' I chickened out.

'Why not?'

'Because you're not—'

'Not your toy boy?' He laughed. 'Well, I certainly hope not. Nat, this is about your financial independence, yes?'

I put my biscuit down, wondering where this was going. 'Yes. But there's more. There's a black-tie benefit later this week and she'd expect you to accompany me.'

He reached across the table to take my hand and it was like sticking my fingers into a blazing fire. Hot flashes enveloped me instantly. Why did he always have this effect on me?

'So let's give them what they want. Something to talk about.'

'Oh, I...' I eyed him doubtfully. 'You really think so? You'd really do that?'

'Why not? Does the idea of holding my hand and kissing me sound that terrible? Your own mum would beg to differ.' His eyes were twinkling and teasing now, and I didn't know what to do with him. Or rather, I did have an inkling of an idea, but *that* thought was off-limits.

'Er... no, of course not,' I managed. 'But I'm a grown woman.'

NANCY BARONE

'And I'm a grown man. What's wrong with that?'

'The fact that you could be my baby brother?'

Again, he laughed and tiny laugh lines crinkled at the corner of his dark eyes. It really was his default mode. 'Nonsense. What are you, thirty-six, thirty-seven? You must have been a baby yourself when you had Sarah.'

I checked his face for traces of sarcasm or shambolic tendencies, but there were none. He really believed I was that close to his age. So who was I to burst his bubble?

'Uh-huh,' I lied. I don't know why, but instead of laughing and telling him my real age, I let the moment pass. And now I'd really done it. I'd definitively lowered the barrier between lodger and landlady. Now he might think all sorts of things of me. Finally.

To be here, in the arms of this man, in this very moment when the rest of my world was in question, would definitely tip the scales.

'Anyway,' I said with fake worldliness, twirling my now empty mug as I got up to put some safe distance between us. 'It's not like I need the real experience. I would know what to write.'

'I'm sure you would. But don't they say to write from experience? How would you know how to write about the thrill of a *new* romance if you don't try it?'

Couldn't argue with that one, could I now? 'Yes, well, the most romantic moment I had was when Neil packed his bags,' I said.

Connor threw his head back and laughed. Only it wasn't exactly funny. My arse was on the line.

'So that's it then? If you have a toy boy you can keep your job?'

'Don't forget the black-tie benefit. It's this Friday.'

He chuckled. 'Okay. Anything to help you, Nat. It is in London, right? I'll drive us.'

'Thank you, Connor. But we can take the train.'

'Nat,' he said. 'I'm happy to drive.'

I shrugged. 'Okay, then. Thanks.'

'No trouble at all,' he said in his charming Irish lilt.

This was it. Now I had to tell him about the hotel room. And the *one* bed in that hotel room. But how? And, moreover, how could I possibly justify making him sleep on the floor after what he was doing for me? He was taking me all the way in his own car, pretending to be my toy boy, as if that wasn't humiliating enough, and now he even had to sleep on the floor? No, I couldn't allow that. I wondered if I still had those padded pyjamas I'd bought in my teens for when I'd gone camping that one time. I hoped that the hotel had very thick carpeting.

'Uhm, actually, there is one more thing...' I faltered.

'Shoot.'

'We're going to have to share a room.'

His eyebrows shot up and for the life of me I couldn't tell if it was amusement or annoyance. An embarrassed silence ensued, and I began to babble to cover it up.

'I already checked for another room, but they're fully booked. Maybe I could book you at another hotel nearby?'

He shook his head and raked a hand through his dark curls. 'No, Nat – how would it look to all your friends if I went and slept in another hotel?'

I thought about it. 'Not too good, I guess.'

'So we'll go ahead with the plan. No problem.'

'Are you sure?' I checked. 'I mean, one thing is hearing a rumour, and another is feeding it with evidence.'

He shrugged. 'It's important to you. This little fib would let you keep your job. And don't worry about anything else for now.'

As much as I was dying to stick my nose in his business and ask what his *girlfriend* thought, I nodded and let go of it.

'Okay. Thank you.'

'No worries.' He clapped his hands together resolutely, taking a deep breath as if to give himself courage before throwing himself into the fire. I didn't know whether to be offended or grateful. 'Right, so,' he said. 'This Friday?'

I nodded. Date night. Even I could see the connection. 'Have you got a suit? I can get you one in Truro tomorrow.'

He stood up. 'Hold it there, Nellie. I may be pretending to be your toy boy, but you're not buying me a suit.'

'Are – are you sure? I mean, you wouldn't need one if it weren't for this, so—'

'Are you insinuating I don't have a social life?' he asked, and I suddenly realised I was the village idiot. Of course he did. I wondered how he was going to juggle us both, even if I was only the pretend lover.

He stood up and clapped his hands again. 'Right, then. Get your best dress pressed, Nellie. It looks like your research is about to begin.'

12

Only You

Friday night, the night of the black-tie benefit, and I was an utter, complete mess. Everything was wrong – my hair, my make-up. Even my dress, which had always suited me, now seemed frumpy. The last time I'd worn it I had felt classy and composed. And now, who did I think I was fooling in a spaghetti-strapped gown? Good thing I had the shawl to make me look more staid.

Standing by what Maggie and Octavia had said, word had already got out that I was bringing my toy boy, and I envisaged curious eyes ready to dissect me. Not because I looked bad per se, but because they'd be measuring me up against Connor, who would look good in a fig leaf, judging by the rare but precious glimpses I'd had of various parts of his body, from the washboard tummy to the lean hips that his low jeans had never even tried to disguise.

'Nat?' Connor called from the downstairs landing as I was putting on my earrings. 'You ready?'

'Yup, coming,' I called back as I grabbed my wrap and

my clutch and opened my bedroom door, my heart in my mouth. God, did I feel like a fraud or what?

I almost forgot my overnight bag. I had brought two kinds of nightwear, depending on the turn the evening would take. One was a T-shirt and an old pair of pyjama bottoms and the other was… well, let's say classy, even if the intentions behind it were not very subtle. How deluded was I, to even remotely think I had a cat in hell's chance at a night, let alone a relationship with Connor, when there was someone else in the picture. I should have had my head examined by Dr Simpson, too.

Clueless of how I was going to make it through the evening without worrying myself sick, I threw myself down the stairs, all the while trying to look poised and calm.

And there he was, standing in a black suit and tie, so elegant I had hardly recognised him, twirling his car keys around his index finger. His black curls were tied back in a sleek man bun, and the hint of stubble gave him a sexy edge. As if he needed it. Next to him, I'd look like a bloody matron. So I balled up my wrap and shoved it into my bag. Was it too late to call the whole thing off?

'Wow,' he exhaled as I wobbled down the stairs, feeling for all the world like Scarlett O'Hara in one of her numbers and hanging on for dear life lest I tripped and landed in a heap at Connor's shiny leather feet. 'You look… just… wow.'

And despite myself, I giggled at the cheek of him. The dashing, dapper gentleman taking out his older lady-friend (who was a schoolgirl at heart) poking her head out for a night on the town.

'You don't look half bad yourself,' I said as he gave me

his arm. Actually, he looked like sex on a stick. 'And by the way, you don't have to start now,' I lied, waves of guilt washing over me.

'Start what now? In case you hadn't noticed, I'm *naturally* gallant,' he said in mock hurt. Ah, that may have been true, but the question was, could we pull this off tonight?

'And you, Natalia Amore, if you don't mind my saying, are very, very, uhm, beautiful. Hey, what's that worried look?' Connor asked, his fingers stealing to his chin. 'Do you not approve? Should I have had a shave?'

'No, it's not that. I just...' I looked at him helplessly and he grinned.

'I know you. You're feeling guilty. But don't. Because tonight, we are a couple, and we will dazzle their pants off while you parlay yourself into your dream contract.'

'But won't you get bored listening to that stuff all night?'

'With you? Please.'

I nodded. He was already in toy boy mode. 'Has the agency sent the sitter yet?'

'Bang on time, too,' he answered as a younger version of Emma Thompson sauntered in, caught sight of us and smiled. 'You look lovely.' Then she eyed Connor. 'Both of you. Have a good time.'

She seemed all right to me, of course, but I still couldn't bring myself to leave everyone. Connor took my hand. 'We're going to be late if we don't leave now, Nat. The girls are already in bed, so it's a no-brainer.'

'And is she okay with Mum?' I whispered as he turned me towards the door.

'Nat – she's a trained carer. Let's go already.'

'Right. Let's go.'

We descended the outside steps and walked to his Jeep where he opened the door for me to climb in. When he shut the door, he remained at my window, chin resting on his forearms. Gosh, he really should be in pictures.

'What's wrong?' I asked. 'Is my lipstick smudged or something?'

He laughed. 'Not that you need any of that crap, but you do look great. So just enjoy yourself and you'll smash it.'

I smoothed my updo back and nodded as my heart kept jack-hammering its way into my throat. 'Okay, let's do it.' We had a long drive ahead of us. It would have been so much easier to just change at the hotel, but I really wanted to get this over with. Plus, Connor and myself alone in a hotel room before a party was not a good idea.

'You sure you're all right?'

'I'm fine. Thank you.'

But he was still there, studying me. I looked into his eyes and for a moment I swear I thought he was going to kiss me. But then he broke the spell and pulled away to round the car and get in.

To say I was nervous would be like telling someone on death row that it might hurt a bit. What if someone started asking us questions? I hadn't thought of that. Oh God, I never was a good liar.

Connor backed out of the drive and shifted into first gear and turned to me. 'So, let's get our stories straight,' he said as if he'd read my mind. 'How long have we known each other?'

'Well, let's say we were friends first, for about two years.'

'Okay, so where did we meet?'

I thought about it. What was one of my favourite places?

'At Sainsbury's in Truro – the cakes section. We kept bumping into each other there.'

'And then one day I just said something to you about sharing one over a coffee in your village?' he suggested. What a smooth operator.

'Perfect. So we met up in the village a few months ago and have been together since.'

'Okay,' he agreed. 'How serious are we?'

'What? Oh.'

He chuckled as he slid me an amused glance. 'You haven't really thought this out, have you, Nat?'

I shrugged. 'I didn't think you'd say yes, to be honest.'

'Now why wouldn't I? Okay, so we're serious enough to be living together.'

'Yes.'

'Have I told you that I love you?'

I baulked. 'What?'

'You're right. It's none of their business, but I suppose your closest friends will ask. So what will you say?'

'I don't know. It depends on how it's going.'

He rounded a bend and looked at me.

'You mean you want to see if we're credible enough. Well, why wouldn't we be? You're a gorgeous woman; I'm a man with excellent taste.'

'Ha. Thanks.'

He grinned. 'It's the truth. You will dazzle everyone, including Octavia Hounslow.'

'You don't know Octavia Hounslow. Nothing impresses her.'

'*You* will, you'll see,' he assured me, patting my hands resting in my lap, his thumb (accidentally?) grazing my upper thigh, and I almost jumped from the electric charge searing through me.

If I was waiting for the doors of the ballroom to open and to be announced like they do at high society parties, I was wrong. We were let into a huge hall festooned with white lilies and dazzling crystal chandeliers descending as if from the heavens above. Everywhere I turned, tuxes and black or white haute couture shimmered before me. Maggie would've recognised every single label, whereas I only recognised the faces. Thirteen years in the industry had given me that much.

Connor swallowed visibly, pulling at his bow tie as if it was choking him to death. Then he exhaled and turned to me, offering his arm. 'Shall we?'

I had to hand it to him. He was doing this just to please me. I nodded, my legs rubbery. But as I swept in on his arm, looking for Octavia, we were met with quite a few curious glances from friends, colleagues and members of rival publications, some of whom had still expected to see Neil at my side as he had been for the past thirteen years.

And I knew that it was not just because Connor was a new face. He was the face every woman wanted to wake up next to, and I knew it was true because every woman in the room – and some men – suddenly turned to us, eyes shifting as they summed us up, then quickly, furtively, or so they thought, turned back to their conversation partners with an urgency to know, exactly who that was next to Natalia Amore. What was his name, where did he come from exactly and was he my man or an escort? The answer was halfway in between, I guess, although I hadn't paid Connor to be here.

'And here she is, the belle of the ball...' a shrill call reached us.

I whirled around, recognising her voice. Octavia The Hound, looking for all the world like a white popsicle stick – flavourless and gelid – in a frosty white dress so tight it looked like it had been poured onto her and solidified.

I swallowed. 'Hello, Octavia. Please meet Connor Wright. Connor, this is Octavia Hounslow, editor-in-chief of *Lady* magazine.'

'Her boss,' The Hound emphasised as she stretched out a slim hand for him to take. 'It's lovely to meet you, Connor,' she murmured, unable to take her eyes off him.

'It's my pleasure, Ms Hounslow,' he answered amiably.

'So – how's tricks?' she asked me, still watching him.

I nodded. 'Good, thank you. I've already started on my article and hope to—'

'Excellent, excellent,' she said. 'Must circulate. Connor, maybe you can save me a dance for later?'

If Connor was surprised, he handled it with panache. 'Oh, you'll have to ask Natalia. I'm hers.'

'Oh? Oh!' I exclaimed. 'No, no, by all means.'

Octavia slid him a smile so slimy you could have slipped on it. 'I'll come back for you then,' she assured him. And then she turned to me. 'Nat, keep up the good work.' And before I could even open my mouth, she was off into the crowd, weaving in and out like the rattlesnake that she was.

'That went well,' he said through a false smile, so obviously struggling not to pull at his collar. If I knew him, he'd have given the earth to be in our garden in his cut-offs right now. So would I, truth be told.

'Well, if she loves you, we're done here,' I said. Not that I cared about fooling anyone else, assuming I could.

'Not just yet,' he said, wrapping an arm around the back of my waist.

When I looked up at him in question, he simply grinned. 'You can't be in a posh place like this without having a dance.' And with that, he twirled me out onto the dance floor, leading like a pro, his stance elegant. My, he certainly had risen to the occasion.

'Where did you learn to do this?' I asked in amazement. 'I didn't know you could dance!'

'Blame my mother,' he said. 'She was so obsessed we all had to take lessons while growing up.'

'Gardening, building fences, tree houses, surfing, dancing – what else can you do?' I asked in awe as he swung me to and fro. 'I bet you can play an instrument.'

He shrugged. 'I strum the guitar every now and then – we had a band, years ago. Used to play at Temple Bar.'

'Really? That's amazing!'

He laughed. 'What's amazing is that I haven't stepped on your toes!'

'There's always hope,' I said, giggling.

He really was the perfect charmer – gallant, attentive, humorous and worldly.

On the final notes of the song, Connor dipped me, his strong arm supporting my slanted body, his beautiful face inches from my own. I gasped at the sudden turn of events, and his closeness. His lashes almost swept mine, his eyes were seriously dark, or darkly serious – I still can't decide which – searching, delving deep into mine. And his mouth looked utterly delicious.

Blame the booze, blame the peer pressure, blame whomever you want, but before I could understand what I was doing, and utterly unable to stop myself, I took his face in my hands and bloody kissed him smack on the mouth with everything that was inside me – my desires, my urgency, my fears.

It lasted forever, but not long enough. It was a kiss that had everything in it. Attraction, passion, kindness, humour, affection. It was naughty and intimate. How did I manage to put all that into one kiss? And how did it wipe me out in a few seconds?

Was this me, falling even deeper into my case of insta-love? I had already been hanging on a wing and a prayer, trying to resist my wild attraction to him, but the evening had left me absolutely shell-less. All of my defences and good resolutions to behave myself and try not to fall for him hook, line and sinker had gone down the drain.

'Nat…?' he whispered, his eyes searching mine as he pulled away slightly. Was that surprise I read on his face? Surprise that *I'd* kissed him, or, worse, surprise that I'd *kissed* him? Now what was I going to do?

As my mind was reeling, I became aware of a sudden buzzing sound – the crowd cheering us on. Oh my God, what had I *done*? I had given everyone what they wanted, and what I had been dreaming of for weeks now, but was it also what *Connor* wanted, or had I embarrassed him, or worse, offended him?

You'd think it would be easy to tell at this point, but he

stiffened and brought me back up to a standing position as the applause filled my ears. How the hell had I got myself into being the centre of attraction? I shied away from attention normally, but tonight, knowing that my job was on the line, I had given it my all. Only I'd forgotten to warn Connor. I'd forgotten to warn myself as well.

The rest of the evening was spent circling and chatting, Connor still by my side, still pulling at his collar and fidgeting even more than before. As the minutes went by, he became more and more uneasy and agitated, bouncing on the balls of his feet as if ready to run away. It was as clear as the chandeliers hanging above us that he wanted to retire to the hotel room. But whether he wanted to retire with *me* was extremely doubtful.

After we said our goodnights, we climbed into the lift where we avoided looking at each other. Was he panicking, like me? Was he wondering how to tell me that I'd crossed the line? That pretending to be my boyfriend was one thing, but to actually kiss him was another, and in front of everyone, to boot? Well, he would be bloody right.

Connor pulled out the key card to room number thirteen – my lucky number, incidentally – opened the door and stood back for me to enter. I swallowed, and, without looking at him, stepped inside, waiting for him to read me the riot act, feeling just like I used to when I'd done something humongously wrong and was awaiting a good bollocking from my mother.

The first thing he did when we got inside was remove his

tie and his jacket. The ball was in my court, obviously. How to handle this?

I cleared my throat. I wasn't that gullible, nor brazen enough, to expect him to continue the charade in private. It would have been nice, though, to be in a real relationship, and to have someone to talk to, make love with and then cuddle up to and still find him there the next morning to share breakfast in bed. But that was fantasy.

'Well, thanks so much for doing this, Connor. You may have well and truly secured my job.'

He coughed. 'Right – my pleasure. You can have the bathroom first,' he said, still not looking me in the eye.

I stopped and turned. 'Oh. Okay. Thank you.'

As I slid open the bathroom door, I couldn't help but notice the irony of it all. We were alone, had a gorgeous luxury hotel bedroom with a huge bathtub positively screaming for soapy sex, and we couldn't even look at each other. I brushed my teeth, noticing my eyes in the mirror. They were getting dangerously moist. *I'm not going to cry*, I told myself. *I will die first*.

I rinsed and turned the bathtub tap on nice and high, until the water cascaded like Niagara Falls, the echo filling the room.

I sat on the toilet lid, drew my knees up to my chin and dialled Maggie's number.

'Nat? What's up? I thought you'd be swinging from the chandeliers by now.'

'I'm stuck in the toilet,' I whispered.

'Uh-oh. It's those damn canapés, isn't it? Try drinking a lot of water.'

'No, I don't mean that. I'm hiding out in the loo – because of the kiss.'

'What are you talking about? That was an Oscar-winning kiss!'

'Exactly! It wasn't real or planned and I don't know how he's taken it. He hasn't spoken to me since except to say: *You can have the bathroom first.*'

'Ouch. So what's your plan?'

'I have absolutely no idea, Maggie. All this time, I was hoping that something was slowly but surely happening between us. Gosh, what did I think, that a bloke like him could actually be…?' I wiped my eyes. I wasn't as strong as I'd thought.

'But, Nat – the chemistry between you is absolutely *sizzling*. Everyone can see that.'

'Well, everyone except for him, apparently.'

'Nonsense. What are you going to do then?'

'I'm going to camp out in the loo until I'm grey and old.'

'Don't be silly. Get out there and tell him that you fancy him.'

'You must be out of your mind. I can't do that. I'm old-school.'

'But you kissed *him*.'

'An isolated aberration. I'm never doing that again.'

'Nonsense. Now you go out there and get things going.'

'Are you not listening to me, Maggie? He's not interested in the least.'

'How are you ever going to be certain if you don't go out there and find out?'

I heaved a heavy, exhausted sigh. 'Okay. I'll talk to him.'

'Not too much talking, though. Nat.'

'Ha.'

'Good luck!'

'Yuh,' I croaked.

I took a quick bath, dried off briskly and, wrapped up in a fluffy robe, stood with my hand on the handle of the adjoining door, debating. I had two options here. If I pulled out my old pyjama bottoms I would be sending a clear message that it had been a farce for me, too.

If, on the other hand, I'd decided to push the boat out and pull out the lacy number, things could go another way. Or... they could go completely awry. He could just stare at me and cough in embarrassment and there would be nowhere to hide. No other room to storm out to, no other bed to sleep in.

Or I could simply stay here, and camp out all night in the bath.

And to think that I'd initially debated whether to have a fling with him. If he'd seemed inclined, maybe I'd have initiated one. But to be fair, Connor had never really actually, openly flirted with me. Except for maybe the odd spaniel-eyed look which, I now understood, I had grossly misinterpreted. Because, in all honesty, even if I were uninhibited and decided to try and encourage him, what were the actual chances he'd even be remotely interested in me? If he had been, wouldn't he have continued to kiss me, perhaps in the lift, like you see in the movies?

In any case, I was not interested in pity nights. I wanted the real thing, even if for now, due to a tremendous lack of courage, I had to settle for my parallel world, and in my mind I rewound the scene to earlier when we got into our room.

I should have stretched my hand out to him. His eyes would have widened in surprise at first, but then he'd be so allured by my *overwhelming* sex appeal that, unable to resist me, he'd let me kiss him and caress him and undress him until he was ready and waiting for me. And of course he would have kissed me back, as if not a soul had been watching us. Just him and me, utterly and *desperately* powerless to restrain ourselves, like in some old romantic black and white movie.

But what if I actually did go back into the bedroom now and initiate something and we did go all the way? What if things were awkward tomorrow morning, independently of how well I'd done? I had no sex-o-meter. I had no idea, outside of bloody Neil, what was acceptable or not, what was super-hot and what was kinky.

I opened the door a crack, but he was nowhere to be seen, so I stepped further into the room. 'Oh my God, he's *gone*,' I whimpered to myself.

And then his head suddenly appeared from behind the other side of the bed.

I jumped and gasped.

'Sorry,' he said, 'I dropped the room key. Didn't mean to scare you.'

'Neither did I,' I answered, and then instantly fell apart. 'Connor, I'm so so sorry about – that kiss – it was totally out of line and not what we'd planned and—'

'Nat,' he said, running a hand through his hair, which he'd let loose and wild. 'It's okay.'

My mouth fell open. 'It is?'

He came to stand opposite me. 'Of course. I understand completely. It's important for your job.'

Oh. 'I – I don't want you to think I've taken advantage of the situation...'

'Nat, believe me. I'm okay with it. Now, if you'll excuse me, I'll go have a shower.'

With my heart lying so low it could have slipped under the plush carpeting, I watched him go.

I changed into my own pyjamas – a cotton, prudish thingy with a high neck, and got into bed, completely disconsolate.

When he came out, he was wearing a pair of pyjama bottoms and a T-shirt. I stared at him, trying to gauge the temperature. He sat on the bed, facing me, his mouth opening and closing as if he wanted to add something, but had thought better of it.

Please say something. Anything, I begged him silently. *Just get me out of my misery.* At this point I'd have even appreciated a joke about putting a barrier down the centre of the bed, but he simply leaned in, and for a minute I thought he was going to kiss me. But he only gave me a peck on the cheek. Which was a clear message: *End of Farce. Don't expect any of that to continue tomorrow morning when you wake up, because it's not happening.*

As if he hadn't been clear enough, he removed himself to the far, far side of the bed. I had a feeling he'd have plastered himself to the opposite wall if he could have.

Not that I was expecting a night of reckless, untamed passion, or anything. But to think that tomorrow reality would be quite different, and that Cinderella's chariot would once again become a pumpkin and that I'd no longer be in this room with him was definitely an anti-climax.

I'd wanted to at least sit and comment further on the evening, but of course it was of no real interest to him. He'd done me a monumental favour and now wanted the evening to end, whereas I wanted it to go on forever and ever.

Any other woman would have been able to take that kiss straight from the party to the bedroom by keeping that sexual tension live-wire hot. But me? I was the anti-allure. The one who could never think of a sexy thing to say, or be comfortable throwing herself at a man. I just couldn't. I simply wasn't a flirt.

I had no idea how to parade myself in front of men, nor would I feel comfortable in doing so. Besides, even on the theoretical level, I was totally clueless. Even now, as he was lingering, not quite sure how to curtail the evening and murder my dreams without seeming to be rude, I took in his beautiful presence. Okay, I was actually admiring the way his wide shoulders tapered down to that lean waist, I admit it – all the while wondering what I had done wrong. How had he changed so quickly, out of the blue from crowd-wower back to my tenant? Was he that good an actor that he could switch the sex-o-meter on and off that quickly?

I could have screamed: *If you're not going to kiss me here, at least tell me I haven't got a chance in hell, but don't keep me hanging anymore!* I needed this. I needed a fling like I needed to exhale.

And then he suddenly rolled over to face me. 'Nat? I, uhm, need to tell you something…' he mumbled apologetically.

Oh, no, please don't tell me that you don't fancy me. Please wait until tomorrow at least? I power-yawned and rubbed my eyes, partly to hide the moistness gathering behind my eyeballs.

'Mmmh, can it wait until tomorrow? I'm absolutely knackered.'

His mouth snapped shut. 'Sure. Of course. It will keep. Goodnight, Nat,' he whispered. 'Sleep tight.'

'Good, uhm, night, Connor,' was all I managed. How would *you* have slept that night, thinking of what could have been but never would, because it had all been a farce? Exactly.

The next morning when I woke up Connor was in the shower. With my luck he'd come out fully dressed, if last night was anything to go by. Trying to stifle my disappointment, I reached for my mobile that bleeped, startling me, and I saw there were over three hundred WhatsApp messages, all from colleagues and friends, varying from *Woohoo!!!* to *You Go Girl!!!* to *Who is your Apollo???*

And then, one single message from Maggie:

I hope you managed to swing from those chandeliers in the end?

Oh, the painful irony of it all! I grimaced as I continued to scroll down, when instead I should have been grinning. The stage was set. The word had spread and I was the new sensation with my old column back, thank God. And yet, I couldn't be any more miserable. How could I act normally after what I'd done? Did I just pretend it had never happened, or act like I was aware it was only a one-night ruse?

I had an entire five hours to think about it on the way

home. During which Connor chatted about this and that amiably enough, and yet, I couldn't help feel that we were blatantly ignoring the white elephant in the Jeep. Had I endangered our friendship?

When Neil came for Mum later that afternoon, he examined her more briefly than usual, as if he was in a hurry. He was cursory with her and not up to normal boring small talk about the weather or *Coronation Street*.

'Right, Mum, everything's okay. I'll be back tomorrow,' he said as he snapped his bag shut and walked out into the hall where, just before the front door, he whirled around to face me.

'I hear you were at the annual black-tie benefit in London last night.'

I bristled. 'And?'

'And you didn't think to invite me? Do you know how many contacts I make every year at those benefits? You should have told me. But instead you take bloody Casanova with you.'

If he wanted me to take the bait, I would gravely disappoint him. 'You and I are no longer together, Neil. When are you going to accept that?'

His jaw worked. 'Never. I am never going to accept that. You will always be my wife, Natalia. No matter what you say – or who you sleep with.'

'Out,' I said. 'Get out now. And don't come back. I'm getting my mother another GP.'

He snorted. 'You wouldn't dare.'

'Watch me,' I said, reaching past him to open the front

door, all the while holding his glare. In the bad old days I used to cower and heel like a dog. But not anymore.

As he was debating whether to challenge me, Connor's Jeep pulled up on the kerb, and Neil flashed the vehicle a murderous look.

'This does not end here,' he said under his breath.

Connor swung his long legs out of the Jeep and ambled up the drive, humming to himself as usual.

'Hiya, Doc,' he greeted him with his usual cheerfulness, which Neil had never bothered to reciprocate. They both knew there wouldn't be any wasted Christmas cards between them.

'Connor,' Neil greeted back through gritted teeth and took his leave, his back stiff with anger.

'You okay?' Connor asked, looking me up and down. 'You look frazzled. Is your mum all right?'

I shook my head clear and looked up at Connor. 'Yes, she's fine thank you.'

He frowned. 'It's Neil giving you grief, isn't he? I told you he wasn't over you.'

I snorted. 'Oh, he was over me the minute he fell into bed with someone else,' I said before I could stop myself. I bit my lip. 'Sorry, too much information.'

He came to stand opposite me and grinned. 'Never. Is there any news from the grapevine about last night?'

'Ah, yes. The word is out. And you have major consensus.'

He threw back his head and laughed. 'It's not about me. You were the star of the evening.'

'We'll see about that. I have a Skype conference call with Octavia on Monday.'

At that, he made a mock face of terror and crossed his

fingers. And that was it. Not a word about the after-ball, during which we'd opted to go straight to bed. Because for Connor, it was clearer than ever: this was all one big lie for my benefit.

A moment later the girls came in from the garden and he clapped his hands together, his eyes bright with mischief. 'Who wants to help me build a tree house?'

The girls gasped, holding their cheeks. 'A tree house? Oh, Auntie Nat – can we? Please?'

Connor's eyes swung to mine, and the twinkle in them made me want to gush like a thirteen-year-old. Despite myself, I grinned. 'Of course you can, darlings.'

And in the next second they were all over him in a swarm of hugs and kisses so affectionate that even Mum awoke from her dozing. 'Eh? What's happening?'

'Connor and the girls are going to build a tree house, Mum. Isn't that fun?'

'A tree house? How lovely, Connor! Are you going to get your kit off and swing from the branches, too?'

'Mother!' I pleaded.

He put his hand on her shoulder. 'Only if you join me, love.'

'You're on,' she agreed enthusiastically.

The zoo had nothing on this place.

'When do we start?' Amy wanted to know, doing the happy dance. I had *never* seen Amy do the happy dance. Not even on the last day of school last year. I know because I had been the one to fetch them.

'Now,' Connor said as Zoe slid off his lap. 'Are you ready, sweetheart?'

She looked up at him with such love that it frightened

me. They were seriously getting attached. What happened when he had to leave? Was Yolanda right about letting the twins get too close to someone who, at the end of the day, was not part of the family, and who would be gone very soon?

The girls would miss him terribly. And I would miss him terribly. It was almost worth not selling the house.

I glanced at the girls at the bottom of the garden, already fussing about how high the tree house should be built.

'Higher!' Amy shouted as Zoe climbed the ladder.

'Zoe! Please get down right now!' Connor and I both called in unison.

But the girls only laughed.

I wrung my wrists, torn between protecting them and letting them grow confident of their abilities.

So the two of us stood guard under the tree, ready to catch them should they have fallen. I looked over at Connor who was biting his lip and eyeing me. 'Thank God I'm not a father, I'd have had a thousand heart attacks by now.'

I chuckled. 'You'd be a great dad, Connor.'

He shrugged. 'Yeah, well, who knows.'

'For what it's worth, the twins will be devastated when you leave.'

He leaned forward. 'So will I. How will you feel, Nat?'

Only yesterday we had a deluxe hotel room all to ourselves which turned out to be completely useless, and *now* he started flirting with me? I lowered my gaze from that playful twinkle in his eyes. 'I'd miss you, too. You must know that.'

He chuckled. 'Must I?'

I wiped the sweat off the back of my neck. When had it

got so hot? All I wanted to do was scream: *Stop flirting with me if you're not prepared to take the consequences.*

'Nat – let me reassure you – until you need the room back, or sell up, I'm not going anywhere.'

I tried not to sag in relief *too* visibly, but I felt my face stretch in an ear-to-ear smile.

'You promise?' I said before I could stop myself.

'I more than promise, Nat. I swear on my life that I won't go unless you tell me to.' He grinned. 'And even then I'd try to convince you to keep me.'

Which was good enough for me. 'Okay, then,' I said, pushing my fringe behind my ear and pretend-shooing him away. It seemed that all was forgiven and that we were back where we'd started, i.e. square one. Which wasn't all that bad, considering that I could have lost him completely due to my recklessness. 'Go and build your tree house, now.'

He pulled his gloves back on and buckled his tool belt.

'Delicious, isn't he, with that strut?' Mum said, craning her neck to admire his derrière as I walked back into the house.

'Mum.' I laughed, seeing as he was out of earshot. 'You've got to stop looking at his bottom.' Dearie me, could mother and daughter think of nothing else lately?

At that, Connor turned around and slid us an amused gaze. I slapped my hand over my forehead. 'You see, he heard you? You're going to get us into trouble one of these days, Mum.'

But she only laughed. 'What's wrong with looking? You can start worrying when I jump his bones, but for now, while my ankle is like this, I'd say he's safe. But not for long. You can go first, if you want.'

I shook my head, but I was happy whenever she was like this. She had never been any fun before. Dr Simpson had been right. There was a silver lining, in the sense that her personality hadn't deteriorated further, but if anything, she had mellowed. I liked this new version of my mother. Now I felt that I could actually talk to her, and not just cower at her harsh judgements.

And I suddenly realised that between Neil and the other version of my mother, I had been kept in a vice. And now I felt, well, if not free from my obligations as daughter to an ill mother, at least liberated from my self-doubt as a wife. Neil had said that no one else would want me because I was always so demure and insignificant. But instead, thanks to his betrayal, I'd discovered that not only was I strong, but that I had also found my self-confidence again.

As Mum read her *Good Housekeeping* magazines, tearing out the recipes she liked, I worked on my column, all the while watching the happenings with Connor under the oak tree. Even at a distance of a hundred feet, I *missed* him. I longed to have him close by, but I couldn't risk it with the excuse of going down there to check up on them. I was like an open book, and I knew that if I wasn't careful, even the twins would suss me out.

Did he have any idea of how much I fancied him? Had he read in between the lines of my kiss? He was probably having the time of his life, teasing me like that. He must have known I found him sexy. And even outside the house, women's reactions when he passed by were more than obvious. But what did he do? Like the gentleman that he was, he kept everything polite and PG-14. It was positively infuriating.

I watched as he climbed the ladder, talking and laughing with the girls. They adored him, too. It was more than obvious. In a matter of weeks he had managed to become indispensable to the entire family.

And then I wondered what his relationship had been like with his ex-wife, and why that had ended.

On the Monday I sat down in my chair for my video chat with The Hound, ramrod straight, reasonably optimistic that our ruse had secured my job.

'Well, hello, talk of the town!' Octavia called as she appeared on my computer screen, and I saw her mobile at her ear as she was actually still on the phone with someone else. Typical Octavia.

'Sorry, love, gotta run. I have a meeting with Natalia *Amore*,' she said as she winked at me. 'Yes, precisely *that* Natalia Amore – not that there's anyone else like her, is there? After all, she is one of my top writers. Laters!' she called and hung up.

'Natalia, so glad to *see* you!' she called and I kept fighting the urge to look behind me to see if there was indeed another Natalia in the room. But no, it was only me. Only a few days ago she wanted my arse out, and now she was glad to see me, just because she thought I was sleeping with a gorgeous, younger man? 'That was quite a stir you caused. So spill the beans! Where's he from, what does he do, how did you meet?'

Maggie had been right. We had been believable, apparently.

I coughed and cleared my throat. 'H-he's from Dublin,

and we met…' I floundered, trying to remember the story we'd made up '…at Sainsbury's. In the cakes section.'

'Yes, yes?' she prompted as if her life depended on it, although actually that was only true for me. 'But how did you actually decide to go out together?' Which was clearly something that she couldn't, for the life of her, figure out.

'Well, we were talking about Danish cinnamon rolls when he said, "Seeing as we both have a sweet tooth for cakes, why don't we share some along with some coffee in the village?"'

'Excellent,' she cackled. 'And then?'

'And then?' What did she mean by that exactly? Gosh, I hoped she wasn't angling – or in her case, demanding the details of what never happened. 'How long has this been going on?' she asked.

'Oh?' I shrugged. 'A couple of months.'

'Right. And what does he do?'

'He's a lawyer with an IT company.'

'So you're living together now? God, that was quick. Most women can't get a man to commit to a mobile phone provider, let alone a relationship. So, what's the arrangement? I know he's younger, so are you his sugar mama?'

Meaning, did I pay him? 'Absolutely not,' I assured her. 'We were friends for a long time before we realised that we, uhm…'

She studied me at length through the screen, and I knew that any minute she was going to tell me that the jig was up, and who the hell did I think would fall for that?

But instead, she said, 'Excellent. I can't wait to read your next article.'

'So I'm keeping my monthly column?'

'Sort of. You'll provide a monthly account of your own experience about living with a younger man.'

'Thank you, I'm very gla— I beg your pardon, Octavia? Did you just say monthly account? You want another article about Connor?' *Oh my God in heaven.*

'Absolutely yes. Two thousand words monthly. And no more hiding.'

'Hiding?'

'Yes. I want pictures galore along with your articles. This will make the older ladies swoon. We want to know every detail of your glamorously naughty life. Or shall I say naughtily glamourous?'

'The older ladies?' I aped. 'But... but... I thought you said you wanted to uhm – rejuvenate the magazine...?'

'Of course. But there will always be a portion of Old Faithfuls reading us and we need to keep their interest, otherwise they'll run for our rival publications. Demographics of women your age are sky-high.'

I could have told her that – in fact I *had* told her that, but she hadn't listened. Now of course, it was all *her* bright thinking. But who cared? I had my income back! Provided I could talk Connor into lying just a little longer.

This was it. This was my chance to not only keep my job, but to be a double-pager, and not just the measly single-paged writer who has to say it in eight hundred words. A double-pager would be just the ticket.

So it would be fair to say that, through no fault of my own, Octavia – and half the capital, apparently – had fallen for it, hook, line and by-line. But now to run it by my accomplice. Because one thing was an evening, but how on earth was I going to ask Connor to keep up the farce, and live the lie indefinitely?

If done on a regular basis, he'd have to be seen with me as much as possible. I couldn't ask him to fake it for the rest of his life. Not after that kiss that almost killed me.

13

White Lies Have Tiny Legs

If until now I'd been blissfully ignorant of all the implications of The Farce, now I was absolutely terrified. Things I'd never thought of were now rushing to the fore.

Namely, how the hell was I going to tell Connor that I still needed him to lie for me? A night out and free champers was one thing – but now? With what courage could I ask him to sustain The Farce – and for how much longer? Octavia Hounslow was smart. For how long could I keep fooling her? I'd have to think of something, and quick.

'So how did that go?' Connor asked as I sauntered into the kitchen.

'She, uhm, offered me a double-paged column of my own.'

He put the kettle down and took my hands in his. 'That's brilliant, Nat! Huge congratulations! Not that I had any doubts. This calls for some champagne! I know – dinner tonight, how's that?'

I bit my lip, eyeing him.

'What's wrong?' he asked.

Spit it out, Nat, I told myself.

'She… she wants the topic of my entire column to be my life with you, the younger man. Oh, Connor, I really want this job, but I'm aware that it's not fair because it would bind you.'

He was silent and I could tell that he was uncomfortable with all this. If one night had been a lot to ask, imagine the foreseeable future.

'Bind me…?'

I shrugged. 'You know, the seasonal parties, the company dinners and stuff. If she gets wind that you and I aren't an item, I'm toast. But I know I can't ask you to do that for me. You have your own life and I shouldn't be putting you on the spot like this.'

He sat down at the table. 'Listen, Nat. I'm quite a private person and I hate to lie. But this is about you and your job. How can I say no to helping you? Of course I'll do it.'

'But – you're too young to waste your time when you could actually be in a relationship.'

His eyebrows rose.

'With someone else,' I hastily added. 'Unless, you already are?'

And now, hopefully, he'd put me out of my misery by spilling the beans on Felicity, or whoever his secret girl was. And whoever she was, I doubted very much that she knew what bed he'd been sleeping in right after the ball. Tendrils of guilt slid down my neck and into my heart. I was *not* going to be the other woman, not even by mistake.

He smiled. 'It's only temporary. And believe me, I've had more relationships than necessary in the past. And now I want to concentrate on other things in life and other kinds of relationships. Plus, you know?'

I looked up at him as he squeezed my hand. No, actually, I didn't know. What was only temporary, the farce, or his current relationship? This was confusing.

He grinned and caressed my cheek with his forefinger. 'I'm being selfish here, Nat. Being around you, in this house with your family makes me feel good, like I actually have a place and a purpose in life.'

Okay, now I was *really* confused.

'So if you're asking me if I'm okay being seen with you and pretending there is something between us, the answer is yes because I want to help. Besides, we should let fate decide.'

Let fate decide? Did that mean that we actually had a chance? Now I was flabbergasted. Was it possible that Connor, so young and handsome, although not as free as the wind, was interested in me after all? And that he was two-timing his girlfriend, like Neil had been two-timing me? Because if so, I couldn't accept to be in that kind of situation. I could never do to another woman what had been done to me.

'Fate?' I echoed. 'Just make sure you don't hurt anyone, Connor.'

His mouth snapped shut. 'I'm trying not to, Nat. Truly I'm not.'

Ah. Bingo.

Over the weeks Connor became my creative sounding board for my toy boy scenario. I worked like a madwoman, pounding out onto my laptop all sorts of dinners and dates and funny scenarios that I'd imagined happening between Connor and me. Connor would read it and cackle in delight, and give me a thumbs up. The fun part of dating and starting a relationship. Oh, if only an iota of it had been true.

One day Yolanda video-called me on my mobile.

'Natalia – hi! How is everything? How are my girls?'

'Your girls are blossoming, Yolanda. They are just beautiful and smart and you'd be very proud of them.'

'I *am* very proud of them,' she pointed out.

'Oh, no, I meant if you were— Of course you're proud of them. They have your beauty and your brains.'

That seemed to mellow her instantly. 'And school? Sports? Friends?'

'Bless them, they're on every team now, thanks to—'

'Your tenant?'

'Connor, yes. He… he spends many afternoons coaching them. You should see Zoe, how she's come out of her shell! And Amy – the way she now waits for her turn! She's developing the art of patience and sportsmanship like no other.'

'And where are you during all this?'

'Oh, half the time I'm with Mum, while the other half I'm cooking or cleaning or working…'

'So you leave them alone with him? A total stranger?'

'Don't start on me again, Yola. I'm not in the mood.'

'Okay, okay, I'm sorry. I didn't call to fight. I need a favour.'

Ah. That explained the quick apology. 'What do you need?'

'I need you to keep the girls a little longer,' she said. 'Until Christmas.'

'Yola, are you serious? When are these poor girls actually going to get to see you?'

'Nat – come, on, work with me here. They've extended my show by another few episodes and I'll never make it back for when I said.'

'I thought you said you wanted to take the girls on a cruise.'

'I do, but it will all have to wait. Listen, can you keep them or not? Because I can always call the nanny.'

The idea of a stranger taking care of my nieces made my skin crawl. 'Of course I'll keep them with me, Yola, but don't you miss them at all?'

'Of course I miss them, but I have no choice. My career is on the rise now and I have to ride the wave. Not that you'd understand.'

'Of course not,' I agreed, my voice dripping with sarcasm. 'But it would be nice if you could find the time to actually speak to them yourselves.'

'Is it my fault if I'm five hours behind?' she snapped. 'You think I don't care about my girls? Would you rather I be worried sick about them?'

Jesus. 'Yolanda, I'm sorry but I have to get back to my column now. Talk soon. Text me a video chat time for over the weekend and I'll have the girls have an afternoon nap so they can stay up late enough to talk to you, okay?'

'Right,' she said. 'See you.'

'See you,' I said, but she had already hung up.

As it turned out, in the end I decided not to find Mum

another GP. Not that I couldn't. But I didn't want to remove a familiar face from my mother, while she still recognised him, that is. Also, I didn't want to make things worse between Neil and myself for the girls' sake. After all, we belonged to the same family, and the last thing I needed was to prolong the feud.

'Mum says you're going out with Him With The Face again tonight?' Neil asked, or rather accused, as he snapped his briefcase shut. So much for peace.

He was jealous of Him With The Face. Not that I could blame him. You might think that the charm would complete the ensemble, but that still wasn't it. What Connor had was intangible. It was a presence, a warmth, a soulfulness that you didn't expect from someone looking like him. And you didn't expect someone looking like him hanging out with someone like me.

'And?' I prompted.

'Well, who's watching Mum in the meantime?' he threw at me.

'First of all, Neil, let me make this clear once and for all. She is not your mother. She's mine.'

'Not that you'd notice,' he snapped. 'You should be staying home with your mother, not showing off your new boyfriend.'

Oh, if he only knew.

'He's not right for you, Natalia.'

'And you are?'

'Of course I am. I love you. I always have.'

'Yeah, especially when you were with the other ladies.'

'I thought we were past that.'

'You may be, but I'm not.'

'When are you going to actually forgive me for that tiny indiscretion and take me back?'

'Tiny indiscretion? Neil, you were seeing her for months before I found out – if not years.'

He sighed. 'Look, I promise to behave myself. If you take me back, we can work on our marriage. You won't have to work so hard and I'll provide for you. I'll make your life better.'

I huffed in disbelief. 'That's what you promised me when you proposed, Neil. If anything, apart from our daughters, you've made it worse. I gave up everything for you.'

'What, you mean your writing career? It's not my fault you write for that silly rag, is it?'

See what I was up against? 'Keep your opinions about my choices to yourself, Neil.'

'I'm sorry. I just want another chance, Nat.'

'Would you take me back if I'd cheated on you?'

He baulked, his eyes clouding over. Whether with disappointment that I would even think of such a thing, or worry that I had, I didn't know.

'Exactly. Goodbye, Neil.'

Later that day, I decided to take the girls for a stroll down the footpath to the beach. Connor was just getting in through the orangery, his laptop under his arm.

'Hey,' I said as the girls were putting their sandals on by the French doors at the back. 'Just in time. Would you like to join us for a beachcomb?'

He came through, his harried expression fading at the idea and already he was smiling. 'Love to. Just give me a sec to change.'

'Hurry up, Connor,' Zoe said, jumping up and down. 'I want to catch crabs!'

I suppressed a laugh and he chuckled and ruffled her hair. 'You guys are so cute,' he said, our eyes meeting. 'Be right back. Ice creams are on me!' he called as he ran up the stairs.

As we dug our bare feet into the sand, I relished the feeling of freedom while it lasted. Only here, down in Wyllow Cove, did I feel relaxed. All my thoughts and worries seemed to fade.

As we strolled up the beach, my mobile phone beeped. It was Hannah Williams, the real estate agent selling Lavender Cottage. I only hoped she wasn't the bearer of bad news, i.e. that there were other more determined buyers than me.

'Aren't you going to answer that?' Connor asked.

I nodded, my fingers shaking as I tapped on the green dot.

'Mrs Amore? It's Hannah Williams. When would it be a good time to come and look at your house?'

Ah – so no news on Lavender Cottage yet. Excellent. 'How's tomorrow morning at ten?' I suggested. The girls would be at school and Mum would be up. They could take pictures of her room first so she could have her nap when she wanted.

'Perfect. I'll bring my equipment to make a video tour and take some shots.'

'See you then.' When I hung up, I felt strangely elated.

'You're doing the right thing, Nat,' Connor said.

I nodded. 'I know. People would kill for a house like that, but to me it's only bad memories of Neil.'

Connor studied me kindly. 'I told you, he wants you back. Big time. And he's willing to wait.'

I shrugged. 'Well, he's going to have a long wait.'

'That's what I like to hear,' he said, winking at me. Oh, one more flirt and I would absolutely throttle him. Or, worse, kiss him again.

'Connor!' Amy called from the rock pools. 'Are you coming or what?'

'Catch ya later,' he said with a grin and then jogged over to where the twins were crouched, scanning the pools for a catch, like two tiny seagulls.

What did he care who I ended up with? It was as clear as day that he wasn't interested in a fling or a romantic relationship. He'd had countless chances to start something, and if he hadn't, it was simply because there was nothing to tell. He saw me as a friend, and that was that. So why didn't my little breaking heart understand that?

Exhausted of waiting for a catch (believe me, I knew how they felt) the girls decided to run to the end of the beach. Connor and I lagged behind, just enjoying being out in the sun.

'Hi, Nat; hi, Connor,' John Baird, the recently divorced school caretaker, saluted as he strolled by us.

'Hi John,' I said, 'This is, uh, Con—'

'Hi, mate,' he saluted, high-fiving him, slowing down long enough to say, 'I did like you said, by the way.'

'And did it work?' Connor wanted to know.

John shrugged, but a huge smile spread across his fair face. 'Looks like it. Can't thank you enough, mate.'

'Sure, any time,' Connor answered, his eyes sheepishly swinging to mine. 'See ya.'

'You know John?' I asked.

He stuffed his hands into his pockets and looked at his feet. 'Yes. I uhm, gave him the number of my divorce lawyer.'

'Oh. Well, I hope he's good.'

'She. My lawyer was a she.'

'Right.'

And then silence fell between us again. I took a deep breath, absorbing everything around me, from the salt air to the cry of the gulls to the green cliffs kneeling to the sea in a gesture of reverence. 'I really love it here...' I whispered.

He breathed in deeply. 'I can't think of anything more beautiful than Cornwall.' He grinned. 'Well, maybe just one thing.'

I smiled inwardly, but said nothing as warm tingles of pleasure danced around my face.

We spent a good hour strolling down the golden sandy beach, chasing seagulls and breathing in the fresh, salty air that clung to my hair and lips. Connor was his usual friendly self, giving the girls piggyback rides, running off with them into the distance under the turquoise sky that wouldn't have been out of place in the Mediterranean. If paradise had a branch on earth, it was certainly Cornwall.

When we got back in, Connor brought us some iced tea and gently rubbed Mum's shoulders. 'How's that, love?'

She placed her hand on his, gripping his fingers. 'Hmm,

nice. Strong hands. I wonder what else you can do with them.'

'Mum!' At this point I was beyond mortification. I just wanted to zap myself into nothingness.

But Connor only chuckled. 'You keep flirting with me like you do and you'll leave me no choice but to tell you,' he said and Mum clapped her hands in sheer delight. 'You naughty boy, you!'

He tapped the front of his forehead. 'Oh, I forgot the lemons. You see, Beryl? You start batting your baby blues at me and I go and forget everything – including myself.'

I watched him as he sauntered across the patio and through the orangery into the kitchen.

'Oh, isn't he absolutely luscious?' Mum said. 'You should go for him.'

I almost choked on my drink. 'Me?'

'Yes, you, Yolanda. I bet he'd love to cook your eggs.'

Yolanda, always Yolanda. I sighed at the sheer irony of it. *I* was the one killing myself here for our mother while she was on the other side of the world caring only about herself and her career as usual.

The next day after I dropped the kids off at school, I stopped over at The Rising Bun to pick up some dessert for after dinner, and maybe a treat to get me through the day. I was feeling peckish although I'd just had breakfast. Could it be I was subsuming my other desires?

Oh, get over yourself, Natalia, my inner voice said. *And don't be so pathetic. The bloke is off-limits. Find something else to do*. Which was what, alongside my sweet tooth, had brought me here to The Rising Bun today.

I grabbed a cup of cappuccino and wolfed down a chocolate doughnut as I browsed the selection of cakes. There was no end to Dora's talents: carrot cake, lemon drizzle, peanut butter cheesecake, Victoria sponge, chocolate brownies and almond cake among many others. I would have taken them all home with me where I would take care of them and shelter them under my beautiful glass cake bells. I'd look at them every day and they would nourish me and feed my sadness.

But I had to set a good example for the girls, so in the end I opted just for one thing: a huge, chocolate mousse. Feed a fever, starve a cold, I knew that much, but what did one do with a rampaging attraction?

At the till, Felicity was there as usual, and also as gorgeous as usual and I couldn't help but feel a pang of jealousy. I had been suspicious of her for some time now, mainly because she was the most beautiful girl in the village. What if I was right and it really was her? If I were a bloke with any woman in Wyllow Cove at my disposal, I'd definitely chose lovely Felicity, no bones about it. She was a great baker, had the smile of an angel and always had a kind word for everyone.

'Hi, Nat,' Dora called as I came in. 'Oh, that Connor is such a lovely chap, isn't he?'

Yes, I was sure she'd think so, with Felicity on the shelf.

'Felicity thinks the world of him.'

Was it so obvious to everyone in Wyllow Cove that Connor and I actually were not a couple? Apparently we were only a 'thing' for the media, but not in real life. There was no fooling my villagers.

'I don't know what we would've done without him,' Dora continued. 'I only hope that Felicity will be accepted over in Dublin.'

She was meeting his *parents*?

'Oh, I'm, uhm, sure she will be,' I stammered.

'Hi, Nat,' she said, eyeing me as I washed down my doughnut with the dregs of my cappuccino.

'Hey, Felicity, how's it going?' I managed.

'Good, good, thanks. How's Connor?'

Bingo. Was she sussing me out to see if I knew about them? I cleared my throat. 'He's fine, thanks. Why don't you call him and ask him yourself?'

'I will, when we get the results back. We're a bit on edge, you understand.'

Results? Oh my God in heaven. I scratched my head. 'Sorry, Uhm. Did you just say... results?'

She grinned. 'Connor helped me apply to a course at Trinity College. I'm awaiting their response any day now.'

'Oh!' Thank God! 'Well, good luck, Felicity.'

'And to you, Nat. You two make a lovely couple. I'm so happy for you.' Then she looked around and muttered, '*I never liked Neil.*'

'Oh. Uhm, thank you,' was all I could think of in response. Ah. So if there was a mysterious girl to be spoken of, it was not Felicity. One down. Another thirty to go, based on my calculations of eligible women.

I paid for my mousse and left, deciding to make a quick tour of the village, blushing as everyone waved knowingly at me. One lady, Dawn Hawkins, who ran the pet shop, even gave me a knowing thumbs up and a wink. Two down. How the heck was I going to find out who my competition was? At this point every single (and married) woman was a possibility.

'Hi, Nat!' came a call from behind me. I turned to see Joe Tehidy, the owner of the angling shop.

'Hi Joe! Is it a good day for a catch?'

He looked up at the sky. 'Just as good as any. How's Connor?'

'You know Connor?'

He blanched. 'What? No, not really. My wife told me his name and that he's living with you. Talk about good catches, eh?'

What the hell was going on? Was I on *Candid Camera* and didn't know it? Or was there such a thing as *The Amore Show* and I was the unknowing main character? This was all so surreal. Everyone knew Connor. Only I didn't know Connor – at least not as much as I would have liked to.

Exhausted by all the possibilities and calculations of who might be his woman, I reached the quay and fell onto a bench, my bag at my side and the mousse on my lap. A seagull came to investigate and I jumped and the mousse slid off my knees, but I lurched forward to grab it and caught it just in time before it upturned and splatted on the pavement, my fingers digging into a corner of the dessert. That had been close. With my index finger I scooped up the sweet goo and stuck it into my mouth. Hmm, it was especially good today.

So if it wasn't Felicity and it wasn't Dawn, who the heck was it? If I only knew what kind of woman he liked, I'd have a better chance at finding out who my rival was. Listen to me. I was already using the R word. Was I presumptuous or what?

There was still some chocolate on the side of the lid, probably the main reason why that seagull was still lingering, eyeing me maliciously. So I scooped up that, too.

Whoever this mysterious woman was, she was not my rival in the least. I mean, I wasn't hers. There was literally no contest, because Connor had come here to Wyllow Cove especially for her. I wasn't even in the picture. I was only the landlady. The thought sobered me tremendously and suddenly I felt defeat looming over me like a dark shadow.

I surreptitiously stuck my finger along the side of the mousse and carved out a tiny dollop so it would still be presentable for dinner. Okay, so even if I knew her identity, there was absolutely nothing I could do. I was not a couple-buster, having been on the other end and not wishing that kind of pain on anyone.

I took another dollop to my lips and almost swooned at the pleasure. Somebody somewhere had definitely overrated sex. They should try Dora's cakes and rephrase their claim. Or maybe they'd simply had a better partner than Neil. Self-sufficient (in every way, towards the end), arrogant Neil was never even a spark in bed, let alone fireworks like you read in novels. Oh, how I *longed* for that feeling.

But for now, all I had was dessert, and I was using two fingers to scoop it into my mouth. If my luck was anything to go by, I'd have to rely solely on my own attraction for Connor to even begin to get a sense of what he would be like to make love with. If even the sole thought of having sex with that Irish Apollo made my heart do the Riverdance, I could only imagine how many times I'd die if we ever actually came skin to skin, eye to eye, mouth to mouth for real, and not just the fake, albeit delicious, kiss we'd shared at the black-tie benefit.

As my fingers went to take another scoop of mousse, I looked down and realised I had literally carved the mousse out from the sides, and before I knew it, it slowly, inexorably collapsed upon itself like a giant chocolate sinkhole.

'Oh, no...' I moaned. I had absolutely no self-control anymore. What the heck was wrong with me? I was never one to pity myself, but, as I watched this former beauty slide to one side, I couldn't help but think that this mousse was like my problems. I'd picked at it from every side, unable to attack it directly, afraid of acknowledging that, yes, I wanted to attack it viciously and get rid of it – via my mouth. Some passers-by gave me a funny look, but said nothing. What could you say to a woman sitting on her own in public devouring a chocolate mousse twice her size?

And the not so funny thing was that I couldn't stop. Scoop after scoop, I ate the whole bloody thing, even as my throat began to constrict, I just shoved it all down, just like my fears, my worries and my beefs. And in a few minutes, it was gone – even the last smears at the bottom, the tray shining like new.

I didn't have the guts to go back in there and buy another one, so I went to the supermarket and bought some ice cream instead, hoping that with the chocolate sauce I still had somewhere in the pantry that it would be enough. Maybe even crumble some Oreo biscuits in there to make it look like I'd actually tried.

On my way to pick up the girls from school I dabbed at my mouth and tried to calm down. I hadn't been this upset since I saw Neil with his bit on the side, and I realised that I couldn't let a rival reduce me. Besides, I couldn't let my nieces see me like this. So I stopped the car by the side of the road and pulled out a bottle of water and splashed my face fresh again.

I got home, composed myself and checked on Mum who was watching the tail of her favourite morning show.

'I'm back, Mum, is everything all right?'

'Super,' she said, not taking her eyes off the screen. 'Connor's made me lunch.'

'But it's only eleven o'clock,' I said.

She shrugged. 'I was hungry.'

'That was nice of him. What did he make you?'

'An egg-mayonnaise sandwich,' she said. 'Shush now, I want to hear the end of this.'

I sighed under my breath and went into the hall to listen for Connor. All I could hear was faint tapping on a keyboard, and then his mobile chirped discreetly. I heard him answer, and then chuckle. Was it her, my nemesis? I didn't want to pry. It was none of my business, so I went back to my second desk in the orangery and turned my laptop on. And stared at a blank screen. Now what? Should I have written about the dangers of eating too many sweets? And speaking of such, my stomach began to complain. It served me right for being such an out-of-control glutton.

Maybe I should write an article about self-control, or the lack thereof. Because, among other things, I was dying to go back into the hall and find out if he was talking to *her*. As if it would make her identity more obvious.

But I stayed with my arse glued to my chair, determined to be a proper landlady in every way, although I think I'd already passed that boundary when I'd asked him to be my pretend toy boy. Which made me wonder – had he told her about this favour he was doing me? And was she okay with it? If so, she must really trust him. Or, au contraire, had he kept things on the quiet, seeing as one night in London could be justified with a vague work excuse?

As I still stared at my blank screen, Connor came downstairs. 'You're back – hi,' he said, sticking his head into the kitchen.

On the counter, I noticed a familiar bag, the sight of which made me want to hurl. Or faint, whichever came first.

I groaned. 'You went to Dora's too?'

He stopped and looked at me as if caught in the act. Bingo! He shrugged, scratching his face as he did when he was embarrassed or put on the spot. 'I've got a very sweet tooth.'

I groaned inwardly.

'Look, I'm just popping out, so I won't be around for lunch.'

Lunch. With who? That was it. I was absolute toast.

I turned in my chair and gave him a smile so dazzling I might have cracked a tooth. 'Hot date?' I said, my lips stretching.

He looked at me funny. 'Your face…'

I stopped smiling. 'What do you mean?'

He came into the room to peer down at me, his face so close to mine that I actually thought he was going to kiss me. Oh, God, the glint in his eye – he really was going to kiss me!

I sat up straight in my chair, not wanting to look like a slouching slob, as he reached out with a long finger and slowly caressed my bottom lip, back and forth. Oh, the sexual charge of his touch!

'You've got chocolate on your lip,' he said with a grin.

I slouched again. 'Oh. Thanks.'

And I watched, sitting up again, as he stuck his index into his own mouth and licked it off, his eyes never leaving mine in a naughty, naughty message that said, *Get your kit off now*. Oh. My. God.

My pulse shot straight for the stars and I don't know how I didn't just collapse at his feet. Actually, I was feeling kind of funny. Not hilarious funny, but dizzy. I tried to fight it as his face began to dance in front of me and split into two. And then I saw nothing else.

The next thing I knew I was waking up in Connor's arms.

Wait, how had I managed to get here and not remember one single, luscious moment of it?

But we weren't in my bedroom, or his, for that matter, and the bed was not a bed. It was hard.

'Can you hear me?' he was saying.

I looked up at him, trying to focus. I was lying on the kitchen floor with my feet up, cradled by Connor's strong arms.

'Hi,' I whispered. 'What's happened?'

He exhaled in relief. 'You gave me a bloody heart attack, that's what's happened,' he murmured, caressing my face.

In the distance, I could hear a wailing sound. I tried to get up, but his large hand on my chest gently pushed me down again.

'Easy there, luv,' he said. 'That's the ambulance. Do not

move,' he warned me as he got up to open the front door. 'She's in here, thanks,' he said, and two women darted to my side, one strapping a blood pressure reader around my arm while the other one ripped my shirt open and applied a stethoscope to my chest and I cringed as Connor got a view of my generous bosom.

'I'm fine, now,' I said, trying to sit up but the woman with the stethoscope pushed me back down.

'We'll be the judges of that,' she reassured me, only to nod at the other woman who said 'One twenty over eighty. Perfect. What were you doing when you collapsed?'

Being kissed by a hot man, I wanted to say. 'Nothing. Just talking to my friend Connor.'

'Were you having sex?' she insisted.

'Of course not!' I whispered. If only. That would be a great way to go, actually.

'I was just brushing some chocolate off her mouth,' Connor said.

One of the paramedics turned to him, eyes wide. 'That explains it,' she said.

I rolled my eyes. Granted, he was hot, but *really*?

'Chocolate contains a high dose of caffeine, which can send the system into overdrive, but you'd need a huge amount to have that effect on you,' she explained. 'Just how much did you have?'

I lowered my eyes to the floor in shame. 'A mousse.'

She shook her head. 'A portion of mousse wouldn't do that. Not even a big one.'

I lifted my eyes to her, feeling the shame wash over me in huge, Hawaiian tidal waves. 'Not a portion of mousse. An... entire mousse.'

Intake of breath. 'All by yourself?'

I nodded.

'Okay,' one of them said, pulling out a syringe. 'We're going to give you a muscle relaxant. You'd better take it easy for the rest of the day. Drink plenty of liquids and don't exert yourself. Have a few cups of chamomile as well, that should do the trick.'

'So she'll be okay?' Connor sighed with relief.

'Absolutely, let's just get her onto this daybed here and put this throw over her, and get a chamomile going. And no sugar for a few days, just to err on the safe side.'

He nodded and gently scooped me up in his arms and put me on the daybed in the corner. I wanted to wrap my arms around him and never let him go. *My hero*.

In the space of a few minutes, they wrapped up and left, but not before one of them scribbled something on a piece of paper and handed it to him.

He fussed over me and I took his hand. 'Thank you for saving my life,' I whispered.

He grinned. 'And thank you for nearly ending mine.'

'What's that piece of paper she gave you, a prescription?' I asked.

He shook his head. 'A... number to call in case we need them again,' he said, turning red.

'Liar,' I said. 'She just gave you her number, didn't she?'

He turned red. 'Yes.'

'And are you going to call her...?'

'Of course not.'

'Why do you have this effect on women?' I said as the muscle relaxant kicked in. 'Why do you have this effect on me, Connor?'

'Hush...' he said softly.

'Connor...'

'Sleep a little, now.'

And I did.

The next day Connor came down the stairs looking like a million dollars in a pair of tatty jeans and an old Radiohead T-shirt.

'Nat, look for a sitter and call the carer. Tonight I'm going to wine and dine the hell out of you.'

'But—'

He took my face in his hands. 'Natalia. I know it's hard on you because of Beryl. And the twins. You have so many responsibilities. I understand that. But you're not going to be of any use to anyone if you're not also taking care of yourself.'

'Myself?'

'Yes, remember you? Don't you deserve a break too?'

Put like that, it made sense, in theory. But in practice, it meant abandoning my mother who was becoming more and more restless and dependent on me as the days went by.

I dragged out a long, tired sigh and he took my hand. I looked up at him. 'She was always so stern and strict and unaffectionate. But at least she was my mother in her right mind, you know?'

'I know, Nat. But you never can tell what the silver lining can be.'

'Yeah.' I snorted, unable to understand.

★

The days of summer slipped by, difficult with Mum but at the same time we managed to snatch some moments of joy and comfort with the girls, out and about in our beautiful Cornwall, or just simply enjoying the garden or the beach. If I looked back today, all I would be able to recall was a myriad of colourful flashes as if from the perfect ice cream commercial, the warm sun on our tanned skin and the girls' laughter and the taste of strawberries in our mouths, watermelon fights and the cry of the seagulls above. Long walks on the beach, soothing chats around the patio table as the sun went down and tea lights floating in glass bowls.

And so many unspoken words between Connor and me, conveyed only by lingering glances and prolonged chats in the semi-darkness after everyone else had been put to bed. Oh, the thrill of wanting to say something, and the will to prolong the bliss of uncertainty just a little while longer.

He was always so kind and caring. On any random day, he'd hand me a cup of tea and I'd look up to see him looking down at me, not exactly smiling or grinning, but with a serenity and total interest in such a mundane task, and I got the feeling that the wellbeing and happiness exuding from him was not only contagious and therefore good for me, but also that it was somehow connected with him being here in my home, and, perhaps, with my family, if not solely me. We got along like hot chocolate syrup on ice cream, and we, as they always say, literally completed each other's thoughts and sentences.

Being together was uplifting, exciting and I couldn't wait to wake up in the morning just to see him, even if to share a cup of coffee and to share our plans for the day. He was always interested in what I had to say and asked questions that I hadn't even considered, but when I thought about them, I knew they were important.

After weeks of intermittent banging and sawing, Connor, with the unwavering help of the twins, finished the tree house. It was huge, almost as big as a real bedroom, with PVC windows that opened and closed. And even pink and purple curtains. There were bean bags for chairs set around a small coffee table, and shelves on a couple of the walls where Connor had hung bunting and fairy lights.

'Can we sleep here tonight?' Amy asked.

Connor glanced at me for help.

'Girls, I don't really want you sleeping in a tree at night out of my sight.'

'Then you come and sleep with us,' Amy suggested.

'Please, Auntie Natty?' Zoe begged.

I rolled my eyes as images of a sleepless night lay ahead of me. 'All right, girls. Just this once.'

'And we want Connor, too,' Amy added.

At that, Connor's eyes swung to mine.

'Oh, well…'

The last thing I needed was to share the same sleeping space with him again.

'We want both of you,' Zoe said with a firm nod.

'Maybe we can take turns,' he suggested.

'We'll see,' I said, and everyone had the sense to leave it at that for now.

But after dinner, the two were already up there.

'Auntie Nat!' Amy called from the top of the ladder. 'Come on!'

'Coming,' I called, gathering the last things we'd need in a canvas bag. Jumpers, flashlights, an extra pillow, a hot water bottle if someone got cold, and some snacks and hot drinks. This would be an interesting evening, going back and forth making sure Mum slept through the night. From my bedroom, I can usually hear her, but from all the way down to the bottom of the garden? Highly unlikely.

But as I looked up from the bottom step, Connor stuck his head out to look down at me, and I swear, he had the look of a five-year-old on his face.

With just a remaining three rungs to go, I transferred my bundle to him, and then he reached out to take my arms.

'I got ya,' he assured me and practically lifted me into his arms. 'Girls,' he groaned in mock exertion. 'What did Auntie Nat eat for dinner, boulders?'

They laughed and I slapped his shoulder. 'Only kiddin',' he said into my ear, causing my entire body to shiver. 'You're a tiny little thing, aren't ya?'

And before I could answer, he gently deposited me opposite him.

'Yayyy!' Zoe clapped, throwing her arms around me. 'Now the whole family is here!'

My eyes swung to Connor's, but neither of us said anything.

'You forgot someone,' Amy corrected her. 'Let's hope Nana didn't hear that.'

'She can't all the way from here, sweetheart,' I said.

'Ah!' Connor said, pointing to a shelf behind me. 'Shall we let Auntie Nat in on our secret?' I turned around and there it was – the baby monitor.

He shrugged. 'Now we don't have to worry about not hearing her if she wakes up.'

'You think of everything, don't you, Connor!'

'Glad you said that,' he said, clicking a little button, and suddenly, the inside of the tree was alight with twinkling fairy lights.

'Oh…' I gasped, realising all too late that I sounded like an eight-year-old. Connor chuckled. 'Fairy lights for my little fairies.'

'Right – let's crack the crisps open!' Amy said.

'But we've just had dinner,' Zoe said.

'Fine, if you're not hungry, I'll have yours too!' her twin shot back.

At that, Zoe looked at me in a panic and I cradled her with my arm. 'No one is taking your share, darling. Amy just likes to joke, is all.'

For a while we sat, identifying every single chirp, scratch and call as the night grew darker, and before we knew it, the girls had drifted off to sleep.

'You comfortable?' Connor whispered as he turned off his flashlight.

I snuggled up in my jumper. 'Yes, thank you. You've built them such a beautiful tree house,' I whispered.

In the darkness, I felt him grin. 'And you've built them a loving home, Natalia.'

Natalia. He hadn't called me that since I had banged my head into the doorjamb when he'd moved in.

I shrugged. 'They're my sister's babies and I love them. Like my own, actually.'

By the light of the fairy lights, I saw him nod. 'Yes, I can see that. Who wouldn't? They are adorable.'

You're adorable, I wanted to say, *for everything you do. And I wish I could tell you how I feel about you. Not only for being the man that you are, but for all you've done for*

Amy and Zoe. And for Mum. And me. Thanks to you, I can finally trust again. And I wish I had been born just a few years later, or you a few years earlier, and that I had met you instead of Neil. We could have had a great love, if you only felt for me what I feel for you.

'Goodnight,' I whispered.

'Goodnight, Nat.'

But it was easier said than done. Hours later, and I was still wide awake.

Somewhere above us a bird shifted in its nest. Connor's arm was flung over his eyes as he lay on his back, the blanket wound around his feet.

Even Mum's steady breathing came over the baby monitor. The entire world was asleep except for me.

That was when Connor stirred and sat up, looking in my direction, and I smiled.

He smiled back and got to his knees. 'You're not sleeping either?'

'No.' I sat up. 'No, I'm wide awake. You?'

'Me, too,' he said.

In the darkness of the tree house, I blinked.

'Care for some lemonade? Or I could bust out the adult goods?'

I smiled. 'Wine?'

'Your favourite.'

'Oh, go on, then.'

I saw his outline as he turned around and fished out a metal flask and two paper cups. 'This way we can destroy the evidence in the morning,' he said, and I could hear the amusement in his voice as he poured a glass for me, and then one for himself and I recalled how attentive he'd been during the evening of the black-tie benefit. He may have looked like a playboy up for some fun, but I was the only one in that room who knew what a warm family man he could be. There was no one like Connor Wright.

If only I could destroy the evidence gathering in my heart. Every day that went by I was getting more and more attached to him. I loved everything about him, from his face, to his voice to his hands and his big broad shoulders. The way he moved, the way he horsed around with the twins, and the way he teased my mother. And the way his eyes met mine, like there was some secret we were keeping under wraps – something only the two of us knew. I loved him, inside and out, no bones about it anymore.

'Here,' he said, taking my hand and guiding it to the paper cup. 'Cheers.'

'Cheers,' I repeated and we both took a sip. It was delicious.

'Hungry?' he said.

I thought about it. 'Yes, I kind of am. Are there any snacks left?'

I heard him fishing around in his bag and then he wrapped my hand around a mini-quiche.

'Connor, please tell me you didn't make these...'

'Well, I'm no Yolanda Amore...'

Ah. 'So you figured out she's my sister.'

He dipped his head. 'You don't need to be a rocket scientist, do you?'

I felt as if I'd betrayed him by not telling him. 'We tend to keep it quiet,' I explained. 'Yolanda's paranoid about all the sickos out there on social media and all.'

'And she's right to be so. But you are doing a fantastic job protecting them.'

'Neil doesn't think so,' I said, realising the wine was already taking its toll.

'Oh? How so?'

'He thinks I made a huge mistake having a lodger. And a male one, to boot.' Oops, had I said 'male' or 'hot'? I was definitely loose-tongued and feeble-brained after a drink or two.

'Nat, he must know that I would never do anything to hurt those two little angels.'

I took another sip. 'I know. I think he's just jealous that he's being replaced.'

He looked up at me, and even in the dim lights, I could see the question in his eyes.

'Replaced as an uncle, or as someone close to you?' he pursued.

That question caught me off guard. Up until now it had only been farcical banter for the sake of my career. But I knew that somewhere in the village he was seeing someone.

'Well, that's hardly possible, is it,' I tittered.

'No?'

'Well, you said you came to Wyllow Cove for love.'

His fingers rasped against his beard in the semi-darkness. 'Did I?'

'You did,' I assured him, but he didn't volunteer any more information, and, biting down on my tongue, I let it go. For now, at least.

'I'm sorry,' I said. 'It's really none of my business.'

'I need to stretch my legs. Would you like to go for a walk around the garden?' he whispered.

'Okay,' I whispered, and together we climbed down the ladder, one of the monitors in my back pocket lest Mum woke up and needed me.

Together we walked the entire length of the garden and back in companionable silence, listening to the night noises. The roaring of the sea in the caves below us sounded hushed from this height and it soothed me.

Without a word, like he'd done that day on the coastal path, Connor took my hand. 'Are you all right?' he murmured and I nodded, whispering, 'You?'

'I'm more than all right,' he said. 'I'm actually quite happy.'

'So am I,' I breathed.

When we reached the patio table, I poured us another glass of wine and we sat for a while, chatting quietly even though the baby monitor was set on one-way only.

And thus we spent the next few nights in secret *rendezvous*, watching the girls fall asleep in the tree, then sneaking down with the baby monitor for a nice walk in the grounds and finally, one last glass of wine.

Eventually the evenings became particularly cool, and I made the twins start sleeping in their room again. Our walk around the grounds, however, had remained a habit we kept religiously. We'd do the tour and then come back to the patio for one last glass of wine before turning in.

And then, late one evening, between the offer of a throw around the shoulders and lingering, entwining fingers, something shifted.

I can't recall who moved first, but as were talking and laughing under our breaths, surrounded by the cover of the night, he suddenly looked up at me and our eyes locked, glistening in the dark. I could barely see his face in the candlelight, but the stillness of his muscles, and the hitch in his breath told me all I needed to know. Before I could open my mouth, he slowly reached across the table, his eyes scanning my mouth, and touched his lips to mine.

When I gasped at the delightful sensation, he pulled back to check my expression, and seeing what he'd evidently hoped to see, he pulled me out of my chair and took my mouth with more urgency.

'Nat,' he breathed. 'I've been wanting to do this for ages.'

I gulped for breath as I pulled him closer to me. 'What took you so long?'

His mouth travelled down my jawline, nipping briefly at my earlobe and I moaned as he took me in his arms.

'I want you so badly, Nat,' he breathed as his hand stole to the buttons down my shirt, his eyes resting on mine, waiting for a sign.

When I nodded, it was like a dam had exploded, and he scooped me up into his arms, his mouth replacing his hand under my shirt, and oh God, when was the last time I'd felt desire, especially like this, so intense that I could hardly breathe?

I tried to think, but no coherent thoughts managed to form in my mind, only new sensations, and coloured fireworks bursting behind my closed lids.

'My room,' I begged, but as he carried me through the orangery and into the kitchen, my mind cleared slightly.

Sarah had the hearing of a dog. 'No, not there, they'll hear us.'

Downstairs was another no-go as Mum sometimes slept very lightly.

'Where, then?' he whispered urgently in between kisses, and then his beautiful face broke out into a grin. 'Five bedrooms in this house and not one viable.'

'Get as far away from the house as possible,' I gasped as I wrapped my arms around his neck and kissed him again while he changed direction and carried me out into the garden and across the lawns, all the way down to the furthest, most secluded corner.

I grabbed the bottom of his T-shirt like my life depended on it and he let me pull it up and over his head, gasping as my hands roamed along his smooth skin over lean muscle.

'Jeans off,' I whispered as I transformed into someone I had never met before.

'Yes, ma'am,' he answered, taking my mouth, his hands roaming over my breasts as I shimmied out of my shorts.

He pulled at my shorts, licking my skin once it had been exposed to the cool summer night. My body responded as he resurfaced, whispering really naughty stuff into my ears, and before I could help myself, I lay naked under him and groaned, 'Oh, *Connor*, love me...'

And then, he suddenly stopped as if I'd hit him over the head. What was happening? Why was his lovely body not on top of mine anymore?

I sat up, more dazed than confused. 'Connor...?' I whispered, but he moved aside, pulling his jeans back on.

'I'm sorry, I can't.'

What? Weeks of dreaming this very moment, of dreading

doing the wrong thing and talking myself in and out of it over and over, and now, *he* couldn't do it? What had I done wrong? I tried to retrace my steps, but all I got were flashes of hands on naked flesh, and shallow breathing teamed with whispered naughtiness.

He gently pulled me up, bundling my naked body into the throw I'd had wrapped around my shoulders. But I wasn't about to let him dump me like a sack of potatoes.

'Let me down,' I said.

He hung his head and let me slide down his body, which was still aroused. So what the hell had happened between us? If he still wanted me, why didn't he *want* me?

'Let me help you to your room at least.'

Help me to my room? Was this a joke?

'I can walk, thank you,' I snapped as I reached down to retrieve my clothes, conscious of my naked butt. Just what had I done wrong? And then it hit me. I had said *Love me, Connor.* I hadn't meant it that way. I mean, I had, of course, but only physically. I hadn't asked him for anything else. Better make it clear to him. But how? I couldn't just say: *I only wanted the sex, which you didn't want to give.* As much as I'd wanted him, and still did, I didn't want to seem that needy.

As I flung my arms into my shirt, he took a step closer, caressing my cheek with his index. 'Forgive me,' he whispered. 'But it's better this way.'

Better for who, the woman you came here for but actually never talk about? I wanted to snap, but instead I shoved my feet into my shoes with an embarrassed 'Goodnight' before I fought my way back inside and up the stairs, struggling to keep my breath even as tears streamed down my face. My dream of having found a man like Connor had ended once and for all.

The next morning, I woke up as the dawn birds were singing. When I caught sight of myself in the dresser mirror, wild-haired and puffy-faced, I wanted to die.

The house was silent, and by the time I'd showered and dressed, I was certain that Connor was holed up in his room due to the embarrassment of last night. But when I checked the drive for his Jeep, it was gone.

14

Because You Thought You'd Figured Him Out

In the cold light of day, I realised that if he was still with the other woman, then *I* had been about to be the other woman, and stopping himself had been the right thing to do. Perhaps not many men would have had the decency to stop. If only Neil had behaved similarly with his little bit on the side. But none of this had any bearing anymore, as I now knew what my place was, i.e. Connor's landlady for another few months. I wondered how I was going to be able to look him in the face for the duration of the rest of the lease. Or if he'd have the decency to find somewhere else to live. Which would mean that I wouldn't see him anymore, not even as a friend, or a friend to the twins.

At that idea, I pushed down a stab of panic with a surge of dignity instead and forced myself to think of something else – anything else – and made a mental list of my chores for the day. Only my duties towards the girls and my mother would get me out of bed.

So I peeled myself off the mattress, washed my face, brushed my teeth and hair, all the while avoiding looking at myself in the mirror, lest my reflection said to me: *I know what you did*. And then I dragged myself downstairs and to Mum's bedroom.

'Good morning, Mum. Did you sleep all right?' I asked as I opened all the windows wide, catching sight of the garden where I'd made a fool of myself.

But today her mood was no better than mine.

'Ready for your ablutions?' I asked, trying to inject as much cheer as possible into my voice. 'I've got your favourite flowery dress ready, and after breakfast we can take a walk around the grounds. Your leg has healed nicely now and you're doing very well. What do you say?'

I needed this. I needed Mum to cooperate today of all days in order for me to stay absolutely and totally upbeat to avoid falling apart completely. At least for today. Tomorrow, we'd see.

Mum sat up and stared at me as if I'd fallen straight into her bedroom via the roof.

'Who the hell are you?' she demanded.

I looked at her in dismay. *Please, Mum. Not today. Please recognise me. I need your support and the kind words that you have managed to unearth after so many years. I need you to be the mother that you never have been. I need you more than ever now.*

I sat down on the bed next to her and took her frail hand. 'I'm your daughter Natalia, Mum.' *Do you not remember me? Please try to remember.*

'Natalia?' she whispered, searching the depths of her cavernous mind.

I nodded. 'Yes, Mum, remember me?' I bit my lip as I'd read to never use that phrase.

'Of course I remember you. You're my little baby.'

I smiled. Better than nothing. At least she was kind again now.

'You are my pride and joy,' she added, and I realised she thought I was Yolanda again.

She tapped her finger in my direction and smiled. 'Ever since the day we brought Yolanda back from the hospital and you took her into your arms so tenderly, I knew that you had a heart of gold. You have always been special, Natalia.'

I stared at her. And swallowed. She *remembered* me after all.

'And where's Giovanni?'

I sat back. 'Giovanni?'

'My son,' she said, disappointed that I wouldn't remember.

I shook my head. 'Mum, there is no Giovanni. You don't have a son. You have two daughters, Natalia, the eldest, and Yolanda.'

'Yolanda…' she said, searching again.

'That's right, Mum. Natalia and Yolanda.'

'For Christ's sake, stop calling me Mum,' she said. 'I don't even know you.'

'I'm afraid she won't be getting any better, Natalia,' Dr Simpson informed me when I finally managed to get him on the phone. I swiped away my silent tears. I knew I was being a big baby, but I still needed my mother, however cold she had been with me.

'She is creating false memories to fill in the gaps that she can't account for,' he explained.

'It's so strange,' I said. 'She can remember stuff from the distant past. She can even still play the piano.'

'That's because she learned it when she was a girl. That part of her brain hasn't shrunk yet.'

'Shrunk?'

'Sorry, it's terminology my colleagues and I use when discussing patients.'

'I understand,' I said.

'Nat! Nat!' my mother called.

'I have to go now, Dr Simpson, she's calling me again,' I said.

'Be strong, Natalia. And be patient, above all.'

'Thank you. I will,' I promised, and hung up to go to her room, but before I got there, I found her in the hall, frozen, clutching at the walls, as if afraid to move. She should not have got up without my assistance, she knew that, but had forgotten once again.

'What is it, Mum? Did you hurt your ankle?' I asked, gently taking her by the elbow.

'Where's the bathroom?' she said.

'Here, let me take you,' I offered, but she shook me off. 'I don't need your help.'

'But you'll fall,' I insisted. I knew I had to humour her in everything, but I couldn't let her fall and break her other ankle as well, could I?

Eventually we got to the bathroom and back to her room, where, exhausted, she collapsed into bed and fell asleep immediately.

I turned off her bedside lamp and sat on the edge of

the bed for a while, just to make sure she was all right. Of course it would be much easier if I hadn't had to bring my poor mum here rather than let her stay in the comfort and familiarity of her own home.

The next morning I quickly dropped the girls off at school, leaving Mum, technically, on her own to watch her morning show, as I was effectively avoiding asking Connor for anything. In fact, I hadn't actually seen him for two nights and a day now.

'Mum,' I said. 'Would you like to come and sit in the garden? It's a lovely morning.'

But she simply stared at me, and before I could do or say anything, she reached out and clawed at my face, poking my eye and scratching my cheek, and suddenly, I'm ashamed to say, everything came to the fore: Connor refusing me, Octavia's impossible demands, Yolanda's complete washing her hands of her own children, Mum's estrangement from reality and even Neil's obvious disdain of my life choices.

'Mum, you're driving me nuts!' I hollered in exasperation and she simply stared at me as if I was the one who'd lost her marbles. I wiped the blood away from my face and reached for a tissue. The scratch was deep and hurt like hell, but I just dabbed at it as I realised that I had committed the unforgivable sin.

I had lost it. She didn't know she was ill. She couldn't connect the dots between her bouts of incoherence. To her, she was just fine. *I* was the one not making any sense to her in her poor, poor mind. This fragile old woman was just a shadow of her strong self – a faded, incomplete memory. A husk. And I had shouted at her. It wasn't her fault.

Everything else in the past had been. She'd been a terrible mother to me. She had been completely indifferent while I, a small child, had needed her love and attention. And I'd suffered in silence for years, watching while she doted on Yolanda.

But now that our mother needed care and attention herself, Yolanda was nowhere to be found, whereas I was. And I resented it. I also resented myself for this, feeling the lowest of the low.

I immediately sank to my knees before her chair.

'Oh, Mum! I'm so sorry!'

But she just looked at me, and not vacantly like before, but exactly like when I was growing up and she'd caught me doing something very naughty. I wasn't expecting that, not anymore, and it had come as a shock, an unexpected window on the way she had been until only a few weeks ago. But that woman, no matter the look on her face now, was gone forever.

'Please forgive me, Mum…'

I remained on the floor, my head in her lap, clutching her hands, and bawled my eyes out. I cried for the mother that she'd been, for the one I'd instead wanted, and the one I'd never had. I cried also because I was resentful that it had to be me and only me dealing with this. Yolanda always emerged from the dung heaps smelling like a rose, nothing ever touching her. I resented the turn our lives had taken, and how I was having to put all her needs before mine and my own family's when she had never done the same for me. And because Yolanda was very similar to Mum, I cried for the twins, and their future. I also cried for Sarah's broken heart, and my own.

'Hey…' came Connor's kind voice at my side, his warm hand on my shoulder as he gently pulled me up.

When he saw my blood, he started. 'What the f— Did Neil do this to you?' he demanded fiercely but at the same time gently putting a finger under my chin so I had to look at him while wiping the rest of the blood off my face with my tissue. 'Where is he? Did he just leave…? I'm going to fucking kill him—'

I took his hands. 'No, please, it wasn't him. It was my mum. She took a sudden swipe at me and I didn't see it coming.'

My mother looked back and forth between us and shrugged as if to say, *I don't know what the hell she's talking about.*

His eyes widened and he turned to look at her in surprise. 'We've got so much to learn about this,' he said, caressing my face. 'But it'll be okay, Nat. I promise you.'

It would have been nice to let him put his arms around me, but I couldn't afford that anymore. Not after he'd so harshly pushed me away. It turned out he wasn't Mr Right after all. He was the last person I needed to see right now – the personification of my shortcomings and thwarted desires.

'Go away,' I sniffed, swiping my cheeks. 'I'm fine.'

'No, you're not, and I know part of it is my fault.'

At that, I shrugged. What could I say about that? *Yes,*

you broke my heart because I'm madly in love with you, even if you're a huge, selfish jerk?

'Cry if you need to, Nat. But know that it'll be okay.'

I blew my nose and checked my face in the mirror to make sure my eye was still there, all the while refusing to look at him. 'How do you figure that? Everything is falling apart.'

'No, it only seems that way right now because you are exhausted,' he said, taking my hand. 'Come on, let's get that pretty face of yours cleaned up before the girls see you. Besides, it's just a moment. In a half hour you'll be stronger than before. Women are like that.'

'Did your ex-wife tell you that? Or your new girlfriend?' I asked as he poured some disinfectant on a cotton ball and gently dabbed at my face, blowing on it to relieve the sting like you do to little children.

'Okay. For the record, I don't have a girlfriend.'

'What? Promise?' Crap, I shouldn't have said that.

He grinned, and after hours without seeing him, it was like the sun had finally come out. 'Promise. There you go, honey. Good as new.'

Honey. He'd called me honey. No one had called me that in a long time. Shame that it was just a word.

The halcyon days of the summer were rapidly fading for me personally and privately, leaving nothing but a bitter aftertaste in my mouth. The memories of golden sunlight and happy picnics and late-night whispered chats were good and gone, along with my slowly blossoming happiness that had frozen like a flower caught in the frost.

Neil had been right about one thing – Connor did end up hurting me, even if it was all my fault for being such a naïve dolt who had jumped at the first sign of affection. I was an idiot. A needy, weak idiot who had way too much confidence in everyone, including myself.

Perhaps I'd been too happy, too soon, about my divorce. Perhaps, rather than jumping straight to the happiness and raring to get on with the rest of my life, I should have hung back and grieved a little, like most people do.

But divorcing Neil had actually energised me, making me realise how much love, affection, respect – and good old sex – I'd missed out on, because I had only really had Neil in my life, all my life. So after him, I had not wanted to miss out on a thing, and Connor had seemed to me like the refreshing gift from above that I'd deserved after twenty years of misery.

But it had all been a mistake. So I continued to dedicate myself body and soul to the twins, my mother and my column. At the end of each quasi-silent meal, I no longer lingered at the table for a chat with Connor. And when the girls were out, the entire house took on a subdued atmosphere, instead of the joyous, boisterous one it normally had.

All I wanted to do was hide under the duvet all day – actually, make that all week – until I found the courage to look him in the eye again.

All this time I'd basked in the warmth of his kindness and the complicity we'd built together, day after day. I had always had doubts about that other woman, but our growing attachment had made me think that he actually had deeper feelings for me, and that I actually had had a chance at love. That night had been a lesson for me.

★

The next day, I went for a quick grocery run, leaving my mother with Sarah who was working from home that day. But when I got back and arrived at the end of Abbot's Lane, I found a squad car parked out front. I still don't know how I even managed to walk the distance from my car to the kerb as my legs turned to rubber, my mind rushing to catch up with events. Was it Amy? Zoe? Did they get knocked down in the street? Did Sarah collapse? Did Mum have a stroke?

They were all in the living room: the agents, Connor, Sarah... and my mother, pale and shaken with a robe wrapped around her. Beneath that, she was only wearing a slip. I dropped my bags.

'Mum – what happened?'

She looked at me, tears streaming down her cheeks.

Connor was holding her hand. 'I tried calling you, but you'd left your mobile at home.'

'We found her wandering the streets,' one of the agents said.

Wandering the streets?

'I wanted to go home!' she bawled. 'But I got lost. Why did I get lost, Nat? Why can't I remember my way home anymore?'

I knelt before her. 'It's okay, Mum. They've changed the streets a little bit. Everyone is getting lost now, you know? It's not just you.'

She looked up at me, hope opening her face. 'Really?'

'Of course,' I said. 'Yesterday I had to ask someone the way. Everything is so different now. But we'll get used to it,

Mum. I promise you,' I lied, biting my lip, fighting to keep the tears behind my eyes.

'It's all my fault!' Sarah cried, slapping her hands to her cheeks. 'You told me to be careful, but I only left her in the garden for just one moment. Just one moment, and when I came back, I found her dress on the grass, and her walking stick was gone!'

'It's not your fault, Sarah,' Connor said. 'If anything, it's mine. I must have forgotten to look the back gate.'

At that moment, Neil arrived through the open door. 'Sarah? I got your message – what in God's name?'

He practically threw himself at my mother's feet, checking her for fractures. 'Mum? Are you all right?'

'Who the hell are you?' she demanded, kicking him in the thigh. He winced, and opened his medical bag and began checking her blood pressure.

'It's okay, Mum,' I said, stroking her arm. 'This is Neil, a friend of ours. And he's also your doctor.'

'Doctor? I don't need a doctor. I'm not sick.'

He checked her blood pressure, which was fine, all things considered.

'I can't believe you left your sick mother,' Neil said hotly.

'I didn't leave her alone, you know.'

'Yeah – I do know. Sarah called me – her *father*, absolutely terrified because her grandmother had disappeared into thin air. I told you she'd be loopy and to keep an eye on her!'

'Please lower your voice. I have enough problems and I don't need you on my back as well.'

'Problems? Wining and dining your toy boy is now a problem?'

'He's not my toy boy, Neil.'

'That's enough, Neil, not in front of the ladies,' Connor said quietly but firmly. Neil ignored him.

'Not your toy boy? Half of my colleagues are snickering behind my back about this.'

'I knew it was about you, Neil. It always was.'

Connor cut in again. 'Neil, I'm really not at my most patient right now, so I suggest you cut her some slack and go home.'

Neil turned around to face Connor, whose gaze had hardened. 'Are you suggesting I leave my own home?' He challenged.

'You don't live here anymore. You're only upsetting everybody and it's the last thing they need.'

Neil snorted and turned to me. 'Do you really believe that a man his age could actually be interested in you? Because if you do, you're beyond sick in the head. And perhaps you're not the right person to be taking care of your mum. You need help.'

'That's it, we're done here,' Connor said, taking Neil firmly by the arm and frogmarching him out of the house.

'You're absolutely right about that,' I snapped after him and, after giving her one of her sleeping pills, I put my mother to bed and decided to face the last piece of the problem. So I went out to the garden for some privacy. It was a little less warm than it had been lately, and I welcomed the late summer winds to cool me down. I dialled Yolanda's number and she answered immediately.

'Hi, Nat, how are things?'

Oh, just peachy, I wanted to say. *Apart from trying to seduce our lodger, running away from home wearing nothing but her smalls and slippers, Mum is driving me absolutely bonkers.* But I swallowed down my sarcasm. There were better ways to catch honey or whatever the saying was.

'Nat? What is it?'

I sighed. 'Mum's becoming more and more difficult, and she's not getting any better, Yola. She's losing it more and more and today she even took off on me.'

'Where?'

I groaned inwardly. 'Halfway down the road into Wyllow Cove.'

'You lost our mother? What the hell, Nat! What if she'd gone the wrong way and taken the coastal path above the cove? She'd have fallen to her death!'

I couldn't even contemplate that scenario. But she did have a point, of course.

'I can't bloody believe you would let her out of your sight!'

There was no point in dragging Sarah into it. All she'd done was tried to help.

'And I don't understand. First you tell me she can barely walk and now she's so fast you turn around and she's gone? What were you doing at the time, Nat? Screwing your tenant?'

'I beg your pardon?'

'You heard. You're so obsessed with this bloke, it's all you ever think about!'

'Funny, seeing as all I ever manage to think about is taking care of your daughters. And instead of giving me grief, why don't you come home, put your career on the backburner for your own kids – God knows you can afford it – and while you're at it, give me some help. She's your mother too. You do remember that?'

'Nat! I told you this show was important for me.'

'Yes, you told me. A million times. One more gig, one more book, one more year. But the fact is, my dear Yolanda, that your girls spend more time with me than with you – I'm surprised they don't call me Mum instead.'

She huffed. 'Look, Nat – I'm sorry. This will be the last show for a while. And then I can stay home a whole year while I write my next book. I just need to depend on you right now, okay?'

I wanted to growl that it was not okay, that she needed to get her act together. 'You know I love your girls as if they were mine. But *you* are who they need.'

Another huff. 'I know. I'll do my best. Just give me until the New Year. And then I'll come home. With a gazillion presents. I promise.'

'What about Mum?'

She groaned. 'I'm sorry, but just what do you want me to do?'

'Agree to get her a part-time carer. At least when I can't be there.'

'A carer? You never know who you bring into the house that way. I'm already not happy with you exposing my girls to some stranger, no matter how good-looking he is.'

'I never told you he was good-looking.'

She huffed. 'I had a chat with Lizzie and Sarah, okay?'

'About Connor? What the hell for?'

'I just wanted to make sure you weren't being reckless.'

'Reckless? Me? Have I not always been the one with her head on her shoulders? Have I not always been the one to pull you out of trouble every time you went and did something stupid? And now you have the cheek to call me reckless?'

'Don't say that, Nat. I was just worried about you. After your divorce from Neil, I just worried that you might be lonely, or drifting.'

'Drifting? I have never been so focused or happy in my entire life!' I hollered down the phone. 'And Connor has never been part of my plans, no matter what everybody seems to think!' And for the first time ever, I hung up on her. The gall! Only she could rile me like that.

I sat in silence, listening to my thumping heart and my heavily sedated mother snoring without a care in the world, as if she hadn't just been roaming around the village in her smalls. Well, at least the disease spared her the humiliation of realising what she'd done.

A minute later, Lizzie dialled my mobile. 'Mum! Sarah told me – how is Nana?'

'She's fine, sweetheart. Just a little frazzled. Sarah needn't have disturbed you.'

'Are you kidding me? She was frantic. I was just about to drive down when she called me back. She said that Nana has completely lost the plot now? Is that true, Mum?'

That was one way of putting it.

'I'm afraid her disease is progressing, my darling. The medication doesn't always work. Some days she's well, and others she's not.'

'Mum? Is she going to be all right?'

I sighed. 'For now, pet. But she will progressively get worse.'

'It's so strange to see her like this,' Lizzie observed. 'Nana isn't Nana unless she's in control, right?'

'Yes, love.' That was true, as far as her granddaughters were concerned. To me, she had been nothing but scathing. The fact that she had become nice to me was lovely, on one hand, but on the other, it actually worried me, because it meant that she wasn't herself.

And now her Wandering Ulysses complex was becoming worse and worse. To not find her in the same room was already disconcerting. To find her at the end of the garden, reaching for the gate was even worse, but to think that actual harm could have befallen her sent shivers of terror down my spine.

Later that evening, twins and Mum sorted, I removed myself from the kitchen where Connor lingered. Better to stay away from him for the moment until I got a grip on my own emotions.

As I was settling down into bed anticipating a lovely quiet evening with my new Milly Johnson and a nice cup of hot chocolate, I became aware of a scratching sound. She did this, now, as she was falling asleep. She'd run her nails over the ribbed headboard and it was extremely unsettling, like someone breathing raggedly.

After Mum had done a runner, I was now suspicious of every time she turned in her bed, and the baby monitor, which was supposed to have made my life easier, actually made it even harder, because every time she moved or moaned, it kept me from falling asleep and sometimes even jolted me awake.

Every little move she made I was aware. When she coughed, the sound would bounce out of the monitor and onto my walls. When she began to breathe evenly, I knew she was falling asleep. When she began to snore, I could finally surrender to my own rest, knowing that she wouldn't be going anywhere for a few hours. But then she'd suddenly stop breathing and the reptilian or mothering part of my brain would alert me to the fact that all was not as it should be, and was she still breathing? Or was she silently suffocating in the study downstairs? And that would send me flying down the staircase in a panic and throw the door open, only to watch as she turned on her side and started snoring all over again. I had become, in effect, her mother.

As I was cooking the kids' favourite dish for dinner, Connor got in.

'Hi!' he chirped as he came in through to the kitchen. 'Ooh, lasagne, one of my favourite things in the whole world!'

'Good,' I said.

He gave me one of his knicker-melting grins. 'Apart from you, obviously. I'm *particularly* a fan of yours…'

And with that, he leaned in to kiss my cheek.

'No!' I said, moving away from him. 'You don't get to do this – it's not right.'

'Do what?' he said.

'Play these games. One day you seem interested in me and the next—'

And with that, he put his hand under my chin, taking me by complete surprise. It was the first time since we had almost had sex that he had come anywhere near me, and I had missed him. I'd missed the smiles that had only been for me. I had missed him being so close that I could reach out and touch him if I wanted to. And I certainly wanted to. Oh, how I wanted to.

'Nat...?' he whispered. 'Do you trust me at all?'

I closed my eyes so I wouldn't see him. Damn me, and this attraction I had for him. 'Open your eyes, Nat.'

I did as I was told and saw the most solemn expression I had ever seen on his face.

'If I confused you that night, I'm sorry, but I've got other things going on and I didn't want to get you mixed up in them. But please believe me when I say that I would never, ever do anything to hurt you. Do you believe me?'

Did I believe him? 'Yes.'

'Thank you. I will tell you everything as soon as I can, okay?'

Unable to speak, I nodded.

The next day Yolanda video-called me. 'Hullo, how are things?'

'Good,' I answered.

'How's Mum?'

'The same, really.'

'Right.'

'And how are the recordings of your new show going?'

'Absolutely great. Do you want to know the title we've picked?'

'Ooh, of course I do. What is it?' I asked, happy for the distraction.

She flipped her dark mane from one shoulder to the other and flashed me one of her famous television smiles. 'Simple – *That's Amore!*'

I baulked. 'What? You can't use that – that's the name of my column!'

She frowned. 'Is it?'

'You know it is.'

'No matter,' she said. 'They're two completely different things.'

'It actually does matter, Yolanda. I don't want to be mixed up with you.'

She snorted. 'Trust me, you won't be. You only have a small picture for your column – no one really cares who you are.'

'Gee, thanks.'

'I only meant to say that people don't really care who the writer is. They just read the column and that's that.'

'Actually, I'm pretty well known too. Just because I'm not on television doesn't mean I don't count.'

'Jealous much?'

'Yolanda, are you really talking down to me again? I thought we'd sorted this out years ago.'

She huffed. 'Look, I understand it's your surname too, but I need it more than you.'

'How so?'

'Because my show is about Italian cooking!'

'And my column is about life and love, if you'd ever cared to read it.'

'I have read it. Once or twice.'

Only she – and Mum – managed to make me feel this way. I huffed in exasperation. 'Jesus, Yola…'

'Can I help it if I don't have time? If it's any consolation, I've heard it's really good.'

'Just – let's move on, okay?'

She shrugged. 'Okay. What else did you want to talk to me about?'

'Uh, your arrangements with the girls?'

'What do you mean? I thought you said they could stay. You haven't changed your mind, have you?'

'No, I haven't changed my mind, but don't you think we – and by "we" I am including them – don't you think we should know what your plans are? Will you actually *be* here for Christmas, or are you just going to send another parcel like you did for their birthday?'

'I don't like the judgement in your voice, Natalia.'

'Well I'm sorry if my thoughts permeate my tone, Yolanda. They're your girls; when are you going to start taking responsibility for them?'

She took a long slug of her drink, but only after adding, 'You should be grateful for the time with them, seeing as you're an empty-nester now, husband included.'

'I *am* grateful for the time with… What did you just say?'

She kept her face hidden in her glass while looking straight at me. It was the trick we used to use as kids with Mum. We'd tell a blatant lie and act indifferently about it, having figured out we had a better chance of being believed that way. Only becoming a mother had taught me that it didn't work. Yola, on the other hand, had not yet tallied up enough mothering hours yet to have cracked that arcane trick.

She shrugged. 'I'm simply saying that you have more time on your hands because you work from the comfort of your own home. Look at me – I'm always flying off to another country. I have no schedule or routine, and my girls have that now, thanks to you.'

I wanted to counter that she could actually hire a nanny and take them with her while home-schooling them, but that would have meant me not seeing them growing up, so I shut up, the whole purpose of my argument now a moot point.

'In any case, I'll be home after Christmas. I have to shoot a Christmas special. The flight is so long it barely warrants the time and effort to go and come back.'

'Not even to see your daughters?'

'Come on, Nat, you're laying it on thick. Do you think I actually like this life?'

I studied her face on the screen. She hadn't changed since we were kids. She had always been selfish and restless, and flighty. Much more adventurous and fearless than myself. This was the life that fit her like a glove. The lifestyle she craved – minimal responsibilities, her every need catered for, and in the spotlight at all times. Amy and Zoe were just pretty little accessories to her. Loved ones, granted, but more a thing to boast about than to care about.

'Yes, Yola, I actually think you do.'

She shook her head. 'Why is it that you are always ready to judge me? Even when I started this job, you raised your eyebrows!'

'Because you didn't understand how much quality time with your girls it would rob you of. You don't act like they're a priority, but a burden. That's not motherhood. Being a mother means putting your kids first. Always. Why can't you understand that?'

She stared at me as if I'd slapped her. 'If I had done that, I wouldn't be the celebrity I am today. I can afford anything I want, for myself and my girls – even a trip around the world. Can you say the same? No, because you settled with a silly magazine job. Easy to do, when your doctor husband brings home the bacon.'

'Have you thought that maybe before a trip around the world, your daughters need to know that their mother hasn't abandoned them, and that she loves them?'

'I tell them that all the time,' she protested.

'Do you, Yola? Because when I read them a bedtime story, I have to screen the ones mentioning mums, which only trigger questions and self-doubt. No matter how many times I tell them that you love them and that you're working hard for them, I see that it's just not enough.'

Yolanda groaned and bit her lip. If I knew she was capable of guilt, I'd believe her acting antics. But no one knew Yolanda as well as I did.

'Right. I said I was sorry. So, are you okay with keeping them?'

'I am. But if you're going to break their hearts again, I'd rather you did it yourself this time,' I said. And before she could object, I called them. 'Amy, Zoe! It's Mummy on video chat, come!'

The answer was a loud slam of the door, followed by the thundering of footsteps on the stairs. How the heck could two eight-year-olds make all that noise with their tiny feet? But mine had been no better.

'Mummy, Mummy!' Zoe cried, sliding to a halt before my desk.

'Mum, what the hell, why haven't you called?' Amy debuted.

I sighed. That was the twins for you, so different, and yet both so fragile. Amy could put up as many shields as she wanted, but I could tell by the look on her flushed face that she was overwhelmed with joy.

'Darlings!' Yolanda called, covering her mouth in awe. 'Look at you, you've grown so much!'

So I left them to it.

The next Saturday morning when I came downstairs, Connor was on the patio doing French braids for the girls before their football game.

'You don't have to do that, Connor – let me,' I said, taking the comb from his hands.

Connor stuffed his hands into his pockets. 'I don't mind. I'm used to looking after my nieces.'

'He's as gentle as you, Auntie Nat,' Zoe assured me.

I turned around and smiled at him despite myself. 'Is there anything that you can't do?'

'What? Oh...' He laughed. 'Yeah, lots. But, most importantly, I can make you smile.'

I smiled again and patted Zoe's rump. 'Done. Off you go, darling. Get your things and don't be long.'

'I won't, Auntie Nat,' she promised.

I gathered my mobile from the counter, my keys, made

sure I had everything I needed in my football bag – face towel, clean clothes, baps, fruit and drinks included.

'You are so lucky to have such lovely nieces,' Connor said.

'So are you,' I reminded him.

He grinned. 'Yeah.'

'And what do they call you, Uncle Shane?' came Sarah's voice from the doorway.

We both turned to her.

She stood, her face red with anger. I took a step towards her. 'Sarah?'

She moved past me to stand before him, her chin high. 'Or are they just another lie?'

'Sarah, what are you talking about?' I asked as I spied a passport in her hand.

'I'm talking about our friend *Shane*, here. How the hell do you explain this?' Sarah demanded, waving it before his face.

'Sarah!' I gasped. 'What are you doing going through Connor's stuff?'

'Dad warned me – he said to keep an eye on him, and he was right!'

'What are you talking about…?'

'His name isn't Connor! He's been lying to us the whole time!'

I opened my mouth to say something – anything – but nothing came out, and it felt like my head was expanding, as if it was about to explode. I called upon all my inner strength to keep my voice low.

Connor's hands shot to the back of his head, his hands raking through his hair as he breathed in deeply.

'Oh, Jesus.' He looked up between Sarah and me. 'Sarah, I need a minute alone with your mum.'

'Like hell I'm leaving you alone with her!'

'Please, Sarah,' he said softly. 'You know that I would never hurt her – or any of you. A moment is all I ask.'

I eyed my daughter, wanting both to protect her and myself from all this. But I didn't have a choice. 'Go, Sarah. The girls have been looking forward to this game all season and you're going to make them late.'

Her eyes swung to me in doubt and she finally nodded. 'Okay. But I'm calling Dad,' she huffed, pulling her phone out of her pocket.

'You'll do no such thing, Sarah. Now run along.'

Her eyes widened. 'Mum – this bloke lied to us, he could be anybody, for Christ's sake!'

He raised his hands. 'Sarah—'

I gestured to him and the chair in the corner. 'You. Sit there.'

'Okay,' he said, his hands falling to his sides as he sat.

'Sarah,' I said. 'This is my problem and I will take care of it. The girls are waiting for you.'

Sarah, who had been high on adrenaline, now came down on a soft sob. 'Okay, Mum. I will. But you!' she cried, her finger shaking as she pointed at Connor. 'You watch yourself.'

When the front door slammed behind her, he made to get up but I backed away and he sat again, hands raised. 'I meant what I said. I wouldn't hurt you for the world, Nat.'

'You already have.'

He lowered his head. 'Yes.'

'And you wormed your way into our household under a false name.'

'Yes.'

'So give me one bloody good reason why.'

He took a deep breath. 'You know, deep inside, that you can trust me.'

'Trust you? I don't even know who you are! Nor why you're here, filling our heads with *lies*! It was all too good to be true!'

He bit his lip, spreading out his hands once again. 'I'm an idiot, Nat. I wanted to tell you but I could never find the right moment. I'm *so sorry…*'

'Why did you lie to us?' I cried.

His shoulders hunched under the weight of his words. 'Because I didn't want… Yolanda… to know it was me.'

My heart sank. 'Yolanda? Why? What are you, one of her stalkers who can't afford a ticket to New York so he settles for the next best thing instead?'

'Stop it, Natalia,' he said, getting angry. I'd never seen him angry before. But then, I'd known him for what, five minutes? 'I'm not a stalker and I'm not here to hurt anyone.'

'So what is it, you have a crush on her, and were hoping to wheedle your way into her life through the girls and our family?'

His mouth clamped shut and his eyes fell to the floor. 'Neither of those things, Nat.'

'Well, then what!' I shouted. 'Why did you come into my home? Just so you could trample all over my heart?'

It was too late. I'd said it, and now there was no turning back. No hiding from my own words.

He got to his feet and made to take my arms, but I backed away.

His eyes widened in hurt as his arms fell to his sides again and he hung his head. 'I've been trying to tell you since I got here. But I never had the courage.'

'What are you hiding from me? Tell me!' I crossed my arms in front of my chest and kept my distance.

'It's a relief actually, to confess,' he whispered, almost as if to himself as he ran a hand through his hair and looked up at me. 'I was younger, in my final year at uni. One night, while playing at Temple Bar with my band, I met a woman. She was a lot of fun. I took her back to my place where she spent the night.'

Images of Connor, no – *Shane* – with another woman stabbed me in the heart but there was no room for my pain. He'd *lied* to me! 'And that interests me how?'

He scratched his face and rubbed his mouth. 'We both knew that it was never going to be more than one night. So we said our goodbyes, and I never saw her again. Until a few years later, on the cover of a cookbook. And then I saw her on her own cooking show.'

My heart shot to my throat and my mouth suddenly went dry. 'Yolanda? You slept with my *sister*?' I gasped.

'I swear I didn't even know who she was at the time and I had almost forgotten about that night until I saw her on an old show featuring her children. All it took was one look at them – I recognised their eyes and their gestures – just like my own nieces, and instantly I *knew*.'

'Knew...?' Shards of panic shot through my veins. No. Oh, no, no, no!

'And then it all came back to me,' he said. 'Yolanda told

me that she was on the pill so there was no danger of her getting pregnant, so we didn't use any protection. It was silly, I know, but—'

Oh my God in heaven. 'So you think that the twins are—?'

'I know it, Nat. Zoe and Amy are my daughters,' he whispered, getting up and taking my arms. 'My own flesh and *blood*...'

His daughters? Impossible. Absolutely impossible. I mean, what were the odds? But of course one night was more than enough. 'H-how can I believe you?' I said.

'I know I was wrong to not tell you straight away, but honestly, if I'd rung your doorbell and said, *Hello, I had sex with your sister years ago and I'm pretty sure I'm the father of her children*, what would you have said?'

The thought alone of him having sex with my sister was enough to blow my mind and make me run a thousand miles. But this wasn't about me.

'But Yolanda couldn't have kids until she had IVF!' I assured him.

'Well, apparently she could. Although she told me she was on the pill...'

'So she doesn't know that you know?'

'No. I wanted to do it slowly.'

'I'll say,' I spat.

'Nat, hear me out – this is a delicate situation. I don't want to upset anybody.'

'It's a bit too late for that.'

'I'm so so sorry, Nat...'

'Does Yolanda even know that Piers isn't... their father?' I asked, finally sinking into the chair opposite him.

'I don't know, I haven't spoken to her since.'

It was true that they looked nothing like Piers, but still…

'Ask Yolanda if you don't believe me. See if she doesn't recognise me. Although I was hoping to do that myself when she returned, but if it means regaining your trust, Nat—'

'Trust?' I cried. 'You talk about trust? You came into my home with the intent of gleaning information about my family under a false name! And then, when the twins moved in, you couldn't believe your luck!'

'True,' he whispered. 'I had never imagined I'd be able to spend time with them and get to know them.'

'You had it made. They practically fell into your arms. And you talk to me about trust? And all in such a dishonest, despicable way. You lied to me.'

'Nat…'

'You could have told me!' I cried. 'You could have spoken to me and explained how things were, rather than just passing yourself off as a prospective lodger! I can't believe you did this! Oh my bloody God!'

'I wanted to tell you, Nat. But I didn't know how and then the entire situation mushroomed and… You think this was easy for me? I had everything to lose! If you doubted me one iota, you'd have called the police and kicked me out. I couldn't risk losing contact with the girls, never being allowed to see them again.'

I watched him. I'd never seen him upset before. Well, in effect, I hardly knew him.

He clenched his fists. 'From that day, when I saw them on TV, I lost any sense of inner peace. I only have the best intentions. You have to believe me. I have to *be* with my daughters. I can't just turn my back and pretend they don't exist.'

I leaned forward under the weight of everything he was saying, trying to put it all in a semblance of order and logic. But it all kept scrambling and re-scrambling in my mind and I was more confused than before.

'I came to see how they were doing,' he added. 'And I'd heard somewhere that Yolanda was divorced.'

'And you wanted to take his place,' I scoffed and he stared at me as if I'd slapped him.

'No, Nat – it's not like that,' he whispered. 'Christ, don't you *know* me by now? I was just wondering how they must have been missing their father, and whether it was the right moment for me to step up to the plate. Probably not, as it is, but I can't just discover I have two daughters and walk away.'

I groaned and buried my head in my hands.

'Nat...? I know you're going to be livid, but there's more.'

My head snapped up. 'What more could there possibly be?'

He bit his lower lip, studying his hands. 'I secretly carried out a DNA test, just to be sure.'

'You *what?*'

'I took a strand of hair from Zoe and Amy's brushes. I know I shouldn't have, but they are my priority. Look, here, I have a copy of the results in my wallet,' he offered and dug into the back pocket of his jeans.

I unfolded the sheet of paper containing the results that would change a good many lives, recognising the address of the medical centre in Truro at the top. And there it was, the truth, in black ink.

If my first reaction was to be furious, my second was to realise he'd done the right thing. There would have been no point in alarming anyone, especially Yolanda and the girls until he had been sure. But now he was, with a truth the size of Truro cathedral.

'I'm so sorry, Nat…' he whispered. 'I know I've hurt you, but if you would only—'

'You can't be here, right now,' I said. 'I need you to leave, please. Now.'

His eyes fell to the floor, and his jaw worked in total silence. Then he slowly nodded. 'Of course. You're absolutely right. I'll go upstairs and… pack.'

'Thank you.'

In five minutes he was back down with his duffel bag strapped over his shoulder, a look of complete desolation on his face. He cleared his throat. 'Your keys,' he whispered, handing them to me. 'Please forgive me, Nat.' And with that, he opened the front door and quietly slipped out of the house, and our lives.

As I climbed the stairs, it all came back to me, a collage of instances when he'd been very fatherly. Like the time he'd pulled up Zoe's socks up for her. Or the time he'd kissed the top of Amy's head after he'd finished braiding her hair. Or the time he'd held Zoe in silence without any apparent reason.

All this time it had been sitting under my nose – the huge, blatant truth, and I had been so wrapped up in myself and my own feelings about a complete stranger that I had been utterly blind to it.

I had failed my sister and her babies terribly. I had let myself be fooled – for the second time in my life – by the charm of a handsome man who had only used me and my stupidity to get what he wanted. How could I have believed him so instinctively? I was never wrong about people. But this was the biggest mistake of my life. I couldn't bring myself to believe it. But all the evidence was there.

It took an entire night of tossing and twisting in my bed, debating and thinking, and yet, I still didn't know what the right thing to do was.

I thought of the consequences of not telling Yolanda, because, whatever her mistakes in the past were, she didn't deserve them to come back at her in such a way. And the girls would only be confused about all this.

But I had no right to keep this monumental information from her either. Yolanda had a right to know.

It needed to be done serenely and clearly, and I was the only one who could bridge the gap between Yolanda and her former lover. The irony of it did not escape my notice.

The next morning I rose early and went for a stroll down the coastal path to the beach in the effort to clear my frazzled mind. And who, of all people, did I bloody bump into? Exactly.

He – *Shane* – was coming towards me, his hands stuffed in his pockets. We both stopped, face to face, just a few feet between us.

'Hi,' he said softly, his eyes searching mine.

'I think you know what you have to do,' I whispered.

He nodded. 'I've been thinking about it all night. I have to tell Yolanda. And I have to do it now.'

'Yes,' I whispered, wondering how the girls would take

such news. It was one thing to be fond of a friend, but another to discover at eight years of age that your friend wasn't your friend, but your father.

'Nat – I'm so sorry I lied to you. But I did it for everyone's good.'

I held up my hand. 'I don't want to hear it anymore. Just do what you have to do.'

He ran his hand through his hair again. 'Okay,' he said. 'Can you please video-call her, and prepare her? I don't want to scare her. She might have forgotten all about me after all these years.'

I very much doubted that. One did not simply forget someone like Conn— Shane Wright. I heaved a huge, exhausted sigh, actually ready for bed again.

'Let me send Yolanda a message first,' I said, feeling a hundred years old. 'Give me a moment.'

'Okay. Thank you,' he whispered as I pulled my mobile out of my pocket, my heart hammering all the way to my head. Poor, poor Yolanda. I didn't want to be her in that moment. I typed the message:

Hi Yola. All okay here. Got a minute to Skype?

A moment later Skype began its familiar chiming and when I pressed the answer button, her beautiful face filled my screen. I pasted a huge fake grin on my own face, feeling the muscles pulling out of place, and a surge of pity for the shock she was about to receive.

'Hey,' she said. 'Is everything okay?'

'Everything's fine,' I said, stalling for time. 'How are you?'

She sighed. 'Busy as usual. What's up?'

I hesitated and looked sideways to the stranger before me.

'I want you to meet my tenant,' I said. 'His name is Shane and I believe he's an old friend of yours, too, Yolanda...'

She frowned. 'Shane? I know loads of Shanes.'

'Well, one in particular is here, and he has something very important to tell you.'

'Oh?'

I beckoned to him to move in next to me. As Yolanda set eyes on him, her face went from curious to frozen. I checked the connection, but it was fine. And then I saw the recognition in her eyes. But I didn't only see recognition. I also saw trepidation and I knew she had immediately connected the dots. She had known all along!

'You...?' she whispered, and then: 'What are you doing with my sister?'

'Hi, Yolanda,' he whispered, wiping his palms along the length of his thighs. 'I guess we've both got a lot of explaining to do.'

I moved further towards the shore line to leave them their space. But even with the sound of the waves lapping onto the sand, his deep voice drifted over to me.

'...spend time with them... whatever makes you feel comfortable...'

Then, after what seemed forever, he came to stand next to me, his gaze lost on the horizon as he passed me my mobile. 'Yolanda wants to speak with you.'

He looked as if he'd dropped a hundred-pound burden from his chest.

I stepped away and began to walk up the beach. 'Hey…'
I whispered. 'How are you?'

She raked a hand through her hair. 'What can I say? It's
all so bloody surreal…'

'Is what he said true, then?'

Yolanda bit her lip and nodded. 'I-I met him one night
and he was so charming, so fun and flirty,' she confessed.
'The exact opposite of Piers. And we had crazy-amazing
sex. Piers and I were doing IVF because I couldn't get
pregnant. And when I did, I just knew Shane was the father,
and as the girls grew up, I could see it. Jesus Christ, what
were the odds?'

I nodded. Exactly what I'd thought.

'But how come you never contacted him? You knew
where he lived,' I asked.

'Yeah, can you imagine me, Yolanda Amore, celebrity
chef, cooking up a scandal with a hot university student?
No. Plus, in the morning we agreed to go our separate ways,
no hard feelings.' Yolanda took a deep breath. 'Is it true,
that they get along well?'

'Like a house on fire,' I said, despite myself. 'You should
see the way he keeps Amy at bay, and encourages Zoe. I
swear you wouldn't recognise them.'

She leaned forward, closer into the screen. 'That's it, Nat.
I'm coming home. It's time to give those girls of mine some
roots.'

'But they can still spend time with me?' I begged.

She rolled her eyes. 'Of course.'

'Thank you, Yola. Thank you. And Connor – Shane – he
may have lied to us, but he honestly does love the girls. I

can see it in his every gesture.' Which was nothing but the truth.

She smiled. 'I know. I can't wait to come home and see how it goes.'

'You'll be fine, Yola.'

'Nat?'

'Yeah?'

'I can't begin to express my gratitude for all you've done for me and the girls.'

'We're family, Yola,' I whispered.

'Yes,' she whispered. 'But nobody does family better than you. Will you be there, by my side?'

'Of course.'

She nodded as she swiped a tear and my heartstrings twitched.

'Hurry home, Yola.'

She smiled. 'I'll be on the first plane back.'

'What about your show?'

'Screw the show. My family is more important. Besides, we have insurance for stuff like this.'

I grinned. 'Okay, then. We'll be waiting.'

She blew me a kiss and her face faded to black.

'Nat?' came Shane's voice from behind me. 'I wanted to thank you, from the bottom of my heart for understanding and giving me the benefit of the doubt.'

I stood there, trying to take in all that had happened, trying to remember all the things he'd said, to see if there had been any indications, any clues or slips anywhere. And then, his words came back to me. *I did it for love.* So he hadn't come for the love of a woman. He had come for his daughters. But even so, how would I personally ever be able to trust him again after this charade that had lasted all summer, after all his lies?

'I can't be anywhere near you, uhm… Shane,' I whispered, turned, and ran all the way home.

Once inside, I swiped my eyes and went in to check on Mum.

She was in her chair, taking her morning nap, lightly snoring as usual. I tucked the coverlet around her and finally crept up to my own room to have a jolly good sob before the girls got up and I'd have to pretend everything was okay.

The next morning I woke up feeling like an empty hot water bottle, absolutely drained dry. After a night of crying and tossing, I slowly crawled out of bed and into the shower, which did absolutely nothing to wash away the feeling of utter betrayal clinging to me. I tried to put myself in Shane's shoes. But I wasn't doing a very good job of it.

When I went downstairs about ten minutes later, the doorbell rang. It was Shane. His eyes were red and his voice raw.

'I didn't want to leave without saying goodbye,' he simply said, his eyes not quite meeting mine.

I sighed, and it took me all the energy I had. 'I need no more explanations, Shane,' I said, the new name sounding alien. 'I'll have Yolanda call you when she flies in.'

'Nat…'

'No. You sort yourselves out. And please don't call me.'

His shoulders slumped. 'As you wish. If you change your mind, I'll be at a friend's down the coast in Little Kettering.'

'Goodbye, Shane,' I whispered and closed the door on my very own heart.

What had been my love, my family, those who needed me, now no longer did. My own girls were grown up, Yolanda would soon be back for her kids, and now even their father was on the scene. I was superfluous to say the least. So maybe it really was finally time for me to start thinking about my own life and my own little dreams.

15

The Homecoming

A few days later Lizzie, Sarah and I piled the kids and their things into my car for the five-minute drive to their own home. Yolanda was due in less than an hour. Once there, the girls shot to their rooms and I busied myself with airing the downstairs areas.

Lizzie kept stealing me worried glances. I smiled at her and shook my head. 'It'll be all right, Lizzie. Yolanda and Shane will sort it out.'

'I'm sure they will, Mum. It's you I'm worried about.'

'Me?' I echoed.

'Mum – we'd all have to be blind to not see that you have feelings for him.'

I shrugged. 'Maybe I had feelings for Connor. I have no idea who *this* bloke is.'

'Maybe, if you just gave him a chance, Mum?'

'Sweetheart, Shane Wright has a lot on his plate now. He certainly doesn't need any more complications in his life. Besides, there was nothing between us.'

'But there still could be, no?'

I thought about it. 'No, Lizzie. There's no room in a relationship of any kind, for lies.'

'But he tried to tell you, didn't he?'

'Tried is not enough, Lizzie.'

And then we heard the sound of a car door slamming shut in the drive. 'That's Aunt Yolanda's taxi. No more of this in front of her. This is none of her business, okay?'

Lizzie went to say something, but her mouth snapped shut at the look on my face. She nodded.

'Good girl.'

'Mummy, Mummy, Mummyyyy' the girls hollered as they flew down the stairs and flung the front door open. They threw their arms around Yolanda who grabbed them fiercely. After a seven-hour flight, she still managed to look amazing in a white trouser suit.

'Oh, my beautiful, beautiful girls! I've missed you so much!' she cried as tears sprung from her eyes and I had one or two to wipe away myself.

After a long moment, she looked up at me. 'Thanks you so much, Nat. How were they?'

'Absolute gems,' I assured her.

'Mummy, did you bring us any presents?' Amy asked.

'Oh yes, my darlings! I have lots and lots of presents for you in those two suitcases! The purple one's for you, Amy, and the pink one is for you, Zoe.'

'Yayyy, thank you, Mummyyyy!' they shouted, and soon it was like a piñata had burst in the room as shreds of tissue paper flew into the air and rained back down on the two happiest girls I'd ever seen.

God willing, Yolanda was back to stay, at least for a

while. That would be enough time to get to know them again, while introducing the idea of Shane Wright as their real father.

After a quick Indian take-away, Lizzie drove back to Truro and Yolanda went upstairs with the girls to read them a bedtime story while I did the washing up. Yolanda would have a lot of questions when she came back downstairs. I only wished I had the answers.

'So,' she said as she came into the kitchen. 'What a crazy story, huh?'

Crazy was an understatement. I finished drying the last glass, put it away and filled the kettle as Yolanda sat back, finally relaxing.

I pulled out the mugs, coffee and sugar. And almost cried with nostalgia when I remembered that I'd given Shane salt instead of sugar in his coffee, one day, a million years ago.

'Tell me everything from the beginning,' she urged me.

So I did. Minus how he'd agreed to be my public toy boy to help me keep my job. And minus my attraction to him that was only mildly reciprocated while awaiting for the real deal, i.e. her, the mother of his children.

'Now it's your turn,' I said as we drank from our mugs.

She plonked hers down on the table with a thud and rolled her eyes. 'Oh, God, where to start? About the Temple Bar, you know. Imagine my shock when I found out I was pregnant. I was a horrible wife and I'm a horrible mother,' she blurted, reaching for a napkin to wipe her eyes.

'Don't say that,' I offered. 'You're just busy. Very busy.'

She looked up. 'You know what Bill said to me the other

day after my Zoom chat with the kids? He said, "You see more of your crew than you do your own girls." And it hurt like hell, Nat – because it's true. And you know why that is?'

I shook my head. Offering my opinion, that she was too ambitious for her own good seemed an unkind thing to say, especially after this mega brick had fallen on her head. Well, our heads, truth be told.

She wiped her eyes and blew her nose. 'Because I've always known Shane was the father. And I've been so racked with guilt all these years!'

'Did you ever think of confessing to Piers?'

She snorted. 'Why do you think he left me, Nat?'

'Piers... knew?'

'Oh, he was no idiot. I was away for at least six weeks. All he had to do was do the math.'

I stared at her. 'Yola... but you never told me any of this – I could have been there for you.'

She shrugged, blowing her nose. 'It wouldn't have changed anything, Nat. Piers was probably sick of my crazy hours and travelling anyway. But it helped me to forget. It still does.'

I put an arm around her shoulder. 'Yola, I had no idea, I'm so sorry.'

She looked up at me. 'I know you think I am a terrible mother and I deserve it. But all these years I was just trying to run away from the guilt. Certainly not my girls. I love them to pieces and have made the decision to be a more hands-on mother. I'm going to finally stop and stay home for a bit. I'll write that next book, and learn to be a proper mum.'

My hand flew to my heart. 'Oh, Yolanda, you don't know how happy the girls will be!'

She dried her eyes. 'But I'll need your support, Nat.'

'Of course.'

'Especially now that Shane is in our lives. The girls wouldn't stop going on about him.'

'W-what are you going to do about him?' I asked her.

She leaned forward and took my hand. 'Is he a good man? Besides the lie?'

I hesitated. 'He loves the girls and wants to be a good father for them.' Which was true. The fact that he had stepped all over me to do so was only a side effect.

'So you think he would be good for them?'

I thought about all the laughs and the horsing around and the picnics on the beach and the tree house and how they gravitated around him. 'Yes. Shane is perfect for them.'

For me, not so much. But he'd be perfect for Yolanda, and the realisation that he would think so too had hit me all too soon.

Nostalgia of what could have been, and what was going to become of his new family had my insides in a twist. I realised that I had gone from being the driving force of the family to the odd one out. Now that Yolanda was back, she wouldn't need me as much. Nor would the girls. And it was only right that they all made up for lost time.

'Okay. Because I want to meet him tomorrow.'

'He's gone to stay in Little Kettering,' I informed her.

'I know,' she said. 'We exchanged phone numbers. He's at Mitchell's, an old university buddy. I've invited Shane over tomorrow morning for a cup of coffee and a chat on how to do this. And if we fit, we'll see what's what, and take one day at a time.'

I exhaled. It had already begun. 'I'm going home now, Yolanda. I think I will step back for a few days. You all need time as a family to sort this out among yourselves.'

She got up and hugged me. She rarely hugged me. 'I understand. Thanks for your help, Nat. I don't know how I would've managed any of this without you.'

'You'd have managed, Yolanda,' I said. She always did.

The next few weeks went by in an absolute blur. Hannah Williams had lined up a series of viewings for The Mausoleum and within the week I received a generous offer from the very first family that had viewed it.

Without wasting a minute, I made my own generous offer on Lavender Cottage, which was accepted. Serendipity trying to get back into my good books?

It took me and a crew of movers another week to pack up my stuff alongside Mum's few belongings. She watched me come and go, most of the time amused, if a little confused.

'It's all right, Mum. We're finally moving out of this place,' I said, sitting on the arm of her recliner. Everything else that Neil had left behind I had donated to charity, and oh what a feeling of liberation that had given me!

'Where are we going?' she asked.

I bent down and kissed her paper-thin cheek. 'We're finally going home, Mum.'

'About time. I hate this old folks' home,' she sentenced.

I laughed and patted her hand. 'From now on, Mum, I'm going to live next door to you.'

'Okay, but no smothering me,' she said.

I beamed at her. 'No smothering. I promise.'

After a lunch of tomato soup and hot rolls, I went to Lavender Cottage for another look. Although it needed massive renovating, I wasn't in the least bit fazed. The peeling wallpaper and the scuffed floorboards could be sorted. All the house needed was new plumbing, new electrics and a facelift. Nothing, compared to what I'd been through. For the first time in my life, I was finally home. The heartache due to losing Connor, a man who had never actually existed, would have to wait.

I was weeks away from exchanging contracts with both my buyers and my seller, but Sarah had already found a delightful little flat in Truro, so Lizzie, Liam and I helped her move her things in.

Personally, I had only got as far as moving out of The Mausoleum, spring-cleaning Mum's cottage and moving my stuff into my old bedroom up in the eaves. It was so small that I still don't know how Yolanda and I managed to get twin beds in there without sleeping on top of each other.

Sleeping with Yolanda had been a nightmare. She had always talked and talked, well into the night. Good luck to Shane with that. He'd discover her idiosyncrasies for himself now.

I wondered what was going on at Yolanda's place that very moment. No doubt she and Shane were hammering out the details of their new situation and making plans for the future. Sorting out a family routine and setting ground rules. I was determined to stay out of their lives and trudge on with my own. I, too, was making a brand-new start. And my own decisions.

And speaking of, the very next day I took the train into London to tell Octavia that I wouldn't be doing any more toy boy articles.

When she shook her head and sucked air in through her teeth, I made another flash decision before she could say anything.

'And I'm handing in my resignation. Effective immediately.'

To which she simply answered. 'Suit yourself. Those articles were your meal ticket.'

'I don't need a meal ticket, Octavia,' I replied. 'I'm going freelance. Good luck with *Lady*.' And as I got up from my chair, warm, tingly tendrils of pride zapped across my skin and I exhaled in relief. Finally! I was getting my life back.

On my way out, Vera, our Agony Aunt, called out to me. 'Oh, Nat, we're going to miss you around here! This letter arrived for you a few weeks ago but we forgot to forward it to you. I'm so sorry. I hope it wasn't important.'

I looked down at the thick white envelope, which I pocketed with a shrug. Probably one of Octavia's legal beauties to bind me to the toy boy column. I'd have plenty of time to read it on the train home. And rip it to shreds.

After having said my not-so-teary goodbyes, I took a bus to the train station and bought myself a cupcake to celebrate my freedom. Who cared if I didn't find anything immediately. I had enough to tide me over while I searched for a new job. Financial independence was now, finally, the least of my worries. Right now I had other things to think about, such as my mother and getting Lavender Cottage renovated.

Once settled in my seat, I ripped the envelope open to

stare at Shane's bold writing as my heart began to pound inside my temples.

Dearest Nat,

This is the sixteenth draft of this letter. I know because I counted them all.

Never has telling the truth been an issue for me, but this time I find it almost impossible and I wish I could skip this part completely and save you the disappointment. But I owe it to you, my dear friend.

Ever since I arrived in Wyllow Cove I have been met with nothing but kindness and trust, and it hurts me to have betrayed that trust, especially yours as I find myself involved in your wonderful household and family almost as if it were my own.

But I had no choice but to lie to you.

Many times I tried to tell you, and you will recall my moments of quiet when I silently willed myself to find the courage to tell you. But every time I tried, either something else came up or I just lost my courage.

So, here it is Nat. I lied about two things – my name, which is Shane Wright. And I lied about the reason why I came to Wyllow Cove, or so to speak. I told you I had come for love. That much is true. I came to fall in love.

Many years ago, when I was a uni student in Dublin, I met a woman at Temple Bar and took her to my place. The next morning we said our goodbyes and I never saw her again – until I saw her face on the back of one of my mother's new cookbooks. And then she appeared on my TV screen in a cooking show. Even then, I thought nothing of it, but when, during her spring special, she enlisted the help of her daughters to bake some cookies, all it took was one look, and I immediately knew. Those two little girls were the photocopies of my own nieces Marian and Emilia. They were my own flesh and blood.

That moment split my life into two. The day before I'd been playing pool and surfing with my friends and the next – I couldn't sleep. All I could do was trawl the internet for as much information on Yolanda as I could. And all I could think of was Amy and Zoe – of the man they called Daddy instead of me, and whether he loved them as his own. And I cursed all the years spent without being able to watch them grow, change their nappies, witness their very first steps and hear their first words and take them to their first day of school.

So the very next day, without telling anyone or having even a trace of a plan, I got into my car and took the ferry to England. It took me forever to get to Wyllow Cove, and still I had no plan. How do you show up at someone's home with this kind of news? And then, while looking for a place to stay, I came across your ad in the paper. I knew who you were because I'd done my due diligence. But I didn't know the girls would be coming to stay with you, and oh, Nat – when I first saw them, I wanted to hug them to me and hold them forever and tell them I was their daddy. It took me all the restraint I could find to avoid dropping this bomb on you all that very day.

And I had to be absolutely certain, so I took a strand of the girls' hair and had their DNA tested. There is no doubt that I am their father.

Please believe me when I say that I had no intention of deceiving anyone, least of all you, my dear, sweet friend. But who would have ever believed me? Sometimes I find it hard to believe it myself, but there you have it, the full truth.

And now, I am looking for the courage to send this to you, but not to the house. I am sending this to your work, where you'll be able to read it and digest it before going home.

I harbour no bitterness towards Yolanda for keeping me from my daughters, but now I need to be allowed time with them.

I only hope that you will be able to find it in your heart to forgive me. I never meant to hurt you, Nat.

Your friend,

Shane

I bunched up the pages and folded in on myself, stifling a sob. His *friend*? All this time I had hoped for him to feel the same way for me. I had wanted to be his woman. To hold him, kiss him, be with him. And now, more than ever, I had never felt so alone.

16

The Key to My Heart

In the following three weeks, as the plumber and the electrician worked on Lavender Cottage, I gave myself the task of collecting all of Mrs Pendennis's things and called someone from her estate who came round to collect them. It was sad to see her things go, and it hit me that one day someone would be doing the very same thing with my stuff. Those days I was capable of only sad thoughts and reminisced about life.

So I kept a framed picture of dear old Mrs Pendennis with her family and left it on the inside windowsill overlooking the garden, next to a vase of her favourite daffodils. She had been passionate about her flowers, and now she could watch her garden change throughout the seasons, year after year, even if she was no longer on this earth. It was the least I could do for her.

I also had a connecting door put in between my mother's house and Lavender Cottage and concentrated on moving her back home among her familiar things.

Personally, I didn't need much besides a new bed, a sofa, a table and chairs. Everything else would come later as I developed the need for it. It was strange, but refreshing, not to be surrounded by all of Neil's things in my new home. I was finally free of the past.

But it was also strange coming through my new door and not straining my ears to hear where the girls were, nor hear Shane's voice. Would I ever get used to it? I had tried to not think of him, what he was doing or what he was up to with the girls – or Yolanda, and desperately trying not to picture him alone with her. It was as plain as the nose on my face; he hadn't called or even texted me because he now had all he'd ever wanted. They had their new life and I had to go on with mine, no matter how much it killed me. But all the time I'd planned to leave The Mausoleum, I had never pictured myself starting over and being miserable.

When I got in from grocery shopping later that day, I pasted a smile onto my face for the benefit of Felicity whom I'd asked to watch my mother while I was out.

'You okay, Nat?' she asked as I dropped my bag onto the bench by the entrance.

I knew she was dying to ask why I wasn't by Shane's side in his new life as a father. The whole village must have been wondering what was going on.

'Perfectly all right, Felicity. Thanks for watching my mum for me.'

She shrugged. 'No problem. Beryl's always a hoot. But you look knackered. Do you want me to make you something to eat?'

'No, thank you, Felicity.'

'Do you want company?'

I shook my head and smiled weakly.

'Okay, then. If you're sure, I'll go.'

'Thanks. How much do I owe you?'

At that, she backed off in horror. 'Absolutely nothing, Nat. Call me whenever you need me.'

'Okay, thanks.' I'd make it up to her tomorrow.

Once alone, I sat back and listened to the sounds of my old, new house; Felicity's retreating footsteps on the flagstone floors, the creak of the front door, and the fire crackling in the hearth.

It was perfect. It was the house I'd always wanted since I was a little girl peeking over the garden wall. So to celebrate my new life, I poured myself a glass of chilled white wine, curled up on the sofa and bawled my eyes out.

The next morning when I checked my emails, I sat back in surprise. All seven of the magazines I'd applied to were offering me a permanent fixture with them! All I had to do was have an informal chat with them in video conference if I had any questions, and then decide who- and how many- to go with.

So I scheduled one interview a day, jotting down my impressions and comparing notes throughout the week. They all offered me conditions that were far better than *Lady* magazine. Apparently this was the year of Out With the Old and In With the New contenders! Suddenly I was the hottest thing since microwaveable dinners. I gave myself a pat on the back. I would never have to worry about a job or my finances again.

But if I kicked arse by day, nights were another story.

Every evening, without fail, after I put my mother to bed, I lay awake staring at the ceiling. Because if I had taken my life by the horns, my heart was still a mangled mess.

What was Shane doing this very moment? The girls must have been over the moon with their family complete. Had they got into a routine by now? Were he and Yolanda sharing her huge king-sized bed? If they'd done it once before, even if for only one night, it wouldn't be too difficult to do it again.

Thoughts of him kissing Yolanda, caressing her the way he did the very night the twins were conceived piled up in my mind and there was no wiping them to one side. With every memory that I pushed away, a new one took its place: the first time I ever saw him in his Zenyatta Mondatta Police T-shirt. The first time he touched me. The first time he held me. The first compliment he ever made me. The night I'd kissed him in front of everyone at the benefit ball. The time we'd almost made love in the garden… How could I ever, ever forget him? It didn't matter what his real name was or where he lived or even if he had a million children. I *missed* him.

My mobile rang and I fished it out of my bag, my heart hammering, but it was Yolanda. Even though I was dying to know how everyone was, I didn't want to be told by my sister.

'Hello?'

'Nat? Were you asleep?'

'Of course not,' I said. 'How are things?'

'Absolutely perfect!' she answered. 'You were right – what a man! We're a perfect fit – and he loves the girls, and they're crazy about him.'

A perfect fit. Of course. I was not surprised. 'That's good. I'm glad it's working out.'

'How about coming over for dinner tomorrow night? I want you to be there when we tell the girls.'

'You haven't told them yet?'

'We wanted to do it with you. After all, you're more than just their aunt.'

'Thank you, but that's—'

'Plus we can get you up to speed on the latest.'

'The latest?'

'We've got news!'

Oh my God. It had taken them less time than I'd expected. My head began to pound alongside my heart. 'I can't tomorrow tonight, Yola. I've got stuff to do.'

'All right, I guess I can keep it under wraps for just a little longer!'

'Right,' I said, suddenly exhausted. My arms and legs had no strength left in them, and my heart was as empty as a conch shell.

I considered trying to put her off indefinitely, but my masochistic side got the better of me. I wanted to know how he was, what he was doing. But was I going to be able to look him in the eye?

Yolanda's concrete and glass villa was at the opposite end of the cove and a short drive from my old house. As I pulled up, the front door burst open and out piled the girls, making a run for me and throwing their arms around my neck.

'Auntie Nat! Auntie Nat!'

'Oh,' I suddenly cried. 'I've missed you guys!'

At the front door, lingering, were Shane and Yolanda, exchanging glances. He looked completely at home with them. God, facing them was going to be more difficult than I'd thought.

I pasted a smile on my face and, with my arms around both girls, trudged up the drive as if going to the noose.

'Hey...!' Yolanda said, embracing me, and over her shoulder his dark, unreadable eyes met mine.

A lump formed in my throat. I couldn't do it. There was no way I could fake my way through this evening.

'So what's the news?' I asked once inside, wishing I could just liquefy and slide under the floorboards.

'Well, first things first, Shane's parents are flying in next week to meet us!' Yolanda said. Her cheeks were bright red and I'd never seen her this happy my entire life, and I was happy for her. But why did it have to be with him, of all men? Oh, God, I was a horrible sister.

'Oh. Wow, that's uhm, great, Yola. I'm happy for you.'

'And there's more!'

Of course there was. Only I didn't know if I could take it.

'Shane is going to legally recognise his paternity so the girls will take his surname for all intents and purposes.'

'Oh...' was all I could say, still unable to look at him. If he was disappointed, he didn't show it.

'I'll... go check on dinner,' he murmured and disappeared down the corridor. It had taken him a very short space of time to slip into their lives, living in Yolanda's home like he'd been there since the beginning. As if he actually belonged there.

I stood tall and smiled for my sister's benefit.

'Congratulations, Yolanda. I'm very happy for you and the girls.'

'Wait – there's more. Last, but not least,' she said, shoving her hand under my nose and I was suddenly blinded by a huge shiny rock on her third finger. 'He proposed last night!'

'Oh my God!' I cried. *Really* cried. For her, for me, for all of us.

'I haven't been this happy since the girls were born, Nat!' Yolanda laughed.

Crikey, did she have to rub it in? She'd got the boy, for the umpteenth time, while I was left standing alone at the umpteenth party. I got it. Nothing new. 'I'm happy for you, Yolanda. Truly I am.'

And that was when Shane came back into the room. 'Uhm, Yolanda? Your broccoli soufflé isn't looking very, uhm... soufflé-ish. It's kind of sunk.'

Yolanda shot up. 'Oh no – be right back!'

I swallowed as he came to stand opposite me, his hands stuffed into his pockets, his spaniel eyes fixed on me. What next, was he going to ask me to be happy for them?

'Hi again, Nat,' he whispered.

I swallowed. 'Hello, Shane.'

'Can I please have a word?'

I nodded stiffly.

'Thank you.'

'Listen, Nat,' he whispered. 'I know I screwed up with you tremendously. And I'm so sorry. Can you ever forgive me?'

I was silent, willing the tears back into my eyeballs. Shane was the last person I wanted to be around, but for the good of the girls, we had to be civil to each other.

'I don't know what to make of any of this. You slept with my sister and oh, gosh, had two kids with her. How is that supposed to make me feel?'

'I know,' he whispered. 'But can't we be civil with each other, for the girls' sake?'

Civil? I wanted to roll in the sheets with him forever and ever, cook him my best recipes, walk down the coastal path hand in hand until we needed Zimmer frames and had to remind each other of our medication, and he only wanted to be *civil*?

'For the girls' sake, I'll t-try…'

'Thank you. I'm really looking forward to the future.'

I'll bet.

'And I have to thank you. For making it all possible.'

That much was true. I had made the transition an easy one. The girls loved him, he and Yolanda had resumed their relationship, albeit years later. She was the mother of his children, and she was beautiful and successful. A perfect catch for him. So what the heck was I still standing around here for? My work was done.

'I'm sure you'll all be very happy together,' I said and swallowed, the words burning my throat. 'So, when's the big day?'

'In December,' he answered.

Only two months away. 'Wow, you move fast.'

He blushed. 'Yes, well, I've been waiting for this moment for a while now. I couldn't have done it without you. I'm just so sorry that I had to lie to you.'

I looked up into his dark eyes, and the entire world I would be missing out on. Everything that I had thought we had been slowly building together – the quiet evening chats alone in the garden, his dependability, his help with my mother and the kids, the fact that he had helped me with my job, cheered me up, given me confidence in my skills. And the subtle flirting/non-flirting that kept me going. How silly I had been, to think that it could actually mean more than that.

I had thought it had all been his way of showing me he cared. But, as it turned out, he didn't care in that way at all. Because he was marrying Yolanda, the mother of his children. And they would be a proper family. All they needed was a dog and their lives would be more than perfect.

'I want my girls to continue living in a happy environment. But I can't start a new life with them knowing that you are not on board.'

'Of course I'm on board. I love those girls and want every happiness for them. I'll do whatever it takes.'

'Then will you forgive me? Can we be friends again?'

'Friends?' How could I possibly be friends with him without my heart breaking completely? Without feeling stabs of pain every time he looked at Yolanda? But, I understood, it wasn't all about me. It was about my nieces, two little innocent girls who had no fault whatsoever and who needed a united family. And who were looking at a new, better life with their real father. Who was I to rain on their parade?

'Let's just say we'll be civilised.' I closed my eyes briefly, unable to bear the weight of tears roaring like a river fall behind my lids. 'After all, not only are you the twins' father, but you're also going to be my, ah, brother-in-law.'

His eyebrows shot up. '*What?*'

I heaved a huge sigh and squeezed the bridge of my nose. 'Yolanda told me.'

'Nat,' he said, taking my arms and peering down into my face. 'Yolanda is getting married all right – but to Bill, her producer – not me!'

I gawped at him, his image blurry from my tears that had managed to break through after all my efforts. 'You're not... marrying Yolanda?'

'Nat, *Nat*,' he said softly. 'Do you really think that I could ever have feelings for Yolanda, when I'm absolutely, positively, head over heels in love with *you*?'

I blinked again and a few hot tears landed on my cheeks, running down to my chin. '*Me?*' I croaked. 'But – she said you proposed last night.'

He laughed. 'No – Bill swung by to pick her up last night. Great bloke, by the way. The girls and I had pizza and played Monopoly in front of the fire. *He* proposed – not me.'

'So you don't love Yolanda...?' was all I could say. 'All this time, you weren't waiting for her to come back so you could...?'

His fingers traced my jawline to where my tears had gathered and he wiped them away with his thumbs as his eyes caressed my face.

'Sweetheart, let me make this clear for you, once and for all. I love *you*, not Yolanda. And not because you have taken care of the girls so stupendously well, nor because I am so happy when I'm with you, or because you're so hot and it's been pure hell trying to keep my bloody hands off you. I love you because you are you. And I always will love you. *Only* you.'

He *loved* me? Like, in real, real love? Oh, my God. Apart from when my daughters were born, was this not one of the best days of my entire *life*?

'But… but,' I faltered. 'You never said! You never gave any sign of having feelings for me!'

He huffed, his eyes bright. 'How could I, knowing I was lying to you? I had absolutely no right to do so. Not until I told you the truth.'

'Then why didn't you? Why did you leave me in the dark all this time?'

'Oh, I tried – a thousand times a day! But every time you looked up at me with those beautiful, trusting eyes… I just didn't have the heart to. I didn't want to ruin everything between us. And I eventually did.' He ran a hand through his hair, his eyes sad. 'That night, in the garden, when we were about to make love…'

I buried my face in my hands, remembering what I'd said to him. *Love me, Connor.*

'Please, I'm embarrassed enough as it is.'

'I wanted you so so badly, Nat. Truly, I did. I wanted to make love to you like I'd never wanted anything in my entire life. But in that moment, when you called me by a name that wasn't mine, it suddenly hit how horribly I was deceiving you, when instead you trusted me completely. It had nothing to do with me not wanting you, Nat. Oh, I wanted you all right. And I still do.'

As I listened to him, my cheeks flooded all over again. The man who had been on my mind from the day we met, the one who was not for me for so, so many reasons, now wanted me too?

'Are you sure…?'

His face softened even more. 'Oh, Nat, did you really think there could be anyone else besides you?'

I shrugged. 'I dunno...'

He bent down and kissed my tears. 'I'm so sorry, Nat...' he whispered. 'I'm so sorry for letting you doubt for a single moment what my feelings were. It was so difficult, not giving in to my feelings right from the start. Because the moment you opened your front door, I was love-struck. But knowing what I was going to do, I couldn't take advantage of you like that. And I wanted you to believe me when I finally did tell you.'

I looked up at him and he took my hands in his. 'I know a lot has happened in the past few weeks. But it's still *me*, Nat.'

I huffed, unable to speak.

'Have we still got a chance to be happy together?' he whispered, kissing my new tears.

'I-I don't know,' I stammered. 'I just need to... to take stock.'

He raked his hand through his hair and nodded. 'Okay, I understand. I deserve this. I should've never lied to you. Some way to start a relationship, huh?'

I said nothing.

He sighed, biting his lip. 'I understand this is a bit overwhelming. Do you need time to think about it?'

I nodded. 'Yes. No. I don't know...'

He took my hands in his. 'It's okay to be confused, Nat.' Then he brought my fingers to his lips and kissed them, one by one.

'Th-that's not helping,' I stammered.

He closed his eyes. 'Perhaps, you could give me another chance to start all over again?'

'How?'

He stepped back and held out his hand, a huge smile on his face.

'Hi, my name is Shane Wright. I'm from Dublin where I live on a huge farm with my huge family. I'm an IT lawyer. I have two lovely daughters and I am looking for the love of my life. She has to be half-Italian, kind and generous and sexy as hell. She has to be a columnist and must also have a potty-mouthed but adorable mother. Do you by any chance know where I could meet someone like that?'

'Can we just skip to the good part?' I asked, and he smiled, so I wrapped my arms around his neck and kissed him smack on the mouth, his five o'clock beard soft against my face. I inhaled his fresh scent, wanting to bury myself inside him, or the other way around, it didn't matter. I wanted to be as close to him as I possibly could. I wanted to take him home and bolt the door and finally have my wicked way with this beautiful, kind man.

'I've wanted this from the minute I met you,' he murmured as he continued to kiss me and nibble at my throat.

'And you drank that entire cup of salty coffee,' I reminded him.

He shrugged. 'I didn't want to embarrass you. You were so nervous that day.'

'But from now on, promise you'll always be honest with me?'

'Entirely,' he promised before taking my lips again in a knicker-melting kiss.

'Well, then, if we're going down this road, I have my own confession to make,' I finally said, drawing for breath.

He gently pushed my fringe off my face in a loving caress. 'Oh, yeah?' he whispered against my lips. 'What's that?'

'I'm not thirty-six. I'm thirty-nine.'

'Oh, I knew that.'

I pulled away. 'You knew?'

'It's on the contract, silly.'

'Oh. Right.'

'But as long as we're doing confessions,' he said. 'Do you remember me disappearing every Tuesday and Thursday?'

'Uh, ye-es?'

'Well, this is why,' he said, going to the drinks bar in the corner and ducking under it. He emerged with a huge object covered by a sheet.

'Come closer,' he beckoned me. 'I hope you don't mind, but I made two. One for the girls, and a special, specific one for you.' And with that, he whipped off the cover and… there it was. *My* doll's house, with its white picket fence and the purple door and shutters and tiny furniture.

'Oh, my God! How did you…?'

'I copied it from that picture you showed me. Not bad, is it?'

'Not bad? It's exactly the same! Thank you, Shane, for caring enough to do that.'

He took me into his arms. 'I care much more than that, Nat.'

'Nat?'

We turned to the door where the girls stood with Yolanda. 'Are you ready for that family chat now?' she asked us and I nodded, detaching myself from Shane.

Zoe and Amy glanced at each other. 'Oh-oh. Is somebody sick?' Amy asked.

Yolanda laughed. 'No, darling, everyone is fine! But we have some news regarding our family.'

'Oh God, you're not marrying Bill, are you?' Amy asked.

Yola glanced at me. 'Maybe. One day.'

'But do you like him?' Zoe wanted to know.

'Of course I do. And he likes me, too. But I have some news about another man in our lives.'

'Is our real daddy coming back?' Zoe asked.

Yolanda exchanged glances with us. This was not going to be easy.

'What Mummy is trying to say is that… well, Mummy and Uncle Connor are very, very old friends. Many years ago they met and made you. We didn't see each other for a very long time. But now we've agreed that he should stay in Wyllow Cove.'

I watched their little faces as they tried to understand. And then a twin set of eyes nearly popped out of their lovely faces. 'You mean Connor is our father?'

Yolanda caressed their shoulders. 'Yes, my darlings. Connor is your real father. Only his real name is Shane. And you like him, right?'

Their faces swung to his as they reached out to grab each other's hands, something I had never seen in the eight years of their lives.

'And he is going to move in with us?' Amy asked.

'No, my darlings. Your father is going to live down in the village.'

'But we can see him whenever we want?' Zoe wanted to know.

Yolanda nodded. 'The only thing that will change is that you get to finally live with Mummy all year, but you can have lots and lots of sleepovers with Daddy whenever you want!'

Shane stepped forward and knelt before them. 'We'll take you to your football, your ballet, your sports club, parties, parks and we can all go away together on holidays,' he promised. 'Nothing has changed. We all love you very much.'

Shane, Yolanda and I exchanged glances as it dawned on the girls that they were no ordinary family.

And then suddenly, as if released from a catapult, they bolted through the sliding glass doors and shot down the garden, running and screaming, long locks trailing behind them. 'Yayyyyy!' they cried in unison, hugging each other in absolute glee, running around in circles, arm in arm, first this way and then that, singing and whooping.

'Well, that's settled, then,' Shane said with a happy sigh, his dark eyes glistening. 'Yolanda, I can't thank you enough.'

'Please. You've given them what I couldn't. A father. And Shane?'

'Yes?'

'Hurt my sister and I'll break your legs. Are we clear?'

'I promise,' he said, putting his arm around me. 'I love Nat with all my heart, and I'm going to make her very happy.'

I blushed as Yolanda came forward and placed her hand on my forearm. 'You'd better. And thank *you*, Nat. For everything you've done. For making me see the importance of family.'

I shrugged, blushing. All these years that I'd waited for

a simple thank you and now I didn't know what to say. 'So when are you going to marry Bill?' I asked.

Yolanda shrugged. 'I want the girls to get to know him better and see that he really is a great bloke.'

'We'll make sure that it all goes smoothly,' Shane promised.

Yolanda smiled at him. 'You know, Shane, when Nat told me she had a male lodger, I was worried about all sorts of stuff.'

'I understand.'

'I'm sorry again for never telling you. I just thought you wouldn't want to know. My own ex-husband didn't.'

The girls shot back in through the French doors, finally jumping all over Shane, covering him with kisses as, overwhelmed, he swiped his red eyes before they met mine. 'We're such a huge family now!' Zoe cried. 'I can't wait to meet our Irish nana and all of our aunts and uncles and *cousins*!'

'Oh my God, imagine all the presents!' Amy echoed.

I laughed, swiping a tear.

'Okay, girls, time to wash up for dinner. The soufflé is a total disaster, but who cares?' Yolanda said.

I laughed as she led the girls out of the room. Shane took my hand. 'You okay?' he whispered.

'I'm fine. Enjoy this, it's a one in a million event.'

'Not anymore. I plan on keeping everyone as close as possible.' Shane smiled. And then gripped my elbows, his eyes suddenly wide. 'Oh my bloody *God!*'

'What?' I said, instinctively clutching his arms in return.

'Me mam! I forgot all about her!'

'You mean you didn't tell her any of this?' I gasped.

'I was going to keep it to myself until I had a happy ending!'

'And did you get your happy ending?' I teased him.

He pretended not to understand. 'Are you kidding me? When I tell her I've met both Natalia and Yolanda Amore, she's going to freak.'

'Ha-ha. But seriously, how is she going to react?'

'She'll be over the moon. She's always badgering me about finding the one. And now I've found my three!'

The next Friday night, at the annual Media Ball, held at our old haunt, The Langham Hotel in London, in the presence of hundreds of colleagues – columnists, travel writers, bloggers – the works, and Shane was at my side, as my real date this time.

Octavia, of course, was there, wearing her customary white, and eating him with her eyes as usual.

'Hello, Octavia,' Shane said pleasantly.

'Hi, Connor, looking good as usual,' she said with her flirty mouth. She still called him Connor because we had decided to not make our business known to anyone until we felt that the right moment had come.

'So are you, Octavia.'

'And what are you up to these days, Natalia?' she asked as she took a sip of champagne.

'Oh, uh, nothing much. I'm currently working on a new article.'

'Freelancing, I imagine,' she said. 'Maybe that is what you need. I find that uncertainty always adds that certain edge. Good for creativity, and you certainly need it. And may I suggest you keep away from writing stuff like that last article of yours – The Clark Kents of the Noughties? Ugh.'

'Actually, Octavia, I am writing a very specific article.'

'Oh?'

'Yeah. It's my first note as editor-in-chief for *La Mode*.'

Octavia spluttered her drink, coughing until coughing turned to wheezing and Shane had to whack her on the back.

'You okay?' he asked.

'Yuh,' she croaked, her mascara running like she'd been crying for hours.

'Don't worry, Octavia,' I said. 'I will put in a good word for you – if I care to.'

'I beg your pardon?'

'Oh. Didn't you know? We're acquiring *Lady* magazine and, well, a few people have to go, so…'

And then Octavia's knees bent and only her plus-one, who was returning from the bar with more drinks, stopped her from hitting the floor. His champagne glasses toppled and spilled all over her couture while someone else threw a glass of ice-cold water in her face. Which brought her to, but she had to be escorted out of the ballroom.

'Poor Octavia,' I said. 'I hope she'll be okay.'

Shane threw back his head and laughed while his arm circled my shoulder. 'Remind me to never piss you off.'

I turned to him. 'I love you, Shane. I've loved you since the moment you stepped over my threshold in your Zenyatta Mondatta T-shirt. I fantasised you had come to make wild love to me.'

'Ah, well, we needn't fantasise any longer. Let's go upstairs to our room, sweetheart,' he whispered as he gently nipped the side of my throat and I shivered with pleasure.

'Let's,' I murmured.

In the lift, Shane patted his pocket. 'I think I've lost the key.'

'Shall I give you mine?' I said as the doors pinged open.

He exhaled in relief as he held out his hand. 'Saved the day again, you have, my love.'

I reached into my clutch and pulled out a heavy, iron key.

Shane chuckled. 'What's that, the key to your heart?'

I shook my head. 'It's the key to Lavender Cottage. Mr Wright, will you come and live with me?'

Shane stared at me, his dark eyes solemn, as I produced the real key to the room I had previously relieved him of. So far my plans were ticking along perfectly.

He took the room key off me and took me by my waist, his mouth taking mine as we backed through the door.

'You beat me by a minute,' he whispered into my mouth and then he got down on one knee, a small velvet box in his hand. 'Natalia Amore, will you do a man a miracle and marry me?'

My hand shot to my heart. 'Shane…?'

'I love you, Nat, with all my Irish heart, and I swear to you that no one will ever love you more.'

'Oh my God,' I whispered. 'Yes, Shane, yes!'

He pulled me to him, lifting me off my feet, kissing me deeply. And then he pulled back and grinned. 'Recognise the room?' he whispered.

'Is it... the one from... the last time? Was it number thirteen? That explains a lot.'

'Uh-huh. I believe that you and I have some unfinished business to tend to,' he murmured as he gently nipped at my throat.

I knew thirteen had to be my lucky number after all.

Epilogue

One rainy afternoon in December, the entire Wright clan flew to Newquay airport in Cornwall to watch Shane officially become a father during an official ceremony.

The girls were over the moon and Yolanda looked like a dream in a gold dress. But I was the one who was dreaming.

We had all finally obtained our happily ever after and couldn't wait for the ten-minute official meeting to be over to go down the road where we'd booked a reception hall to celebrate.

It was barely big enough to house the whole of Shane's family – his brothers and sisters and nephews and nieces were all there, surrounding Amy and Zoe with hugs and kisses and presents, along with stories of Shane's adventures. It was true that his youngest nieces Emilia and Marian were the spitting image of Amy and Zoe. And they were such a close-knit family, just as he had said.

And Old Mary, Shane's Mam, was not old in the least. She was a sprightly, warm-hearted, cake-baking matriarch, widowed at a young age, who'd raised her children with love and dignity.

'I've been following your career for years and you are

every inch the lovely girl I imagined you were,' she said to me above the din as I sat down opposite her at the table.

'Oh, that's so kind of you, Mary, thank you!'

'And your work – love it! That article you wrote a few months back, "The new, twenty-something Clark Kents of the Twenty-twenties"? Pure genius!'

I grinned as I reached out for a devilled egg. 'My old boss thought it was drivel.'

Mary dismissed the thought with her hand. 'What does she know. I am so happy my son has bagged such a smart, funny, kind and beautiful woman! What else could a man want?'

I laughed and Mary reached across the table to squeeze my hand and I basked in the warmth of her genuine affection.

Afterwards, Mary sat with Mum at the end of the table and read my articles to her from her tablet. Mum tittered at my humour, slapping her hand against her armrest. There certainly was a first time for everything. 'She gets her sense of humour from me, my girl.'

'Well, she is one talented girl,' Mary said.

'So is your son,' Beryl replied.

Mary nodded and turned to smile at me. 'Looks like we have a lot to talk about. I want to know everything about Nat when she was little.'

And to my surprise, Mum began to fill her in from the early days of her pregnancy, not missing a detail of my first few years of life.

'You remember all that, Mum?' I asked, my throat constricting.

She tapped her temple. 'It's all in here, love,' she said.

'And in here,' she added, indicating her heart. 'I only regret that I suffered from post-partum depression for many years after that, and could not be the mother that I wanted to be.'

My hand stole to my heart. Depression? If I'd only known. That explained all the times I needed her and she wasn't there.

Mary grinned and took her hand. 'You and I have a lot to talk about, Beryl.'

Of course, there would be days when Mum was out of it. But today, she was present – and that was what mattered the most.

And it got even better: Yolanda took a year off to write the cookbook of her life and to spend quality time with her daughters and Bill. Shane and I saw the girls on a daily basis, picking them up from school and helping them with their homework and ferrying them around and we all spent our weekends together. Lizzie and Liam came down from Truro for Sunday lunches with Sarah, who had finally obtained that promotion, and had just started seeing a lovely man named Jeremy.

'How are my girls?' Shane whispered into my ear, making me shiver with delight as usual.

I giggled. 'We're fine – all three of us.'

'What? Are you *pregnant?*' Lizzie gasped, and there sounded a biblical silence in the reception room.

I eyed Shane uncertainly. Because, at eight weeks, I wasn't even showing yet. We hadn't actually mentioned it because we wanted it to be all about Amy and Zoe for as long as possible, and especially today, when the paternal acknowledgement became official and we celebrated the birth of a new and improved family.

'Dibs on the first one out!' Amy called. 'The oldest ones are always smarter!'

The tension was released and we were hugged and kissed from every direction as Zoe whispered to us, 'Don't tell Amy, but she doesn't know that the first one born is actually the youngest.'

'Is that so?' Shane said.

'Yes, because the first one to be con— Uhm, conceived, comes out last. So much about being smarter!'

Shane caressed her cheek and winked at her as we crossed our hearts to keep her secret.

'Listen to her. Are you sure she's only eight?' Shane said with a chuckle.

'And we were worried about them,' I replied. 'They're going to be just fine.'

Shane pulled me to him. 'I'm so happy I think I might just bawl, Nat,' he said, his eyes moist.

'No crying.' I laughed. 'From now on, only happiness and love.'

'And that's a promise,' he whispered as he kissed my lips.

I knew I had finally made it in life now that I'd gone from living in a big house with very little love, to a big love, much more than enough to fill one little Cornish cottage.

Acknowledgements

With each book that I write, the list of people to thank becomes longer and longer.

First and foremost, many thanks to my amazing editor Hannah Todd for her patience and hard work, Helena Newton for her attention to detail, Cherie Chapman for her gorgeous covers, Vicky Joss for shouting about my books from the rooftops and everyone at Aria Fiction. You are a fantastic team!

Also, many thanks go to my agent Lorella Belli who makes me feel like a pro!

I couldn't have gone anywhere near even mentioning such a delicate issue as mental illness without the help of Doctor Maria Accetta, a systemic therapist who has vast experience in Alzheimer's disease. She is also vice-president of a rehabilitation centre which focuses on helping both patients and their families cope. Thank you, Maria- we need more people like you!

An affectionate shout-out goes to my Facebook fellow fans of AT, you have been a huge support and I truly enjoy your messages of praise and encouragement. You lot come up with the best suggestions for the names of my male characters!

Another crucial presence is that of our beloved book bloggers, thank you for taking the time and sharing your knowledge with other readers!

To my family and friends, thank you for putting up with me, even on-line. Although currently out of reach, you are forever in my heart.

And finally, as always, I would like to thank you, Dear Reader. Your support and kindness always keep me going through thick and thin, and your reviews cheer me up no end! I do hope you enjoy Dreams of a Little Cornish Cottage, and please do keep your eyes peeled for my next Cornish adventure!

Stay safe,

Nancy Barone

About the Author

NANCY BARONE WYTHE grew up in Canada, but at the age of 12 her family moved to Italy. Catapulted into a world where her only contact with the English language was her old Judy Blume books, Nancy became an avid reader and a die-hard romantic.

Nancy stayed in Italy and, despite being surrounded by handsome Italian men, she married an even more handsome Brit. They now live in Sicily where she teaches English.

Nancy is a member of the RWA and a keen supporter of the Women's Fiction Festival at Matera where she meets up once a year with writing friends from all over the globe.